P9-EMH-631

Praise for Stephen R. Lawhead's
SONG OF ALBION Book One:

THE PARADISE WAR

"A splendid tale of action and excitement"

Madeleine L'Engle, author of *A WRINKLE IN TIME*

"A mistral wind amongst so many dull breezes...
Elegantly written and speedily paced...Will
please almost every shade of fantasy fan."

Fear

"Savagely beautiful and bloodily poetic...Celtic
twilight shot with a brighter, fiercer light and
tinged with modern villainy."

Michael Scott Rohan, author of
THE WINTER OF THE WORLD

"Well paced, exciting and very well re-
searched...An epic struggle between Light and
Darkness."

Forbidden Planet

"Reminiscent of Tolkien...A world of vivid
imagery. This book is a delight."

Bookstore Journal

"Lawhead evokes the best of British fantasy. He
breathes with the Celtic mythos in a beautiful
voice that is all his own."

Encounters

Other Avon Books by
Stephen R. Lawhead

THE DRAGON KING TRILOGY

BOOK ONE: IN THE HALL OF THE DRAGON KING
BOOK TWO: THE WARLORDS OF NIN
BOOK THREE: THE SWORD AND THE FLAME

THE PENDRAGON CYCLE

TALIESIN
MERLIN
ARTHUR

THE SONG OF ALBION TRILOGY

BOOK 1: THE PARADISE WAR

Avon Books are available at special quantity discounts for bulk purchases for sales promotions, premiums, fund raising or educational use. Special books, or book excerpts, can also be created to fit specific needs.

For details write or telephone the office of the Director of Special Markets, Avon Books, Dept. FP, 1350 Avenue of the Americas, New York, NY 10019, 1-800-238-0658.

STEPHEN R. LAWHEAD

BOOK TWO
SONG OF ALBION

THE SILVER HAND

AVON BOOKS • NEW YORK

If you purchased this book without a cover, you should be aware that this book is stolen property. It was reported as "unsold and destroyed" to the publisher, and neither the author nor the publisher has received any payment for this "stripped book."

To Donovan Welch

AVON BOOKS
A division of
The Hearst Corporation
1350 Avenue of the Americas
New York, New York 10019

Copyright © 1992 by Stephen Lawhead
Cover illustration by Daniel Horne
Published by arrangement with Lion Publishing Corporation
ISBN: 0-380-71647-X

All rights reserved, which includes the right to reproduce this book or portions thereof in any form whatsoever except as provided by the U.S. Copyright Law. For information address Lion Publishing Corporation, 1705 Hubbard Avenue, Batavia, Illinois 60510.

First AvoNova Printing: October 1993

AVON TRADEMARK REG. U.S. PAT. OFF. AND IN OTHER COUNTRIES, MARCA REGISTRADA, HECHO EN U.S.A.

Printed in the U.S.A.

RA 10 9 8 7 6 5 4 3 2 1

Contents

*"Since all the world is but a story,
it were well for thee to buy the
more enduring story, rather than
the story that is less enduring."*

The Judgment of St. Colum Cille
(St. Columba of Scotland)

Hear, O Son of Albion, the prophetic word:

Sorrow and be sad, deep grief is granted Albion in triple measure. The Golden King in his kingdom will strike his foot against the Rock of Contention. The Worm of fiery breath will claim the throne of Prydain; Llogres will be without a lord. But happy shall be Caledon; the Flight of Ravens will flock to her many-shadowed glens, and ravensong shall be her song.

When the Light of the Derwyddi is cut off, and the blood of bards demands justice, then let the Ravens spread their wings over the sacred wood and holy mound. Under Ravens' wings, a throne is established. Upon this throne, a king with a silver hand.

In the Day of Strife, root and branch shall change places, and the newness of the thing shall pass for a wonder. Let the sun be dull as amber, let the moon hide her face: abomination stalks the land. Let the four winds contend with one another in dreadful blast; let the sound be heard among the stars. The Dust of the Ancients will rise on the clouds; the essence of Albion is scattered and torn among contending winds.

The seas will rise up with mighty voices. Nowhere is there safe harbor. Arianrhod sleeps in her sea-girt headland. Though many seek her, she will not be found. Though many cry out to her, she cannot hear their voices. Only the chaste kiss will restore her to her rightful place.

Then shall rage the Giant of Wickedness, and terrify all with the keen edge of his sword. His eyes shall flash forth fire; his lips shall drip poison. With his great host he will despoil the island. All who oppose him will be swept away in the flood of wrongdoing that flows from his hand. The Island of the Mighty will become a tomb.

All this by the Brazen Man is come to pass, who likewise mounted on his steed of brass works woe both great and dire. Rise up, Men of Gwir! Fill your hands with weapons and oppose the false men in your midst! The sound of the battleclash will be heard among the stars of heaven and the Great Year will proceed to its final consummation.

Hear, O Son of Albion: Blood is born of blood. Flesh is born of flesh. But the spirit is born of Spirit, and with Spirit evermore remains. Before Albion is One, the Hero Feat must be performed and Silver Hand must reign.

Banfáith of Ynys Sci

1

Doomsayer

We carried the body of Meldryn Mawr down from high Findargad to be buried in the Hill of Kings. Three horses pulled the wagon: a red and a white to draw the bier, and a black to lead them. I walked at the head of the dark horse, guiding the great king's body to its rest.

Six warriors walked on either side of the bier. The horses' hooves and the wagon's wheels were wrapped with rags, likewise the spears and shields of the warriors. The Llwyddi followed, each man, woman and child carrying an unlit torch.

Burial of a king has been observed in this way from time past remembering. The wheels and hooves are muffled, so that the bier may pass silently through the land; the weapons are covered and the torches unlit, so that no eye will mark the passing procession. Secrecy and silence are maintained so that the gravemound will never be discovered and desecrated by an enemy.

As night drew its cloak of stars across the sky, we arrived at Glyn Du, a narrow valley tributary to the Vale of Modornn. The funeral procession entered the black glen, moving beside the still, dark water. The deep-folded valley was darker even than the sky above, which still glimmered in blue twilight. The gravemound loomed on its hill as a mass of thick-gathered shadow.

At the foot of Cnoc Righ, the Hill of Kings, I kindled a small fire to light the torches. As the people took their places, forming two long lines on either side of the path leading up the hill to the entrance of the cairn, the flame was passed from torch to torch. This is the *Aryant Ol*, the radiant way along which a king is carried to the tomb. When the people had assembled, I began the funeral rite, saying:

"The sword I bear on my thigh was a wall, high and strong—the bane of marauding enemies! Now it is broken.

"The torc I bear in my hand was a light of keen judgment—the beacon of rightwise favor shining from the far-off hill. Now it is extinguished.

"The shield I bear on my shoulder was a platter of plenty in the hall of honor—the sustenance of heroes. Now it is riven, and the hand that upheld it is cold.

"The pale white corpse will soon be covered, under earth and blue stones: Woe my heart, the king is dead.

"The pale white corpse will soon be covered, amidst earth and oak: Woe my heart, the Ruler of Clans is slain.

"The pale white corpse will soon be covered, under the greensward in the tumulus: Woe my heart, Prydain's chieftain will join his fathers in the Hero Mound.

"Men of Prydain! Fall on your faces, grief has overtaken you. The Day of Strife has dawned! Great the grief, sharp the sorrow. No glad songs will be sung in the land, only songs of mourning. Let all men make bitter lament. The Pillar of Prydain is shattered. The Hall of Tribes has no roof. The Eagle of Findargad is gone. The Boar of Sycharth is no more. The Great King, the Golden King, Meldryn Mawr is murdered. The Day of Strife has dawned!

"Bitter the day of birth, for death is its companion. Yet, though life be cold and cruel, we are not without a last consolation. For to die in one world is to be born into another. Let all men hear and remember!"

So saying, I turned to the warriors at the bier and commanded them. The horses were unhitched, the wagon was raised and its wheels removed. The warriors then lifted the bier shoulder high and began to walk slowly towards the cairn, passing between the double line of torches, moving slowly up the radiant way to the gravemound.

As the bier passed, I took my place behind it and began the *Lament for a Fallen Champion,* singing softly, slowly, allowing the words to fall like tears into the silence of the glen. Unlike other laments, this one is sung without the harp. It is sung by the chief bard and, although I had never sung it, I knew it well.

It is a strong song, full of bitterness and wrath at the way in which the champion's life has been cut short and his people deprived of his valor and the shelter of his shield. I sang the lament, my voice rising full and free, filling the night with harsh and barren sorrow. There is no comfort in this song: it sings the coldness of the tomb, the obscenity of corruption, and the emptiness, waste, and futility of death. I sang the bitterness of loss and the aching loneliness of grief. I sang it all, driving my words hard and biting them between my teeth.

The people wept. And I wept too, as up and up the Aryant Ol, and slowly, slowly we approached the burial cairn. The song moved to its end: a single rising note becoming a sharp, savage scream. This represents the rage of the life cruelly cut short.

My voice rose to the final note, growing, expanding, filling the night with its accusation. My lungs burned, my throat ached; I thought my heart would burst with the effort. The ragged scream burst and faltered in the air, dying at its height. A truncated echo resounded along the sides of Glyn Du and flew up into the starry void—a spear hurled into the eye-pit of night.

The warriors bearing the king's body halted at the sound. Strength left their hands, and the bier pitched and swayed. For an instant I thought they would drop the body, but they staggered, steadied themselves, and slowly raised the bier once more. It was a dreadful, pitiful moment, speaking more forcefully than the words of my lament the anguish and heartbreak of our loss.

The bearers moved to the entrance of the cairn, where they paused while two men with torches went ahead of them into the tomb. The bier entered the gravemound next, and I followed. The interior was lined with stone niches, small chambers containing the bones of Prydain kings whose shields covered the openings.

Meldryn's body was laid in the center of the cairn, on its bier, and the warriors saluted their king, each man touching the back of his hand to his forehead, honoring Meldryn Mawr for the last time. Then they began filing out one by one. I lingered long, looking upon the face of the lord I had loved and served. Ashen white, sunken-cheeked and hollow-eyed, pale his brow, pale like bone, but high and fair. Even in death it was a noble countenance.

I considered the shields of other kings on the walls of the cairn: other kings of other times, each a lord of renown who had ruled Prydain in his turn. Now Meldryn Mawr, the Great Golden King, had relinquished the seat of power. Who was worthy to take his place?

I was the last to leave, consigning the king's body to its long sleep. One day, when death's handmaidens had finished their work, I would return to gather the bones and place them in one of the empty niches. For now, however, I bade Meldryn Mawr a final farewell and stepped from the cairn. Passing slowly down the shimmering pathway of the Aryant Ol, I raised my voice in the *Queen's Lament*.

As I sang, the women joined in, blending their willowy voices with mine. There is a measure of solace in the song and as I sang I became the Chief Bard in more than name only. For I sang and saw the life of the song born in my people; I saw them take strength and sustenance from its beauty. I saw them live in the song, and I thought: Tonight I grasp Ollathir's staff, and I am worthy. I am worthy to be the bard of a great people. But who is worthy to be our king?

Gazing upon the faces of all those gathered on the slopes of the Cnoc Righ, I wondered who among them could wear the torc Meldryn Mawr had left behind. Who could wear the oak-leaf crown? There were good men among us, fine and strong, chieftains who could lead in battle—but a king is more than a war leader.

Who is worthy to be king? I thought. Ollathir, my teacher and my guide, what would you have me do? Speak to me, old friend, as you did in former times. Give your *Filidh* benefit of your sage wisdom. I wait on your word, Wise Counsellor. Instruct me in the way that I should go...

But Ollathir was dead, like so many of Prydain's proud sons, his voice but an echo fading in the memory. Alas, his *awen* had passed out of this worlds-realm, and I must find my way alone. Very well, I thought, turning to my task at last. I am a bard, and I can do all that a true bard can do.

I placed a fold of my cloak over my head and raised my staff high. "Son of Tegvan, son of Teithi, son of Talaryant, a bard and the son of bards, I am Tegid Tathal. Listen to me!"

I spoke boldly, knowing there were some who would rather I remained silent. "Most mournful of men am I, for the lord who upheld me has been wickedly killed. Meldryn Mawr is dead. And I see nothing before me but death and darkness. Our shining son is stolen from us. Our king lies stiff and cold in his turf house, and treachery sits in the place of honor.

"It is the Day of Strife! Let all men look to the edge of the sword for their protection. The Paradise War is begun; the sound of warfare will be heard in the land as Ludd and Nudd battle one another for the kingship of Albion."

"Doomsayer!" Meldron shouted, thrusting his way through the crowd. He had dressed himself in his father's clothing—siarc, breecs, and buskins of crimson edged in gold. He wore Meldryn Mawr's gold knife and belt of gold discs fine as fish-scales. And, as if this were not enough, he had bound back his tawny hair that everyone might see the king's golden torc around his throat.

My words had found their mark. Meldron was angry. His jaw bulged and his eyes glinted like chips of flint in the torchlight. Siawn Hy, Meldron's champion, sleekly dark and smooth-faced, followed at his lord's right hand.

"Tegid is confused. Pay him no heed," Meldron cried. "He does not know what he is saying."

The Llwyddi murmured uncertainly and Meldron rounded on me. "Why are you doing this, bard? Why must you persist in frightening everyone? We have enough to do without listening to all this careless talk of yours."

"I see that you are busy indeed," I replied, facing him squarely. "Busy stealing Meldryn Mawr's belt and torc. But do not think that by wearing your father's clothing you will take his place."

"No one talks to the king this way, bard!" snapped Siawn Hy, thrusting himself closer. "Watch your tongue, or lose it."

"He is no bard," Meldron said. "He is nothing but a doomsayer!" The prince laughed abruptly and loudly, waving me aside with a flick of his hand. "Go your way, Tegid Tathal. I have had a bellyful of your meddling. Neither you nor your spiteful tongue are wanted here. We do not need you any more."

Siawn Hy smiled thinly. "It seems you are no longer useful to the king, bard. Perhaps your service would receive greater esteem elsewhere."

Anger leapt like a flame within me. "Meldron is not the king," I reminded them. "I alone hold the kingship; it is mine to give as I choose."

"And I hold the Singing Stones!" Meldron bawled. "No man can stand against me now."

His boast brought a murmur of approval from many standing near. It became clear to me how he had managed to gull his followers and to work Llew's inspired achievement to his own advantage. He had claimed the gathered fragments of the song-bearing stones and had made of them a talisman of power.

"Your courage is misplaced," I told them. "The Song of Albion is not a weapon."

Siawn's sword flicked out, the blade a streak in the shimmering torchlight. He leaned close and pressed the point against my throat. "We have other weapons," he hissed, his breath hot in my face.

His threat was rash and reckless. The people surged around us, uncertain which way to go. Attacking a bard before his people could only bring disaster. But Meldron, with his heavy-handed authority— backed by Siawn Hy and the Wolf Pack—had them cowed. They did not know whom to believe any more, or whom to trust.

I regarded Siawn Hy with icy contempt. "Kill me now," I taunted. "For Meldron will never be king."

Siawn forced the swordpoint deeper. I could feel his strength gathering behind the point. The blade bit into my flesh. I gripped my staff and made ready to strike.

A voice cried out from the crowd. "Look!"

Another shouted. "The cairn!"

Siawn's eyes shifted to the gravemound. Surprise replaced malice and the blade faltered.

I glanced towards the hilltop. In the torchlight I saw something move inside the cairn. A trick of fickle light, I thought; a flicker of flame, the smokeswirl from the upraised torches. I made to turn away but saw it again... something up there... moving in the darkness...

As we strained forward, all saw the form of a man emerging from the cairn.

A woman cried: "It is the king!"

"The king!" the people gasped. "The king lives!"

A tremor of fear and wonder shivered through the host.

In truth, I thought it was the king returned to life. But the thought vanished at once. It was not Meldryn Mawr struggling back to life.

The man stepped from the gravemound, straightened, and began striding down the Hill of Kings towards us. I caught the golden glint of the champion's ring on his finger.

"Llew!" I shouted. "It is Llew! Llew has returned!"

The name of Llew rippled through the gathered throng. "Llew... it is Llew... Do you see him? Llew!"

Truly, the Otherworld traveller had returned. The Llwyddi melted before him, forming a shining path as he passed among them. He looked neither right nor left, but advanced with resolute steps down the hillside.

I watched him, and saw how the sight of him both astonished and heartened the people: they hailed him, hands stretched to touch him, torches were lofted before him. "Llew! Llew!" they shouted; how easily his name leapt to the tongue.

I watched him striding down from the Kings' Hill on the radiant way and I thought to myself: on this frame the Swift Sure Hand may yet stitch a king.

2

Return of the Hero

"Greetings, brother," I said, as Llew came to stand before me. I would have embraced him as a kinsman, but his jaw was set and there was dread purpose in his eye. "I am glad to see you."

He offered no greeting, but confronted Siawn Hy. "It is over," he said—though he spoke quietly, his words were unyielding—"Put away that sword. We are going home."

Siawn Hy stiffened. The blade in his hand swung instantly from my throat to Llew's. But Llew grasped the naked blade with his bare hand and jerked it aside.

"Take him!" shouted Meldron, reaching for his knife.

A dozen spears swung towards Llew. But the spearheads, still wrapped in their cloth coverings, wavered uncertainly. The warriors of Meldron's Wolf Pack obeyed, although they were reluctant to assault their own champion. The crowd surged dangerously, pressing more closely; some shouted defiance at Meldron's order. The people did not understand what was happening, but clearly they did not like it.

"Llew!" I cried, sweeping the spears aside with the butt of my staff. "Hail, Llew!" I raised my staff and called to the crowd. "The champion has returned! Hail him, everyone!"

The Llwyddi cried out with a mighty voice. Llew turned his eyes to the people gathered all around, torches held high, peering expectantly at him. It came to me that Llew did not know what his appearance meant to those looking on: Meldryn's champion emerging from the Hero Mound. A dead king had gone into the dark portal, a living man had come out—mysteriously, inexplicably, yet in full sight of all: an Otherworld hero declaring his equality with the king we had just buried.

Before Meldron could react, I raised my hands for silence and said, "The king is dead, brother, but you are alive. You are back among your people, and that is cause for celebration."

The people greeted this with loud approval. Meldron's frown deepened as he sensed his moment slipping away. He had exaggerated his support, and underestimated the people's regard for Llew.

Still he sought to recapture the advantage. "What do you mean, coming here like this?" he demanded.

"I have come to honor the king," replied Llew slowly. His eyes flicked from the prince to Siawn Hy. Something passed between Siawn and Llew that I did not understand. But I saw Siawn bristling with anger, and Llew's face harden once more as resolve returned. "And to do something I should have done long ago."

"You speak of honor," Meldron sneered, "but you steal it from the dead."

"Llew was the king's champion," I declared—thinking it prudent to remind everyone that Meldryn Mawr had chosen Llew for this honor; it was the king's final act, and the one which had caused his death. "Who would deny the king's champion the right to pay homage to his lord?"

"You are not in authority here, bard!" Meldron said, his voice vengeful and brimming with spite. "You and your kind may have deceived my father with your sly words and cunning ways. Do not think to deceive me."

"Why speak of deception, Meldron?" I asked. "You are surrounded by wise advisers," I told him, watching Siawn twitching with malice. "Could it be that you do not trust them?"

"I trust the blade in my hand," the prince spat. "I trust my warband. Better the company of warriors, than the empty words of a bard."

Having pressed the matter too far, Meldron did not know how to retreat with dignity. Rather than embrace Llew, which would have increased his own support—for clearly, the people esteemed Llew greatly—he chose to mock and revile.

The prince turned to all those gathered close about. "Llew has returned! We have nothing to fear, now that my father's champion is once more among us." He spoke with undisguised contempt. He slowly raised an accusing finger and pointed at Llew. "Yet I cannot help thinking," he continued, "that if Llew had honored the king as highly as he claims, Meldryn Mawr would yet walk among us. How is it that the king lies dead and his champion lives?"

What the prince hoped to accomplish by this rash speech, I knew well enough: to poison the people's good feeling towards Llew. Apparently, he thought that casting doubt upon Llew's loyalty and ability would aid him. But, instead of sowing doubt, all he managed was confusion.

The people looked at one another in bewilderment. "What is Meldron saying? It was Llew who saved us from the Coranyid!" Several even protested outright: "Paladyr killed the king! Paladyr it was—not Llew!" they shouted.

Yes, I thought, Paladyr killed the king. And where is Paladyr now?

But I held my tongue. If suspicion is to be loosed, let it roost in Prince Meldron's roof, I thought. Oh, but it is a chancy thing to malign a hero who has rightly earned the clan's affection. Meldron showed poor judgment in the attempt, and people have a way of remembering these insults and redressing them.

Having done all he dared for the time being, Meldron called for the procession to depart, then turned and thrust his way through the gathered host. Siawn Hy allowed himself a slender smile, then hurried after Meldron. The Wolf Pack moved away awkwardly, taking their places behind the prince.

I was relieved to see them go, and equally relieved to have Llew beside me once more.

"I feared you dead," I whispered. People streamed by us, every eye on Llew. Some saluted him outright with heartfelt greetings and expressions of respect. Most were too awed to speak, however, and simply touched the back of their hands to their foreheads as they passed.

Llew smiled ruefully. "I should have told you what I intended," he said. "I thought it best to go alone. I am sorry. It will not happen like that next time."

"You mean to leave again?" I asked.

"Yes," Llew replied, tensing again. "I am sorry, Tegid. That is how it must be. You understand."

"But I do not understand," I confessed.

"Then you will just have to accept what I am telling you."

"But you are telling me nothing."

He made no reply, so I reached out and gripped his arm; it was rigid beneath my touch. "Llew, we are brothers, you and I. We have drunk from the same cup and I will not let you go again without hearing a better explanation than I have heard just now."

Llew frowned unhappily, but he remained silent and turned his eyes to watch the departing Llwyddi. I could see it was hard for him, this decision he had made. He wanted to tell me, I think, but simply did not know where or how to begin. So I suggested, "Say nothing yet. We will wait until the others have gone ahead and we will follow at a distance so that we will not be overheard. You can tell me as we walk and no one will disturb us."

Llew agreed, and we waited until the last of the procession had started back through Glyn Du. Then we struck off after them, walking a long while in silence before Llew found the words he sought.

"I am sorry, Tegid," he said. "I should have told you, but I thought you would prevent me."

"Prevent you from leaving?"

"From doing what I had to do—what I must do," he said, and I could feel the turmoil seething within him. I made to speak a soothing word, but he prevented me, saying, "No, Tegid, not yet. I have to say this."

He was quiet a little longer. We listened to the soft swish of our feet through the long grass. Ahead, the first of the procession had reached the entrance of the glen and were dousing their torches in the stream. By the time we came to the place, all that remained was the lingering scent of steam and smoke. The procession had moved out into the Vale of Modornn. A pale moon had risen and we could see, drawn in silver on the darkness of the valley floor, the long lines of walkers stretching out before us.

It made my heart ache to see it, for it seemed to me as if we were a dying race walking through the fading light into oblivion's darkness. But I kept this to myself, and waited for Llew to speak his heart to me.

He began again as we moved out from the mouth of the black glen. "There is a war raging in my world," said Llew softly. "It is not a war of swords and spears—I wish it were: we could fight the enemy then. But the enemy is here," he struck his fist against his chest. "The enemy is within us—it has poisoned us and made us sick. We are sick inside, Tegid. Siawn and I have been poisoned, and we have brought this poison to Albion. If we stay here, we will poison everything—we will destroy everything."

"Llew, but for you it would have been destroyed already. You saved us when no one else could."

He seemed not to hear me, for he continued as before. "Simon—Siawn has already spread the poison far. He has put ideas into the prince's head—ideas that have no place here in Albion."

"He would have little trouble there. Meldron was ever greedy for more than he was given."

"I believe the murder of Meldryn Mawr was Siawn's idea. He thought kings were chosen by right of succession, and he—"

"Right of succession?" I wondered, halting him. "I know nothing of this right."

"*Dilyn hawl,*" he said, choosing other words. "It means that the kingship is passed from father to son. In our world, that is how it is done. Simon—Siawn Hy, that is—did not know that it was done any other way. He thought if Meldryn Mawr died, the kingship would pass to Prince Meldron directly."

"He told you this?"

"Not in so many words, no. But I know Simon; I know how he thinks. And he convinced Meldron that together they could change the way kingship was held and conferred—they could alter the rites of sovereignty."

"So that is why they tried to silence the song," I said. "And that is why they hold the Singing Stones now."

"The Song of Albion..." he grew silent, remembering.

"They think the stones will give them power," I informed him. "They hope to use the song as a weapon."

"Then it is even worse than I thought," Llew muttered. "If I had done what I set out to do, none of this would have happened."

He stopped walking and caught me by the arm. "Do you hear, Tegid? All those people—your clansmen, Tegid, the king and all the others—they would still be alive if I had done what I came here to do. Meldryn Mawr and all those who fell to Lord Nudd would still be alive."

"What do you mean, talking this way?" I said. "It is only because of you that any of us remain alive now. We owe our lives to you."

"It is only because of me so many have died!" he insisted. "Tegid, listen to me. I came here to take Simon back, and I failed. I allowed myself to be charmed, to become enchanted with this place and to believe that I could stay."

"If you had not come," I replied, trying to soothe him, "Meldron and Siawn would have succeeded."

"Tegid," the grim determination was back in his voice, "Simon must be stopped. He does not belong here—I do not belong here, either. We must go back to our own world. I must take him away from here, but I need your help, brother. Help me, Tegid."

I gripped his arms in the way of kinsmen and said, "Llew, you know I will do anything you ask. But I would ask something of you."

"Ask, then. I will do it if I can."

"Let me make a king of you," I said.

He recoiled. "You have not heard a word I said," he cried, shrugging my hands from him. "How can you ask me such a thing?"

"You were the king's champion. By the Hero Feat you saved us when no one else could. The people respect you; they would support you before Meldron."

"Tegid, it cannot be!" He started walking again—quick, angry steps.

I walked beside him. "I cannot allow Meldron to become king. He will not perpetuate his atrocity by my hand. Yet I must give the kingship to someone—and soon."

"Give it to someone else."

"There *is* no one else."

He whirled to face me. "You do not understand! Simon has to be stopped before he destroys everything. I have to see to it that he goes back where he belongs. Do you hear what I am telling you?"

"I hear you, brother," I replied softly. "But think what I am saying. As king you could stop Siawn Hy and Meldron. You could undo all the wrong that Siawn has done by taking the throne."

He made to turn away, but I caught his shoulder and held him fast. "Hear me, Llew," I said earnestly. "You say that Siawn has spread a deadly poison here. If that is true, then stop him. I am offering you the chance to do that."

3

Tán n'Righ

"Long in my grave and cold I will be," I vowed, "before ever I give the kingship of my people to that hissing viper Meldron. If he were a snake, I would lop off his head and throw his writhing body into the firepit."

"But Meldron has made himself king."

"He is not the king! Only sovereignty can make a man king. And only a true bard can confer sovereignty," I declared. "I alone hold the kingship of Prydain. And it is mine to give as I choose. That is the ancient and honorable way."

We sat alone on the hillside below ruined Sycharth, talking quietly. I thought it best to speak in secret, away from Meldron's eyes and ears, and I knew no one would intrude so near to the devastated stronghold.

Llew shook his head slowly. "I do not like it, Tegid. Do you expect Meldron just to step aside while you hand the crown to someone else? He would have killed us tonight if the people had not prevented him."

"And they will prevent him again. You saw how it was; they will not let Meldron harm you. They esteem you highly, Llew. They respect you. Given a choice between you and Meldron, they will follow you."

Llew was silent for a long time. Then he said, "Very well, Tegid. I will do it." Before I could reply, he raised a finger and quickly added, "But only until my task here is accomplished. Then you will have to choose someone else to be your king."

"Agreed," I said quickly.

"I mean it, Tegid! I will be king only until I can find a way to get Simon back to the other side where he belongs. Do you understand?"

"I understand."

He glared at me.

"Only until Siawn Hy is subdued. I understand, brother. Truly."

The tension went out of him at last. "How do we go about this kingmaking then?"

"There are many ways kingship may be conferred," I told him. "I will use a way that Meldron does not know—an ancient way. I will use the *Tán n'Righ*."

"King by fire?" Llew wondered. "That sounds painful—is it?"

"No," I replied, "not if you do it right. But it is necessary that you listen carefully and do everything exactly as I tell you."

We talked far into the night, head to head, huddled in our cloaks, shivering, and watching the campfires below. Dawn was not far off when we finished.

"Now what?" asked Llew, yawning.

"We will rest now. And you will stay out of sight. Meldron must not find an excuse to challenge you. Also, he must not become suspicious or he will interfere. I know where you can hide."

I told him where he could sleep in seclusion, and we rose and stood together. "Are you certain that it can be done in one day?" Llew asked.

"One day is all I need. Leave everything to me. I will come for you, or send someone, when all is ready."

We parted then and went our separate ways. As I walked down the hillside to the camp my thoughts were already racing fast and far, far ahead. Yes, there was much to be done, and it must all be done quickly. The ceremony would take place that night!

I worked through the day—quietly, and without undue haste. I assembled stones from the four quarters—black from the north, white from the south, green from the west, and purple from the east. I drew water from a fresh-running spring. I gathered the nine sacred woods: willow from a moving stream; hazel from among the rocks; alder from the marshes; birch from the waterfall; yew from the open place; blackthorn from the hidden place; elm from the shady place; rowan from the hill; oak from the sun. To these, the *Nawglan*, the Sacred Nine, I added holly with its bright array of spears; elder with its potent purple berries; and apple with its sweet, smooth hardness.

I burned these in a fire built on a flat stone. Then I carefully collected the ash and put it into a leather pouch which I tied to my belt. When I had made these preparations, I returned to camp and set about gathering wood for the Tán n'Righ, the King Fire. For this, I took live embers from each of the hearthfires which the people had burned the night before, and firewood from the stockpile of each camp.

The only difficulty lay in obtaining the ember and branch from the prince's fire. But the Goodly-Wise smiled on me, and Meldron—bored with the duties of the camp, which he considered beneath him—rode out to hunt at midday. I had only to wait until he and the warriors of his Wolf Pack were out of sight. I helped myself to what I needed and he was none the wiser.

At dusk I summoned Llew from hiding and hastened back to camp to await Meldron's return from the hunt.

In the time-between-times, the light of a new-risen moon on my left, the setting sun on my right, I kindled the King Fire within a circle of stones gathered from the four quarters. Then I summoned the people with the aurochs' horn. The sound had not been heard among us since Meldryn Mawr led us to Findargad, and the clansmen were alarmed to hear it now. They gathered quickly, circling the fire ring. Then I called Llew from my tent.

As Llew stepped forward to take his place, Prince Meldron thrust his way forward through the host, Siawn Hy at his side. "What is this, Tegid?" Meldron called. "More of your foolishness?"

I did not acknowledge the insult, for I did not want to give them leave to speak.

"Put off your boots," I told Llew. When he had untied the laces and pulled the buskins from his feet, I said, "Spread your cloak on the ground behind you."

He did this, and turned again to me. "Remove your siarc, and belt, and breecs," I told him.

Llew hesitated at this command, but obeyed. "Lay aside your clothing," I told him, "and come before me."

In full view of the gathered clan, Llew reluctantly stripped off his clothes, placing them on the outspread cloak as he removed them. Then he stepped before me and I bade him walk three times in a rightwise circle around me.

"This is embarrassing," he growled through clenched teeth as he passed the first time.

"Keep walking."

"They are laughing at me!" he whispered as he completed the second circuit.

"Let them laugh. They will squeal like stuck pigs soon enough."

He continued, walking slowly, and, completing his third circuit, came to stand before me once more. "Can we get on with it?"

"It is of highest importance. You must be seen to possess no blemish," I told him. "Stretch forth your right hand."

He put out his right hand. "Now the left," I directed. And as he stretched forth his left hand, I stooped to the fire and caught up two burning branches which I had prepared. I pulled them out of the flames and stepped behind him. "Remember," I whispered as I moved behind him. "Say nothing. And do not twitch a muscle."

Taking a branch in either hand, I began moving the flaming brands over his naked body. Beginning at the heels, I worked the torches up along his calves and thighs, over his buttocks, and along his ribs, and then along his outstretched arms. Llew stood rigidly, looking neither right nor left, but staring straight ahead, his eyes fixed on the rising moon.

I worked the flames over his chest and stomach, down over his groin and genitals, legs and feet. The hair on his chest and legs singed where the flames touched his skin and filled the air with the stink of burning hair. His jaw bulged, and he glared murderously at me, but he did not wince or cry out.

"Llew!" I said loudly, rising to stand before him face to face. "You have displayed yourself before the people. I find no blemish on you."

At this, one of the Wolf Pack shouted, "How can you see through all the soot?" They all laughed again, even now thinking no ill—which only shows how ignorant they were.

"As flames cleanse and purify," I continued, carefully replacing the branches in the fire. "I proclaim you cleansed and purified of all corruption." Taking up the pouch at my side, I poured the contents into my left hand and with the fingertips of my right hand, I marked Llew with the Nawglan, saining him with the Sacred Nine: on the sole of each foot, across the stomach, over the heart, at the throat, upon the forehead, down the spine, and around each wrist.

The Llwyddi watched, mystified. I stole a glance at the prince and saw that his haughty smirk had faded, and he now appeared mildly concerned by what he saw before him. Siawn Hy looked on with cool menace in his hooded eyes.

When I finished, I stepped once more before him. "Lift your voice, Llew. Declare before the people: who do you serve?"

He replied as I had told him: "I serve the people!"

"Whence comes your life?"

"The life of the people is my life!"

"Where will you reside?"

"I reside in the will of the people!"

"How will you rule?"

"I will rule in the wisdom of the people!"

"How will you obtain?"

"I will obtain in the wealth of the people!"

I raised my hands before his face, palms outward. "I have heard your declaration," I called in a loud voice, so all could hear. "Let it be so confirmed!"

So saying, I turned and retrieved the firebrands. Quickly, so that he would not have time to think about what was happening, I thrust a burning brand into each of Llew's hands—flame-end downwards. The fire raced up the length of the branch, and instantly Llew's hands were engulfed in flames. Yet he stood before them, grasping the firebrands as the fire licked at his flesh. He did not scream or cry out; he did not flinch or drop the torches.

The people gasped. Prince Meldron and his scoffers gaped stupidly.

"With flames of fire," I proclaimed, "your declaration is confirmed."

Llew raised the burning brands above his head and slowly turned round so that everyone could see that the fire consumed the branches but did not burn his flesh.

With every eye on the marvel of the fist-clenched fire, no one saw my hand reach under my cloak and withdraw the torc. The firebrands lifted high, Llew's back to me, I stepped behind him and slipped the golden torc around his neck. And then I raised my hands over him and said, "By authority of the Tán n'Righ, I declare you king!"

I turned to the people and lifted my voice in song:

"By authority of wind when it gusts sea gales, you are king.
"By authority of sun when it whelms dark night, you are king.
"By authority of rain when it greens far hills, you are king.
"By authority of earth when it heaves high mountains,
you are king.
"By authority of stone when it births bright iron, you are king.
"By authority of bull and eagle and salmon and all creatures that swim and fly and tread the hidden places of earth, sky, and sea, you are king.
"By authority of the Goodly-Wise, who with his Swift Sure Hand establishes and upholds all things in this worlds-realm,
you are king."

The song ended, I raised my staff and proclaimed, "Behold! Llew,

Sovereign of Prydain, King of the Llwyddi! Pay him heartfelt homage! Prepare to do him honor!"

Some were already in the act of kneeling, when the prince's voice stopped them. "No! No! He is not your king!" Meldron dashed into the fire circle and seized Llew's torc, tearing it violently from around his throat. "I am the king!"

Before anyone could lift a hand to prevent him, Siawn Hy had a spear in Llew's ribs, and he was shouting, "Meldron is king! Meldron is king!"

Siawn pulled Llew's arms down and knocked the firebrands from his hands. He gestured to the foremost of the Wolf Pack, who stepped into the circle, glancing nervously at the people gathered close about. I noticed they avoided my eyes.

Meldron, raising the torc above his own head, declared himself king, saying, "Hear me now! I hold the torc of the Llwyddi kings! The kingship of my father is mine by right!"

"There is no such right!" I countered. "Only a bard can bestow kingship. And I have given it to Llew!"

"You have no power here!"

"I am the chief bard of our people," I replied, calmly, confidently. "I alone hold the sovereignty. I alone hold the power to confer kingship."

"You are nothing!" the prince roared, clenching the torc in his fist and shaking it in my face. "I hold my father's torc. I am king!"

"And I tell you that holding a torc will not make you a king, any more than standing in the forest will make you a tree!"

Some laughed at this and Meldron's rage deepened at the laughter. I rushed on, recklessly. "Go ahead! Wear the golden torc, and command the *gosgordd* of warriors," I challenged. "Array yourself in fine clothes, and lavish gifts of gold and silver on the yammering pack who clamor after you. Do all you will, Meldron! But remember this: Sovereignty does not reside in the torc, or in the throne, or even in the might of the sword."

I turned to the people. It was time for them to act, to put down Meldron once and for all. "Listen to me! Meldron is not the king. You have just seen a kingmaking: Llew is the chosen king. Resist Meldron! Defy him! He has no power here. He can do no—"

Then, before I could say another word, Meldron screamed to his Wolf Pack, "Seize them! Seize them both!"

The Captive Pit

"I am sorry, brother."

I might have been speaking to the mud at my feet. Llew sat with his knees drawn to his chest, his head resting on his arms. In the dim light of the pit, he was a shadow—a morose and miserable shadow.

After seven nights and days in Meldron's captive pit, I did not blame him. The fault was mine. I had underestimated Meldron and his readiness to overthrow the long-honored ways of our people. I had misjudged the support he enjoyed among his warrior band, the Wolf Pack, and their willingness to uphold him against their own kinsmen. Yes, and I had overestimated my own ability to exploit the respect the people felt towards Llew. They might have exalted Llew, but Meldron was known to them, and he was one of their own. Llew was the outsider, the stranger in our midst.

Nevertheless, I had thought—no, I had believed in my blood and bones—that the people would not stand by and let Meldron challenge their last remaining bard. A king is a king, but a bard is the heart and soul of the people; he is their life in song, and the lamp which guides their steps along the paths of destiny. A bard is the essential spirit of the clan; he is the linking ring, the golden cord which unites the manifold ages of the clan, binding all that is past with all that is yet to come.

But fear makes men blind and stupid. And these were troubled times. I should have known the people would not challenge Meldron to the shedding of blood. In the Day of Strife, even brave men would not risk their lives for the truth by which we have ever lived.

"I am sorry, Llew."

"Stop saying that, Tegid," he muttered. "I am sick of it."

"I did not mean this to happen."

He raised his face to the low black roof above his head. "It is my own fault for letting you talk me into it. I never should have listened to you."

"I am sorry, Llew—"

"Stop it!" His head whipped towards me. "It—it is..." he struggled to rise above the lethargy of our predicament but crumpled at the effort and slipped back into his misery. "What is the use? It does not matter."

He was silent for a long time, and I thought he would not speak again. But then he said, "I remember now, Tegid. I can remember everything—I could not remember it before."

"What do you remember?"

"My own world," he answered. "Until I went back, I had all but forgotten it even existed. I did not want to remember, you see? And I almost succeeded in forgetting altogether. But for Simon, I would never have considered going back, and I would have lost it."

I watched him in the darkness of the pit. He had never spoken to me about his own world, and it is not our way to inquire. Those of other worlds who sojourn among us—the *Dyn Dythri,* the strangers—are treated with respect. We accept them and include them; we teach them our ways and allow them the freedom to prove themselves and earn what honor they can.

Once our race journeyed in their world, and we gave them gifts to ease the burdens of their lives. But no more. The rift between the worlds has grown ever wider, and the bridge is treacherous and dark. We still welcome the strangers among us, but we do not willingly journey to their world, nor do we encourage them as we once did.

"It had changed," Llew continued, speaking earnestly. "The

world, my world, had changed. It was even worse than when I left—and I think only a day or two had passed on that side. No color, no life—everything fading away, decaying, disintegrating."

He seemed to be trying to work something out in his mind, to explain it to himself, perhaps; so I did not intrude on his thought but let him speak.

"It is the Paradise War," he continued. "What happens here, in this world, affects life over there. Profes— I mean, my friend Nettles, told me; he explained it all to me. And I believed him. But I had no idea it could be so—that the change could be so devastating. It was as if the world was disappearing before my eyes."

I remembered what he had said about Siawn Hy poisoning our world—or at least corrupting the weak Prince Meldron. "Corruption is always a potent enemy," I observed.

"It is more than that, Tegid," he replied quickly, shifting in the darkness to lean towards me. "Much more than that. There is a balance, you see—a harmony between this world and the other. Simon has upset the balance; his ideas, his schemes—just his presence here has changed things."

"And changes in this world provoke changes in the other world," I offered. "I understand."

"Believe me, if there is going to be anything left worth saving—of either world—Simon must be stopped."

"I do believe you, brother," I replied. "But before we can save the world, we must first save ourselves."

"We have to get out of here. We have to get free!" He rose—as he had risen countless times before, to push against the timber planks over our heads. But it was useless, and he soon collapsed again.

"Will he kill us, do you think?" he asked after a time. "Now that he is king—"

"Meldron is not the king. You are the king."

"Pardon me," he scoffed bitterly, "I keep forgetting."

"I have given the kingship to you," I told him. How many times had I told him already? "You are the king. And I do not know what Meldron will do," I replied. "If I knew, we would not be here like this now."

"Do not tell me that you are sorry, Tegid. I will not hear it yet again."

After seizing us during the kingmaking ceremony, Meldron had dragged us up to the ruined caer and imprisoned us in the refuse pit behind the hall. He had covered the pit with charred timbers and sealed them with a mound of rubble and filth from the burnt-out stronghold. There he left us under guard. What he intended doing with us, I could not guess. And it occurred to me that Meldron did not know, either.

He feared killing us outright, I surmised, or we would be dead already. He had stretched the support of the people to the breaking-point; any further trouble and he would lose what little favor he now enjoyed. Neither could he let us go free to incite rebellion against him. So, until he could think of a better way to deal with us, we would remain his prisoners.

The pit was watched day and night to prevent anyone from helping us to escape. There were at least two guards at all times, and often more. We could sometimes hear them talking as they came and went, changing watch duties. We knew when they changed because the new guards brought us water and a little food, which they lowered to us through a small chink in one of the planks.

So the days passed. Llew and I remained in our stinking, filth-smothered prison, locked away from the light, and any who might help us. And with each passing day, Meldron despised us the more— yet he could not rule unopposed while Llew and I remained alive. This thought alone cheered me. For, in this small way at least, we were preventing him from beginning his wrongful reign.

One night, I awakened to a small scraping sound. I disregarded it at first, thinking it nothing more than the gnawing of the rats which had taken over the caer. But I gradually perceived that the slow scrape–scrape–scrape had a definite rhythm.

Someone was digging.

I waited, listening in the darkness. The sound grew louder, and I ventured speaking to the digger. "Who is it?" I asked, hardly daring to raise my voice above a whisper.

Llew was asleep. But he stirred when I spoke. "Tegid? What is it?" he said, rolling onto his knees.

"Shh! Listen!"

"Be quiet down there . . . you will wake the warriors . . ." The voice was that of a child.

"Who are you?" I persisted.

"It is Ffand," came the reply. "Now be quiet."

"Who is Ffand?" Llew wondered.

"Who is with you, Ffand?" I asked, pressing my face against the roof timbers of our crude prison.

"No one is with me," she answered, and the scraping noise began again. It continued for some time, and then it stopped.

"What are you doing, Ffand?"

"Shh!" the whisper was sharp, insistent. Silence followed. And then: "It was one of the warriors. He woke up, but he is asleep again. I have to leave now."

"Wait—"

"It will be morning soon."

"Ffand! Wait, I—"

"I will come back again when it is night."

"Please—"

But she was already gone. I slumped back to the floor.

"Who is Ffand?" asked Llew again.

"She is the girl who keeps your dog," I explained.

"My dog?" he wondered aloud, and I could tell he had forgotten all about Twrch. "Oh, yes . . . my dog."

"You gave Twrch to a little girl. On the way to Findargad—"

"Before the battle of Dun na Porth," he said. "I remember. I never learned her name."

All that long, long day we waited. Night could not arrive soon enough. The darkness of our prison deepened and we held our breath, listening for the slight scraping sound to come again. When it did not come, we brooded over what could have happened to her: maybe she could not get away tonight; maybe the guard would not sleep tonight... Or worse: maybe she had been discovered and caught... What would they do to her if they caught her?

We had given up hope when the slow scrape–scrape–scrape began again. "She has returned!" I whispered. "Ffand!" And I tapped lightly on the beam above my head. "Ffand!"

A moment later her voice answered, "Shhh! Be quiet! They will hear you!"

I made to speak again, but Llew cautioned me. "Let be, Tegid. Let her work."

I settled back, and we listened to the rhythmic scraping sound above us. But it had no sooner begun than it stopped. And it did not begin again that night. We listened long, but the sound did not come again.

We waited through the next day, anxious and uneasy, hoping she had not been discovered. Wondering why she had stopped...

Ffand did not come the next night, and we feared the worst.

So dejected were we that we did not expect her again. So, when the scraping sound began again on the following night, we were startled by its suddenness, and realized we had been waiting— waiting for it and willing it to begin again.

She worked all through the night, stopping only twice: once to rest—she said her hands were tired—and once when one of the guards woke to relieve himself.

She did not return for the next two nights. But we knew now not to be concerned. Little Ffand was obviously canny and capable. She would choose her times well and would not risk discovery needlessly. In any event, we had no other course but to await her pleasure.

Ffand returned on the following night to tell us that King Meldron had announced he would be holding court in the morning. "He has said we must all get ready to leave this place. He says we are moving to Caer Modornn."

"When?"

"Very soon," came the reply. "At dawn the day after the court."

Llew laid a hand to my arm. "Ask her how long it will take to free us? Can she do it tonight?"

"Ffand," I said, my cheek hard against the plank above, "can you finish tonight? Can you free us tonight?"

There came a little silence. And then, "I do not think so."

"Listen, Ffand, it must be tonight. They will come for us tomorrow. We must be free tonight."

"I will try."

"Maybe we can help," said Llew. "Ffand, tell us what to do."

The scraping sound began again—more quickly this time, and louder as the girl began working harder and faster to free us. She did not stop or slacken her pace but worked through the night. Scrape–scrape–scrape . . . scrape–scrape . . . scrape–scrape–scrape . . . all through the night.

And then . . . there came a dull thud, as if something heavy had fallen away.

"There!" Ffand's voice came down to us. "It is done."

"Good. Tell us what to do, Ffand," I said.

"The timber is loose now," came the reply. "But it is too heavy for me to move—you have to do it."

"Which timber, Ffand? Knock on the one we are to move."

A sturdy thump sounded on a timber at one corner of the pit. "Good. Now listen very carefully, Ffand. We will do the rest. But you must leave us now. I want you well away from here."

There came no answer.

"Ffand?"

"I do not want to go."

"You must. I do not want you to get hurt if anything goes wrong. Go now."

Llew spoke to the timber. "Ffand—" he said, earnestly, "listen to me."

"Yes?"

"Thank you, Ffand. You have saved our lives. But you must get far away from here if all your hard work is not to be wasted. Understand? Besides, think of Twrch—what will happen to him without you? I want you to look after him a little longer. Will you do that for me, Ffand?"

"Oh, very well," she sighed.

"One more thing," I said quickly. "How many guards are there?"

"Only two tonight, and they are sound sleepers." She paused, putting her face close to the timber. "Fare well."

"Ffand?"

No answer.

"She has gone," I surmised. "Ready?"

Llew knelt beside me at the far end of the pit. Together we gripped the timber, working our fingers into the cracks between the beams on either side. At last I understood what Ffand had done: using the heap of rubble to shield her from the guards, she had scraped through the debris and soil at the end of the pit and freed one beam. It still bore its weight of rubble, but by shifting the heavy timber back and forth a little at a time, we began to loosen, and at last to withdraw it. Debris and filth rained down on us, falling through the crack we made. But we worked at the plank, sliding it back and back until there was a gap large enough for a man to squeeze his shoulders through.

Then we squatted on our heels, staring up at the hole we had made and listening. When none of the guards stirred, I said, "I will go first."

I poked my head cautiously through the gap. As Ffand had said, there were two warriors on guard and both were asleep. I forced myself up into the hole, wriggling and kicking my way until I was able to pull myself through.

I knelt, tense and sweating, behind the heap of debris that covered the pit. The guards slept some distance away—as far from the stench of the place as possible, I suppose. That is why they had not heard Ffand, or us.

"Come," I whispered to Llew.

A few moments later, he crouched beside me. Quickly, quietly, moving with exaggerated care through the tumbled wreckage of Meldryn Mawr's once-great stronghold, we hastened, ever watchful for other guards. But we met no one else, nor did I wonder. The caer was a charnel mound, stinking and desolate. The warriors to whose lot it had fallen to become guards could not have been chosen for a more detestable task.

I marvelled at little Ffand's courage. The child had dared what bold men shirked.

We hurried to the place where the gates had stood, and there paused to overlook the plain. I could see the campfires arrayed below, and, towards the curve of Muir Glain, the horse pickets. By skirting the camp to the east, we could reach the nearer horses without being seen.

But we would have to make haste—already the sky was lightening in the east. It would be dawn soon and people would begin stirring. We wanted to be well away before anyone knew we had escaped.

Without a word, we started down the track from the caer. Staying clear of the nearer tents, our hearts racing wildly, we traced the perimeter of the camp, reaching the nearest stake line just as the first rays of the sun broke above the horizon.

There were sentries on watch: two of the Wolf Pack—careless and indifferent, it is true, but present nonetheless. So we paused to decide how best to take the horses without alerting the watchers. Presently, one of them rose from their campfire and walked off along the line of horses. The remaining sentry stayed slumped at the fire, apparently asleep.

"It is now or never," said Llew, and he made ready to dart in among the horses. But he had not stirred a step when we saw two horses back away from the picket and begin walking towards us. We watched mystified, until they turned and we saw a slender, frail-looking girl—Ffand, it was—between the animals, holding tight to their halters and leading them to meet us.

She came to where we waited at the far end of the picket. She was younger than I remembered, thin, her face smudged with dirt, her smile gap-toothed, her hair bedraggled, her clothes filthy from her digging.

"Beautiful girl!" exclaimed Llew softly.

"May the Gifting God bless her richly," I murmured, scanning the pickets for any sign of the sentry's return. I saw no one, and a few moments later Ffand stood before us, offering us the reins.

"I did not know which ones belonged to you, so I chose the best," she said happily. "Did I do right?"

"You have done wonderfully!" I told her.

"I love you, Ffand." Llew placed a big kiss on her round cheek. A sudden flush of delight lit her face.

We gathered the reins and swung onto our mounts' bare backs. "What about Twrch?" Ffand asked.

"Can I trust you to keep him a little longer, Ffand?" Llew asked. She nodded solemnly. "Good. I will come for him one day."

"Fare well, Ffand," I told her. "We will not forget how you have helped us."

"Fare well!" the young girl replied. "I will keep Twrch safe."

We turned our mounts to the north and rode for the river. Across the marshes lay the wooded hills and, beyond, the wide Vale of Modornn. We would cross the River Modornn and strike east into Llogres, for there was no longer any help to be had in Prydain. A ride of two days would bring us to Blár Cadlys, the principal stronghold of the Cruin king.

We reached the edge of the marsh and Llew called out. "Wait! Listen!" I halted.

In the distance I heard the sharp blat of the horn sounding the alarm. Our escape had been discovered.

5

Hunted

Mist hung thick and dense over the marshlands. We drove straight towards the heart of the fen where the fog haze was heaviest. If we could avoid the hunters there, we would have a chance of escape.

But, before this small hope could take root, I heard the hounds: the sharp, savage, heart-sinking howl of a hunting hound in pursuit. There were three of the king's pack left, and Meldron had not hesitated a moment in sending them after us.

Llew gained the edge of the fen just ahead of me, and disappeared into the mist. I followed, nearly colliding with him at the water marge.

"Which way?" he asked.

"Dismount! Send the horses on!"

"We can lose the hounds in the fog."

"They would track us by the sound," I told him. "Send the horses on and we may yet elude them."

He slid from the horse's back and slapped it on the rump. "Hie!" The horse bolted riderless into the fen. I slid into knee-deep water, and sent my mount on with a slap and a cry—then followed Llew's quickly vanishing form.

I was sorry to lose the horses so soon, but this way offered our only chance of escape. Dogs can run a horse to exhaustion, and with their keen noses there would be no eluding them. In the marsh, however, the dogs would have to rely on their ears; they would pursue the horses, and the riders would follow the dogs.

The water was cold, the sun dim and distant. We proceeded to a nearby stand of rushes. "Go in there," I directed. The leaves were dry—new growth had not yet come—and the dead stalks rattled as we entered. After a dozen steps, I halted. "We wait here," I explained. "As soon as the riders pass, we will run to the river."

"If they do not ride over us first," Llew pointed out.

"Listen!"

I heard the splatter of a horse's hooves, and the snarl of a dog. Clenching our teeth, we hunkered down in the water and pulled the rushes around us.

A little distance away, we heard another horse strike the water marge and splash into the fen. But a heartbeat later, another rider followed . . . and then two more.

Once in the marsh, the mist diffused the sound of the riders, so that they seemed to come at us from every direction. It was impossible to tell where they were, or how near. Llew and I squatted in the water, shivering, listening to the sound of the hunters all around. We heard them directing one another, heard them calling to the dogs, heard the dogs baying and yelping.

The sound steadily diminished as the hunters moved farther away. We waited, shivering, in the water. The fog swirled in the air and I could see blue sky above us as the rising sun burned through the marsh-haze. "We should move," Llew whispered. "The fog is clearing. They will see us."

He rose and started forward.

"Wait," I whispered, grasping his wrist and pulling him back down beside me.

The plunge of hooves striking the water was the only warning we had. A horse careered into the rushes. The rider, sword in hand, slashed as he came.

Llew hurled himself to one side, and I dived to the other.

The startled horse reared. The rider struck with his sword.

Thrashing, Llew staggered to his feet, and ducked beneath the horse's belly as the rider struck again. He grabbed the warrior's sword arm and pulled him from his mount. I swung out at the horse, swatting it on the flat of the neck. The frightened beast bolted into the fen beyond.

The rider shouted. Llew struck him in the face with his fist—once, and again. His struggling ceased.

We froze, listening.

There came no answering cry, no shout of discovery.

"Help me get him up," Llew said. We heaved the unconscious rider onto our shoulders and dragged him back across the fen to the water marge where we left him.

"The river is that way," I said, looking east. "With speed we might reach it before they circle back this way."

"To the river, then," Llew replied.

We floundered across the wetlands, skirting the edge of the marsh, scrambling now over soggy hillocks, and now through water to our thighs. Our lungs burned, our hearts raced, our muscles ached, but we struggled on towards the looming wood which marked the near bank of the Modornn River.

Streaming cold water, our clothing sodden and heavy on our limbs, we gained the brushline and forced our way through thickets of elder, willow and hazel. Thorns raked at us. We penetrated the brush and drove through the standing wood, making for the steep bank down to the river.

At high tide, the Modornn is a wide, shallow expanse of grey-green water. At low tide, it is a broad sweep of mud cut through by a single deep channel. Either way we would have to swim, but I hoped the tide would be high enough to cover our tracks across the muddy stretches either side of the channel.

By the time we reached the river's edge, I could see that the tide was on the ebb. The water level was falling, but there was still enough water to cover our tracks; and if we hurried, we could reach the farther shore before the mudflat became exposed.

Without a backward glance, we lurched across the tidal estuary:

sprawling, falling, hauling one another upright, and fighting on through the mud. We floundered through the channel and slithered across the shallows on the far side. Sticky, foul-smelling muck sucked at our feet and legs.

By the time we reached the far bank, the water scarcely filled our footprints. But we dragged ourselves into the undergrowth and lay on our backs, gulping air—listening for the sound we dreaded: the shout of discovery and the clatter of hooves across the estuary.

We waited, but the shout never came. The hoofbeats did not sound.

When it appeared we had eluded the pursuit, at least thus far, we drew together the ragged remnants of our strength and staggered deeper into the wood, away from the bank. Only then did I begin to hope we might yet escape.

We had eaten little since our capture—dry bread and sour beer which the guards let down to us—and hunger had sapped our endurance. We walked east, away from the river, and stopped in a clearing to rest and let the sun dry our clothing.

There we listened intently for any sound of the chase. We heard neither hound nor horse. And slowly the quiet of the wood began to calm us.

"We have no weapons, no provisions, no horses," Llew said, rolling onto his side. "Can we expect a welcome cup from the Cruin, do you think?"

The Llwyddi and the Cruin have often met face to face on the battleground. But just as often have we feasted one another. Meldryn Mawr always enjoyed King Calbha's respect, if not his friendship. "Well," I observed, "a bard is welcome anywhere."

"Then lead on, wise bard," Llew said. "And let us hope Lord Calbha is in as sore need of a song as I am of a hot supper."

We rose on tired legs to begin our journey through the wooded hills and boggy lowlands to the Cruin stronghold at Blár Cadlys. All that day we walked—with much backward glancing and many a pause to rest and to listen for the sound of pursuit. We reached the grassy banks of a secluded stream as the sun slipped behind the hills.

There, weary and footsore, we stopped for the night, drinking our fill from the stream, and then wrapping ourselves in our cloaks to rest and sleep in the long, winter-dry grass. I woke at dawn and roused Llew. We washed in the stream, and then continued on our way.

Four days we journeyed thus, sleeping at night beside a stream or pool, and moving on at dawn. Four days on foot through dense wood and reeking bogland. It was too early for berries, and we could not stop to catch any game. But we kept starvation at bay with shoots and roots that I knew how to find; and we drank from fresh streams and pools.

At the end of the last day, and the end of our strength, we came in sight of the Cruin settlement. Hungry beyond words, we stood at the edge of the surrounding wood and watched the silver smoke rising from the cooking fires within the caer. The scent of the smoke brought water to my mouth, and a sharp pang to my empty stomach.

Blár Cadlys is built atop a great oblong hill which guards the entrance to Ystrad Can Cefyl, the Vale of the White Horse, the principal route into the heart of Llogres. On the broad plains of the sprawling valley run the huge herds of horses which give rise to the Cruin boast: horsemen second to none. Indeed, the boast is not without a shade of truth.

"Do you think they know what has happened to Meldryn Mawr?" Llew wondered.

"No, they could not know yet—unless..."

"Unless Paladyr has preceded us?"

He spoke my thoughts exactly. "Come, we will soon discover what they know."

We stumbled from the wood and staggered up to the caer—but slowly so that they would have time to mark our approach. And they did. For, as we set foot on the track leading to the gate, three warriors appeared at the breastwork of the gatehouse. The foremost of them called out to us, commanding us to halt and declare ourselves.

"I am Tegid Talaryant," I shouted back to him. "Chief Bard to Meldryn Mawr of the Llwyddi. The man with me is champion to the king. We have matters to discuss with your lord."

The porter regarded us doubtfully, exchanged a brief word with his fellows, and then replied, "You claim to be men of esteem and honor, yet you come to us as beggars. Where are your horses? Where are your weapons? Why do you come to us ragged and on foot?"

"As to that," I answered, "I deem it no man's affair but my own. Yet it may be that Calbha will think it worth his while to welcome us as befits men of our rank and renown."

They laughed aloud at this, but I stopped them quickly enough. "Hear me now! Unless you take my message to your lord, I will declaim against you, and against all your kinsmen."

That gave them something to think about.

"Do you think they believed you?" asked Llew, as the three discussed my threat.

"Perhaps not. But now we will see how far they trust their luck."

Apparently the Cruin guards were not in a wagering mood. For, after a short deliberation, one of the three disappeared and but a moment later the gate opened. Four warriors emerged from the caer and came forth to conduct us to the king's hall. They did not speak, but motioned us to follow them.

I had once been in Blár Cadlys with Ollathir, and found it little altered from the way I remembered it. Yet there were changes: grain stores increased in number, and two warriors' houses now where there had been but one. Outside the artisans' huts men worked at fashioning spear shafts; the cattle pens had been enlarged.

As we neared the hall, one of the warriors hastened ahead to alert his lord. King Calbha received us outside the hall. Broad-shouldered and bull-necked, he wore his dark hair and beard short, and his moustache long. He strode towards us, a hand on the hilt of his sword, and a mild frown creasing his wide brow. Those with him watched with interest to see how the king would deal with us. "Greetings, Llwyddi," the Cruin lord said, but he did not extend his hands to us. "It is long since we have welcomed your tribe within these walls. I cannot say it is a pleasure I have missed."

"Greetings, Lord Calbha," I replied, inclining my head

respectfully. "It is long since the Llwyddi have ventured across the Modornn. But no doubt you will soon acquire the pleasure of welcoming us with greater frequency."

The Cruin king's eyes narrowed. He had heard the implied warning in my words. "Let them come," he replied. "Whether in peace or in war, they will find us ready to receive them."

He eyed us head to heel, and what he saw did not impress him, for his scowl deepened. "Why have you come here like this?"

"In Prydain," I answered, "a bard is shown the comfort of the hearth before he is asked to sing."

Calbha rubbed his jaw. "In Llogres," he said slowly, "a bard does not wander through the land like a fugitive of the hostage pit."

"Your words are better than you know, lord. And if my throat were not so parched from thirst and my belly so slack from hunger, I would tell you a tale worth hearing."

Calbha tilted back his head and laughed. "Well said, bard. Come into my hall. Eat with me and drink; take your ease and sleep. Want for nothing, you are my guests—you and the mud-loving champion with you."

I raised my hands and gave him a blessing. "Let peace attend you while we shelter beneath your roof, and may all men call you Calbha the Generous from this day forth."

This pleased the lord of Blár Cadlys. He went before us into the hall and called for the welcome cup to be brought to him. The brewmaster hastened forward, bearing a goodly-sized silver bowl. He offered the bowl to his lord, who took it and drank a deep draught.

"Drink! Drink, my friends, and refresh yourselves," Calbha said, wiping his moustache on the sleeve of his siarc. He passed the bowl to me and I drank, thinking I had never tasted ale so rich and good.

I then passed the bowl to Llew, who should have drunk before me—he was Lord of Prydain, after all. But I thought it best not to reveal his rank at this time. He paid no heed to the slight, being only too happy to clutch the bowl between his hands.

Chairs were produced, and we sat with Calbha, passing the welcome cup between us until it was empty. The king would have filled it again, but I prevented him, saying, "Your ale is the best I have had in many, many days. But if I drink more now I will not be able to sing."

The king made to protest. Llew spoke up just then: "Lord, as you see, we are no fit guests to sit with you." He spread his hands to his torn and mud-spattered clothes. "Allow us to bathe, and you will find us more agreeable companions."

"I see that you have travelled hard," Calbha conceded. "Wash yourselves and come to me when you are ready. I will await you here."

We were conducted to the yard behind the nearer of the two warriors' houses where there stood a great stone trough full of water which the warriors used to bathe when they had finished their practice in the yard. A basin was brought to us, and tallow soap, and cloths to dry ourselves. We stripped off our dirty clothing and stepped into the trough. The water was cold, but we sank into it gratefully and felt ourselves revived. We lathered hair and limbs, taking it in turns to ladle water over ourselves with the basin.

While we were washing, a woman came and removed our clothes, replacing them with fresh garments, so that when we had finished we did not have to face our filthy rags again. As we dried ourselves, Llew abruptly asked, "Why did the Coranyid attack only Prydain?"

The question caught me unawares. It was true that Lord Nudd and his vile warband had, in their unrestrained frenzy of hate, destroyed nearly every settlement in Prydain. Yet this Cruin stronghold—near to Sycharth though it was—had escaped destruction. Why only Prydain? Why not Llogres? Why did Lord Nudd concentrate his wrath on Prydain alone, while Llogres—judging from Blár Cadlys—stood unmolested?

"Your question is astute," I replied at last. "I cannot answer."

"But you knew the Cruin would be here," he persisted. "You knew, Tegid. You never doubted it."

"I did not stop to consider. I only thought to escape—and this was the nearest refuge," I told him.

Llew pursued. "That may be so. And yet you assumed the Coranyid had not destroyed the Cruin. That is not like you, Tegid."

We dressed quickly, pulling on the clean clothes we had been given, and making our way back to the hall. The fire had been kindled on the hearth, and chairs had been placed around it. Calbha was seated, and some of his advisers and members of his warband had joined him—perhaps twenty men in all. A dark-haired woman sat beside him, and his warriors stood nearby with cups in their hands, talking loudly.

"Who is the woman with Calbha?" Llew asked.

"It is Eneid," I answered. "She is the queen."

Lord Calbha and his wife had been head to head in conversation when we entered. At our approach they stopped their talk; the queen straightened and regarded us with interest. We came to where they sat. I greeted the queen, who inclined her head and said, "My husband tells me you have travelled from Prydain on foot, and slept in thickets and fens. I hope you will find the hospitality of Blár Cadlys more to your liking."

"Thank you, lady," I replied. "Already we are more comfortable here than we have been at our own hearth."

The queen rose then, saying, "You will be hungry. Sit with my husband. He is eager to discuss with you. While you talk, I will attend to more agreeable matters elsewhere."

She offered me her chair and waved Llew to the empty seat nearby; then she took her leave of us.

"You are the first guests we have had in a very long time," the king said. "My wife will deem it an insult if you do not eat and drink your fill at every meal. For myself, I would be happy to hear word of what passes in the lands beyond the Modornn."

"Ask what you will, lord. I will tell you all I may."

"Tell me this, then," Calbha said as we took our places next to him, "have you escaped from Meldryn Mawr's hostage pit?"

Calbha was direct—to the point of rudeness. Yet he had promised us the freedom and comfort of his hearth. I saw no ill intent in him, or in his brusque manner, and decided to answer him forthrightly, matching his directness with my own. "Yes. We have escaped from the captive pit at Sycharth and have come to you for help."

My free admission caused a small sensation among Calbha's men. He silenced the talk with an upraised hand. "A bard and a champion in the captive pit?" he mused. "It is not like Meldryn Mawr to waste the abilities of such skilled men needlessly. Your crimes must be great indeed."

"We have committed no crime, lord," I replied, "save one only: displeasing one who has wrongfully proclaimed himself king."

If my first reply struck sparks, these words lit a flame. The king's advisers and warriors began clamoring as one. "Tell us!" they cried. "What does this mean? A new king? Who is it? Tell us!"

Lord Calbha leaned forward, concern creasing his brow. "A new king? What of Meldryn Mawr?"

"Meldryn is dead. Killed by his champion."

This disclosure silenced the hall. Calbha's eyebrows raised in wonder, and his eyes turned to Llew.

"No," I told him, "Llew is not the murderer. The deed was done by Paladyr, the man Llew replaced."

"Who is king now?" Calbha asked.

"The Great King's son, Meldron, calls himself king now," I answered. "He has seized the kingship for himself."

Lord Calbha shook his head in disbelief, and his advisers fell to muttering among themselves. "What has happened? You are chief bard—or so you say—how could you allow the kingship to be challenged in this way?"

"I bestowed the kingship as I saw fit," I replied simply. "Prince Meldron disagreed with my choice. He seized us and threw us into the pit."

"Ah!" said Calbha understanding at last. "So that is the way of it."

"Yes."

"And what of Meldron? Will the warriors support him?"

"They will."

"I see." Calbha paused, turned to one of his advisers and beckoned the man forward. The two spoke together privately for a moment, and then the king turned and said, "I know this Meldron. I am reminded that he led the Llwyddi warband in the northern troubles some time ago."

"That is so, lord," I answered. "He is an able war leader. Meldryn had given him authority over the warband."

"What is in Meldron's heart—peace or war?" the Cruin lord asked, revealing his own heart to me in that question. I knew then that I was right to trust him.

"Meldron will do all to advance himself, whether through war or peace—though he deems peace much the slower course."

"But what of the king?" Calbha asked. "You said you had given the kingship to another. What happened to him?"

I had determined the mood of Calbha's court and could now disclose what I had deliberately held back. "He sits before you, lord," I answered, touching Llew on the shoulder.

Calbha turned his gaze to Llew, and observed him for a moment before answering. "I did not know I received a king at my hearth. I trust my ignorance did not offend."

"Lord Calbha," Llew answered, "I am not so much a king that you should take note of me. Neither am I a man to imagine offense where none is to be found. Indeed, I come to you as an exile and have found acceptance denied me elsewhere. I thank you for that, and I will not forget it."

Llew's answer could not have delighted the Cruin king more. At once all questions ceased and jars appeared and our cups were filled. We drank, and the queen and her servants entered the hall. Others hastened to bring the tables so that food could be served. We ate our fill that night, and slept secure beneath Calbha's stout roof.

6

Safe Haven

We spent the next days at Blár Cadlys resting and regaining our strength. King Calbha proved himself a considerate host. He did not stint with food or drink, neither did he try to exploit our distress for his gain. And there was much about our predicament which a less honorable lord might have used to his own benefit. But Calbha left us to our own counsel and did not make any demand upon us. I grew to trust him.

And since he had earned my trust in this small matter, I decided to trust him in the greater: I told him all that had happened in Prydain through the unnaturally long Sollen season. I told him of the destruction wrought in Prydain by Lord Nudd and his demon Coranyid. He sat silently astonished as he listened.

When I finished, he replied, "Sollen was overlong, and more fierce than is common, it is true. Yet we did not mark it strange for all that." He shook his head slowly. "But this... Prydain destroyed, you say? It is more than I could have imagined."

Calbha could not illuminate the mystery of Prydain's destruction. He knew nothing of Lord Nudd's attack, so he could not answer why Llogres had escaped the demon horde's vengeance.

"What do you want of me?" King Calbha asked, perceiving that we had come to the purpose of our visit at last.

"I ask your aid in helping us restore Llew to the throne of Prydain," I told him.

He tugged on the end of his moustache thoughtfully. "You ask for aid, and I would give it," he said at last. "Yet it is not my blood that would be shed in such a fight. Therefore I will put the matter to my chieftains and leave them to decide."

He sent men at once to summon the nobles and chieftains from the settlements round about. They arrived in Blár Cadlys, fifteen strong, and when they had assembled in the hall the king bade me stand before them. "Speak, bard," the king invited, "we will hear you now."

I stood before them and once again related all that had happened through the season of snows. I told them Sycharth was destroyed, and Prydain's population devastated. I told them of Lord Nudd and the demon host, and how the Great King had met his death by treachery. I told them how the prince had wrongfully seized the torc, and suggested that Meldron was woefully vulnerable to attack, and if we were to act quickly, we could crush the usurper before he had time to amass strength and power in the land.

And then I appealed for their support in helping Llew to establish himself in his rightful place as king of the Llwyddi. Calbha thanked me and asked me to leave them, whereupon the Cruin lord and his chieftains sat in deliberation over all I had said.

All through the day they held council while Llew and I took our ease, savoring the warmth as Gyd stretched gentle, healing hands across the raw Sollen-ravaged lands. Llew was quiet and thoughtful. I could see he was contemplating something within himself and did not disturb him. On the evening of the second day we were brought before the king's council to hear the result of their considerations.

The hall was dark and smelled of stale smoke. No fire burned in the hearth. We approached the king's chair and stood before him; we were not invited to sit. I could see by the faces gathered in the gloom—closed and solemn—that Calbha's good will had come to an end. Nor did he soften the blow, but spoke with his customary forthrightness. "We have heard the warning in your words, bard," he said. "And we believe it to be the saving of many lives. For this, we are beholden to you. Even so, we cannot support you against Meldron."

"Lord Calbha," I replied, "I accept your decision although it stirs grave apprehension in my heart. For, in revealing Meldron's weakness, I have placed the lives of my kinsmen in your hands—yet I have asked no pledge of faith in return."

"That is so, you have asked no pledge," he agreed readily. "I tell you the truth, I am content to let the matter rest as it is. I will not take arms against the Llwyddi or seize lands in Prydain."

I made to thank him, but the Cruin lord held up his hand. "All the same, I am persuaded that Meldron will not be so easily appeased. For you to abide here will inflame Meldron's anger against us, and I have no wish to give him cause for war. Therefore you must be gone from here before the sun sets tomorrow."

The Cruin noblemen murmured gruff approval over their lord's decision. "But because of the trust you have shown me," Calbha continued, "I will give you horses of your choice from among my own; also I give you any weapons you desire, and whatever provisions you consider most helpful to you." He regarded us hopefully. "What say you to that?"

"You are more than fair, Lord Calbha," I answered, inclining my head respectfully. "We accept your gifts."

But Llew spoke up. "Your generosity is great, Lord Calbha. Yet I cannot help but wonder—if it extends so far, might it extend a little further?"

"Yes?" the Cruin lord asked warily. "Speak it out. What would you have?"

"We would have a boat, Lord Calbha."

Calbha regarded Llew discreetly and tugged on the end of his moustache. "A boat?" he repeated, slowly glancing around at his advisers; none seemed to disapprove of the request. "Very well, I will give you a boat. But, for a boat, I will ask something of you in return."

"Ask then," Llew replied. "What may be done, that I will do."

"I ask your pledge of peace between us as long as we both rule."

"Lord, if I am a king, I am a king without a realm or people. But by whatever authority I hold, I pledge you the peace of my rule as long as I live."

This was said with simple and forthright conviction, and it pleased Calbha immeasurably. Having exchanged pledges, King Calbha ordered a cup to be brought and he and Llew drank. I marked the event well, for it was the first time Llew's kingship had been acknowledged in deed as well as word.

At dawn the next morning, Calbha led us to the stockade where he had brought twelve horses from which we were to choose our mounts. All were excellent beasts, and I was prepared to choose for both of us, but Llew turned to Calbha and said, "We have a long journey before us, and no doubt many dangers. The horses of the Cruin are renowned throughout Albion, and indeed, these far surpass all others I have seen. If you were in my place, which would you have?"

This gave Calbha the opportunity to demonstrate his superior knowledge of horses, which he did with great zeal. "Any of these will bring a goodly return in trade," he said. "All will serve you well." He paused and allowed himself a wink. "But you are right to ask my advice, for it is not always the fleetest foot or sleekest coat which will serve best."

He turned then and entered the stockade, walking among the horses, patting them, stroking them, letting his hands play over their flanks. Llew walked with him, and they talked together, examining each horse in turn and discussing its merits. I watched as the two talked together. Again I thought how Llew seemed more resolved and purposeful. His manner was different. For the first time since emerging from the Hero Mound on Cnoc Righ he appeared confident and determined.

Calbha and Llew inspected the horses and, after long consideration, chose two: a leggy black mare, and a roan stallion with white fetlocks. Both were spirited animals, young and strong. And, when they had been saddled, Calbha himself rode with us to the coast on his piebald mount—a bold black-and-white stallion.

Like the Llwyddi, the Cruin kings had long maintained a stretch of coastland along Muir Glain for a shipyard. Unlike the Llwyddi, however, the Cruin had never cultivated a fondness for the sea. They much preferred their horses, and the solid earth beneath their feet.

Nevertheless, their boats were seaworthy and stout: black, thick-planked, low-riding, with heavy square sails. And, though he had but four boats large enough to transport both us and our horses, Calbha insisted on giving us the best of the four. While his boatmen readied the vessel for us, the Cruin king paced the shingle, worrying over each small detail and calling commands to his men as they secured the horses in the center of the boat.

I think he was sorry to see us leave. He had no bard, and he would have liked me to stay with him. Also, he had come to respect Llew; but for his fear of Meldron, he might have found a place for Llew in his warband.

So King Calbha helped us as he could. And, when the time came for us to push away from the shore, he stood with his arms crossed upon his chest and watched until we had gained deep water and raised sail.

"He was good to us," Llew said, settling himself beside me at the tiller. "I would like to repay his kindness one day."

"Well, now that you have your boat, where will you go?" I asked, turning my eyes to the sea spreading bright before us. "The sea is calm; the wind is fair. Meldron is far behind us. Where will you go?"

"To Ynys Sci," he replied without hesitation. "There we will receive a welcome worthy of us."

So we sailed for Sci—fairest of Albion's scattered isles—hastening over the whale-track to our safe haven. Our boat was not fast, but it would have sailed itself, I think. We had only to keep the sails full and the prow divided the sparkling water. We travelled secure in the knowledge that Meldron could not follow us—there were no boats left in Sycharth. Once out of sight of Muir Glain, we felt bold to go ashore where and when we would to make camp and find water and fodder for the horses.

In all, it was an agreeable voyage—save for the fact that the land we passed was empty and forsaken. Prydain was a wilderness. We saw no sign of anyone, and it caused me to wonder whether we would find Sci inhabited when we arrived.

When, after our days on the broad-swelling sea, we sighted the rocky headland of Sci, I stood at the prow and scanned the cliffs above the bay. "There!" I shouted, pointing to the slender smoke plume rising from the kitchens behind Scatha's hall. "Nudd has not carried them away after all!"

"Good," replied Llew. That was all he said, but I could tell he was much relieved. During his long sojourn on the island, he had given his heart to the place. "So far as I have one," he once told me, "Ynys Sci is my home."

But he had another reason for wanting to come to Sci. The island was well beyond Meldron's reach; it would be long before the usurper could venture here in search of us. Yet, remote as it was, Sci held commerce with all of Albion: the sons of noblemen and champions came from every realm to Scatha's Isle to learn the warrior's art. Through them we would discover how matters stood in Caledon and Llogres.

These thoughts were on my mind as we sailed into the shallow, sand-rimmed bay. Our arrival had been seen and we were greeted by Boru, chief instructor in Scatha's school. He rode down to the beach from the clifftop caer to greet us.

"Tegid!" he cried, when he saw me standing at the prow. He lashed his horse into the swirling surf, leapt from the saddle, and waded out to meet us. "Tegid, it is good to see you. Welcome!" I threw him the rope which he wrapped around his hands and began walking backwards to the beach. "And who is with you, Tegid?"

"Boru!" Llew said, leaping from the boat. "Do you not know me?"

The lanky warrior halted at the voice and stared. "Llyd?" he said. "Can it be?"

"Llyd it is—or was," I answered. "He is Llew now. Much has happened since we were last with you."

"Greetings, brother!" Llew splashed towards him, extending his hands in the kinsman's welcome.

"Llew, is it?" Boru laughed, dropping the rope and gripping Llew's arms tightly. "So you have won a proper name at last. Tell me all about it!"

"In time, in time," Llew said. "Tegid is bursting to tell you everything."

Boru helped secure the boat and unship the horses, which we rode bare-backed across the beach and up the narrow, winding track to the caer. Scatha's caer has neither wall nor gate—her renown as a warrior is all the fortress she requires. Thus we rode directly to the hall entrance and dismounted.

"Smell the air, Tegid!" said Llew, drawing a deep breath. He turned his face to the sky. "And look—ahh, the sunlight!—it is like nowhere else."

Boru went before us into the hall, throwing aside the oxhide covering the doorway and calling loudly. It was not Scatha who answered, however, but Goewyn, her golden-haired daughter. She rose from her seat at the hearth, surprise giving way to pleasure as she hastened to welcome us.

"Welcome, Tegid. It is good to see you. It seems an age since you left here, yet it is but one season."

She turned politely to Llew. Her smile faltered as her eyes played over his features.

"Goewyn...I—" Llew began.

At the sound of her name on his tongue, she said, "Llyd?"

He nodded. She stepped hesitantly nearer, raising her hands to touch him, but holding back.

"Llyd he was," I explained, "but no longer. The man you see before you is now named Llew, and he is king of Prydain."

"Is this so?" Goewyn's eyes grew wide. "A king?"

"It was Tegid's doing," Llew admitted. "It is a long story."

"That is a tale I want to hear! King of Prydain?" Boru hooted in genuine surprise. "Who would have guessed it?"

"You have changed," Goewyn said softly. "And in more than name only. You are not the same man who left here only a season ago." She lifted a hand to touch his hair, his face. Then, as if reassured that the man standing before her was the one she remembered, she embraced him. "I have missed you."

This last was said to Llew alone—truly, the welcome in her soft brown eyes was for him alone. I saw how easily she gave herself to him, and knew that through the dark, snow-plundered days of Sollen, she had carried a glowing ember within her heart. This ember kindled a flame the moment she embraced Llew, and it began burning brightly from that moment.

And why not? They knew each other well. Llew had spent seven years on the island: training as a warrior through three seasons of the year, and resting during the cold fourth season—resting and taking his ease with Scatha's three beautiful daughters, each of whom served in the court of a king, and each of whom returned to winter on Ynys Sci when most of the warriors-in-training had gone home to clan and kin.

Obedient to Meldryn Mawr's command, however, Llew had not returned to Sycharth, but spent the wild, cold Sollen seasons on Sci with those few whose privilege it was to remain in that bright company.

I turned to Boru. "How many warriors are here?"

"Sixteen," he replied. "They have gone hunting on the far side of the island and will not return until they have run the legs off their horses. No others have arrived yet."

"Where is Scatha?"

"She is riding," Goewyn replied. Remembering her courtesy, she moved away quickly. "You are tired from your journey. Sit, please, and rest. I will bring food and drink."

She hastened away, and Llew watched her until she disappeared from sight behind a screen at the far end of the hall. "It is good to be here. I feel as if I have been away forever."

"Sit, brothers," said Boru, drawing together chairs for us. He lowered himself into a seat and folded his long arms over his chest. "What tidings from Meldryn Mawr? Where are your warrior-cubs?" he asked, beaming at us.

I wondered at this. Could it be that those on the island knew nothing of what had passed in the world beyond their shores?

"What have you heard from Prydain?" I asked, taking my place.

"Not a whit; not a whistle," Boru answered. "But that is not surprising. The sea froze between Sci and the mainland this year. I have never seen it so cold—I thought it would never end."

Just then Goewyn reappeared, with Govan fairly dancing behind her. Sisters they were, but as unlike as two women may be. Goewyn's hair was golden and fine as flax, her skin fair and white; Govan's hair was tawny and her skin deep-hued, as if kissed by the sun. Govan's eyes were blue where her sister's were brown. And whereas Goewyn was tall and elegantly graceful, Govan was nimble, lithe, a delight in motion. She was rarely quiet, and never still. Wherever Govan was there was laughter—or tears, it is true—but seldom silence.

Accordingly, they came laughing into our presence. Govan approached Llew directly. She raised wide eyes to meet his, searching his face, fascinated by the change she saw there. "Llyd?" she whispered in a voice made small by awe. "What has happened to you?"

"It was a hard winter," Llew replied.

"My sister told me you were changed, but . . ." Delighted by the alteration in Llew's appearance she laughed, letting the words go.

"It is good to see you too, Govan," Llew replied.

"You were ever welcome here," Govan told him, suddenly solemn—suppressed laughter tugged at the corners of her mouth. "And you shall be no less welcome now that you are a king."

We heard the hollow sound of hoofbeats outside and, almost before they ceased, she was there—Scatha, clothed in a scarlet cloak and mantle, with a girdle of plum-purple. Her long hair was unbound and wind-tossed from her ride. Her cheeks glowed with her exertion, and she entered the hall with eyes alight, for she had seen our boat on the beach and knew she had guests to welcome.

"Tegid!" she called upon entering. "Greetings and welcome to you." She turned to Llew. "And to you also—" Scatha hesitated, stepping closer and scrutinizing Llew carefully. "Llyd? Is it you?"

"I have returned, Pen-y-Cat," he answered, using the informal title which her warrior pupils bestowed upon her: Chief of Battle.

"Come to me, son of mine," she said. All who had mastered their skills in her hard school she recognized as her sons.

Llew stepped before her. She placed her hands upon his shoulders and gazed long into his eyes. "Yes, it is Llyd," she said, and, leaning close, kissed him on both cheeks. "Welcome, my son."

"I am called Llew now," he told her simply.

"And he is a king!" added Govan.

"Is he indeed?" Scatha asked, regarding Llew placidly. "This is a tale I will hear gladly." At that moment, servants entered with platters of bread and cold meat, and jars of beer. "Build up the fire and fill the cups," Scatha called to them. Turning to me, she said, "And you, Tegid Tathal, will tell us how this remarkable thing has come about."

"At last!" said Boru. "And here was I, thinking he had swallowed his tongue."

Just then Gwenllian, Scatha's first daughter, entered the hall. She had been riding with her mother, and had seen the horses stabled before coming in. She now joined us, calling a greeting as she glanced quickly from one to the other of us.

Upon seeing Llew, she froze in midstep.

The smile of welcome vanished from her face, and her body grew rigid. I thought she might swoon, for she swayed on her feet—but her eyes remained bright and alert. We all fell silent, watching her. "Hail, Llew, I greet you," she breathed in almost silent recognition, her eyes playing over his features. "You have come at last."

I did not wonder at this odd greeting, for it was Gwenllian whose emerald eyes had first glimpsed the shape of the dire events which had come to pass in Albion. And flame-haired Gwenllian it was who bestowed the prophecy upon Llyd from which he had taken his new name. Seeing him now, wise *Banfáith* that she was, she recognized him despite his altered appearance, or it may be because of it.

The moment passed, and Gwenllian went to him; she pressed his hand and kissed his cheek by way of greeting. Scatha watched this exchange, her features sharp with interest. And even as her daughter stepped away, Scatha's eyes remained on Llew, standing easily now, assured once more of his place among them. I do not know what the Pen-y-Cat saw—perhaps she was remembering the man she had lately sent away, or appraising a strong new ally.

We settled at the glowing hearth, and I began my doleful recitation of all that had happened since Llew and I had last sat in that happy hall. I told them about the harrowing of Prydain by Lord Nudd and his demon host of Coranyid—of Sycharth's destruction, and that of all the settlements large and small throughout the land. I told them of our desperate flight to Findargad, and the long siege brought to an end by Llew's discovery of the Singing Stones by which the dying Phantarch had contrived to save the Song of Albion.

Lastly, I told them of Llew's Hero Feat on the wall at Findargad, and Prince Meldron's treachery which ended in the Great King's death; I recounted Meldryn Mawr's funeral and entombment, and how, in full sight of everyone, Llew had emerged from the Hero Mound. I told them how I had bestowed the kingship upon Llew, and how in retaliation Meldron, wicked seed, had stolen it away and imprisoned us. I described our escape from the hostage pit, and our flight to Ynys Sci.

In short, I told them everything that had happened in the land since we had last sojourned on the island. I knew we would have need of Scatha's considerable aid in the days to come, so I held nothing back. I had already begun to conceive a plan by which we could regain the throne of Prydain.

For their part, my listeners heard the sorry tale in silence, bread and cups untouched at their hands. When I finished, night had deepened and the hall was dark. We sat in a circle around the central hearth, the fire dwindled small. The ticking of the embers grew loud in the silence of the hall. My tale had stunned and astonished. Boru stared into the shimmering coals, his face deep-shadowed and drawn. Scatha and Govan frowned, their eyes glimmering with unshed tears. Gwenllian, erect, hands before her, fingertips together, remained inscrutable behind closed eyes. Goewyn wore a look of mingled pity and pride, and I wondered what she had heard in my words to awaken such a response.

Finally, Scatha raised her eyes, drew breath and said, "I am sorry for Meldryn Mawr's death, and saddened by the shameful actions of his grasping son. Whatever I can do to help you, be assured—it will be done."

Scatha had offered me outright that which I had hoped by persuasion to obtain. I accepted gladly. "I thank you," I replied. "With your help we will make good Llew's claim and establish his rightful reign."

But Gwenllian raised a cautioning hand, "You should know this: my mother is bound by a strong *geas* never to support one king over another in battle, or to raise sword against any who have delivered kinsmen to her tutelage, unless any first raise hand against her." She paused, allowing me to take in the full import of her unhappy words.

I understood the wisdom of this prohibition, even as I lamented its unfortunate effect. For Scatha's taboo meant that we could not count on her considerable skill and support in battle.

"It is true," Scatha replied. "There are some means I am not free to pursue."

"Pen-y-Cat," said Llew, "though your blade alone is worth a hundred, it is enough that you have received us and given us shelter. You need have no fear for your geas. We will find another way to overcome Meldron."

"Well, I am bound by no such vow," Boru said, leaping to his feet. "I will gladly take arms against Meldron and any who follow him. I support you, brother. Whatever I have is yours to command."

"Thank you," Llew told him. "I accept. No doubt I will have need of your strong arm."

"Come," said Scatha, rising, "we will speak no more of this now. You are friends too long absent from this hearth. Tonight we will eat and drink together and rejoice in your safe return." She called for the fire to be built up again, and for food and drink to be served anew. Talk turned to happier things, and we lingered no longer on Meldron and his low treachery.

Night was far gone when we departed to our sleeping places.

Quitting the hall, we followed Boru across the moonlit yard to the warriors' house. Llew stopped abruptly and looked up at the star-spattered sky.

"What is it? What do you see?" I asked.

He did not answer at once. "I had forgotten how bright they are here," he murmured at length. "And how close."

7

Black Beltain

Like noisy gulls returning to their summer nests, the young warriors began flocking to Scatha's school. On the wings of the wind they came—though none from desolate Prydain. This lack was more than made up by others from Llogres and Caledon.

Llew and I stood on the cliff as the first boats discharged their eager passengers. Boys, some as young as eight summers, trooped ashore, their heads full of the glory they would win with skills they had yet to master.

"Scatha's fields will be full this year," I observed. "Another fine harvest."

"Hm?" Llew said absently. He was watching a man secure a boat with no other help but the rope wrapped around his broad shoulders. The man leaned into his task, back heaving, strong legs churning as he dragged the boat onto the shingle.

"There is a stout battlechief," I said, and, catching Llew's rapt attention, asked, "Do you know him?"

"Yes, I think I do," he answered and at once began scrambling down the cliff-track to the shingle below.

I followed, and heard him shout: "Cynan!"

The young man glanced around and a wide grin spread across his face. Wild red curls, bright as polished copper, ruffled like feathers in the sea breeze; eyes cool and blue as chips of ice cheerfully scanned the shore to see who had called him. A thick silver torc gleamed at his throat.

"Here, Cynan!" called Llew, splashing into the water.

"Greetings, friend," he said as Llew came to stand before him. "Cynan ap Cynfarch I am." He continued to smile, but no recognition came into his eyes.

"Cynan, it's me: Llyd!"

The young battlechief paused, keen blue eyes squinting in friendly scrutiny. "No—is it ... Llyd?"

"You remember!"

"Llyd ap Dicter!" Cynan cried. "Is it you, man?"

A strange name: Anger, Son of Fury. What did it mean?

Llew laughed and seized him by the arms. They embraced as kinsmen, talked and laughed, oblivious to the waves surging around them. Taking the rope, the two friends beached the boat and then strode onto the shingle where I stood.

"Tegid," Llew said, "this is Cynan Machae. He is my sword-brother, and it is to him that I owe all I know of humility."

"Humiliation, you mean," Cynan laughed, draping an arm across Llew's shoulders. "Ach, but you were a sorry opponent!"

"Cynan's father is King Cynfarch of Caledon," Llew explained. "His is the largest clan in the south."

"If you are including sheep as well," Cynan added happily. "Good greetings to you. Any man who calls Llyd friend is friend to me."

"Greetings, Cynan Machae," I said. "May your spear fly true as your word."

Llew thrust out a hand to me. "This is Tegid Tathal, Pen-derwydd of Prydain," he explained to Cynan. "He allows me to travel in his company."

"You serve a Chief Bard?" Cynan raised his scant red eyebrows. "You have risen in the world since I last saw you, Llyd."

"Indeed," I answered, "though he will not say it himself. He is Llyd no longer. He is become Llew, and he is the king I serve."

The amazement in Cynan's blue eyes was genuine, as was his

pleasure. *"Clanna na cù!"* he hooted. "The stump of a spearhandler I remember was never yet a chieftain, much less a king." He pressed a finger to the hollow of Llew's throat. "Where is your golden torc, man?"

"Come to the hall and we will raise cups together," said Llew.

"A man of my own heart," Cynan replied. "Lead the way."

They started off across the beach to the hill track, and Llew turned back. "Will you come, Tegid?"

"I will join you in a while. The day is good; I want to walk and think. Save me a jar."

I watched the two of them mount the steep track leading to the caer. Then I turned and began walking west over the strand. The sea glimmered and gleamed like hammered silver, and the sky shone burnished blue. The salt air was crisp and fresh; a pale sun slowly warmed the land and water. The small round rocks beneath my feet sounded hollow as I trod over them, and the gulls circling far above shrieked their shrill cry.

Yes, a good day to walk and think—and I had much to think on. My foremost concern was the raising of a warband to carry our claim against Meldron and regain the kingship. The Llwyddi warband, though much diminished, still numbered eighty. And the prince's Wolf Pack remained intact—an élite force made up of twenty of Prydain's best warriors.

We would have to do more than merely match Meldron man for man. We must overwhelm him. I had no wish to make war on members of my own clan, but a large enough force might mean less bloodshed in the end. Yet, to gather a warband of any size...easier to coax oysters from the sea, or beckon birds from the sky. Nevertheless, that was the task set before us.

I scrambled over the sea-lashed rocks and rounded the headland. The wind hit me full and fresh. I pulled the air deep into my lungs and tramped over smooth wet sand the sea had just abandoned.

The difficulties of raising a warband occupied my mind for a time, but my thoughts drifted. Unaccountably, I began thinking about the night on the sacred mound at Ynys Bàinail—when out of the lowering storm-wrack the Cythrawl, ancient evil, was loosed upon the land. I reached back into the shadows of my memory to that accursed night when Ollathir, Chief Bard of Albion, died.

I heard again the voice of Ollathir, lifted in the secret tongue of the *Derwyddi,* crying out in desperate entreaty. The sacred mound trembled with the sound. I swooned. The last thing I saw was the Chief Bard standing alone with his back to the pillar stone of Prydain, his staff of power above his head, straining to hold the writhing Cythrawl at bay.

Before he died, Ollathir breathed his awen into Llew. I did not see this happen, but I do not doubt that it occurred exactly as Llew described it to me: a dying man's kiss.

Llew possessed the Chief Bard's awen, but he was not a bard. The awen is the bard's guiding vision, it is the illuminating spirit of his craft, it is the essence of knowledge made manifest in power. In a bard like Ollathir the awen was a most formidable tool and weapon. And this Llew possessed but, as he was not a bard, he could not call it forth at will.

This weapon was not lost to him completely, however. I had seen it flash forth from him in the Heart of the Heart, the hidden chamber of the Phantarch deep under Findargad's rock. There, quickened by the power of the Song of Albion, the awen had transfigured him: Llyd, the reluctant warrior, had become Llew, the champion.

The Chief Bard's awen was alive in Llew, but it remained buried deep within. It would be an invaluable aid to us if I could find a way to allow him to invoke it. But the training of a bard is difficult and long. Even so, the disciplined harmony of mind and heart that unites in the song spirit is not granted to all who enter the narrow gate of the Derwyddi, and not every bard can wield the awen as he will.

It felt good to walk so—the wind fresh on my face, the sun warm, and the sea spreading fair beside me. A plan began to take shape in my mind. I was the last bard of my people; all the rest were gone. But judging from what I had seen of Llogres and on Sci, Lord Nudd's destruction seemed to have been confined to Prydain alone. It seemed likely that among the tribes of Caledon and Llogres the bards did not even know what had happened.

It came to me that I might send to them through the warrior-*Mabinogi* who flocked to Scatha's isle. Yes, I would gather the learned brotherhood and tell them all that had taken place. I would apprise them of Meldron's offense against sovereignty, and ask their aid in helping us restore the kingship of Prydain.

In the next days, I talked to the boys and young men arriving on the island and discovered which kings in Caledon and Llogres maintained bards. From the warrior-Mabinogi I learned the names of my brothers and where they could be found. And then I waited, giving myself to the tasks I found in Scatha's service.

Through days as sweet and rich as golden mead, the Wheel of Heaven revolved, turning through its measured course: through planting time and blossom time—when the hills glow with tiny golden flowers, and even the deep-shadowed glens deck themselves in red and purple—the seasons worked their slow enchantment. I watched the signs, marking each day's passing and observing the sacred celebrations and festivals of our people.

I observed also the growing bond between Goewyn and Llew.

They were often together: riding in the fresh dawn light, walking the hills at sunset or the silvered strand by moonlight. I saw how Goewyn watched him, delighting in his presence. It was not dawn's fresh light that rose in her dark eyes, but something brighter still and just as clear and strong.

Llew held himself enthralled by her every grace—by her bright-braided tresses no less than by her laugh, by the curve of her lips no less than by the cool touch of her slender fingers. Llew was not lonely with Goewyn ever in sight.

Rhylla, season of seedfall and song, came in its time, bringing the short, amber-tinted days and frost-tinged nights. The Season of Snows followed, with cold, wet, gusty days. But before the ice-laden gales conspired to end sea travel, the young of Scatha's school departed to their separate realms and the hearths of their clans.

Before the ships departed, I spoke to those returning to the mainland and extracted solemn vows to deliver my message to the bards: at the request of the Chief Bard of Prydain, a *gorsedd* on Ynys Bàinail one moon after Beltain.

I stood on the cliff, the wind lashing my cloak against my legs, and watched the ships setting forth on their homeward journeys. Word of the gathering went with my pledged messengers; I had no fear that it would fail. When the last ship sailed from the bay, I hastened to the hall, warming myself with the knowledge that my plan, so long anticipated, was finally proceeding.

Fortunate indeed are those who enjoy the shelter of Scatha's hall when the cruel wind howls. There is feasting on savory meat and sweet bread and honey mead; there is singing and the matchless music of the harp and tales of wonder; there is sporting at games and hunting and riding in the snow, returning red-cheeked to sip hot ale from steaming cups; there is lavish conversation over a crackling fire; there is warmth in excellent company while the gale claws with icy fingers at the roof-thatch, and the roof-tree groans.

One by one, the days passed and the year's wheel turned. The Season of Ice and Darkness waned; fury spent, winter gathered its flagging forces and retreated. The days lengthened and the wind warmed. The moon moved through its phases until one morning, as a new moon rose in the time-between-times, we observed the rite which marks the year reborn: the kindling of the Beltain fire.

On that day, all other fires are extinguished so that the Beltain flame, pure and perfect, may be the mother of all flames throughout the year to come. In the chieftain's house this fire burns without cease, and anyone needing fire is given live embers from the Beltain bed so that each house receives warmth and light from the same pure flame.

Accordingly, in the dark of the moon, Gwenllian and I gathered the Nawglan, the nine woods whose unique qualities produce such wonderful benefit. We obtained a goodly quantity, which I bundled with strips of rawhide. On the highest hill on Ynys Sci, we cut a wide and shallow trench in the turf—a circle large enough to enclose the entire company of Scatha's house. In the center of the circle, we placed the bundled wood on a newborn lamb's white fleece.

Before dawn the company assembled on the hilltop: Gwenllian, Govan, Goewyn, Llew, Scatha, Boru, the servants and the few warriors who wintered with us. And then, in the time-between-times we kindled the flame. Grasping the greenwood bow, Gwenllian drew the gut line, spinning the length of rounded yew in the deep-cut notch of an oaken bole. At the first glow from the wood, I applied the dried plant called *tán coeth,* which causes the infant flame to burst bright and blush crimson—as if drawing life from the very air.

I have done this countless times. But, this time, as I touched the tán coeth to the wood, the spark glimmered feebly and died in a wisp of smoke. Gwenllian saw the flame fail and drew her breath in sharply; the bow fell from her fingers and her face went white. My heart lurched in my chest.

I glanced to the east, towards the rising sun, even as my hands fumbled to retrieve the bow and yew. The first rays of the sun touched the hilltop and there was no fire to greet the new day. The Beltain fire failed. The year dawned black.

Quickly, quickly, I replaced the bow and spun the yew stick as hard and fast as my shaking fingers would permit—as if speed alone could recover the loss. Black Beltain! How could it have happened? I held my breath, willing the flame to appear.

A moment later, a tiny plume of silver smoke curled from the oak bole. I blew gently on the spark and coaxed it to a flame. In the space of two heartbeats the fire leaped quick and high. If any of the others noticed anything amiss, they did not show it; I think only Gwenllian and I knew. So great was my desire to see the new year begun aright, I turned my face away from the ill-omened flame and instead stood to greet the year renewed.

We baked the Beltain bread then, forming the small loaves of grain and honey and setting them to cook on flat stones at the fire's edge. Gwenllian prepared a porridge of milk and oats and eggs, while I roasted the flesh of fish, fowl, and kine on spits over the fire. Goewyn shared out apples and hazelnuts kept through Sollen's darkness, and Govan poured beer and sweet, yellow mead into

bowls. The fire loaves are all that is strictly required, but other items
are added as the clan desires in order to ensure plenty through all the
year.

Thus, in the new light of the year reborn, we ate and drank and
sang. Gwenllian, her harp against her shoulder, sent the sparkling
melody skyward. She lifted her voice and offered a precious gift of
music to the day. But though I sang, and heard the song rising up like
the smoke from the fire before us, my heart was not in it. Dread had
taken root in my soul and I could not sing true.

When the fire had burned down, I gathered the live embers to
rekindle the hearthfire in Scatha's hall. Then I collected the ash,
dividing it into four equal portions for Gwenllian and her sisters and
myself. The Beltain rite observed, we all returned to the caer.

I put the inauspicious fire behind me, and looked instead to the
coming gathering. I ordered the various matters in my mind, and
weighed the words I would use to unite the brotherhood and rouse
the bards of Albion to action—remembering only too well that the
last gathering had ended in sharp dissension. And then, as the day
drew near, Llew and I readied our boat for the voyage to the Ynys
Bàinail, the Isle of the White Rock, where the gorsedd would take
place.

On a fair, wind-swept day, Llew and I bade farewell to our friends
and raised sail for Ynys Bàinail and the gathering of bards.

I did not know how many Derwyddi would answer the summons,
but this is the way of it: when the chief bard of one of the three
principal realms of Albion determines to raise a gathering, all bards
are bound by vows of brotherhood to attend the gorsedd if no higher
claim prevents them. As Chief Bard of Prydain it was my right to
summon my brother bards.

A gorsedd brings bards from all clans and realms, for the
Derwyddi hold not to ties of blood kinship in the way of other men;
neither do we swear fealty to any lord or chieftain, save the one who
is chief over us. We who hold the kingship for our people are bound
to sovereignty itself: our fealty is to kingship, not the king.

This is how it must be. Kings come and go, but sovereignty remains. Kings are men, and men may fall to vice and corruption, but sovereignty is pure and undefiled at its source. Albion's bards are charged with maintaining the Sovereignty of Albion in its purity. We, the keepers of kingship, are ever vigilant for those who would do violence to that which we have vowed to uphold through all things.

I held our sturdy boat close to the wind so that the prow divided the waves, driving the silver fish before us. I was eager to reach Ynys Bàinail to see who arrived first, and also to tend Ollathir's grave. I had buried him in haste, and wanted to honor him properly now.

"What are you going to tell them?" Llew asked, when he at last turned his eyes from the misty blue mound of Ynys Sci.

"I will tell them that Prince Meldron has raped the kingship of Prydain," I answered simply.

"What do you expect them to do?"

"We will hold council and see what may be done," I answered. "That is why I have issued the call."

Llew nodded, his eyes on the sea's far horizon. "How many will come?"

"I cannot say. I believe the bards of Caledon and Llogres remain."

"Two thirties and two?"

"How do you reckon that number?"

"You told me there were three thirties and three in all Albion," Llew replied. "That makes thirty and one for each of the three realms. Since no bards remain in Prydain—save you alone—that leaves two thirties and two." He smiled. "Well? Have I guessed correctly?"

"Yes, if all answer the summons. Some might be prevented."

"What would prevent them?"

"The need to protect the kingship or the people," I replied. "It is for each bard to determine where and when his skills are required by his people and his king."

"I see." Llew sat down with his back to the mast and his arms folded on his knees. "What about the Phantarch—will you tell them about the Phantarch's death?"

"Of course. It is a matter of highest concern," I said, thinking that even I did not fully comprehend it all. "The brotherhood will decide what to do to restore the Song of Albion."

The Song of Albion has been sung from the beginning of this worlds-realm; from the beginning there has always been a Phantarch to sing it. Hidden in his chamber of stone under high mountains, the Chief Bard of Albion sang the Song; through him the Song of Albion was given life, upholding and sustaining all that existed.

The Phantarch was dead, but the Song remained. For the Chief Bard of Albion had protected it in death, even as he had upheld it in life. By means of strong enchantment the Phantarch had bound the Song of Albion to the very stones that had crushed him and formed his grave mound. This he had done so that the Song would not pass out of the this worlds-realm and Albion fall to utter darkness and chaos. These were the Singing Stones which Meldron now held—and by which he thought to justify his unlawful claim on the sovereignty of Prydain.

"Will they try to recover the Song from Meldron?" Llew inquired. Our time on Scatha's Isle had done much to restore his spirits. The gaze from his clear grey eyes as he looked out upon the sea-swell was steady and untroubled.

"I do not know," I told him. "This has never happened before."

We talked of other things then and ate some of the bread from our provisions. Our stout boat parted the waves, and the gulls hovered above our billowing sail. If the wind held good, three days' sailing would bring us to our destination: Ynys Oer, larger companion to Ynys Bàinail.

We sighted the big island early on the morning of the third day. As the wind remained favorable, we proceeded to sail around the broad northern headland and came at Ynys Bàinail from the west. This made the sea journey a little longer, but saved us a rough walk across the promontory.

As we rounded the headland, the Isle of the White Rock came into view, shining like a beacon in the sun. Shielding my eyes with my hand, I could almost make out the pillar stone on the mound in the center of the island. We sailed past the isle and entered the strait separating the White Rock from its larger island neighbor. Those who go to Ynys Bàinail often camp on the western shore of Ynys Oer and then cross the strait to the sacred isle by curragh, the small leather-hulled boats the Derwyddi keep especially for the purpose.

There is a sandy cove among the rocks on the western shore of Ynys Oer and a stone hut where provisions may be stored, and where a few useful tools are kept for those who visit the sacred isle. The hut stands at the head of a grassy glen where horses can be grazed; through the glen flows a clear-running stream where horses can be watered. Horses are not allowed on the White Rock, nor weapons of any kind, nor any unworthy person; for Ynys Bàinail, Isle of the White Rock, is the sacred center of Albion.

We made landfall on the shore of the rock-sheltered cove and anchored the boat. Llew gathered firewood and fetched water. He moved our provisions from the boat to the hut, and, having done all to make ready, he walked the sea strand to occupy himself.

Meanwhile, I took a curragh and went alone to the White Rock to visit Ollathir's grave. I tidied the small mound and added to its heap of smooth black-and-white stones. Then I sat beside the gravemound until the sun touched the far sea-rim in the west, whereupon I rose and made my way back across the channel to wait for the bards to arrive.

8

The Last Gorsedd

The first bards arrived the next morning; seventeen, and all from Llogres. They had assembled on the eastern side of the island and, having seen our ship the previous day, crossed the headland to join us. At dusk eleven bards arrived from Caledon in two boats. And three boats from Llogres appeared just after dawn the next day bearing fourteen, along with their attendant Mabinogi. Twelve from Caledon arrived on horseback at midday, and the remaining eight followed at dusk.

Thus, all bards of Albion were in attendance. They had received my summons and had come, eager to discuss the signs and portents which they had witnessed since the last gathering.

Most of the brotherhood were known to me, and I greeted them by name. My heart lightened to see them again, for since Ollathir's death I had made my way alone. For their part, the Derwyddi were concerned to see that Ollathir was not with me. Indeed, it was Ollathir they were expecting; they did not know he was dead. But though they saw I now held the rowan staff of Prydain they said nothing, biding their time until I should declare the reason for the gathering.

The gorsedd is conducted with all probity; strict laws of rank and order are observed. It is a most ancient observance and one which is held in highest respect. Wars have been halted in mid-battle to accommodate a bardic gathering! It is not lightly regarded.

Gorsedd is itself a most ancient word. It can be used to designate the chair or throne of a king, for the earliest kings received their sovereignty atop the holy mounds or in sacred groves. The word for throne thus indicates a mound. And, since bards are often buried in these holy mounds, gorsedd also means 'grave'. The sacred mound on Ynys Bàinail was Ollathir's grave; even if he had not died on the mound itself, it is likely he would have been buried there.

The Chief Bard of Caledon was a tall man with a long dark moustache and braided beard. His name was Bryno Hir and, now that Ollathir was gone, Bryno the Tall was the most eminent bard in the Island of the Mighty. Ollathir respected Bryno; he had sought his counsel on many occasions and welcomed his company always.

When Bryno's ship arrived, I made certain to meet him the moment he disembarked. He raised his hands in greeting, "Hail, Tegid ap Talaryant! May your song endure!" Even as he greeted me, his eyes slid past me, searching for Ollathir. He meant no slight; it was an instinctive action.

"Hail, Bryno!" I touched the back of my hand to my forehead out of respect, even though we now shared the same rank. Still, when the time came to choose a new Phantarch, I recognized that it would likely be Bryno Hir. "I trust you journeyed well."

He looked at me, his keen dark eyes searching. "What has happened?" he asked softly.

I walked him a little apart from those who were with him. "Ollathir is dead," I told him simply. Before he could ask how this had come to pass, I added, "And all the rest of Prydain's bards with him. I alone have survived."

Bryno seemed to shrink into himself; the color drained from his face. "How?" he asked in a shattered voice.

I explained briefly, and Bryno listened, shaking his head gravely all the while. When I finished, he turned his eyes to the White Rock. "Yet the sacred center was not defiled."

"Llew," I replied, "the man with me, prevented it. He has received Ollathir's awen, and I have made him king of Prydain."

Bryno was silent for a long moment, searching the meaning of all that I had told him. Wise and far-seeing, the Chief Bard of Caledon rightly understood the peril facing us. "The Day of Strife," he said at last. Then he asked, "What of the Phantarch? Dead?"

"Yes."

He did not ask how this had come about, nor how I knew it to be true. "And the Song of Albion?"

"It was saved," I answered, and told him about Llew's Hero Feat with the Singing Stones.

"Where are the stones now?"

"Prince Meldron has them," I answered. "But with help, I am certain they can be recovered."

Despite this reassurance, Bryno passed a hand before his eyes. He remained some moments in silent mourning for the age he saw passing away before our very eyes. "The Day of Strife," he repeated slowly, heavily, as if the words were weighted with the grief of all the world.

After a moment, he turned to me. "Ollathir tried to tell us, but we would not hear him." He was recalling the last gathering of bards which had refused Ollathir's warning and instead had fallen into discord and dissension.

"Not even Ollathir knew what would happen," I offered. "If he had known, he would never have—"

The bard lifted his hand and gripped my shoulder. "No," he said gently. "We own the guilt. So be it." He glanced at the scattered knots of bards assembled on the strand and drew a deep breath. "There is treachery among us."

"The traitor has answered for his crimes," I replied. "He chose treachery, and treachery claimed him." I then told him about Ruadh, Prince Meldron's bard, and how Llew and I had found his body at the bottom of the dry well shaft in Findargad.

Bryno accepted this and set his face to the task ahead. "You were right to raise the gorsedd," Bryno said. "There is much to be done this day, and in the days to come."

Leaving the Mabinogi to tend camp, we launched the curraghs and plied the narrow strip of water separating Ynys Oer from Ynys Bàinail. Time and again, the small boats crossed the blue-green water until all stood on the white strand. We then made our way up the long, narrow path to the top of the great White Rock, passing through the hole in the rock which leads to the wide plain above. In the center of this plain stands the holy mound, and in the center of the mound, rising like a spike, the great pillar stone. The bards of Albion made their way to the foot of the mound. When all were assembled, we passed three times in a sunwise circle around the base of the mound, and then mounted the steep sides.

The top of the mound is flat, and the perimeter marked with white stones; these form a wheel and the pillar stone the axle. The various orders of bards: *Filidh, Brehon, Gwyddon,* and *Derwydd*—some of them holding branches of white hazel or rowan, or staffs of oak, beech, or yew—all gathered in ranks around the pillar stone within the sacred circle.

Thus did the gathering of bards begin. Since Llew now possessed the Chief Bard's awen, he was allowed to join us atop the mound, though in any other circumstance that would not have been allowed. With Bryno the Tall at my right hand and Llew at my left, I stood before the blue-painted pillar stone and delivered my terrible pronouncements to the assembled Derwyddi: I told of the deaths of Ollathir and the Phantarch, the ruin of Prydain and the slaughter of Prydain's bards by Lord Nudd, and the dawning of the Day of Strife.

At my words, the brotherhood trembled. When I finished, they rent their garments and sank to their knees, pounding the earth with their fists. They filled the air with wailing and loud lamentation, throwing the white dust of the mound over their heads, rubbing it into their hair and beards. They shrieked their outrage to the sun, and called upon the elements to witness their sore distress. Many uttered vows in the dark tongue, binding their spirits to the cause of justice for their murdered brothers.

Llew watched all, grimly, without a word, his arms crossed over his chest. He alone remained unmoved.

When the outcry had exhausted itself, I stood once more before the brotherhood and bade them stand on their feet and hear the prophecy of the champion which the Banfáith had given to us. "Bards of Albion, Wise Men, cease your lamentation! Rise up and hear the prophetic word which I shall speak."

They rose and silenced themselves to hear what I would say. I knew well the words. I had hoarded them in my heart. I had but to open my mouth and speak them out. Yet, even as they stood watching me, I could not. Something stayed me. I stood with gaping mouth and stared at my brothers, and it came into my mind that I looked upon corpses: grey-faced in filthy cloaks, their hair wild, their eye-pits hollow.

When the Light of the Derwyddi is cut off, and the blood of bards demands justice . . .

The words of the Banfáith's prophecy—she had spoken of this time. The Light of the Derwyddi was the Phantarch and the blood of my kinsmen, the bards of Prydain, demanded justice. The gathering had cried out for justice. I wondered at this. Was this how the prophecy would be fulfilled?

As if in answer to my ill-posed question, there came a shout—distant, yet distinct—a cry of challenge. I turned to Llew. He stood motionless, listening. The cry came again: a word—a single shouted word. I heard it and recognized it . . . my name.

"T-e-e-g-i-i-i-d-d!" came the shout for a third time.

Who dared invade the sanctity of the holy isle?

The Derwyddi surged towards the sound. Those closest to the outer rim of the wheel dashed to the edge of the mound to look upon the plain below. Their reaction was instantaneous and fatal.

Seeing the abomination in the sacred place, some bards threw themselves over the edge of the mound, racing down the slopes with shouts of rage. Others fell back, calling to those behind. In the space of one heartbeat, all was confusion. The outcry was deafening. I could not make out what was happening.

"Follow me, Tegid!" It was Llew, pushing through the

churning throng.

More and more of the Derwyddi were racing down the slopes of the mound. I could hear their voices as they ran, screaming, calling on the Swift Sure Hand to strike. But why? What was happening? What did they see?

Llew and I reached the rim of the mound and looked down. Warriors, a band a hundred strong, advanced across the plain below, their weapons and shields glinting in the sun as they came. This is what the Derwyddi had seen—and what had sent them into a frenzy of rage.

"Meldron!" Llew said; the word was a curse between his teeth.

The usurper was there, standing in the midst of his Wolf Pack, ordering the attack upon the defenseless bards. Beside Meldron stood Siawn Hy, spear in hand, shield slung over his shoulder.

Helpless, I watched as my brothers hurled themselves onto the spears and swords of the waiting warriors. "Stop them!" shouted Llew.

But there was no stopping them. Heedless, they rushed to their deaths, defending the sacred ground with their bodies. The cries of the dying assaulted the air.

The bards hastened to the plain, cloaks and mantles streaming, flying to their deaths. Meldron's Wolf Pack struck and struck again. Spears thrusting, swords flashing out from under uplifted shields. The warriors simply stepped over the twitching bodies and moved on.

"Tegid, do something!" cried Llew. "Stop them!"

Bryno Hir appeared beside me. He held his rowan staff in both hands, raised above his head, his face dark with anger, his lips tight over his teeth. He opened his mouth and the air shook to the sound of the *Taran Tafod,* the dark tongue. *"Cwmwl dyfod! Gwynt dyrnod!"* he cried, calling on the clouds to gather and the winds to blow. *"Cwmwl dyfod! Gwynt dyrnod!"*

At his word, wind gusted across the plain and swirled around the base of the mound. Vaporous clouds appeared over the pillar stone, boiling out of the air and spreading across the clear sky.

"Dyrnod! Dyfod! Tymestl rhuo!" Bryno Hir called, swinging his

long staff through the air. The clouds thickened, darkening the plain below. Wind whipped and flattened the long grass. *"Cwmwl dyfod! Gwynt dyrnod! Tymestl rhuo!"*

The sound shivered the air as the dark tongue boomed out from the top of the mound and echoed across the plain. *"Dyrnod tymestl, rhuo tymestl! Terfesgu! Terfesgu!"*

Cold wind shrieked in the heights; clouds—swarming, swelling, surging—streamed over the plain. The storm struck fierce and strong. Rain pelted down in stinging sheets, scouring the plain.

The tempest crashed. Thunder rolled. The warriors advanced, mounting to the slopes of the holy mound. Llew shouted, taking up an oaken staff as a weapon. Bryno lifted his face to the sky and called down the wind and the rain.

The enemy advanced. The remaining Derwyddi descended to meet them; better death than suffering the foeman's foot on the holy mound. And they did die. The attackers, grim-faced and determined, made quick work of the unprotected, unarmed bards. Corpses strewed the slopes like dark boulders. The foemen wiped the gore from their blades on the bodies before them and moved on.

The first warriors reached the top of the mound. I gripped my staff and dashed at them, swinging the stout length of rowan like a club. The warrior—I knew the man; he was a kinsman!—stumbled back. I struck at him with the staff, catching him on the top of the shoulder. He screamed in pain and dropped the sword.

Before I could strike again, a blade flashed, cleaving the staff in two. I heard a rush behind me and felt strong hands on my throat. I tore at the hands and more hands seized me, grabbing my arms and holding them back.

"Llew!" I shouted, fighting furiously. From the corner of my eye, I glimpsed Llew struggling with three foemen. They had him pinned to the ground and were hammering at his face and chest with their fists, trying to subdue him. One of them raised the hilt of his sword and smashed it down on the top of Llew's skull. "Llew!"

I screamed like a beast. I flailed with my feet, and was dragged down. As I fell, I saw Bryno sitting on the ground with his back against the pillar stone. Rain streamed down his face, mingling with the blood flowing freely from the gash in his throat. Blood smeared the pillar stone behind him and soaked the ground. One of the Wolf Pack stood over him, wiping his blade on Bryno's beard.

Blood and rain, and howling wind. The screams of the dying... death... abomination in the sacred center... atrocity and death...

It was quickly over. With Bryno silenced, the storm dispersed, melting away, sunlight breaking through the swiftly-dissolving clouds. I squinted against the light and looked at the bodies of my brothers lying where they had fallen. The holy mound, the gorsedd, had become their grave.

All those not already dead were put to the sword. Llew and I only were saved.

Llew was dragged unconscious from the mound. I was half-thrown, half-carried down the slope to stand before Prince Meldron, who greeted me with a fist in my teeth. Siawn Hy laughed to see it, and his wicked laughter pierced my heart more cruelly than the red-stained spearblade in his hand. His eyes were wild, and cold with hate.

"Did you think you could escape me, bard?" Meldron demanded.

I spat at him. He hit me again, and warm blood filled my mouth

Seeking alliance with the Cruin," he continued, shaking his head in mock disappointment. "That was very chancy. You hoped for support, but Calbha turned you out instead."

Llew groaned where he lay. Meldron stepped to him, grabbed a handful of hair, and snatched his head upright. "Foolish to travel without weapons," the prince observed mildly. "Especially for a king."

"Perhaps he is the king of fools," Siawn Hy remarked.

The prince laughed and released Llew's head. Turning again to me, he said, "You left before I finished with you. I always finish what I have begun; you should know that, Tegid."

"Do what you will, Meldron," I muttered through bleeding lips. "Kill me and be done with it. You will receive nothing from me."

"I want nothing from you, bard," he sneered, "except what belongs to me."

I knew what he wanted, but I would die before giving it to him. "I have given the kingship to Llew. He is king of Prydain."

"*I* am king of Prydain," Meldron insisted with a snarl.

"I will never see you king," I replied.

"For a Wise One, you are very stupid," he said, his voice hard-edged as the blade at his side. "Do you still say that Llew is king of Prydain?"

"Yes, I say it!"

Meldron glanced at Siawn, who smiled wickedly.

"But is it true that a maimed man can never be king?" Siawn asked, leaning casually on his spear.

"That is the truth of it," I replied. "The blemished man cannot be king."

Llew moaned and opened his eyes. Consciousness returned to him and he struggled in the arms of his captors. "Simon!" he hissed, calling Siawn by his former name.

"Good of you to join us, friend," Siawn replied darkly, and then nodded to Meldron.

"Stretch out his sword arm," Meldron ordered, drawing his blade. The men holding Llew forced him up onto his knees. After a struggle, one raised Llew's right arm, and another took hold of his hand and together they stretched it between them. "No!" shouted Llew, struggling to pull his hand away.

"Do not do it, Meldron!" I shouted.

Meldron moved to the kneeling figure. "I want him to see this," he said. "I want everyone to see it."

The third warrior seized Llew by the hair and turned his head to look along his outstretched arm. "N-n-n-o-o-o!" Llew groaned.

My own head was held in a tight grip so that I could not look away. "Stop!" I shouted.

Meldron brought the sword up and dropped the blade sharply. There sounded a dull chunk, the sword rang and Llew's right hand came away in a bright spray of blood. His eyes fluttered in his head and he collapsed.

Meldron picked up the severed hand and held it before me. He removed the gold ring which his father, Mcldryn Mawr, had given Llew and placed it on his own finger. I made to look away but could not. "You see?" he said, dangling the hand before my face by the forefinger, "Llew is blemished. He is maimed. He can no longer be king. Now you must choose someone else."

"I will never see you king."

"So be it," Meldron replied savagely.

The sword in his hand flicked out. Instinctively, I jerked my head back, but it was held fast in the grip of my captors. Meldron slashed the blade across my eyes.

I screamed. The world blazed red—hot red, molten red, and then . . . black.

9

Cast Adrift

We were dragged down from the White Rock to the beach and tumbled into one of the curraghs waiting there. Half-conscious, I felt the boat shoved across the sand and into the water, and we were cast onto the mercy of the waves.

My eyes were on fire. I lay in the bottom of the curragh, aware of nothing but the blazing agony. I screamed, and heard the voices of men laughing in reply. These dwindled and became the voices of gulls. I heard water lapping at the sides of the boat...and I fainted.

I do not know how long I swooned. But the flaming ache in my head roused me and I sat up. The movement brought such pain that my stomach heaved and I vomited over myself. I slumped back and fell over Llew.

He groaned and I remembered his hand. His hand!

I struggled upright, clawing at the side of the boat. It felt as if my head would burst. My face throbbed. I leaned over, scooped seawater into my hands and splashed it on my face. The salt water stung my wounded eyes and the pain flared white-hot—pain like a firebrand burning into my eyes. I gagged and fell back.

My head cleared and I pulled myself upright. Cursing Meldron and my own torment, I stretched my hands over Llew's inert body and began to examine him.

He was lying on his side, his arm bent at the elbow, the forearm hanging down across his chest. I felt carefully along the length of the arm to the wrist and hand. It was whole; he was lying on his wounded arm.

I raised myself up on my knees beside him and, with difficulty, lifted him and rolled him onto his back. The wounded arm came free. Carefully, carefully, I raised the arm and cradled it against me while with gentle fingers I probed the wound.

Blood bubbled from the stump, warm and thick. I think he had been lying on the wound and the weight of his body on the doubled arm had constricted the flow of blood; this had saved his life. By turning him I had started the bleeding again, but I had no other choice; and, if I was to help him, I had to complete my scrutiny. With my fingertips, I softly brushed the raw stump of his arm. Meldron's blade was sharp; the bones and flesh were cut clean.

I lowered the stump carefully, and quickly seized the edge of my siarc between my hands and ripped it. I then tore the cloth into a wide strip and, groping for the side of the boat, I wet the strip of cloth in the sea.

My head felt as if it would burst at any moment. Grinding my teeth against the pain, I forced myself to finish what I had begun. I gathered the wounded arm to me and began to wrap the handless stub with the sea-soaked cloth.

Blood surged from the wound with every pulse of Llew's heart. I could feel it leaking through the cloth. I tore another strip and bound that around the first; and then a third strip, which I used to bind the other two, tying the ends as tightly as I could. I bent the arm at the elbow and nestled it against his chest, hoping he would not bleed to death. There was nothing more I could do for him.

Dizzy and weak from my exertion, I ripped another length of cloth from my siarc; I wet it in the sea and, braving the stinging lash of the salt water, bound the strip around my eyes. I vomited again. And then, strength spent, I slumped back in the boat, groaning with fatigue and pain.

Blind! All was dark and formless to me. I would never again see the faces of my kinsmen and brothers—never again see the light. Blind! My world had become as dark as grief, as dark as the sealed tomb, as dark as Uffern's black pit, as dark as endless death.

I lay curled in the bottom of the small boat and wept bitterly for my lost vision, and for the agony of my ruined eyes—until at last, exhausted by misery, I sank into an empty sleep.

The torment of my slashed eyes woke me. I did not stir, but lay listening for a moment. The wind remained but slight; the wavelets slapped against the side of the boat without force. The tideflow around the islands is not heavy; it would take us but a little distance out from the western shore of Ynys Oer. Then we would be subject to the sea currents and the weather.

If the winds held steady from the north we would be blown south along the western coast of Albion, to be driven aground somewhere on a strip of deserted coastland. If the winds became fitful and erratic—much more likely in this changeable season—we would drift further westward and arrive I knew not where.

At best, landfall was merely a remote possibility. We had no oars, no sail, no provisions. A single large wave would easily capsize us; a small tip of jagged rock would pierce the stretched leather sides of the curragh. We were at the mercy of the wind and rocks and water.

Meldron had been canny. He had not murdered us outright, but left our fate to the sea. That way he could, in all truth, claim not to know how we had fared. He would incur no blood debt for our deaths.

Oh, but the blood debt he owed for the deaths of the Derwyddi was vast indeed. Had he owned a gleaming mountain of gold and all the sheep, cattle, handmaids and serving men in the Three Realms, still he could not have paid it.

Sun and stars, bear witness! Lord Nudd, Prince of Uffern and Annwn, King of the Coranyid, Sovereign of Eternal Night—he it was who had slain the bards of Prydain. But Prince Meldron had slain the rest. No bards were left in Caledon or Llogres. No bards were left in the Island of the Mighty.

No, no...I was yet alive a little longer, and Scatha's daughters were safe on Ynys Sci.

Llew moaned, and came awake with a scream. I raised my throbbing head and put out a hand to him. "Be easy, brother," I told him. "I am here. Be still."

"Tegid!" he began, and then convulsed in agony. He shut his mouth and stifled a cry; the sound emerged as a tortured whimper. My fumbling hand found his back. I could feel him straining against the pain, muscles tight, sweat drenching his clothes. He fainted again and lay still.

I drowsed.

When I woke again, the air was cool on my face and the sea still. I reckoned by this that it was night. Llew must have been waiting for me to awaken, for when I stirred, he said, "Where are we? What has happened?" His voice cracked and his words slurred with pain.

"We are cast adrift," I told him. "Meldron has abandoned us to our deaths."

He was silent for a time, and then said, miserably, "I am so cold."

"Here, take this." I found my cloak and held it out. He took one end of it and I the other; we shared the cloak between us.

"My hand, and your eyes...Tegid, what are we going to do?"

"That is for the sea to decide. It is for us to wait."

We waited: through an endless, everlasting night. All the next day we lay in the boat, hardly moving. When the sun slipped below the rim of the world, we huddled together in the bottom of the boat to keep warm. We drowsed fitfully, never fully asleep for the throbbing of our wounds. My eyes, his hand—what could we do?

The weather held fair and we counted that a blessing. From time to time, Llew raised himself to look around. But we were far from land, and I could get no sense of our location from Llew's spare description.

On the fourth day, the wind rose sharply and swung to the west. The waves grew, lifting our small boat, tossing it from side to side. With each lurch and shudder we were slammed against the sides, against the curved wooden ribs of the curragh. Llew cried out whenever his wounded stump was jostled.

Night gave us no relief. The storm strengthened. The sea heaved; waves swelled and toppled over us. Exhausted, Llew swooned, and I cradled him against me so that he would do no further hurt to himself. I held him and he muttered incoherently as the troubled sea tossed our little vessel. I heard a strange grating sound, and I listened to it for some time before realizing that it was Llew grinding his teeth. I tied a knot in the corner of my cloak and thrust it between his teeth, lest he bite through his tongue.

The gale increased through the night. I heard thunder growling and felt the sting of wind-lashed rain on my face, but saw no lightning flash. As the furious heart of the storm swept down upon us, Llew roused himself. "Sing, Tegid!" he shouted above the shriek of the wind.

I thought him ranting. "Peace, brother. Be easy. It will soon end," I said, thinking that our boat would founder on the next wave and we would be spilled into the sea to drown. We would soon join the bards of Albion in death—but two more among all the others Meldron had murdered.

Llew struggled upright. "Sing!" he insisted. "Sing us to shore!"

Though the wind wailed high and wild above us, and the sea swell crashed on every side, I raised my voice and sang—haltingly at first, finding my way. The gale snatched the words from my mouth and hurled them back in my face. "What is the use?" I shouted.

"Sing!" demanded Llew. "Sing to the Swift Sure Hand, Tegid!"

I lifted my voice in a song of deliverance to the Many-Gifted. I sang the manifold virtues of the Great Good God; I sang the zealous pleasure of the Swift Sure Hand to heed and help all who call upon him.

And as I formed the song and gave it utterance, images, sharp and clear, sprang into my mind. I saw...a steep-sided glen in deep forest, tall pines straining for the sky... I saw a hidden lake and a fortress of timber... I saw an antler throne on a grass-covered mound, adorned with an oxhide of snowy white... I saw a burnished shield with a black raven perched on its rim... I saw a beacon fire burning bright from a distant hilltop, and answered from the top of nearer hills... I saw a rider on a pale yellow horse, galloping out of the mist, the horse's hooves striking sparks from the rocks... I saw a mighty warband washing themselves in a high mountain lake, the water stained red with blood... I saw a white-mantled woman standing in a green bower with the light of the sun flaring her hair like golden fire... I saw a cairn in a hidden glen, a secret, secluded gravemound...

I sang, and the tempest raged. Our leather boat pitched and lurched, now lifted high and now flung low. We were blown over the billowing swell like a fleck of sea foam before the gale. Water cascaded over us, drenching us, chilling us. The salt water burned in my wound and filled my mouth.

With every lurch of the boat, Llew yelped with pain. "Sing, Tegid! Sing!" he kept shouting, and I thought he must be delirious in his torment. Yet he persisted, and so I sang. And the visions swarmed and danced in my head, crazy as the tempest whirling around us.

"Do you hear, Tegid?" cried Llew, his voice swallowed in the wind-roar. "Hear it?"

I listened and heard nothing but the wind's wild shriek, and the water's roar as waves crashed on the rocks—the rocks!

"Do you hear it, Tegid?"

"Yes! I hear it!" It was the sound of waves beating and breaking over rocks. The storm was driving us towards the shore. "Can you see anything?"

"No," he replied. "Wait! I see something. I see the rocks. I can see where the waves are breaking."

"Can you see land?"

"It is too dark."

He grasped my arm with his good hand. "Keep singing, Tegid! Sing us to land!"

I sang and the sound of crashing waves grew to fill the tempest-tossed night. Closer, I could almost feel the jagged teeth of the rocks gnashing in the storm, looming ever closer, clashing out of the darkness to tear and crush and destroy. Water gushed in torrents over us as the sea rent itself on the rocks all around. My voice was drowned in the wave-roar, yet I sang, claiming a small circle of safety for our little boat amidst the sea-wrack.

I felt the sea gather beneath us like a beast, bucking and heaving. We were thrown high, spun around, and flicked as lightly as a leaf in the swirl. Sea-thunder sounded from every side, shattering ear and mind, shaking the soul.

Down into the trough, and up, up again. I heard water sucking rock and felt the boat lurch sideways as the wave pulled away. For the space of a heartbeat, the boat hung between sea and sky. The sea surged, lifting the boat free and hurling it high. We plunged and struck another rock and I heard a sharp crack as wooden ribs gave way.

"Hold tight!" wailed Llew.

I flung my hands out to grip the sides of the boat and felt cold rock instead. I tried to push away, but the boat was already slipping down. In another instant we would be spilled into the seething sea. I gulped air and, with a last shout, cried deliverance from the watery grave yawning beneath us.

The waves retreated and I felt myself falling. The boat fell sideways and rolled over, and over again. Water gushed into my mouth and lungs. The sea twisted my arms and legs, pulling me down into the churning depths. I was tumbled and turned, dragged deeper and deeper.

I struck something hard with my knee, and my right shoulder collided with what seemed to me a hard wall. The weight of water flattened me against this wall, crushing me like a giant hand, forcing the air from my lungs. I fought with my hands to push free of the rock wall.

And then—

Air streaming over me! I gasped, choking on sea foam. Then the water fell away and I found myself pushing against, not a wall, but a stony shingle. A wave crashed over me, first pinning me beneath its weight, then lifting me and hurling me further up the beach. Gasping,

I scrambled like a crab over sea-slick rocks through the back-rushing water.

The sea dragged at my legs. Seaweed tangled my arms and ankles. The wave-surge swelled, rising to my hips, waist, chest. I was lifted again and propelled forward. When the water fell away once more I was on my knees, small rocks hard under my hands.

. I rose and stumbled forward, struck my foot against a stone and sprawled headlong. I heard the roar of the waves crashing in once more. I kicked with my feet for a foothold, but I was pulled back, my hands torn from the rocks as the sea reclaimed me.

All at once, I felt myself caught and held securely. And then Llew's voice straining against the wind and wave-roar, "Tegid! I have you," he shouted. "Stand!"

He clutched me by the arm and lifted me to my feet. Leaning on one another, we struggled further up the rock-bound shore and collapsed on a spit of sand.

"You have done it, Tegid. You sang us to land!" Llew said, and then gasped. I felt him squirm beside me, and realized he was writhing with pain.

"Llew!" I threw my hands towards him. He clutched at my arm with his good hand and moaned—a hopeless, heart-tearing sound. I held him until the pain eased again.

"You sang us to land," he said, when he could speak again. His voice was ragged as frayed rope. "You saved us, Tegid. We were lost."

"The Goodly-Wise heard our song and reached down with his Swift Sure Hand and plucked us out of the sea—and out of the grave Meldron intended."

We lay on the beach, shivering with cold and weak with the pain of our wounds. Llew whimpered from time to time, when the agony was too great to bear; but he did not cry out. Through the night we lay on the sand, as the storm slowly dwindled around us. Then, as dawn seeped into the fleeting rags of storm-wrack to the east I felt the first flush of sunlight warm my face. I sang the song I had been given:

I sang the steep-sided glen in forest deep; the fortress on the lake, and the antler throne high on its grass-covered mound, with the white oxhide upon it. I sang the bright-burnished shield and the black raven perched on its rim, wings outspread, filling the glen with its severe song; and the beacon fire flaming the night sky, its signal answered from hilltop to hilltop. I sang the shadowy rider on his pale yellow horse, and the mist which bound them, and the sparks struck from the rocks. I sang the great warband bathing in the mountain lake, and the water blushing red from their wounds. I sang the golden-haired woman in her sunlit bower, and I sang the hidden Hero Mound.

When I finished, Llew had fallen asleep beside me. I lay back on the sand and, with the sound of the waves sighing on the rocks, I slept.

10

The Nemeton

I could still hear the sea moaning, restless in its stony bed, but the sound abated as we moved further inland. In my left hand I held a length of sea-scoured oak which I used as a staff; my right hand rested on Llew's shoulder as he guided me. From the way my steps seemed always to descend, I surmised that the land dropped away from the sheer-cragged headland directly behind.

After a wretched, pain-racked night on the beach, day had awoken our resolve to rise and toil inland, which meant scaling the sea cliffs of the headland. Neither of us could have done it alone. Even now, I do not know how we survived. It took most of the day, but once the headland was behind us we rested in a grassy cleft between two rocks, and shivered when the sun went down. It was morning once more when we began our slow trek inland.

As we walked, Llew described what he saw before us. "There are hills ahead," he told me, "rising to peaks in the distance. I can see snow on some of the higher peaks."

"What is the direction?"

He paused to take direction from the sun. "South and east, I think," he replied. "The nearer hills are rounded and wooded—mostly oak and beech, and some pine. There is a stream just ahead, but we will have to climb down to it. The wood begins on the other side. We can rest at the stream before entering the wood, and—"

He gasped. His shoulder tensed and he doubled over.

It was another of the fiery pains that afflicted him—sharp, burning arrows of agony that suddenly flared without warning. When this happened, we halted until the attack passed and he could move again. I could but imagine the distress of his wound—perhaps it matched the hot spears piercing my eyes, searing through my head.

"Where are we, do you think?" he asked in a moment, speaking through clenched teeth.

"Are the peaks wooded?"

"I think so," Llew said; he gulped air and straightened somewhat. "They are far away. I cannot be sure, but it looks as if the slopes are dark with trees."

We began walking again. "It may be we have landed somewhere on the coast of northern Caledon. If this is so, the peaks you see before us are the *Monadh Dubh*."

"Clan Galanae, Cynan's people—they are in the south of Caledon," Llew offered.

"Very far to the south. There are few people this far north," I explained. "The land is wild and unsettled. These highlands are prey to violent winds and storms—as we have endured. It is no kindly place you see before us; we will not find any king to receive us."

Carefully we picked our way down the hillside to the stream where we knelt and drank, and then rested. Lying back on the grassy bank of the stream, my thoughts turned to the massacre on the mound. The gorge rose in my throat and a moan escaped my lips. How could I have anticipated such atrocity? Even now I could not comprehend it. How could I fathom such an attack? I could scarcely believe it had happened.

When the Light of the Derwyddi is cut off, and the blood of bards demands justice, then let the Ravens spread their wings over the sacred wood and holy mound . . .

So the Banfáith had said. The words, with dire certainty, were coming to pass. The learned brotherhood had been slaughtered, the light of their wisdom cut off; the blood of bards cried out from the earth demanding justice. So be it!

Resting on the bank of the stream, I let my mind sift these thoughts. In a little while, Llew stirred beside me. "What now?"

"We need rest," I answered. "And time to allow our wounds to heal."

"Are you in pain?" he asked, voice tight and breath measured.

"I do not know which hurts me more, the loss of my sight, or the loss of my brothers. It feels as if my soul has been torn from me."

Llew was silent for a time. "We cannot stay here," he said at last. "There is water, but no food or shelter. We will have to move on."

"We will find shelter in the wood."

Neither of us moved for a long time. Finally, Llew stood up slowly. I felt his hand on my arm as he pulled me to my feet. "I say we follow the stream and see where it leads."

The brush grew thick along the stream bed, making progress wickedly difficult. But the stream soon joined a river. Taller trees grew beside the river, and wide watermeads spread on either side, allowing us easier travel.

We moved slowly, resting long and often. By nightfall we were no great distance from the place where we had begun. But the river valley afforded many hollows and rocky dells wherein we could find good shelter. I had nothing with which to make a fire, but I instructed Llew where to find a number of edible roots—which he dug with a stick and washed in the river. We might freeze in the cold night air, but at least we would not starve.

That night I was awakened by Llew's screams. He was in pain and trembling with cold. I roused him and, with much staggering and stumbling, we made our way to the river where I compelled him to suspend his stumped arm in the icy water until the flesh grew numb. This gave him some relief, but upon returning to our cold camp we were overcome with chills and could get no more sleep that night.

Next day, I made certain that Llew found a flint striker and gathered dry moss a-plenty to use as kindling, so that we be certain of a fire from then on.

"What good is flint alone?" asked Llew.

"There are other stones which bring the spark from flint. I will show you. Indeed," I told him, "I will make a bard of you before we are finished. We will rescue Ollathir's awen yet."

"Lead on, O Head of Knowledge," Llew said. "To hear is to obey."

In this way, we journeyed into Caledon's heart: halting, slow, pain-wracked steps, with much pausing to bathe inflamed wounds in the clear, cold flowing river. During one such pause, I bade Llew unwind the bandage from his wrist. "Describe the wound to me," I said.

"It is mending."

"Describe it. I must know if it is healing properly."

He took a deep breath and loosed the strips of cloth with which I had bound his wound. He groaned—partly with pain and partly with grief—as the cloth came away from his gory stub. "It is black," he said. "There are white flecks of bone in it."

"Wash it in the water and then tell me what you see," I instructed.

He lowered the arm gently and I heard him swish the limb forth and back in the water. *"Clanna na cù,"* he muttered through clenched teeth.

"How does it look now?" I asked when he finished.

"More red than black. Some of the bone chips have washed away. It is bleeding again."

"The blood—is it thick and red? Or is it thin and watery."

"Thick and red, I suppose."

"And the flesh around the wound—is it inflamed and hot to the touch? Or is it cool? What is its color?"

"Well," he answered after a moment, "it is warm to the touch, but not hot. The skin is red and swollen, but not inflamed. Here, you feel," he said, and I felt his hand take my right wrist and guide my hand to his arm. He pressed my fingertips to his wrist. "There."

I gently probed the flesh around the wound. It was warm to the touch, yes, but not feverish hot, as it would be if it were inflamed. When I touched the wound itself, he winced and jerked his arm away. "I am sorry."

"Well? What do you think?"

"I think healing has begun. It should be wrapped again, but with clean cloth."

"Where will we get that?"

I drew my siarc over my head and began tearing it between my hands. Llew protested. "Not your siarc, Tegid. You need what is left of it to keep warm."

"I have my cloak," I replied, and proceeded to rip the cloth into strips. "Now, help me wash them in the water."

Together we knelt at the river's edge and rinsed the strips of cloth. When we had finished, I gave them to Llew, saying, "Spread these on a bush and let them dry in the sun."

Llew did as I instructed him and we slept in the warm sun. When the cloth strips were dry, I helped Llew to bandage his arm, whereupon he said, "Now it is your turn."

I reached a hand to the binding on my eyes. "It is well."

"No," he informed me flatly, "it is not well, Tegid. It is filthy with blood and dirt. You have to change it."

I unknotted the ends and unwound the binding; the cloth stuck to the wound and we had to pull it free, which started the blood flowing again. I bit my lip to keep from crying out. "You have to wash it now," Llew insisted.

With Llew's help, and with difficulty, I lowered my face to the water and gently splashed water onto my face and the raw wound that had been my eyes. The sting of the cold water countered the fire of the pain somewhat, and I felt better for it.

I raised my head from the water and turned to Llew. "How does it look? Describe it to me."

"It is a clean cut," he told me. "The flesh is red and swollen around the gash, and there is some yellowish fluid seeping out. But the blood looks good—it is not watery."

I pressed my fingertips to the edges of the wound and felt the flesh. It was sore and inflamed. "What of my eyes?"

Although he tried to keep his voice level and dispassionate, I sensed that he was disturbed by what he saw. "There is so much clotted blood and swelling... brother, I cannot tell. I think you should keep them covered."

He feared to say what I already knew: my eyes were ruined. Since Meldron's cruel stroke, I had seen neither spark nor blush of light. Brightness of sun and darkness of night was all the same to me. I would never see again.

We stayed two days in a grassy dell, resting, conserving our strength. We ate the roots of water plants that grew in the river, and kindled warm fires from fallen branches fetched from the surrounding wood. Thus refreshed, we moved on, following the river, as it seemed good to me. Day by day, as we walked, I instructed my amiable companion in the lore of wood, field, and forest. Llew welcomed the distraction from his pain which my teaching provided, and he showed himself a quick and able student. He remembered all I told him, and often engaged me in closely reasoned discussions concerning one small detail or another. I had only to tell him a thing once and it was his.

After many days, we came to a waterfall. The river, which had been bending ever southward, became narrower and deeper, and the rocks along the watercourse larger, as the land rose higher in its approach to the mountains. We stopped, the sound of falling water loud in our ears. Llew gazed at the falls before us and said, "We will have to find a way around this rise. The boulders here are too big and the cliff too steep to climb."

"This is one of the gates to the mountains beyond," I told him. As I spoke these words, there surged within me a sudden conviction that we had been led to this place; the Goodly-Wise had directed our steps. "It is for us to go through here."

"Are you certain? I cannot see how we are to climb."

"Well, we will make a start."

Llew made no complaint, but sat down and began studying the tumbled mass of rock before him. After a time he said, "The boulders are big as houses, and smooth—there is no way to climb them. We might find our way among the smaller rocks, but they are covered with thick, green moss and splashing water, so they will be very slippery." He paused and asked, "Are you sure you want to do this?"

"Yes, I am certain."

"We could double back along the river and find another way, perhaps."

"This is the way of our path," I told him. I stood and cast aside the oak branch I used as a staff. "I feel it—this is the way we must go."

Llew offered no further objection, and we began picking our way up the mass of stone. We were instantly wet to the skin from the mist and spray. Speech was difficult over the constant crash and clatter of falling water, but Llew shouted directions to guide me. Straining, slipping, fighting for every precarious foothold, we crawled up the rock face before us.

I moved in close-wrapped darkness, my hands gripping the rock, feeling the cool hardness beneath my grasp. I began thinking of stone: standing stones, pillar stones, the circle stones which mark rare powers on the land. I thought of ogham stones, and stone cairns. And all the stones were carved with the *Môr Cylch*, the life-maze.

I imagined the precise pattern of the curving pathway as if woad-daubed in blue. It seemed to me that I entered the Môr Cylch, blindly placing my feet on the twisting, turning path, trusting to the Maker of the Maze to guide my steps.

"This is as far as we go," Llew called over his shoulder. "We will have to go back and find another way."

He eased himself back to where I perched, pressing my body against the rock. When he spoke again his voice was closer. "It is too steep, too dangerous. What do you suggest?"

"I will lead."

"Tegid, you are—" He stopped himself saying it. "How?"

"I will lead," I insisted.

Whatever his misgivings, Llew did not dispute my judgment. He spoke not a word of fear, but shifted along the narrow rock ledge where I stood. I flattened myself as close to the rock wall as I could, as, with greatest care and difficulty, we changed places. And then I began, slowly and with extreme care, to feel my way up the sheer rock face.

"Watch my hands and feet," I called back to Llew. "Do what you see me do."

"This is insane!" he shouted back.

"Well I know it!"

Nevertheless, we continued our climb. Trembling, halting, fearful for every step, in the sightless dark, I sought the path. Trusting only to my fingertips and toes, I found first one foothold, then a handhold, and another. Step by shuddering step, we climbed. I held the image of the life-maze in my mind, and each foothold became a step along the patterned way.

Up and ever up, we scaled the rocky height. Mist and spray bathed us, drenched us. We paused now and again to gather the ravelled threads of our faltering strength, and then climbed on. Llew called out encouragement to me, urging me on with high-sounding words.

After an age, it seemed to me that the water-roar grew less. "Llew, what can you see?" I called over my shoulder.

"Nothing," he replied. "The mist and spray—I cannot see a thing!"

I made to move on but, try as I might, I could not find the next foothold. Finally, in a fit of desperation I reached as high as I could stretch, pressed my fingers tight to the rock crevice and swung out and up...

I felt my foot strike a step that I could not see, but the rock was slick and my foot slipped away again. But for my fingers wedged into the crevice, I would have fallen. I slid back down.

"Tegid! Are you all right?"

"Yes," I answered, "I will try again."

"No! Wait—"

I kicked out once more and my heel caught on the narrow, unseen edge. I quickly shifted my hands and pulled my trailing leg up until the foot reached the step. I straightened and felt fresh wind on my face. I stretched forth a hand and felt the rock sloping sharply away. Two more quick steps and I was standing on a wide, level surface.

I called for Llew to follow, and he shouted back, "Stay there!

Wait for me."

In a moment, he shouted again: "Tegid, it is too far. The step—I have nothing to hold on to."

I lay on my stomach and extended my hand over the edge towards him. "Take my hand," I shouted.

"I cannot reach it, Tegid," he shouted; I heard the pain and frustration in his voice. "I cannot hold with one hand!"

"Take my hand, Llew. Reach for it, I can hold you. Stretch out your foot to the step and take my hand. I will pull you up."

"No, Tegid. It is too far. I cannot—"

"Take my hand, Llew."

"I tell you it is too far! *I have but one hand!*"

"Trust me, Llew. I will not let you fall." He was silent for a time. "Llew?"

"Very well," he replied slowly. "I will count to three. Ready? On three: one...two...THREE!"

I braced myself. His hand struck mine; my fingers closed on his wrist and held fast. Loose stones clattered away and were lost in the water-roar below. A moment later, Llew was scrambling onto the rock beside me.

"Tegid, you did it!" he said, gasping for breath. "Bless you, brother, we made it!"

We lay panting on the rock. And, as if to reward us for our effort, the sun shone down on us, warming the rocks and drying our clothes. We lay back, drinking in the warmth, listening to the water-voice now small and far, far below.

When we finally roused ourselves to continue on our way, I asked Llew to describe what he saw around us.

"It is the entrance to a glen, I think," he replied. "The river has carved out a bowl-shaped ravine here. Very green. The grass is short and fine. There are many rocks among the trees, and the trees are large. The river ahead is wider here, and deeper, too. The glen is crooked; it bends out of sight a little way along. I cannot see what lies beyond the bend, nor what lies above the ridge of the glen." He paused as he turned towards me. "Well? What say you, brother?"

"Let us follow the river and look for a place to make camp," I answered. "And if you see a likely branch for a staff, I would welcome it."

So saying, we moved on. Llew directed my steps and we clambered over and among the rocks along the riverway. I listened to the sounds around me and sniffed the wind, sifting the air for signs. Amidst the sounds of moving water, I heard birdcalls: the thin cry of the tree creeper, the whistling warble of the dunnock, and high, high aloft the mewing call of a buzzard circling lazily over the trees. Now and then, I heard the splash of a fish, or the furtive rustle of an animal darting into the undergrowth at our approach. I smelled the rich earthsmell of mouldering foliage and damp, rotting wood; and the clean, fresh scent of sun-washed air; and the faint sweetness of flowers.

In a little while, Llew paused. "There is a stand of pines not far ahead," he told me; pain made his voice crack. The climb up the falls had exhausted him, and his wound was hurting him again. "I think we should stop and make camp there."

We made our way to the place, and found a well-sheltered clearing among the trees. The ground was covered in a drift of pine needles, thick and soft beneath our feet; the branches overhead formed a fair roof. There were large stones clumped in a rough ring—these formed a rude caer in which we might build our fire and sleep. After a rest, Llew set about gathering firewood and I turned to the task of clearing a space for the fire.

As I worked, feeling around the circumference of our caer, I heard the breeze sighing in the treetops. The wind was rising, strengthening out of the east as the sun sloped towards evening. It would be a chill night, we would be glad of the fire. This I told Llew when he returned with the firewood.

"Then I will gather more wood," he said. I could tell it was the last thing he wanted to do, but he moved off among the trees.

Feeling my way slowly, I crept down to the river's edge and retrieved several smooth, round stones. After repeated trips, I had assembled enough to make a simple fire ring. As I began arranging the stones for the ring, I caught the slightest whiff of a familiar smell.

I stopped and sat up, raising my head and turning my face to the wind. I waited, but the scent eluded me. Perhaps, I thought, I have imagined it only.

I continued with my work, and in a moment the wind gusted, and I smelled it again. This time I was certain I had not imagined it: oak smoke. I turned my face into the wind. I was still standing this way when Llew returned.

"What is it?" Llew asked, dropping his armload of wood. "What have you heard?"

"Nothing," I replied. "But I have smelled something—an oak fire." I indicated the direction of the wind. "It is coming from that direction. Not far from here, I think."

"A settlement?"

"I cannot say."

"It will be dark soon," Llew observed. "Still, I think we should go and see."

"We will go together."

"Here," said Llew—he stooped and then took me by the wrist—"I brought you this."

He pressed the end of a branch into my hand. The length was slender and the bark smooth; the wood supple, yet resilient: ash, I guessed. "When I find another knife, we will carve you a proper staff," he said.

We moved slowly along the river, following the smoke scent. Soon, Llew remarked, "I can smell it now. We must be getting near—but there is no sign of anyone."

"It might be hunters," I replied.

Presently, Llew stopped. He placed his hand against my chest to halt me. "I see it!" he whispered. "I see the smoke—drifting across the water. The camp must be just a little way ahead."

We continued on, quietly, and, after but a few paces, Llew halted. "I think there is a ford here," he said. Even as he spoke, I heard the sound of water trickling over stones. "We can cross to the other side. Do you want me to go across and see who has made the fire?"

"Guide me. We will go together."

With my staff in one hand, and the other holding to Llew's arm, we crossed the river at the ford. The stones were well placed, and I had no difficulty finding my way across. My feet had but touched the opposite shore, however, when I became aware of a strange stillness in the air, and in the earth itself.

"An oak grove stands before us," Llew told me in a whisper. "The trees are very large."

"Let us go into the grove," I replied. "See that you remain alert."

We started forward, and after a few paces I sensed a change in my surroundings. It was cooler in the grove, and damp—rank with the smell of smoke and the moss-grown trunks of trees and fallen leaves. The air was still, the wood silent. No sound could be heard— no wind shifting the leaves, no stir of small feet in the undergrowth, no bird-cry.

We crept forward cautiously, pressing close to the trees. Llew tensed, touched my arm, and stopped. "What have you seen?" I whispered.

"It is an image of some kind—a carving. Here—"

He took my hand and raised it to the trunk of the tree beside me. The bark had been pared away from the bole, and a figure carved in the smooth wood. I traced the carving with my fingers, and felt a rough-hewn image: a hollow circle with a narrow rod passing through its center. It was a wheel with a spear for an axle.

"There are more of them," Llew whispered. "At least one carving on every tree."

I did not need to see the images hewn into the towering oaks to know that we had come to a place of power. I could feel the stillness of the grove—a silence persisting from time beyond memory, from before men walked upon the earth, from before the forest even—a stillness which overwhelmed all sound, calming, quelling, pacifying. A peace which reconciled all things to itself.

The image carved into the tree trunks identified the grove. It belonged to Gofannon, Master of the Forge. It was his sanctuary we had entered.

"This is a *nemeton*," I whispered, "an ancient place, a holy place. This wood is sacred to Gofannon; it is his place. Come," I said, tugging Llew's arm gently, "we will greet this lord and see whether he will have compassion on us."

On soundless feet we crept deeper into the nemeton. I brushed the rough trunks of the great trees with my hands as we passed, and smelled the sweet dry smoke of burning oak ... drawing near to the heart of the refuge, entering into the presence of the lord of the grove.

11

Gofannon's Gift

"He is here." Llew breathed a barely audible whisper. "He is ... Tegid, he is enormous—a giant."

"What does he look like? Describe him."

"He is twice the height of the tallest man. His arms are knotted thick with muscles; they look more like the limbs of an oak tree than arms. He has rough black hair all over—on his arms and chest, his legs, his hands and his head. He has a long forked beard, and long black hair. He wears it bound tight to his head like a warrior. His face ... Wait! He is turning—looking this way!"

Llew gripped my arm in his excitement. "He has not seen us yet."

"What else? Tell me more. What does he look like? What is he doing?"

"His skin is dark—smoke-blackened. His eyes are dark, too; and he has great, thick black brows. His nose is flattened and immense; his moustache is tremendous—it covers his mouth and curls upwards at the ends. He is dressed in leather breecs only; his arms and chest are bare—except for huge gold bands coiled around each wrist."

"What is he doing?"

"He is sitting on a hump of earth at the entrance to a cave. The cave has a doorway: two square stone posts crossed by a stone lintel.

The two posts have skull niches, three on each side, with skulls in them—birds and beasts, I think—and the lintel is carved with the Endless Knot. The skulls and the carving are washed with blue woad. There is a stone and anvil just outside the cave entrance. Next to the stone, I can see a hammer—huge—it is the biggest hammer I have ever seen. And there are tongs on the anvil."

"Go on," I urged. "What else?"

"He is sitting before a firepit and holding a huge spit in his hands. There is meat on the spit—a whole sheep or deer. He is dressing the meat on the spit—getting ready to roast it. There is no fire yet, and . . . he is looking this way again. Tegid! He has seen us!"

I heard a voice, deep as the voice of the earth itself, stern and commanding.

"Welcome, little men," said the lord of the grove. "Stand on your feet and come before me."

Though it was stern, I heard no threat or malice in the command. Still gripping my arm, Llew drew me with him and we stepped slowly from the outer circle and into the ancient one's scrutiny.

"Hail, lord," I called, "we greet you with respect, and with all worthy regard."

Gofannon replied, "Show me a token of this respect you declare. What gift do you bring me?"

"Great Lord," I replied, speaking in the direction of the voice that addressed me, "we are exiles seeking refuge in a land unknown to us. We were set upon by enemies and cast adrift. We bring only the small benison of the companionship our presence will afford. But if you deem that a gift worth having, we give it gladly."

"That is a rare gift, indeed," replied the ancient one with gravity. "For it is long since I have welcomed men within my grove. I will accept your gift with pleasure. Sit with me and share my food."

We stepped nearer—Llew guiding me with his hand under my elbow—and sat down on the ground.

"Do you know me?" asked the ancient one.

"Great Lord, you are the Searcher of Secrets," I replied. "You are the Delver of Ore, and the Digger of Treasure. You are the Refiner, and the Shaper of Metal, the Master of the Forge."

The deep voice grunted its resonant agreement. "I am that—and more. Do you dare to speak my name?"

"You are Gofannon," I replied confidently, though I trembled inside.

"I am he," replied the lord. I sensed satisfaction in his voice. He was pleased with his guests. "How is it that you know my name and nature?"

"I am a bard and the son of bards, Mighty Lord. I am learned in the ways of earth and sky, and of all things needful among men."

"Do you have a name, little man?"

"I am Tegid Tathal," I told him.

"And the little man with you," Gofannon said, "has he a name? Or do you share one name between you?"

"He has a name, lord."

"Has he a tongue? Or is yours the only tongue to serve you both?"

"He has a tongue, lord."

"Then why does he not speak out his name? I would hear it, unless something prevents him." I sensed a slight shift in the giant's voice as he turned to address my silent companion.

"Nothing prevents me, Great Lord," said Llew softly. "Neither have I lost my tongue."

"Speak then, little man. You have my grant and leave."

"My name is Llew. I was once a stranger in Albion, but I was befriended by the one you see before you."

"I see much, little man. I see that you are wounded," said Gofannon. "You have lost a hand, and your friend has lost his eyes. And I see that these wounds still pain you. How did this happen?"

"Our enemies attacked us in a holy place," said Llew. "The bards of Albion have been slaughtered. We alone survived, but they wounded us and cast us adrift in a boat."

The lord of the sacred grove mused long on this, uttering a low rumble in his throat as he turned our words this way and that in his sagacious mind, weighing out the truth. "I know you now," Gofannon replied at last. Again, I sensed satisfaction in his words. "Come, we will eat together. But first there must be wood for the fire."

His next words were for Llew. "You, little man, will chop the wood for the fire."

I heard the giant rise and move away. Llew whispered, "He means me to cut wood. My hand—how can I use an axe? I cannot do it."

"Tell him."

"Here is the axe," Gofannon said, returning. "The wood is there. Cut enough to last through the night, for we will need it."

"It is my pleasure to serve you, lord," Llew said politely. "But I am injured as you see. I cannot hold the axe, much less cut wood with it. Perhaps there is another way I may serve you."

Though Llew declined with all courtesy, the Master of the Forge remained unmoved. "You had two hands and lost but one. Do you not have another?"

"I do," answered Llew, "but my injury is—"

"Then use the hand that is left to you."

Llew said no more; he rose from beside me and a few moments later I heard the chunk of the axe as he began, slowly, clumsily, to chop. I thought Gofannon's demand harsh but did not consider it wise to intervene in the matter.

So I listened to the dull chunk of the axe, and Llew's breath coming in bursts. And I gritted my teeth for Llew's sake, feeling his pain and frustration as he wielded the giant's axe.

When Llew finally made an end of his work, Gofannon had him carry the wood to the firepit. Llew did so without a word of protest, although I knew his wound must have been pounding with pain after his ordeal. Again and again, from pile to firepit he carried the wood, using his one good hand. Upon delivering the last log, Llew collapsed beside me on the ground.

He was wet with sweat and trembling with exhaustion and pain. "That is over," he whispered through gritted teeth.

"Be easy," I soothed. "Rest."

"Good work!" cried the forge lord. "We will eat now."

So saying, the giant clapped his hands and I heard the crackle of a fire, and soon I smelled the scent of roasting meat. The aroma brought water to my mouth, and my stomach suddenly felt its emptiness. While Gofannon busied himself with his task, Llew lay on the ground, gathering his strength, and I listened to the sizzle of bubbling fat as the lord of the grove turned the spit and the hot juices sputtered in the flames.

By the time the meat was cooked, I was dizzy with hunger.

"Let us eat!" cried the Shaper of Metal suddenly, as if he could wait no longer. I then heard a loud pop and a muted tearing sound and, the next I knew, a steaming haunch of roast venison was thrust into my hands. There came another rending pop and Llew was likewise presented a whole haunch to eat. "It is enough meat for a week!" Llew whispered. The rest of the deer belonged to our huge provider.

"Eat my friends! Eat and be filled," he bellowed happily, and I heard a snuffling sound as our host began to gnaw meat from bone.

Casting off all restraint, I lifted the haunch to my lips and began to eat. I worried the meat with my teeth, filling my mouth greedily, delighting in the warmth and flavor. The savory juices flowed down my chin and neck and onto my chest. I let them flow, I was so hungry.

"Lord Gofannon," said Llew abruptly, "never have I eaten meat this good. Had you given us but a taste of your meal, you would yet remain most generous."

"Where food is taken alone, the repast is meager," answered the ancient one affably. "Yet, where meat is shared among true companions of the hearth, the meal becomes a feast!"

The lord of the hearth laughed then, and we laughed with him, filling the grove with joyful sound. We finished our meal, glowing with the pleasure of warm food in our bellies.

"Drink with me, little men!" cried the ancient one in a voice that rattled the clustered leaves on the oak boughs. He clapped his hands, and the sound was like thunder.

"I cannot believe it!" gasped Llew, leaning close.

I heard a sound like the plunge of a rock into a deep pool. "What has happened?"

"It just appeared," whispered Llew.

"What appeared?" I whispered back. "Be my eyes, man! Describe what you see."

"It is a vat! A golden ale vat—the size of..." he stumbled in his search for words. "It is enormous! Fifty men could stand in it! It could serve three hundred!"

I heard the sound of another plunge, and into my hands was thrust a cup. But what a cup—a beaker the size of a bucket!—and filled with frothy ale.

Gofannon cried, "Drink! Drink, my friends! Drink and be happy!"

I lifted the beaker and quaffed cool, refreshing ale. It was the finest brew, bittersweet and crisp on the tongue, full-flavored and creamy rich—easily the best I have ever tasted, and I have drunk in the halls of kings.

I thought Llew would not be able to lift his cup at all, so I turned to him and offered mine. "Not to worry, brother," he replied heartily, sucking foam from his moustache. "I just put my whole face into the cup!"

He laughed and I heard the sound of the man I knew returning. We drank and laughed, and I felt the torment of my wound and the distress of my blindness begin to loosen and fall away from me like burdens shed at the threshold. Yet it was not the food and drink and mirth alone. We were in the presence of one greater than the forge lord—one whose fellowship itself was a soothing balm, a boon of inestimable value. I forgot my injuries and weakness; in the presence of the Goodly-Wise I was hale and whole once more.

When we had eaten and drunk as much as we could hold, Gofannon said to me, "You have said you are a bard. Have you rank among your kind?"

"I am Penderwydd of Prydain," I replied. "In former times I was Chief Bard to Meldryn Mawr."

Our host made his throaty rumbling sound once more and then said, "It is long since I have heard the song of a bard in my grove."

"If it would please you, Great Lord," I said, "I will sing. What would you hear?"

The Master of Artisans thought for a time, rumbling to himself all the while. "Bladudd the Blemished," he answered at length.

A curious choice, I thought. The *Song of Bladudd* is very old. It is little-known and rarely sung—perhaps because there are no battles in it.

As if listening to my thoughts, Gofannon said, "It is a tale seldom heard, I know. Nevertheless, that is the tale I would hear. A true bard would know it."

"So be it," said I, rising to my feet. Standing before him, I suddenly missed my harp. "I must beg your pardon, lord, but I have no harp. Still, the song will suffer but little for its lack. That I promise you."

"Never say it!" cried Gofannon in a voice that shivered the trees. "Why suffer even the lack of very little, when that little is so easily granted for the asking?"

"Great Lord," I replied, still trembling from the mighty voice, "if it would please you, might I yet have a harp?"

"A harp!" he cried. "You ask for a harp, but you stand there with your arms dangling at your sides! Open your hands if you would receive."

I opened my hands to him, and received a harp. My arms closed around the familiar and comfortable weight, nestling the instrument against my chest and shoulder. I tried the harpstrings and found them melodious and resonant. What is more, the harpstrings were tuned. I struck a chord and the air was filled with a splendid sound, rich and vibrant. The harp was well-made, a delight to play and hear.

I prepared myself to sing, pausing while my listeners settled themselves to receive the song. Then, loosing a shimmering chord, I began: "In elder times, before pigs were known in Albion and beef was the meat of kings, there arose in Caledon a monarch of mighty renown, and Rhud Hudibras was his name." My huge host grunted his approval, and the tale commenced.

"Now this chieftain, a man of esteem and well-loved by his people, had three sons. The first son was a hunter and warrior of vast skill and cunning, and the second son was like the first. Both men enjoyed nothing more than feasting with fine companions, and listening to the songs of bards. Life to them was good if mead filled their cups and a maiden filled their arms.

"But the third son cared nothing for hunting or warring. More pleasant to him was the obtaining of wisdom. Yes, more pleasant to him was knowledge than the harpsong of bards, or the feasting of friends, or even his arm around the slender waist of a girl. Bladudd was his name. Truth and knowledge was ever his delight, and this is the way of it:

"One day, King Rhud called his three sons to him and spoke kindly to them, saying, 'I am ever at your service, my beloved. Good gifts are yours. Speak to me, my sons. Reveal to me your hearts' desires. Ask anything and it will be granted to you.'

"The first two sons answered their father the king. 'Our delight is hunting and feasting, as you know. Therefore, we ask nothing more than swift horses, plentiful game, and a warm fire and a welcome cup shared with good friends at the end of the day.'

"The Great King heard them, and said, 'These things you have already. Is there nothing more that I can give you?' For it was in his mind and heart to bestow good gifts upon his favored ones.

"The sons, strong men and bold, held counsel with themselves and answered him, saying, 'You are right when you say we have that which we desire already. Yet there is one thing we do not have.'

" 'You have but to name this thing, and it is yours, my bold ones,' Rhud, Wise Father, said.

"Up spoke his sons in answer: 'We would have years unnumbered so that we can enjoy the pursuit of these pleasures forever.'

" 'If that is what you desire,' replied Rhud, 'it is easily granted. But is there nothing else?'

" 'You have asked, and we have answered,' replied the two hunters. 'We seek nothing else.'

" 'Very well,' the good king told them. 'Go your way. The thing which you desire is yours.'

"Then the king, Wise Lord, turned to his youngest son, who

stood a little apart, his brow wrinkled in thought. 'Bladudd, my beloved,' the father said, 'I am ever at your service. Good gifts are yours. Speak to me, my son. Reveal to me your heart's desire. Anything you ask will be granted to you.'

"Bladudd, who had been thinking hard the while, replied at once, 'Father, since you are ever a man of your word, I will answer you forthrightly. As you know, the pursuit of truth and the getting of wisdom is all my delight. Yet I desire a thing, and know not if it will bring me pain or pleasure. I hesitate to speak it out for fear it will be denied.'

" 'What is it, son of mine?' asked his father. 'Speak your heart. Withhold nothing from me, and I will withhold nothing from you.'

" 'Then hear me when I say that I desire to journey to a land far away where my knowledge will be increased so that I will know the truth of all things and, knowing the truth, I will gain much wisdom. For I am not lying when I tell you that I have learned all there is to know in this realm—including charms for every enchantment. But what are charms and enchantments next to Truth?'

"When he heard this, Rhud, ever wise and loving father, both groaned and wept for joy. He groaned because he knew the hardship which awaited his beloved; he wept for joy because Bladudd desired a gift worth having above any other. To his son he said, 'Where is this far-off land? What is its name?'

"Bladudd replied, 'It is a realm in the west, beyond the place where the sun sets in the sea. The Land of Promise is its name, and there the youngest child is wiser than the wisest man in this worldsrealm.'

"King Rhud raised his hands and said, 'Go your way, my beloved son. You have that which you desire.'

"That very day Bladudd sailed away in a ship. He journeyed long and travelled far, sailing ever westward towards the place where the sun sets. He did not reach the far-off land in many days, nor even many more days. Six moons passed over his head at night, and then two more. On the night of the ninth moon's birth, Beltain it was, a deep sleep fell upon him. He pulled his cloak over his head, closed his eyes, and soon lapsed into the most profound sleep he had ever known.

"It seemed to him but a short time and he heard a sound like the voice of a flea. He awakened and, pulling back his cloak, he saw a dancing light. He heard faint music in the air. The light shone all around him, coming from the sea. Bladudd sat up straight and, gripping the boat with his hands, put his face into the water to see what made the light.

"If the light shining above the waves was fair to look upon, the light shining under the waves was dazzling. And the music was the loveliest he had ever heard. Yet it was neither the light nor the music which held him. Not at all. The thing which seized Bladudd's attention was the sight of rounded green hills, and apple trees in blossom.

"Where before the sight of fish and seaweed addressed him, now he saw birds and flowers—brilliant birds and sweeping meadows of blue and white flowers. The birds flew to the apple trees and began singing so sweetly that Bladudd thought his heart would burst. It was as if he had been deaf every day of his life until that music began.

"When he made bold to greet the birds, up in a swirl they rose with a flurry of wingbeats. And when they alighted on the ground the birds became fifty young women of matchless beauty. Bladudd gazed rapturously upon these maidens and would have gladly continued gazing from that far-off time to this, except for the sudden appearance of a herd of stags racing over the hilltop.

"When the stags reached the place where the maidens waited, they were transformed into fifty young men as handsome as the women were beautiful. Each man wore a torc of thick gold around his neck; every maid wore a golden crown. They joined one another and began to disport themselves upon the meadows. And their game was marvelous to behold.

"And the grace of this wondrous race made Bladudd's spirit yearn to join them. At once he climbed from the boat and leapt into the water. At the sudden appearance of Bladudd the maids turned into birds once more, and the young men into stags. Both birds and stags fled away over the hill.

"Quickly, Bladudd bethought himself what he might do. 'I will cover myself with a charm of concealment,' he thought. And so he did.

"Thus hidden, he ran to the place where the young men had become stags and, choosing the foremost among them, threw his arms around the comely creature. In this way, the stag and Bladudd ran together side by side over the hill. Yet, though the stag had been first of all the others, because of Bladudd holding onto his neck the stag was last over the hill.

"On they ran and soon saw a mighty caer atop a hill both high and broad. Up to the caer flew the birds, with the stags running right behind. In the center of the caer stood a most wondrous hall. The lands around the caer far and far exceeded any Bladudd had ever seen for beauty, as did the king's hall far outshine all others Bladudd knew.

"Upon entering the caer, the stags and birds changed into elegant young men and women once more. The young men laughed at the stag who had been first among them but was last to enter the caer. Laughing, his companions asked whether their sport had wearied him. 'No,' replied the youth, 'yet when I first began to run, I suddenly felt a weight upon my neck. If death, who clings so tightly to mortal men, had fastened upon me, the weight could not have been greater.'

"The Fair Folk went into the hall then, and Bladudd followed. Invisible in his concealing charm, he found a pillar in the hall to stand beside and clamped his hand across his mouth to keep from exclaiming at all the things he saw. For wherever his eye fell, he saw treasures marvelous to behold, wonders beyond counting in every corner and cranny of the hall. And the least treasure he saw would have been richer by far than any in his own world. On a jewelled throne sat the king. His hair gleamed bright as a flame, and his face shone. If any were handsome in his court—and they were! they were!—the king himself was more handsome still.

"Bladudd thought he would not be discovered. But as soon as he took his place beside the pillar, up jumped the king and exclaimed, 'There is a dead man among us!' This so startled Bladudd that he forgot his concealing charm and became visible to the fair company.

"The king looked upon Bladudd and demanded of him his name and rank. 'I come of blood that would not shame you in a guest,' Bladudd replied proudly. 'Since I am a stranger among you, I claim the same hospitality of you that you would ask of me if our places were changed: the best of meat and drink, a fair woman to be your companion, harpers to fill your ears with praises, the best place by the fire, and a pile of new fleeces for your bed.'

"'Here is a fearless asker,' remarked the king. 'What do you mean, coming here like this?'

"'I came here seeking truth which leads to wisdom,' Bladudd answered. 'I swear by the gods my people swear by, that I mean no one here any harm. Indeed, all my takings will leave you no poorer, for all I desire is some of your knowledge.'

"When the king heard this, he threw back his head and laughed out loud. 'Think you that we part with our knowledge so lightly?'

"'I find it never hurts to ask,' replied Bladudd.

"'That is true,' affirmed the king. 'At all events, I would have thought it beyond the ken of any mortal to find a way to this place, unless it was Bladudd ap Rhud Hudibras of Caledon.'

"'I am that man,' Bladudd declared, astounded that his name should be known among such great and powerful people.

"'Well then,' the king said, 'your wit and fearless tongue have won you a place among us—though not, perhaps, the place you might have hoped for. You shall tend my pigs.'

"Thus Bladudd—who had never seen a pig, much less smelled one—became swineherd to the king of the Land of Promise. These pigs, Bladudd soon learned, were the most remarkable creatures he had ever seen. Their chief virtue was this: as often as they were killed and eaten the pigs were alive the next day. But that was not all. Far from it! For it was the eating of the meat of these pigs which preserved the people of the king from death.

"For seven years, as it seemed to him, Bladudd kept watch over the wonderful pigs—though in all that time he had never the chance so much as to dip the tip of his littlest finger into the juice of a roasting pig, let alone to taste some of the meat. Yet every day at midday the king's servants would come and drive away as many pigs as were needed for that night's feasting. And every morning the pigs would be back in Bladudd's care.

"Canny Bladudd watched and listened all the while. With his pigs he walked the Land of Promise, met the people, talked with them, and learned much. At night, he listened to the bards sing in the king's hall and learned even more. Thus, despite his low estate, he grew in knowledge and was content.

"At the end of seven years, Bladudd was herding the peerless pigs by a stream one day. He heard the blast of a hunting horn and looked up to see a company of men riding recklessly through the brake. Around the riders ran their hounds, and both riders and hounds were in full pursuit of a magnificent stag, white as sea foam, with red horns and ears.

"The white stag leaped the stream in full flight—landing just a few paces from where Bladudd stood—gave a shake of its antlers and disappeared into the woods. The hounds and riders searched for the stag, and though the hounds bayed and the riders looked long, they could not find the trail again.

"Bladudd watched them, and discovered that he saw them as if in a reflection in a pool and not as flesh and blood before his eyes. By this he knew that the stream was one of the boundaries separating one worlds-realm from the other, and that he was looking into the world he had left behind. He saw the bright patterns of their clothes and heard the rhythms of their speech as they spoke to one another, and a potent yearning came upon him. Tears burst from his eyes and he lay down beside the stream and wept for his former life.

"From that moment, Bladudd lost all desire to remain in the Land of Promise and sought to return to his own land once more. He set his mind on returning to his own kin and clan, and ever looked for his chance to do so.

"He watched and he waited, finding his chance at Samhain when the ways between the worlds stand open and crossings can be made. So, gathering his few belongings, Bladudd set off for the ford of the white stag. In secret he left the king's caer, lest anyone try to stop him or talk him out of going. And he left driving nine of the king's pigs before him, for he wanted to bring a boon to Albion.

"This was well, but the pigs squealed as they ran and wakened everyone with their piteous cries. The king heard the sound and gave chase. Bladudd fled, trying one charm after another to elude the king.

"Upon reaching the stream, plucky Bladudd bethought a charm which changed him into a salmon and the nine pigs into silver scales upon his back. But the king took the form of an otter. Then he changed himself to a squirrel, and the pigs to nine nuts in a pine cone. But the king pursued him in the form of a ferret. Whereupon Bladudd changed himself into a heron, and the pigs to nine feathers on his neck. But the king became a plummeting eagle. Lastly, Bladudd changed into a wolf, and the nine pigs to burrs in his fur. But the king overtook him in the form of a hunter on horseback; he shook his spear over Bladudd and the pigs, and changed them back into their own shapes.

" 'What an unfaithful swineherd,' remarked the king.

"Boldly Bladudd answered him. 'Not so, Mighty King. Seven years I have served you well. In all that time you have suffered no loss, for I have kept your pigs safe from predation of wolf and eagle, from wandering lost, from negligence and all such harm as comes to pigs. Not so much as a single hair from the pink hide of the smallest piglet has been lost. And as for the good I have had of them, well! I tell you the truth: I have not so much as laid one fingertip upon the skin of one when it was roasted and afterward licked that finger. Nor have you paid me so much as a kindly word for the service I have done you. Therefore, Bold King, it seemed good to me to select a small tribute from the increase of the herd.'

" 'You stole my pigs!' railed the king.

" 'Not so, Great Lord. I have undertaken to save the honor of your good name and make your renown as high in my land as in your own, by delivering these pigs to my people as a gift from you to them. This

I have done so that no one could think you mean and miserly.'

"The king's face became black with anger. 'That was ill-spoken,' he roared. 'You have no idea of the trouble your meddling would have caused if I had not prevented you. A most terrible and wearisome trial awaited you if these pigs ever set foot in your own lands. Yet, for the sake of the innocent, I will prevent it. You can thank me for my kindness.'

" 'Then I thank you for nothing,' snapped the bold prince.

" 'You came seeking knowledge—'

" 'And knowledge I received—no thanks to you.'

" 'Yet, if you had but learned to give up your selfishness and pride, you would have received a far greater gift than even you could dream of asking.'

"So saying, the king raised his spear and struck Bladudd squarely on the head, so hard that all sense fled him and he fell down on the ground as one asleep. When Bladudd opened his eyes he was in Albion once more; of the king and his impressive pigs there was no sign.

"But there was this: the blow visited on Bladudd by the king had blighted his body so that he lost all beauty and seemliness. His hair fell out, his teeth rotted, his skin became inflamed and his muscles withered. His once-fine clothes hung off him in filthy rags. He looked as one whom Lord Death has groomed for his own.

"So he tried by every means to restore himself. Alas, all he had learned availed him nothing. He could not undo the harm which had overwhelmed him.

"When Bladudd understood this, he mourned. 'A chilly homecoming I foresee for myself. This is not the form of a man to be celebrated by his friends, nor yet praised by bards, far less to win the favors of fair women.'

"He gathered his ragged clothes around him as best he could and made his miserable way to the fortress of his father. The people he encountered shrank from the sight of him, and no one made bold to stop him—until he reached the gates of his father's stronghold. The gatesmen were unwilling to admit him. 'Who are you?' they asked.

'What do you here? What makes you think we would allow the likes of you to see our king?'

" 'Who I am and what I do are my own affair,' the mysterious stranger replied. 'As for your king, tell him I am a man who can tell of marvels beyond imagining. And if that does not move him, tell him I have word of his lost son, Bladudd.'

"As soon as King Rhud heard of this, he ordered the stranger to be brought before him at once. 'Who are you, lord?' Rhud asked politely. 'More to the point, what tidings have you of my son?'

" 'Your son stands before you now,' the stranger replied, spreading his hands wide so that the rags fell from him and he stood revealed for the hideous sight he was.

"The Goodly-Wise King wept. And Prince Bladudd wept. And all his kin and clansmen wept, too. For, as handsome as he had once been, he was now that ugly. After a while they left off weeping, brought the young man bread and meat and good drink and, as he refreshed himself from his journey, he told them his fabulous tale. The king heard all his son told him, and then held council with his chieftains to decide if anything could be done.

" 'It is a sad case, and most lamentable,' said one of the king's counsellors. 'Nevertheless—please, forgive me for what I am about to say—the ways of kingship are clear: the blemished man cannot be king. Bladudd, you must agree, is blemished worse than most. Therefore the prince cannot resume his place among the silver-torced nobles worthy to be king.'

"The wise counsellor spoke the sorry truth. Even blighted Bladudd agreed that there was nothing for him but to hide himself away from the sight of men. He took himself far off and built a house in the forest where no one would see his blemish.

"Thus for seven years he dwelt in his lonely house with but one servant to aid him. In all that time, no man came near him, much less did he see the fair form of a woman. One day, at the end of seven years, his servant came to him and said, 'Bladudd, get up. Someone has come to see you.'

" 'That is a marvel,' replied Bladudd. And glancing around, he asked, 'Where is this extraordinary person?'

" 'Standing without, awaiting your will, lord.'

" 'Admit my visitor at once!' cried Bladudd. 'That is my will!'

"Directly, the visitor was admitted. And upon removing the hood which covered the head, there stood revealed before Bladudd a woman. This woman possessed neither beauty nor bearing. Wall-eyed, gap-toothed, and heavy-lipped, she was plain as mud. Yet she was beguiling to Bladudd by the very reason that she came willingly into his presence and did not flinch or retch at the sight of him, but stood smiling all the while as if Bladudd's grotesque appearance were nothing to her. Warmly she greeted him, showing neither fear nor disgust at his deformity.

"Bladudd was enthralled; he was intrigued. 'Who are you, woman? Where is your home, and what errand brings you here?'

" 'I come from a place well known to you, though you may not think so. And I come seeking you because I have glad tidings for you.'

" 'Then why keep me waiting? I am starving for some good word,' exclaimed Bladudd. 'Tell me these glad tidings at once!'

" 'I have discovered a way to heal you, lord, if healing be a thing you desire.'

" 'Desire!' cried the blemished prince. 'The bards have no word for the magnitude of my desire to be healed. I will tell you about desire! Did you know that I have seen no woman in seven years? Nor man neither, for that matter, except my servant. Of course I desire to be healed!'

" 'Very well,' the woman said, 'follow me.'

"Bladudd was persuaded to follow her at once, but the thought of the dreadful effect his appearance had on his kinsmen made him wary. 'Wait. How do I know you mean me good and not harm?' he asked. 'Forgive me, but you might lead me out to humiliation and disgrace.'

" 'Have it your own way, prince,' the woman replied. She turned on her heel and made to leave.

" 'Wait!' shouted Bladudd. 'Where are you going?'

" 'Make up your mind, Bladudd,' the woman replied. 'Will you accompany me, or not?'

" 'I will,' Bladudd said. He gathered his rags about him and hastened after the woman.

"The blemished prince followed his visitor and she led him to a barren hill, beyond that to a barren moor, and beyond that to a pool of stinking, black, bubbling mud.

" 'Throw off your rags and bathe in the pool,' the plain woman told him as she settled herself upon a rock. 'There is healing in the water.'

"Bladudd peered doubtfully at the smelly ooze. The surface of the mud heaved and sighed, exhaling stinking fumes. It seemed to him more a punishment than a healing. Yet he did not want to offend his visitor further, and they had come a long way. So into the foul pool he went.

"The mud was hot. It burned his skin. Tears ran from his eyes in a stream. But Bladudd, who had borne his sorry affliction with great fortitude, endured the pain for the sake of his desire to be healed. Even so, he could not endure forever. When the scalding mud bath grew too hot he pulled himself from the stinking pool to stand before the woman.

" 'This is splendid to look upon, to be sure,' Bladudd remarked, looking indignantly down the length of his mud-caked form. 'Yet I had hoped for more.'

" 'For that I should leave you as I found you,' the woman told him. 'Nevertheless, your cure is almost finished.' The gap-toothed woman pointed to a willow tree, which Bladudd had not seen before. 'At the foot of that tree is a vat of water. Wash the mud from yourself and you will be surprised at what you see, though you may not think so.'

"Bladudd took himself to the vat, climbed in, and washed. The water was clear and cool, soothing to his mud-blistered skin. He relaxed in the water and forgot his pains. Indeed, he forgot all his former hurts and troubles. When he finally stirred himself to rise from the vat, he had been renewed in his mind. He looked at his poor, ravaged body and, marvel of marvels, saw that his body, too, had been renewed.

"He took himself directly to the woman who sat waiting for him on her rock. 'I am healed!' he told her, gazing with joy down the length of his body. 'Indeed, am not lying when I tell you that I am better now than when the king of the Land of Promise smote me with the haft of his spear.'

"When the woman made no reply, the prince looked up and saw that the plain woman was gone and in her place was the most beautiful maid he had ever seen. Her hair was so pale yellow it was almost white; her skin was fair and smooth as milk, and her eyes were deepest blue and glowed like gemstones; her teeth were fine and even, and her nose straight; her brow was smooth; her neck was slender and elegant; her fingers were long, her arms supple, her breasts soft and shapely. She was the maid of Bladudd's fondest dreams.

" 'Lady,' breathed Bladudd in a small, awestricken voice, 'where is the gap-toothed woman who conducted me to this place? I must thank her for the singular service she has rendered me.'

"The comely maid looked at Bladudd; she looked to the left and to the right also. 'I see no other woman here,' she replied. And, oh, her voice was like melting honey. 'Indeed, I think that you must be mistaken. Or perhaps you believe that I am gap-toothed?'

"At this she smiled so sweetly that Bladudd's knees trembled and he feared he might fall on his face before her. 'Lady,' he said, 'I detect neither fault nor flaw in you at all.'

" 'Nor I in you,' the lady told him. 'But perhaps you would be more at your ease if you put on some clothes.'

"Bladudd blushed and looked around him. 'You are right to remind me,' he replied, espying his filthy rags on the ground where he had shed them. 'Yet I will go without cloak and clothes rather than wear those rags again.'

" 'Rags?' replied the lady wondrous fair. 'You must be used to very fine clothes indeed if these be rags to you.' So saying, she leaned from her rock and lifted the heap of clothing. The startled Bladudd saw that his rags had become the finest clothing imaginable.

" 'My clothes?' he wondered aloud, as well he might, for he beheld cloak, siarc, breecs, and buskins more costly, more luxurious than anything even his father King Rhud Hudibras possessed. 'Are these mine?'

" 'You cannot think they are mine,' the lady replied, smoothing her soft white mantle with slender hands. 'And between the two of us,' she added, 'it seems to me you have the greater need.'

"The astonished Bladudd dressed himself quickly, exulting in the excellent craft of his new raiment. When he had finished, he appeared a king. 'I tell you the truth,' he announced, 'I am no stranger to good things, but I have never owned clothes this fine.'

" 'Will you forget your sword?' asked the lady.

"Bladudd looked and saw that the lady held a golden-hilted sword across her palms. 'Is this mine?' he asked, suspecting a trick. For no one he knew had ever owned a weapon half so splendid.

" 'I see no one but you here before me,' the lady replied. 'And I tell you truly, I am well pleased with the sight.'

"Happy Bladudd strapped the sword to his hip and felt even more a king than before. He gazed lovingly upon the maid. 'Great Lady,' he breathed, his heart swelling with love and gratitude, 'what is your name that I might know you?'

"The maid so fair gazed at Bladudd from beneath her long lashes. 'Do you not know me at all?' she asked.

" 'If I had ever seen you before,' he answered, 'you can be assured I would remember you. If even I heard your name but once, I would live forever on the sound.'

"The maid rose from her place on the rock. She smiled and lifted her hand to Bladudd. 'My name is Sovereignty,' she replied. 'Long have I sought you, Bladudd.'

"The unblemished Bladudd held his head to one side. 'A name like no other,' he said. 'Yet it becomes you most nobly.' Then he took her warm hand and the holding of it filled him with pleasure. 'Lady,' he said, 'will you accompany me to my home?'

" 'And here was I beginning to think you would never ask,' the comely maid replied. She pointed to the willow tree, where two horses now stood tethered. Together the maid and the unblemished prince rode to the realm of Rhud Hudibras.

"When his father beheld his son, restored to him in all perfection, he wept tears of joy, so great was his rejoicing. And he called for a feast to celebrate the return of his once-blemished son. 'You are healed, my beloved!' the king exclaimed through his tears. 'Tell me how this came to be.'

"And the happy prince described all that had happened to him since he and his father had last sat beneath the same roof: the seven years of lonely exile, the coming of his visitor, the bath of scalding mud, the pool, the appearance of the maid, everything. King Rhud heard the tale, shaking his head slowly, marvelling at all he heard.

"'So I asked the maid to accompany me to my home,' Bladudd concluded, 'and here she is.' He turned his loving gaze upon the maid and said, 'I hope she will stay with me forever. Indeed, I do not think I could live one day longer if she removed herself from my sight.'

"'I will stay with you, Bladudd,' the maid replied.

"'Will you yet wed me?' asked Bladudd, his heart beating like a struck drum.

"'I will wed you, Bladudd,' vowed the maid most fair. 'Indeed, I was born for you, and you for me—if only you knew it.'

"So Bladudd and the most beautiful maid in all the land were wed that very day. And on that day did Bladudd also become king. For when his father saw how wise and good his son had become, and how fair and wise was his wife, Rhud Hudibras removed his golden torc and called to his chieftains and his people gathered close about. He called his Chief of Song, and before the close-clustered host, he said, 'Listen to me everyone!

"'I am no longer to be king,' he declared. And the tribes began a lament, for he had been a lord both great and good. 'It is for you to choose one to follow me,' he told his bard. 'Choose wisely now, and choose you well.'

"The bard and the people deliberated a while, and the king

waited. When a suitable time had passed, he said, 'Well? What is your decision?'

"The bard, in the voice of the people, answered with a loud cry, saying, 'We know we shall never find a lord as great and good as you to rule over us, but since you say you must cease to be king—which we will long and bitterly regret—we choose Bladudd. May he be to us a pillar of protection, and a sword of rightwise judgment.'

"Rhud beamed his pleasure, for the people had read his heart aright. And the Chief of Song placed the golden torc of kingship around Bladudd's throat. From that day, Bladudd ruled wisely and well. His keen desire for Truth, and his wife, Sovereignty, stood by him through all things—and through all things did Bladudd prosper.

"Here ends the tale of the Blemished Prince. Let him receive it who will."

The last notes of the harpstrings lingered long in the grove. I took my place by the fire once more, put the harp aside, and drank from my cask of a cup. I heard the silence of the grove deepening as night drew its cloak over us, gathering us to its dark heart.

At last, Gofannon, his voice a quiet thunder from the mound, stirred himself and said, "I have been blessed by the gift of your song—and no less by the gift of your excellent companionship."

"It is for us to thank you, lord," I replied. "Your food and drink are the saving of us."

"Tch!" the giant said impatiently. "Meat and drink satisfy for only a short time and they are gone. But the gift you have given me goes with me and sustains me wherever I wend. By merit of this truth, I grant you a boon: I will give you the virtue of your song."

"Great Lord Gofannon," I said, "we have enjoyed the bounty of your hearth, your kindness and your company. Indeed, you have already granted us more than we had any right to ask."

"Nevertheless," the giant answered, "I will reward you well for the service you have done me this night." I heard a rustle, and the great lord's voice sounded from a place high above me. "We will sleep now," he said. "Rest you in peace by my fire. Worry not. No enemy will intrude upon your repose; nothing will disturb you in my grove."

The voice receded, dwindling, and I realized that the lord of the grove was withdrawing to his cavern. His voice came back to us as he left us to our rest. "My reward will come to you in good time," he said. "See that you are ready to receive it."

12

Druim Vran

"He gave it to you," said Llew. "He meant you to have it."

I was tempted. Never had I held such a harp. "Did he leave anything else behind?" I asked.

Llew paused as he gazed around the camp. "No," he said. "Just the harp. The ale vat is gone, and the cups, and even the leavings from our meal. Everything is gone but the harp. It is yours, I tell you. It even has a strap."

We had awakened to find the grove empty and the forge lord gone. But he had left the harp. Perhaps, as Llew insisted, Gofannon meant it for me. But I had begun to have doubts about our gigantic host.

"You might as well take it, Tegid," Llew urged, "because you cannot leave it lying here."

"You are right, brother," I relented, seizing the strap and slinging the harp over my shoulder. "Let us go."

Silently, so as not to disturb the peace of the nemeton, we crept away—Llew leading and I walking just behind with my left hand on his shoulder, feeling my way with the ash branch in my right hand. We did not return to our camp of the day before but took up the trail along the river once more. We walked a long time. I could tell Llew was thinking, and I had thoughts of my own to occupy me.

The day was warm. We travelled the river marge where the walking was easiest. At midday we stopped to drink from the river, cupping water in our hands and splashing it into our mouths. Then we sat down on the grassy bank to rest.

"Last night was the first since—" he hesitated, "since Meldron— the first time I did not hurt."

It came to me then that my own wound no longer throbbed and burned. I touched a hand to my bandaged eyes and, though still tender, the pain had gone.

"It seems that Gofannon has blessed us as he promised," observed Llew.

"I do not think it was Gofannon," I said, more to myself than to Llew.

"What?"

"He appeared in the guise of Gofannon," I answered, "but I think it was not the Master of the Forge who feasted us last night."

"Who was it, then?"

"Another lord, greater still and more ancient. Perhaps the Swift Sure Hand himself."

"I wonder," replied Llew thoughtfully. "You did not see him when you sang. But I watched him. He changed, Tegid. He was fierce, almost wild-eyed before. But as he listened to the song he took on an entirely different aspect. I tell you, brother, he was changed."

"Truly?"

"If you had seen him, you would agree. When you finished, he could not speak. Nor could I. You have always sung well, Tegid. But last night..." Llew halted, grasping for words. "Last night you sang like the Phantarch himself."

I turned this over in my mind. It seemed to me that while I sang, I could see. With the song in my mouth, the words falling from my lips, I was no longer blind. For the span of the song, I saw the world bright before me—as if my darkness was illumined by the light of the song, as if the vision of the song became my sight.

We journeyed deeper into the wooded hills of Caledon. The land beneath my feet began to rise, inclining towards the mountain peaks in ever higher hills and ever deeper valleys. The river narrowed, becoming deeper, faster, and louder the sound of its passing. Llew led well: he was my eyes.

Nevertheless, as the path rose and the woods deepened to forest, our progress slowed to a tedious crawl. To divert ourselves from our labor, we talked about the land, and about the seasons, and about the movements of the sun across the bowl of the sky. We discussed the star host: the Nail of Heaven, Great Bran the Blessed, the Plow, the Boar and Bear, the Seven Maidens, Arianrhod of the Silver Wheel, and all the rest. We delved into lore both ancient and holy. We talked of things hidden and known, seen and unseen: the powers of air and fire, water and earth; principles and verities: truth, honor, loyalty, friendship and justice. And we contemplated great kings and chieftains, wise leaders and foolish. Yes, we talked long of kingship—the right ruling of people and nations, the secrets of discernment, the sacred order of sovereignty.

As before, Llew took it all in. His capacity was boundless. Llew had a bard's memory. He learned; he remembered. He grew, much as a tree grows when its roots touch the water hidden under the earth— straight and high and broad, casting its branches wide, claiming pre-eminence in the forest. As Ollathir would say, he became an oak of knowledge.

Much of what I told him was known only to the bards themselves. But what of that? There were no bards in Albion any more, and knowledge, like fire, is increased when it is shared.

Alas, though he increased in knowledge, I detected no kindling of the awen spark, no flash of the brilliance concealed within. Ollathir's awen remained a hidden gem, waiting to be revealed when and where it would.

We ate what little we could find, but hunger was our constant companion. We did not thirst, however, for we drank our fill from the cold river freshets. Our bodies grew lean from want and hard from the rigors of the trail. Keen privation drew us close and mingled our souls. Llew and I became brothers of the heart, kinsmen born of a bond stronger than blood.

One day, after many days, we woke to rain and wind out of the north. We stayed under the trees and waited for the rain to stop. The rain continued through the day, and when it finally stopped and the clouds parted, it was too late to travel on. But we walked a little way up the trail just to see what lay ahead.

"We are on a hill overlooking a deep glen," Llew told me. "The hill on the far side of the glen is high—higher than this one."

"What lies beyond it?"

"I cannot see—it forms a wall, steep and high. It will be difficult to climb. It may be that we would do better to go another way."

I nodded, trying to picture the lay of the land in my mind. "What is the forest like here?"

"It is pine, mostly, and close—dense in the glens, but somewhat thinner near the top." He paused to take in the landscape to the right and left. "I think the hill is part of a larger ridge. There appears to be a ridgeway running north to south along the top. If that is so, we might be able to follow it south."

I pondered this for a moment. Were there any old trackways in Caledon? It was possible, although I knew of none. Presently, the wind gusted, changing direction, blowing out of the south as the rainstorm passed. The wind brought with it the scent of pine, strong after a day of rain.

I breathed in that heady scent, and there appeared in my mind's eye the image of a lake: the lake of my vision. Suddenly, I saw the steep-sided glen in deep forest and the tall pines straining for a blue, cloud-swept sky which was reflected in a clear mountain lake.

"What is it, Tegid?" Llew asked; he was growing accustomed to my lapses. "What are you thinking?"

"Let us climb to the summit of the ridge."

Llew did not say no. "We have not much light left. It is high and will likely be dark before we reach the top."

"It is all the same to me."

Llew nudged me with his elbow. "A joke, Tegid? This is the first time you have made light of your blindness."

"Light of blindness? Do you think yourself a bard to speak

in such riddles?"

"The fault is yours, brother—filling my head with your talk." He considered the path before us and sighed. "Come on, then."

We accomplished the descent very quickly. The climb up the other side took much longer. Llew hurried as fast as he dared in the failing light. He might have gone more quickly without me, but not much. And though the bruises proliferating on my shins might seem to indicate otherwise, I was growing ever more adept at finding my way along with the aid of my staff. I could move with some haste.

As the hillside was steep, Llew's directions became more succinct; he spoke only when necessary to guide me. And I wondered if he knew how well, how naturally he led. Was it, in the end, so different leading men? Was it not much the same—picking out the trail, deciding the safest way, strengthening the unsure step with words of encouragement, guiding, going ahead, but not too far ahead—was not trailcraft much the same as kingcraft?

"It is just a little way now," Llew called out from directly above. "You are almost there."

"What do you see?" I asked him.

"I was right about the ridge," he replied. His hand found my arm and he pulled me up to stand beside him. "The view from here is stunning, Tegid. The sun is down now, and the sky is the color of heather. We stand on a high ridge. Before us is a wide, bowl-shaped glen, all but surrounded by the ridge wall. A stream passes through the wall somewhere below us and empties into a lake in the center of the bowl. There are tall trees around three sides of the lake and a broad grassy lea on the fourth side. The lake is like a mirror; I can see the clouds reflected in the water—and stars, there are stars beginning to shine. And it is just beautiful," he concluded. "I wish I could describe it better. I wish you could see it."

"I have seen it," I told him. "And it is beautiful."

"You know this place?"

"I have never been here," I explained. "But I feel certain this is the place I saw in my vision."

"Your vision in the boat—I remember." His voice shifted as he turned his gaze to the lake once more. "What else do you see here, Tegid?"

I delved into my memory of that storm-lashed night and brought forth the glimmering remnant of my vision. "I see a lake. . . I see a fortress, high-timbered and strong. . . And I see a matchless war host—many hundreds gathered around a throne raised upon a mound," I told him, recalling the images. "I see—"

"No, I mean describe it—in detail. Be precise."

I concentrated, holding the images in my mind. "I see," I began slowly, "a stand of tall pines lining the top of the ridge to our right. The slope is steep and densely wooded, rising from the near shore of the lake."

"Go on."

"The lake is longer than it is wide; it stretches almost the whole length of the valley floor. Forest surrounds it on three sides, as you have said, and a wide grassy meadow on the fourth."

"What about the meadow?"

"It forms a plain between the lake and the ridge; a plain perfectly enclosed because the ridge base rises sharply to form a protecting wall at the farthest end."

"What else?"

"The lake is bounded by a rough rock shingle; the rocks are black, the size of loaves. There are numerous game trails and runs down through the forest to the lake."

"That is remarkable," Llew conceded. "Unbelievable. It is just as you describe it." He clapped his hand to my shoulder. "Let us go down to the lake. We will make our camp there."

"But it is growing dark, you said. How will you see the path?"

"I cannot see the path," he replied lightly. "Even now it is too dark. But I do not need to see the path, for you will lead me."

"Do you mock me?"

"It is all the same to you, is it not?" demanded Llew. "Your inner sight will lead us to the appointed place. We will not stumble or go astray. Indeed, we will not put a foot wrong."

There came the croak of a raven. I listened, and heard an

answering call—and then others. Soon the ridgetop resounded with the ragged, raspy clamor. Ravens were gathering in the trees along the ridge for the night.

"Do you hear?" Llew said. "The guardians of this place are greeting us. Come, brother, we will be welcome here."

We stood atop Druim Vran, the Ridge of Ravens... This is the place I have seen, I thought, and I heard again the Banfáith's prophecy: *But happy shall be Caledon; the Flight of Ravens will flock to her many-shadowed glens, and ravensong shall be her song.*

Llew spoke the truth. I turned again in my mind to the vision I had been granted. And yes! I could see the path stretching out before my feet—as if in the full light of day.

"Very well," I said. "Let us prove this vision of mine. We will go down together."

I adjusted the harp on its strap and stepped forth boldly. My foot struck the path as I saw it in my mind. I took another step, and two more. To my surprise, the path of my inner sight shifted slightly as I moved. I saw the narrow trail sloping down before me—less a path than a dry watercourse choked with the tangled roots of trees and loose rock. Dangerous in any light, it would be treacherous for Llew in the dark.

I took a few more steps. "The trail drops away sharply here," I warned, describing what I saw in my mind's eye. "Put your hand to my shoulder. We will go slowly."

Llew did as I bade him, and together we began the long, laborious journey down to the lake. It took all my strength of concentration; despite the cool night, sweat ran freely from my brow and down my back. Each step was a trial of trust, each step a pledge to be renewed—and no easier for the success of the last.

Down we climbed, and down, following the twisting path. Contrary to Llew's brash affirmation, our feet were rarely placed right: we stumbled over stones and tripped on exposed roots; we slid on the loose scree, and branches scratched at us from thickets on either side. Ignoring these small irritations, we persevered.

"Tegid, you are a wonder," Llew gasped with relief when we

gained level ground once more. We continued on a little way to a place overlooking the lake. The trees grew tall; we found a place under sheltering branches and sank down on a bed drifted high with pine needles. "I am tired," he said with a yawn. In a few moments he was asleep where he had dropped.

I, too, was weary. But my mind was quick with excitement. Blind, I had traversed the treacherous way. Guided only by my inner vision, I had mastered the unseen path, and I could feel the newfound power leaping like a fresh-kindled flame within me. The vision granted me was genuine. Step by step, we had tested it and it had held true.

I was blind still, and yet I had found a new sight. And it seemed to me that the sight I now possessed was greater than the sight I had known before. Sight! No longer confined to the limitations of light or even distance. Sight! If I could see beyond the furthest vistas, might I also see beyond the present and into the future...into realms yet to be?

I did not sleep. How could I? I sat wound in my cloak, gazing inwardly at the lake as it was, and as it perhaps would be. I strummed the harp softly and sang, giving voice once more to the vision that burned within me. Goodly-Wise is the Many Gifted; let all men honor him and perform endless homage to the One who sustains all with his Swift Sure Hand.

13

The Crannog

We established our camp in a clearing among the pines on the slopes above the lake. The first day Llew caught two fish, in traps he had made of woven rushes and hidden in the reeds and tall watergrass.

That evening, while Llew cooked the day's catch over the fire, we talked about all that had happened to bring us to this place. We discussed the meaning of the vision, and how it might be fulfilled; and we determined all that we would do. And then, with the vision glowing in our hearts, we ate our meal of fish and talked some more.

Later, however, as I settled back with my harp and began to strum, Llew caught my wrist and held it.

"Tegid," he said urgently, "I want to do something."

"What do you want to do?" I asked.

"We cannot sit here like this," he continued, "or nothing will happen. We have to make something happen. I think we should make a start."

"What is it that you want to do? Tell me and we will do it."

"I do not know," he admitted. "But I will think of something."

He said nothing more about it, then. But the next morning he woke at dawn and left the camp. I woke later and found my way down to the lakeside, thinking to find Llew there as well. But he was not to be found.

I washed, standing in water to my waist, splashing cold water over myself. Upon emerging, I heard a dull, thudding sound. I heard it again as I pulled on my clothes. I turned in the direction of the sound. "Llew?" I called. Then louder, "Llew! Where are you?"

"Here!" came the reply. "Over here!"

I made for the sound of his voice, and found him standing on the broad lea above the lake. "What was that sound I heard?" I asked him.

"It was this," he told me, and placed a large, heavy object in my hands. It was round and smooth and cool to the touch.

"Why are you carrying stones?"

"I am marking out the dimensions of our caer," he replied, retrieving another stone. "These are the markers."

Apparently he had gathered stones from the lakeshore and heaped them in a pile. Now he was walking the circumference of his would-be fortress, using the stones to mark out the walls. We began the circuit of the walls, and he showed me where he had placed the stones.

"This is good," I told him. "But a bard should choose the place to build the stronghold if it is to stand. All the more if it is to be the residence of a king."

"I am no king," he growled. "You keep forgetting, Tegid. I am a maimed man. In this world, men do not follow cripples. That is the truth of it!"

"Yes," I agreed. "That is the way of it! Yet, Goodly-Wise is the Many Gifted—"

"No more! I do not want to hear it."

"Yet you will hear it!" I insisted. "The Swift Sure Hand has marked you; he has chosen to work in you this way. Now it is for you to choose: follow, or turn back. There is no other way. If you follow, more may be revealed."

"It makes no sense to choose me. None of this makes sense."

"I have already told you—it is a mystery."

"And still you persist?"

"I do persist," I answered.

"Why? What makes you so certain?"

"But I am not certain," I told him. "Nothing is certain. You want certainty?"

"Yes!"

"Then you want death."

"This is hard for me, Tegid!"

"It is hard, yes. It is difficult. Life is harsh and it is relentless. You will choose in the end—one way or the other. No one escapes the choice."

"Bah! It is no use talking to you," he cried, and his voice echoed across the water like the cry of a bird.

"The path is revealed in the treading," I said.

"You sound like...like a bard," he replied sourly.

"A bard who cannot help believing that we have been brought to this place for a purpose. And the One who brought us here will not see his purpose fail."

"It has failed already! I *believed* you, Tegid!"

Oh, the pain went deep in him. I realized that now, and I understood that the loss of his hand was the least of it. There was a potent bitterness in him, like a poisoned spring seeping into his soul. He had borne his suffering bravely, but it had been wearing at him all the same. It was behind his impatience of the previous night—and it was behind this impulsive exercise in moving rocks.

"I am telling you the truth when I say there is a mystery—"

"Stop it!" he roared, throwing down the stone he carried. "Speak to me no more of your mysteries, Tegid—and say no more of kingship. I will not hear it!"

He stood seething; I could feel the heat of his anger flow across the distance between us. "Oh, what is the use?" he grumbled; he snatched the stone from my hands and heaved it away. "We do not even have tools enough to cut a willow branch, let alone build anything. If we did, we would not stay here; we would go back to Sci where we belong. It is hopeless, and I am sick of it."

We stood silent for a long time. The sun was warm on our backs, the wind light in the pines. Away on Druim Vran, I heard the squawk of a raven. He is wrong, I thought. *This* is where we belong. "It is not hopeless;" I said, "impossible, perhaps, but not hopeless."

"Bards," Llew grunted. "We cannot stay here, Tegid. There is nothing for us here. If we cannot get to Sci, let us travel south to the Galanae. It may be that Cynan's people will receive us."

When I did not answer, he said, "Did you hear me?"

I stooped to the rock at my feet—I had felt the impact in the earth when he threw it. "I heard you," I told him. "You are right."

"We should travel south?"

"We should make a beginning. But not here."

"What is the difference?" he said sullenly.

I turned towards the lake. In turning, my inner vision awoke and I saw the stronghold; I saw where it should be. "On the lake, yes," I told him. "But not here. Out there."

"You are mad."

"Perhaps." I began walking towards the lake.

"In the water, you mean?"

"Yes."

"Out in the lake?"

"It is to be a *crannog,*" I explained.

"A crannog."

"It is a dwelling constructed on a false island made of timber and stone, and which is—"

"I know what it is," interrupted Llew impatiently. "But if we cannot erect a simple mud hut on the meadow, how are we to build a fortress in the lake?"

At his words, my inner vision shifted and I saw an image of the crannog as it would be. "Not a fortress only," I replied. "A city."

Indeed, the stronghold I saw was large as great Sycharth itself had been. It was an island of earth and timber in the center of the lake—and not a single island only, but a cluster of smaller islands linked together with bridges and causeways to form a great fortress, a caer built on water: round dwellings of wicker and daubed earth, stockades, granaries, storehouses, and, on an earthen mound in the center of the central isle, an enormous timber hall for the chieftain.

I saw smoke rising from cook houses, and from the hearthfire of the hall. I saw sheep and kine and pigs in pens on the crannog, and also on the broad lea where fields of grain had been planted. Many dozens of boats, large and small, plied the water all around the island caer, and children swam and played, and women fished in the shallows.

I saw it all; I saw more. And I related everything to Llew, just as it appeared to me.

"This I want to see," he remarked, and I sensed the bitterness abating, submerging once more. Llew took the rock he held cradled in the crook of his wounded arm, marched down to the lakeside and heaved it in. I heard the splash as it struck the water. "There!" he called back. "I have made a start. What shall we call this water city of yours?"

"But you have already named it," I said, walking down to join him. "Dinas Dwr—Water City—so let it be called."

Llew liked the name and threw another stone into the lake. "Dinas Dwr is begun," he said. "Truly, I hope the Many-Gifted Dagda sends us a boat, or we will be forever building it this way."

"It will take more than a boat. It will take a host of builders and craftsmen. This will be no mean city, brother. It will be a refuge for many, and a beacon in the north for all Albion."

We sat for a time on the stony lakeshore, discussing how the crannog would be constructed. I described the means and manner of building, its advantages in times of trouble, its limitations. Llew listened to all, taking it in, and when I finished he rose. "We cannot perform this mighty work on roots and bark, small fish and the occasional bird," he declared. "Arms that lift heavy stones and timber need meat to sustain them."

"What do you propose?"

"I propose finding some ash saplings and fashioning a few spears so that I can hunt," he replied. "The forest abounds with game—all we have to do is catch it."

"Yes, but—" I began.

He cut me off. "I know what you are thinking. But Scatha always insisted that a man who fought with one hand only was but half a warrior. On Ynys Sci we learned to use our weapons with either hand."

"I never doubted you."

"It may take some practice," he allowed, "but I will revive the skill, never fear."

"How will you cut and shape the ash sapling?" I wondered.

"Flint," he answered. "There is flint on the ridgetop and on the slopes. We can use that to make scrapers and axes and spearheads—as many as we like."

Thus we spent the next day gathering and chipping flint to make the blades we would require. It was easier to work by feel than I imagined, and I soon became proficient in producing stone blades as sharp, if not as durable, as iron. We had no leather to bind the crude blades to the wood, but I used threads from the edges of our cloaks. I braided the threads in threes and then braided the three: three threes, a satisfactory number, and very strong.

While I braided the rope, Llew searched for and selected a sturdy branch to make the haft of the axe. He found a short, thick length of forked oak, and I bound the finished axehead to the branch.

Llew tried the tool on a piece of firewood. "This will work," he announced, hefting the finished axe. "Now to find a good, straight sapling."

"You will find as many as you like along the eastern rim of the ridge," I told him.

"You have seen this?"

"No, but that is where the tree grows."

He was gone for the rest of the day, and returned just before nightfall with not one or two, but six fine, straight ash saplings. Four were green, but two were dry, having been uprooted on the slope. He had trimmed the branches and top, and was ready to begin shaping them with a flint scraper I had made for this purpose.

One of these he made into a staff for me. It was longer than any I had used before, and thinner. But it was easier for a blind bard to wield, I decided. "I am sorry it is not a rowan staff," Llew said. "But perhaps it will serve until a better one is found."

I ran my hands along the smooth, rounded wood. He had done fine work shaping and smoothing with his crude tools, and I commended him. "You have done well, Llew. It is an excellent staff. I want no other."

The next day, while Llew shaped the shaft, I finished work on the spearhead and made another braided thong to bind it. The day was spent by the time we had finished. "Tomorrow we will eat meat," Llew declared, chewing a bit of mallow root. After a moment, he added, "If only we had a little salt."

"We are too far from the sea for that, but savory herbs abound in these woods. I will gather some while you are away."

"Have the fire ready. I will return with our supper," he vowed.

He made good his promise, but it was not a boar or deer which he brought back to roast—only a squirrel. Llew was very disappointed and said he would have used his time better catching fish.

"The deer run too fast," he muttered, as we waited for the squirrel to finish cooking. "They are gone before I can get a decent throw. Without a horse, I will never be able to run them down. And wild pigs are dangerous when the hunter goes on foot." He pondered this for a while and then said, "If I want a deer or pig, I will have to climb a tree above a game run and wait."

"Better to find the trail they use to reach water," I suggested. "Any game on this side of the ridge probably come to the lake to drink. Find the place, and you could await them there."

The next morning Llew hastened down to the lakeside and searched along the shore to find the watering place. I took the staff Llew had made for me and, poking here and there, I foraged in the woods nearby and found a cache of nuts, which I wrapped in a pouch of leaves.

Llew returned at midday to say that he had found the watering place and a suitable game trail leading from the wood. "There is a low place along the western shore; the wood is thick and the lake is shallow. From the tracks I have seen, there are deer and pigs to be had. And not more than a hundred paces up from the watering place, there is a pine I can climb—it is old and big and the undergrowth is thin around it. The track passes beneath one of the larger limbs and I may be able to get a good throw from there. Wish me luck, Tegid."

"I wish you nothing else," I told him. "But are you going now?"

"I think it best. I want to be in place well before nightfall to give my scent a chance to disperse."

"Go then, and take this with you," I handed him the leaf-pouch of nuts. "Good hunting to you."

He took the pouch, and I waited through the remainder of the day. The moon would rise late—well after dark. I did not expect him to return until morning. Nevertheless, I tended the fire through the night so that he could find his way back to camp if he returned while it was still dark.

As night drew on, I took up the harp and began to play. The sweet singing of the harpstrings filled the sphere of night around me—like the glow of the campfire, could I have seen it. I sang softly, a melody of peace and repose, so as not to disturb the serenity of the wood and the night.

The liquid crystalline notes of the harp trickled lightly into the air, the fire creaked softly, and I became aware of another's presence with me. A subtle alteration in the air, a slight trembling of excitement on the skin—I was being watched.

I sensed the visitor just outside the circle of the camp, watching. An animal? No, not an animal.

I stopped singing but continued strumming the harp, listening beyond the harpsound to the faint nightnoise around me. I did not hear what I was listening for at first, but then...the hushed exhalation of a breath.

I stopped strumming, put down the harp, and stood slowly. "Who is here?" I said gently.

No answer—although I thought I detected the quivering of leaves, as if a branch held aside had been replaced.

"Come out," I said—this time with more force and authority. "You are welcome to share my fire."

Still no reply.

"You need have no fear. I will not harm you. Come, join me. We will talk together."

Again there was no answer. But I heard, crisp and distinct, the snap of a twig and the rustling of leaves as the stranger departed. I waited a moment... silence. I was alone once more.

I walked around the fire ring to the place where my shy visitor had been. I leaned on my staff and listened for a time, but there was nothing to be heard. Then, as I turned back to the fire, I felt something beneath my foot. I bent down and picked it up. The object was flat and brittle, with sharp spines or thorns attached to a woody stem.

I turned it over in my fingers for a moment before it came to me what it was: a sprig of holly.

14

Visitors

Llew returned at dawn with a kill—a roe deer which he dropped by the fire and instantly forgot in his excitement to tell me what he had seen.

"It was incredible!" he gasped. "You will never believe—Tegid!" He had run all the way from the lake, dragging the small buck, and was out of breath from the climb to the camp.

"I had to stay awake—" He gulped air. "Or fall...out of the tree...I got cold up there," he gasped and swallowed. "And so I had to...shift around to keep from getting stiff...and I...I was..."

"Calm yourself," I told him. "I can wait."

He drew a deep breath, and another. "I dropped my spear," he continued in a steadier voice. "It fell in the center of the trail. It was dark, but with the moon I could see it below me. I climbed down to get it—" he paused and drew another long breath. "I picked up the spear, and—Tegid, it seems strange to say, but I just knew something was there with me. I felt eyes on me—as if I was being watched. I thought it might be a stag. I climbed back into the tree as quickly and quietly as I could, and made ready to throw the spear if the deer came onto the trail."

Gulping again, he hurried on. "All this time I was cursing myself for not taking better care. I was certain I had lost the chance for a kill.

"But just as I was getting into position again, I heard a sound on the trail. I looked down, and standing directly under the branch where I was sitting—" Llew's voice trembled with excitement, "I saw it, Tegid! You will never believe! At first I did not know what it was. It was just this dark mass under the tree. But it had a face, and I could see its eyes! Tegid, the eyes glinted in the moonlight. It was looking right at me! It saw me! It was just—"

"Yes—what?" I broke in. "What was looking at you, brother?"

"It was—what is the word?—a tree being."

"A tree being?"

"I do not know the word. What do you call it?"

"I cannot tell you, until you tell me what you saw," I replied. "Describe it."

"It was like a man—very tall and thin and covered in leaves and thorns. It had hair, I think, but there were twigs and leaves of all kinds sticking to it from head to toe. Its eyes—Tegid, its eyes were huge, and it was looking right at me. I know it saw me. It knew that I was there. I nearly fell out of the tree when I saw it! This thing just stood there, looking up at me. This thing—this—"

"Cylenchar," I told him.

"Cylenchar?" Llew tried to puzzle out the meaning of the word. "Bashful bush ... timid tree?"

"Tree, or forest, yes," I replied. "Though not bashful—concealed, or hidden. It is a very old word; it means the hidden one of the forest."

"But what is it?"

I held out the holly sprig. Llew took it from my fingers. "He came here, too," I explained. "I think my harp summoned him."

"He—him?"

"The Hidden One, the cylenchar."

"The Green Man," Llew said, his voice low. "In my world we call it a Green Man, or Jack o'the Green. I saw one once—it was ..." He fell silent, remembering the incident.

"What is it, brother? What do you remember?"

"Simon and I saw one—we saw a Green Man, a cylenchar, on the road. Before coming here. We were travelling in Scotland—in

Caledon...beside a lake, like this one..." His voice dwindled away
again.

I placed more wood on the fire. "Sit," I told him. "Rest yourself."
He did as I bade him. "A Green Man," he whispered.

I extended my hand towards the buck he had brought. I ran my
fingers over the pelt and carcass; it was a young animal, small and
supple yet. The meat would be toothsome and tender. "You made a
good kill. We will eat well for a few days."

"But I did not kill it," Llew said. "The cylenchar brought it. Just
before dawn, I heard a sound in the bush, and I readied myself to
throw. I saw—" he paused, swallowed, "—saw a blur of green—
branches, leaves and twigs, bristling, moving—and then it was gone,
and I saw the roebuck lying in the clearing under the tree. It was
already dead. I climbed down. The buck was still warm; it was killed
only moments before. I waited for a while, but nothing happened. So I
picked up the deer and brought it here."

We sat for a time, listening to the crackling fire, wondering if the
cylenchar was even now watching us. He had seen us from the
beginning, I suspect, and watched us as we set about establishing
our camp, making the spears. He had watched us and had brought a
gift of food. It was his way of welcoming us.

"The hidden ones are very old," I said after a time. "When the
dew of creation was still fresh on the earth, they dwelt in the land. At
the coming of men to Albion, they retreated to the forests where they
wait and watch."

"What do they watch?"

"They watch everything. They know all that passes among the
leaves and shadows. They tend the trees and the animals that shelter
within the circle of the trees. They are guardians of the forest."

"You said we have been welcomed. Why would it do that?"

"I cannot say. But we will be watched and I think we will be
protected now."

"And fed."

"Yes, watched and fed. We will set aside a portion of the meat for
the cylenchar—to show our respect and thanks. If the meat is

accepted, we will know that our presence is honored here."

Llew hung the buck by the hind legs from the branch of a tree, cut its throat and left it to bleed; he gathered some willow branches and returned to begin skinning the deer. "You are tired," I told him. "Go to sleep. I will do the rest."

"Are you sure?"

"Yes. I will wake you for supper," I told him. It was only slightly more difficult than I thought it might be—owing more to lack of a proper iron blade than lack of eyesight. Using the flint blade and scraper, I carefully removed the pelt. I quartered the carcass and, as best I could, jointed the haunches. The portions I thought to save, I wrapped in the pelt; the offal I left for the birds and beasts. All this was carried out away from the camp, as I did not wish to foul the campsite with the leavings.

When I had finished, I returned with the meat to the fire, built the flames high and hot and affixed two haunch portions of meat onto the green willow spits Llew had prepared. I set the joints to cook slowly at the fire's edge and waited for Llew to awaken.

We ate at midday, gorging on the succulent venison. We ate until we could hold no more and then went down to the lake to drink and bathe. The water was cold, making the skin tingle as we swam and sported in the water. I missed having soap, and I did not like the wet cloth on my eyes. Llew saw me unwrapping the cloth and swam to me.

"It is time to see how it is healing," I said.

"I agree," he replied. "I will join you." He began unwinding the cloth from his wrist-stump.

"Well? Tell me what you see."

I felt his hand touch the side of my head. He turned my face to one side and then the other. "I will not lie to you, brother," he said solemnly. "It is not good. Yet it is not as bad as it might be. The color is better, I think." I felt his fingers gently probing. "Your eyes were cut deeply. Can you see anything?"

"No. And I think my sight will not come back."

"I am sorry, Tegid." His tone allowed no hope.

"How is your arm?"

"It is healing, too. The skin is still slightly inflamed, and it is very red. But the flesh is beginning to close over the stump. There is still some fluid seeping from the wound. The fluid is watery though, not yellow. I should wrap it again later, but it will not hurt to wash it now. The cold water feels good."

"If we had a cauldron, I would make a poultice for you, to draw some of the inflammation from the flesh..." Even as I spoke the words, my inner vision flickered to life and I saw in my mind's eye a man standing on the shore of the lake with a basin in his hands. He raised the basin over his head and, as the sun broke above the ridge, he threw the basin into the lake. I saw the splash, and the shimmer as the vessel sank.

"What is it, Tegid? What do you see?"

"There is a basin—a bowl of bronze—here," I turned to the lake spreading before me. "It was the gift of a lord to the memory of a newborn son who died."

"Here?"

"In the lake." I pointed to the place I saw in my mind. "Just there."

"Wait here," Llew said. "I will find it if I can."

He accepted my vision without question. At once he began diving in the lake, searching among the rounded stones of the lake-bed for the basin I described. He dived and dived again, but found nothing.

"Stay!" I called to him. "Listen to me; I will direct you."

I made my way up from the water to the shore. As before, the image in my mind shifted as I moved. To my right I saw a large rock, partly on the strand and partly in the water—when I had seen the man, he had been standing on this rock with the basin in his hands. I picked my way over the rounded stones to the rock and climbed up on it. I turned once more to the water. I stretched my hands forth. "Where are you, Llew?"

"Here," he answered. "I am just a little to your left."

I located him by the sound of his voice, and visualized him in place against the image in my mind—and he appeared in my mind's eye in that place. "Raise your hand, Llew."

He raised his hand above his head, and the image of my inner vision responded likewise: they were one and the same.

"The bowl is behind you and to the right," I told him.

"How far?"

I estimated the distance between him and the place where I had seen the splash. "Two paces to your right," I answered, "and seven or eight paces behind."

He turned away from me and my inner vision faded to black. There came a rippling sound as Llew waded to the place I had indicated—and then a splash as he dived. He dived once, and then again. He dived once more. I stood listening, waiting for him to surface. I did not hear anything for a few moments . . . and then . . .

A surging splash and a shout sounding at once. "I have it!" Llew cried. "It is here, Tegid! I have found the bowl."

He charged up out of the water. I held out my arms and felt the chill, wet weight as Llew delivered the basin into my hands. The bowl was broad and shallow; the bronze was thick, and the surface uneven where it had been hammered. Three deep lines had been incised around the rim.

"It is larger than I expected," Llew said; I could almost hear the grin on his face. "It was upside down. Under water it looked like a stone. But it was where you said it would be." He paused, turning away briefly. "I wonder," he added, "what else is out there in the lake?"

I made to answer, but before I could speak I heard the whinny of a horse. "Listen!"

The whinny sounded again, clear in the quiet of the glen.

"It came from across the lake," said Llew.

"Do you see anything?"

Llew said nothing. I could feel him tense beside me. I heard the breeze light on the water, the wind blowing down from the ridgetop towards us across the lake.

"I see him," Llew whispered. "A warrior. He carries a shield and spear. He has come down to the lake to water his horse. He has not seen us—yet."

"Is he alone?"

"I do not see anyone with him."

"Keep watching."

We waited.

"No—there is no one else. He is alone."

"What is he doing?"

"He is kneeling...he is drinking now..." Llew paused. "He is rising. He is looking this way..."

Llew gripped my arm with his good hand. "He has seen us!" he hissed sharply. "He is remounting his horse—"

"Is he coming this way?"

Llew hesitated. "No," he answered, relaxing his grip on my arm. "He is riding back the way he came. He is leaving—" and a moment later, "he is gone."

"Then come," I said, handing the bronze bowl to Llew and stepping down from the rock. "I think we must prepare for visitors."

"Do you think he will return?"

"Yes," I called over my shoulder as I hobbled over the stones. "I think we must assume that he will return, and next time he will not come alone."

We waited through the night, and the next day. And though Llew climbed to the ridgetop and watched the glen most of the day, no one came. I began to think I would be proven wrong, that the rider would not return.

"I walked all along the ridge," he told me when he returned to camp. "I did not see or hear anything." With a weary sigh he planted his spear and dropped onto the ground. "I am hungry, Tegid," he said from across the cold fire ring. "Let us have a fire and cook some more of the deer."

I hesitated. I had not allowed the fire the night before, for fear of drawing the notice of the intruders.

"What do you say?" Llew coaxed. "No one is coming. If anyone were in the woods I would have heard them today. There is no one about."

My caution appeared pointless and a little foolish. "Very well," I relented, "gather the wood. We will build a fire."

Llew piled the firewood high, and I kindled the flame. In no time, all that remained of the deer—the three portions we had not eaten—was turning on the spits at the fire's edge, and the air was tinged with the aroma of roasting venison. The fat sizzled as it bubbled and ran.

Llew, whose hunger could not wait, pulled hot strips of meat from the spit with his fingers and blew on them before tossing them into his mouth. "Mmm," he murmured happily, "this is more like it, Tegid. I have waited all day for this."

While the meat cooked, I brought the bronze basin to the fire. In Llew's absence, I had prepared the poultice. The forest abounded in herbs of many types and, despite my blindness, I had assembled all I needed in a short time. The hardest part was fetching water in the basin and returning to camp without spilling it on the way.

I mixed the herbs with the water and set the mixture aside to mingle its essence. Now that we had a fire, I brought the bowl to the fire's edge to heat it properly. While I waited for it to boil, I prepared a hazel twig to stir the mixture. Llew continued to worry bits of cooked meat from the spit and lick his fingers, and I stirred the basin, smelling the fragrance of crushed herbs.

"What is in that?" Llew asked idly. "If it is an—"

"Shh!" I hissed.

I strained my ears to the wood sounds around us. I heard the tree-creeper, and the thrush. I heard the tiny rustlings in the dry leaves under the bushes ... and I heard the light jingle of a horse's tack.

"They are still some way off," I told him. "Leave the fire. We will hide in the forest until we can determine what they want."

Llew stood, plucking his spear from the ground beside him. But before he could take a step towards me, a voice behind me said, "Hold, friend!"

I whirled to the sound.

"Do not be foolish," the voice said.

Another voice added, "Put up your spear, friend." He spoke to Llew in a voice tight with menace.

And a third said, "Is this a proper welcome for warriors of our rank?"

The first spoke again: "Stand easy."

I heard movement behind and on either side of me. They had left their horses some way away and had come upon us by foot. There was no escape. We were surrounded.

15

Deadly Alliances

"Who are you?" demanded Llew. "Why do you attack us?"

I heard the wary edge to his voice. He had not relaxed. I strained within myself to awaken my inner sight, but my mind's eye remained dark.

"Put down your spear," the first warrior told him bluntly.

"Not until I know why you have invaded our camp," Llew insisted.

"It is not our custom to answer questions at spearpoint," the intruder behind me said.

"And is it your custom to enter a peaceful camp by stealth and force?" Llew replied, his tone flat and low.

"Is this your forest," inquired one of the warriors smoothly, "that you have the right to demand answers of all who sojourn within?"

I heard a brushing step as one of the men shifted nearer. I spread my hands to show I had no weapon. "Peace," I said, "you have nothing to fear from us." I spoke boldly, but without intimidation. "Join us at our hearth."

There was silence. I could feel their eyes on me. "Who are you?" one of the strangers asked.

"I will tell you who I am when you have told me why you spurn our offer of peace and the companionship of our hearth." When no

157

one replied to this, I added, "Perhaps you think it beneath you to sit with us and share our food?"

The first warrior answered. "We mean no one any harm," he said sullenly. "Rhoedd saw men at the lake. We were sent by our battlechief to discover who has come here. Our lord is troubled by news of invaders."

"Who is your lord?" I asked.

"Cynfarch of Dun Cruach," the warrior answered.

"You are far north, man," Llew said. "Where is your battlechief?"

"He waits for us in the glen by the river," the warrior answered.

"Bring him," Llew said. "We will welcome him here."

The warrior made to protest. "Bring him here," I directed. "Tell him that Llew and Tegid await him."

"But we are no—"

"Go!" I commanded, my voice loud in the silence of the clearing. "Return with your battlechief, or do not return at all!"

Without another word, the three turned and disappeared the same way they had come. We listened to them hastening through the brush and, when they had gone, Llew exhaled with relief.

"They were that close to attacking us," he said.

"They were afraid."

"Do you think Cynan is with them?"

"That we will soon discover." I stooped to the basin at the fire. The vessel was hot and the herb brew simmered. "The poultice is ready. Let us see to your wound."

I pulled the basin away from the flames. "Unbind your wrist and bathe the wound in the water."

"It is boiling," Llew pointed out.

"It must be hot to do you good. The heat of the poultice will draw the poison from the wound."

Llew complied reluctantly, complaining all the while. When the brew grew too cold to be effective, I heated it again, placing the bowl at the fire. Llew complained about that, too. Indeed, he was still protesting when our visitors returned.

This time they rode directly into our camp—seven men on

horseback, with weapons drawn and shields ready. "Who are you to command warriors not your own?" a stern voice demanded from among the trees. "Stand on your feet, friends, and let me see you."

"Cynan!" Llew leaped from his place at the fire, overturning the bowl. I heard the hiss of steam as the poultice spilled into the embers.

"So! It is true!" called Cynan. I heard the creak of leather as he swung down from the saddle. "They said Tegid and Llew were camped on the other side of the ridge, but I did not believe it. I came to see for myself, and here you stand."

For a moment all was confusion. I heard the sound of horses snorting and shuffling, of men talking excitedly at once. I heard loud laughter and then Cynan was standing before us. "Welcome, brother!" cried Llew. "Our hearth is humble and our hall has no roof, but all we have is yours. It is good to see you, Cynan."

"And it is glad I am to—" Cynan must have reached out to grip Llew's arms, and discovered Llew's injury. "*Clanna na cù!*" he gasped. "What happened to you, man?"

Cynan turned to me. "Tegid, you—?" I could feel his anger flare like a firebrand. "Who has done this? You have but to speak his name and I will avenge you tenfold! A hundredfold!"

Llew answered. "Meldron," was all he said.

"I will kill him," Cynan vowed.

"Meldron owes a blood debt past reckoning," I said, "but not for our wounds. Truly, this is the least part of what he has done." I then told Cynan and the others about the massacre of the bards on the holy mound.

Cynan and his men listened in stunned silence. When I finished, it was as if they had melted into the night. I heard nothing but the fluttering crack of the fire and the soft, shifting hiss of the night air among the pine needles.

When he finally spoke again, Cynan's voice was a tight knot of anger and despair. "It is even worse than you know," he said. "Meldron has provoked war with the lords of Llogres. He has attacked the principal strongholds of the Cruin and the Dorathi. Many have been killed, and more have fled to the hills and forests."

"When did this happen?" I asked.

"We learned of it just before Beltain. Some came to us seeking refuge, and they warned us that Meldron has sent warriors into Caledon to search out the weaknesses in the land."

"Ah," Llew replied, "that is why you are ranging this far north."

"It is," Cynan confirmed unhappily. "We have been riding the glens and rivers to see if they mean to strike at us from the wilderness where we are not protected."

"Have you seen anyone?" I asked.

"No one—until Rhoedd saw you two days ago," Cynan answered.

"But why did it take you two days to return here?" Llew asked.

"We were camped a day's ride from here," Cynan explained. "I commanded my men to return at once if they found any sign of strangers in the land."

"If he had but spoken to us, we would have welcomed him," Llew told him. "Someone might have been hurt."

"As to that, I am sorry," Cynan replied ruefully. "But if you were spies for Meldron I knew that you would not hesitate to murder my men—even under a sign of welcome. We did not know it was you."

"Well, I am glad you are here. Sit with us," Llew said, "share our food. We have but a little meat and water, but you are welcome to it."

"We have provisions with us and, as we have come unbidden to your camp, you must allow us to contribute our portion," Cynan offered happily.

"I will not say no," Llew replied, and Cynan ordered two of his men to begin preparing a meal.

We sat down together then and, while the others fetched water and wood and went about expanding our camp, Cynan and Rhoedd sat with us and began telling us all that had passed in Albion since our meeting on Ynys Sci. I listened to Cynan's description of the tribes and clans that Meldron had overrun or defeated, and I could not help shaking my head in wonder.

"Cynan," I said, "how has Meldron accomplished this so quickly?

When we left Sycharth he had but a hundred men altogether. How is it that he defeats clans with larger and better-armed warbands?"

"That is easily told," Cynan said harshly. "He has made alliance with the Rhewtani."

The Rhewtani are a contentious clan who rule in northern Llogres. They had long troubled both Prydain and Caledon—until Meldryn Mawr put an end to their warring with a series of stinging defeats. Odd that now they should have joined with Meldron, helping their old enemy's son to further himself. I wondered what Meldron had promised them to secure their aid.

"The Rhewtani," I repeated. "Anyone else?"

"I have not heard of any others," Cynan answered, "but it is said that some of the conquered chiefs have come over to him rather than face defeat and death. Although," he added fiercely, "any chieftain who would do that is not worthy of the name."

We talked of all that had happened in Albion and waited for the food to be served. Our visitors supplied a more than ample share from their provisions, and our meal became a feast of friends. "I am not lying when I say that you are the last men I thought to find here," Cynan said, slapping his thigh.

"After Meldron attacked the sacred mound," Llew told him, "we were taken prisoner. We were cast adrift on the tide and left to die." He told about the storm at sea and related how we had walked inland and arrived at this place—failing, I noticed, to mention the nemeton or the cylenchar in his account.

Cynan and his men listened to the tale with interest. When Llew finished, he said, "Still, it is strange. We had decided to return home, when Rhoedd thought he saw someone hiding among the trees." Cynan addressed Rhoedd. "Tell them what you saw."

"I saw someone watching us across the river," Rhoedd began. "I told Lord Cynan and asked leave to follow. I raised the trail and pursued it until I reached the waterfall. But since I had seen no other sign, I decided to abandon the search. I was about to turn back when I saw someone on the rocks above the falls."

"Did you see who it was?" I asked.

"No, lord," Rhoedd replied. "But he wore a green cloak. I saw that."

"So you continued following?"

"I did that. Not easy to find a way around the falls—and I would still be searching if I had not seen a hind running into a cleft in the rocks. I followed and found a path; it led here, to this ridge. From the ridge I saw the lake and went down to water my horse. It was in my mind to return the way I had come. If I had not seen you across the water, we would have returned to Dun Cruach. The rest you know."

"If and if and if," I observed. "It seems to me you were fortunate beyond reason."

"This is what I am thinking, too," Rhoedd admitted. "I never did see the man who led me to the trail. I know I never would have found it for myself."

"No," I answered, "nor will you see the one who led you, unless he reveals himself. For it was the guardian of this place who brought you here."

"Who is this man, lord?" asked Rhoedd.

"It is no man," I answered. "It is one of the ancient ones." I told them of the cylenchar then, and how we had been watched and eventually accepted by the guardian of the hidden glen.

Cynan and his men were fascinated, and we talked of this—and all that had happened in Albion—far into the night. Dawn's greeters had already begun chirping when we turned yawning to our beds.

Upon rising the next day, Cynan said, "You are welcome to return with us. There is a place for you at Dun Cruach."

"I thank you, Cynan Machae," I replied, "but it is for us to remain here."

"Here? Why, there is nothing here." Cynan turned to Llew. "You are injured. You need food and rest. You will find both at Dun Cruach."

"Again, we thank you," Llew replied. "But it is as Tegid says: we mean to stay."

"What will you do if Meldron discovers you?" Cynan asked pointedly. "You are injured. You cannot even hold a sword. Return with us. We can protect you."

Llew did not take offense. He turned aside Cynan's blunt but well-meaning concern with a gentle reply. "It is not for you to protect me, brother. Rather it is for us to protect one another."

"How so?" demanded Cynan. Llew's refusal rankled somewhat, but roused his curiosity more.

"Listen," Llew said, speaking low so that all drew near him to hear. I could imagine Cynan and the others straining after his words. "Tegid has had a vision—a vision of this place. He has seen a great fortress rising out of the water of the lake. It is an island—"

"An island?" one of his listeners wondered.

"But there is no island," another pointed out.

"Quiet! Let him finish," said Cynan.

"That is true," Llew confessed, "there is no island—yet. It is to be an island made by men. It is an island made of many crannogs, a stronghold of many fortresses: Dinas Dwr is its name. And it will be a refuge and a haven for all of Albion."

"You have seen this?" The question was for me; I felt Cynan's hand on my arm.

"I have seen it, yes," I replied, resisting the urge to say more. Llew had begun; better to let him finish as he would. "It is as Llew has told you."

"Dinas Dwr," Cynan mused. "Dinas Dwr—yes, it is a good name."

"With a fortress in the north," Llew proceeded, "the south would be more secure. We would be like two swordbrothers fighting back to back, each covering the other's weakness, each protecting the other, shield to shoulder, shoulder to shield."

The warriors saw the wisdom of this. Llew had made it live for them in his simple image, and they voiced their approval of the plan. "Meldron will look to attack where we are weakest," Cynan conceded. "I am a wonderful fighter, truly—but even I cannot defend two places at once."

"We will defend the north," offered Llew. "What say you, brother?"

"Well," allowed Cynan, "it is a worthy plan."

"Support me in this, Cynan," Llew said with quiet fervor; there was no pleading in his voice. "Together we can make this vision live."

Cynan was silent for a moment. And then he was on his feet, shouting in his zeal. "It shall be!" he cried. "Earth and stars bear witness, I pledge you all a man can pledge to aid you in this mighty work!"

I stood and raised my hands in declamation, left hand above my head, palm outward, my right-hand shoulder high, gripping my staff. *"The Golden King in his kingdom will strike his foot against the Rock of Contention,"* I proclaimed, in the words of the Banfáith's prophecy. *"The Worm of fiery breath will claim the throne of Prydain; Llogres will be without a lord. But happy shall be Caledon!"*

The warriors acclaimed this solemnly, and backed their lord's pledge with oaths of their own. Then everyone began talking at once, their voices keen with excitement; and I heard in the sound of their elation a vision assuming solid shape, faith taking flesh.

I listened to their eager talk for a time, then rose and, taking my staff, withdrew to the surrounding forest. I wanted to be alone with my thoughts, to understand what Cynan had told us: the Cruin defeated, and the Dorathi; Llogres had already fallen to them. Meldron and the Rhewtani, that was a deadly alliance.

I pondered this but could not hold it in my mind. I heard the branches moving in the treetops and smelled rain on the wind. I could not see the sky, but I knew it was yet clear and the sun burned bright. It would rain before evening, yet for those gathered around our crude hearth the future held no clouds.

I listened to the voices of the men, ardent in friendship over their plans: the fellowship of honorable men is a most potent force. The alliance of Llew and Cynan, born of trust and respect, would be formidable. And anyone seeking to break it by treachery or violence would find it a deadly alliance, too.

Clearly, the Swift Sure Hand was moving mightily: powers long dormant in the land were stirring again; guides and kindly spirits were gathering around us, ancient forces befriending us in unexpected ways.

Happy shall be Caledon ... So be it!

16

A Flight of Ravens

"I will return as soon as may be," Cynan promised. "And I will bring men, tools, and provisions enough to establish a fortress like no other in Caledon!"

"I would settle for a change of clothing and a handful of thatch to keep the rain off my head," Llew told him. "All the same, I will see neither if you do not leave!"

Even as he spoke, the rain which had besieged us for two days stopped. The horses jerked their heads, making their tack jingle in their eagerness to be away once more.

"Very well, we are going. But I am leaving Rhoedd behind—and weapons enough for all of you."

"We can look after ourselves," Llew protested mildly. "We do not need a servant. If you meet Meldron on the trail, you will need Rhoedd's spear."

"Nevertheless, he is yours to command," Cynan insisted. "Do not be stubborn about this."

"Very well, I accept," Llew replied, and bade Cynan farewell. The others were already waiting on the trail; I heard them shout as Cynan took his place at their head, and then the drumming of the horses' hooves as they wheeled their mounts and disappeared among the trees.

"Well," said Llew, returning to where I stood leaning on my staff, "we have a horse and a warrior to command. Our warband is begun."

"Scoff if you will," I told him. "Great kings have begun with less."

"Since you say it, I will believe it," he replied, with a lightness of voice I had not heard in a very long time. "For myself, I am content with Rhoedd here. And between you and me, Tegid, he looks like one tough nut. I am certain he is contrary enough for ten men."

Rhoedd laughed at this. "Cynan warned you!" he said cheerfully. "Did he also tell you about my foul temper?"

Thus began the close companionship of the forest hearth which we were to enjoy through the season of warmth. Rhoedd became a boon and blessing to us: tirelessly resourceful, and shrewdly ingenious, he aided us in everything and increased the bare comforts of our camp.

Most days Llew and Rhoedd hunted or fished in the early mornings, and spent the rest of the day gathering the roots and other edible plants that were our food. We bathed in the lake in the early evening, and ate our meals by the fireside at night. Then I would take my harp and sing, sending silvery song aloft on the fragrant smoke of our oak-fired hearth. In this way, then, we filled the days waiting for Cynan's promised return.

One day Rhoedd appeared breathless at the lakeside where I was drawing fresh drinking water. He and Llew had left to hunt but a short while earlier. I answered his call, and turned to await him as he came running to me.

"What has happened? Is Llew hurt?"

"Lord Llew is unharmed," Rhoedd answered. "He sent me to bring you. We have seen men on the river trail below the ridge."

"How many?"

"Six—maybe more. They were too far away to be certain. They will arrive before midday. Llew is watching the track."

I retrieved my staff and Rhoedd led me up the slope to the ridgetop—pausing at our camp to gather the extra spears and shields Cynan had left us. We hastened along the ridgeway west for a time, and then down a long, steep path where we joined Llew, crouched behind a cluster of rocks part way down the slope.

"They are almost upon us," Llew said. "I think Rhoedd and I can take them, but we will need you to help us, Tegid. We must make certain they do not leave this glen."

"Meldron's spies? Is that what you are thinking?"

"Who else? Cynan warned us they were searching out the land."

We discussed ambush tactics, and made a plan by which we might subdue the invaders. "There is a place east of here, where the glen narrows," said Llew. "The rocks come right down to the river's edge. Their horses would be no use to them."

"And further east?" inquired Rhoedd.

"Further east, the valley opens to a wide plain."

"Then our best chance will be at the narrows," Rhoedd agreed.

We hastened back up to the ridgetop and east along the trackway until we found the place. We took up a position overlooking the river trail below, and then sat back to wait. The day passed midday and we did not see or hear any sign of our approaching visitors. Llew grew impatient.

"What is taking them so long? What are they doing?"

"Perhaps they have turned off the trail," I suggested. "Perhaps they are watering their horses."

Llew sent Rhoedd down for a closer look, charging him to take care that no one should see him. Waiting for Rhoedd to return was no less maddening than waiting for the invaders. Llew marked the time by tapping the butt of a spear on a rock—the sound, I thought, of bone rapping against bone.

Then the tapping stopped. "What can be keeping him?" he blurted at last.

"Listen!"

A moment later, we heard Rhoedd on the trail; he crouched before us, breathing hard. "I have been down to the valley," he told us when he could speak. "I found them. They are making camp."

"Did anyone see you?"

"No."

"Do you know them?"

"They are not of any tribe or clan known to me. I do not think they are from the north at all." He paused, softening his disdain for our benefit. "They looked like southern men to me."

"Meldron..." Llew muttered. "How many did you see?"

Rhoedd answered, "There are six."

"If they are Llwyddi," I said, "we may know them. I might speak to them."

"Why?" wondered Llew. "After what they did to the learned brotherhood—what could you possibly have to say to them?"

I turned to Rhoedd. "Take us to the place where you saw them."

Though the track was rough and arduous, we managed some speed with stealth. We crept as close as we dared. "Tell me what you see," I said, touching Rhoedd's shoulder.

"Six men—with horses," Rhoedd said. "It is as I have already told you."

"Describe it!" I urged. "Details!"

Rhoedd must have looked to Llew for explanation, because Llew said, "Do as he says; tell him what you see."

"Well, there are six men," replied Rhoedd slowly. "They have six horses with them—three red roans, a yellow, a grey, and a black. They are good horses. The men are—well, they are men—"

"Are they dark or fair? What are they wearing?"

"They are dark, mostly; dark and unshaven—hair and beards plaited. They are wearing long cloaks, though it is warm. They do not carry weapons, but I see bundled spears and wrapped swords on the horses. At least three men have shields."

"That is better," I prompted. "Go on—what else?"

"They are wearing arm rings and bracelets—gold and silver. One man has a gold arm ring, and a gold brooch on his cloak. He has the look of a champion; he alone wears a torc, but it is silver, not gold. They all wear the blue on their sword arms—the image of a bird, maybe a hawk or eagle—I cannot tell from here. I think they have travelled far. They appear weary and ill at ease, and their faces are gaunt."

"Splendid!" I told him. "You have something of the bard in you, Rhoedd."

"It will be difficult to take them all at once," Llew said. "We have five spears between us, so Rhoedd and I ought to be able to stop three before they reach their weapons."

"And the other three?" I asked.

"We will have to fight them outmanned," Llew conceded. "Still, if we strike quickly we may overcome them."

"If we waited until nightfall," Rhoedd said, "we might stand a better chance. We could attack them while they slept."

"But they will have their weapons ready to hand then," Llew pointed out. "No warrior sleeps unarmed in strange country. Besides, they will probably post a watch for the night. I say we go now."

He and Rhoedd fell to discussing how best to make the first moves of their attack. As I listened to their talk, I felt increasingly troubled; not from fear—more a feeling of wrongdoing.

"Tegid, take this," said Llew, pressing a knife into my hand. "If any should try to escape—"

I dropped the knife as if it had burned my palm. "We cannot do this," I told him. "It is not right."

"I do not think any will come this way," Rhoedd reassured me. "It is just for your own defense."

"That is not what he means," Llew said. "What is it, Tegid?"

"We must not attack unarmed men. It is a thing Meldron would do, and it is vile."

"Well, what would you do, Tegid Tathal?" Llew said, and I could sense his exasperation.

"Welcome them."

"Welcome them," mused Llew dryly. "Well, Tegid, that is certainly something Meldron would never do."

"Lord Bard," Rhoedd began, "if we welcome them and they are spies, we will be dead before the sun sets."

"But, Rhoedd my friend, if we attack them and they are men of peace, we will be murderers."

"What do you suggest?" Llew asked.

"Let us receive them as strangers to our hearth." So saying, I gripped my staff and stood.

Llew rose quickly and laid his hand on my arm. "I will go first," he said, and stepped slightly ahead of me so that I could follow him without stumbling, or fumbling awkwardly and thereby demeaning myself before the strangers.

Together we three moved out from the cover of the trees and strode boldly to the stranger's camp. "Greetings, friends!" Llew called. "Peace to you, and to your lord, whoever he may be."

Our sudden appearance surprised them. I heard the clatter of dashed utensils and the shuffle of feet as the strangers scrambled for weapons and whirled to confront us—then silence for the space of three heartbeats while they determined how to receive us.

"Greetings," replied one of the strangers slowly. "You have come upon us by stealth."

"That is true," Llew replied. "Forgive us if we have caused you distress. Yet, if your intentions are peaceful, it will be well with you here. If strife is your aim, you will find warmer welcome elsewhere. If nothing prevents you, I would know the name of your lord and what brings you to this place."

"We accept your welcome gladly," replied the stranger. "We bear you no ill will, friend, and hope to pass through these lands without giving offense to any who live here. Indeed, we would esteem it an honor if you would tell us who is the lord of this place, so that we may greet him as best befits his rank."

Llew made to answer, but I spoke up, saying, "You speak with some skill, friend. How is it, then, that you have neglected to answer the question put to you? Or perhaps you have a reason for concealing the name of your lord."

"I did not answer," the stranger replied ruefully, "because that name above all others has become bitter to me. I conceal it for the purpose of forgetting it. I am telling you the truth, when I say I wish I had never heard it."

It came to me then who these men were, and why they had come. "Put aside your hurt and woe," I said. "Though you may not know it, the Swift Sure Hand has brought you here. If you would honor the lord of this place, it is he who has greeted you and even now stands before you, extending his hand in peace."

"This place is unknown to me and we did not expect anyone to receive us, much less to welcome us. If my speech or conduct has offended you, I beg your pardon, lord. Such was never my intent."

"I see that you are a man to speak your mind," Llew replied easily. "Yet I perceive no insult in either word or manner. And I tell you again, you are welcome here. We are camped beyond the ridge; it is a rough hearth, but its freedom is yours. Come, take your rest."

The strangers agreed, and we started up the track. Llew bade Rhoedd lead the way, and the six strangers followed, leading their horses. Llew and I came last.

"Why did you tell them I was the lord of this place?" Llew demanded as soon as the others were far enough ahead not to overhear.

"Because you are."

"What will they do when they learn I am lord of nothing more than a wide place beneath the trees?"

"Do you not know who they are?"

"No." He paused to consider what he had seen and heard. "Do you know?"

"Yes."

"How?"

"Their coming has been foretold."

"Well, are you going to tell me? Or will I grow old wondering?"

"They are the Ravens."

"The ravens? What ravens?"

"Happy shall be Caledon," I said, repeating the words of the Banfáith's prophecy, *"the Flight of Ravens will flock to her many-shadowed glens, and ravensong shall be her song."*

"Six warriors," Llew observed sourly. "Not much of a flock, is it?"

"It will grow," I told him. "You will see."

"I will tell you what I see," Llew replied, accusation sharpening his tone. He stopped walking and turned me to face him. "You are determined to bring about this prophecy one way or another. You know that it cannot be, and yet you stubbornly persist in making me the center of it."

"No more stubbornly than you persist in denying it," I remarked. "The prophecy was given to you. The Chief Bard's awen was given to you."

"Yes!" The word was a vehement hiss. "And this was given to me, too!"

I did not need eyes to see that he was shaking his stump at me.

"I did not come here to be king of anything. I came to take Simon back," he snapped, "and as soon as I can think of a way to do it, that is what I am going to do. And that is *all* I am going to do."

He turned away abruptly, and started climbing the slope. From somewhere high above, I heard the ragged squawk of a raven. At once my inner vision awoke. Into my mind came the image of a raven perched upon the back of a throne made of stag antlers—the image from my vision. And with this first raven, I saw others—many others, a flock, circling the throne, circling, soaring. Even as I watched, more ravens gathered in the way that ravens will—the first drawing more to their numbers, and yet more, until an immense cloud filled the sky, their black wings flashing in the sunlight, their black eyes deadly and bright.

"Llew!" I called after him. "Let us settle this now and be done with it."

I heard his footsteps halt, and then begin again as he retraced his steps to me. "How?"

"Are you willing?"

"I am willing," he declared. "What do you suggest?"

"The warriors who have come to us," I began; "we will let them be the test."

"How so?"

"I tell you they are the Flight of Ravens whose coming has been foretold to us."

"The prophecy again—"

"Yes, the prophecy again. The prophecy is the path. Gofannon, the cylenchar, and now the Ravens—these are the lights along the way. By them we know the path is true."

He did not reply, so I pressed him. "If the prophecy can be proved true, will you put aside your doubt and follow the path set before you?"

Llew took his time considering. "It is a hard thing," he said at last.

"Harder than a one-handed man becoming king?"

"No harder than that, I suppose."

"Then why do you worry?"

"Very well," he agreed, reluctance dragging down his voice like a weight. "Let us put this prophecy to the test for once and all. Tell me now who you believe these men are."

I replied without hesitation, trusting to the insight that had come to me. "They are Rhewtani."

"Perfect." Llew spat the word. "Just what we need."

"But they are not spies or traitors. They are honorable men. Indeed, they have placed honor above their lives. For, when their false lord made disgraceful alliance with Meldron, they chose to live as outcasts rather than serve a traitor."

"They have abandoned their lord. That does not sound very trustworthy to me."

"Do not say they have abandoned their lord," I replied. "Say rather that they are seeking a lord worthy of their loyalty."

"Rhewtani," Llew mused. "Most interesting. But that is not enough. What else?"

"You will find that the one who addressed you is the battlechief, and those with him are the best of the Rhewtani warband. If you tell them who you are, and what you mean to do in this place, they will pledge themselves to you."

"Better..." Llew replied, and I could sense him warming to the challenge. "Something more—but it has to be something difficult."

"Would anything less satisfy you?" I said and paused to think, holding the image of the ravens in my mind. "By this," I said at last, "you will know the path is true: they are the Ravens."

"You told me that already."

"Yes, but they have not heard it. And it is their true name," I explained. "When you ask of them they will tell you: 'We are the Ravens.' Now then, do you agree?"

Llew drew a deep breath, and I knew he was squaring himself to the test. "I agree. Let it be as you say."

17

Glorious Schemes

The strangers were making a picket for their horses among the trees when we joined them at the camp. Llew waited until they had finished and invited them to sit with us. The six ranged themselves on the ground around the fire ring.

"I see you are men used to better lodgings," Llew said. "Yet it may be that a sky-roof shared with honorable men is more to your liking than a king's hall and the company of traitors."

"That is the pith of it," replied the foremost warrior. "We would live as outcasts rather than sit at meat with false lords and wicked schemers."

"We are not unlike, then," Llew assured him swiftly. "We, too, have abandoned hearth and kin rather than suffer injustice or further the shameful aims of evildoers."

The warriors shifted uneasily. Their leader hesitated, and then asked, "Do you know us, lord?"

"I do know you," Llew replied with conviction. "I believe you are Rhewtani warriors."

"That is true," replied the warrior chief. "We are the Ravens of Rhewtani."

"Clanna na cù!" Llew murmured.

I heard a slap, and knew the man had smacked his arm with his open hand. "This was once a mark of honor—"

They all wear the blue on their sword arms, Rhoedd had said, the image of a bird ...

"—but it has become hateful to us. It is a mark of disgrace." The warrior slapped the tattoo again, his voice grew sharp with bitterness. "We would cut it out if we could."

"No," Llew told him, "let it remain a mark of honor. For you have given up rank and esteem rather than serve a faithless king. Meldron may have stolen the respect of your king, but you did not allow him to steal your honor as well. For that, you are welcome here."

At Meldron's name, the strangers murmured in amazement.

"Who are you, lord, that you know these things?" asked their chief, mystified.

"I am called Llew. And the man with me is Tegid ap Tathal, Chief Bard of Prydain."

The warriors exclaimed at this revelation. Their leader said, "But we have heard of you!"

"We heard you were dead!" added another.

"Not so dead as some would wish," Llew replied.

"It is also said you were the king of Prydain," the warrior asserted, making of his words a challenge.

"I was—" Llew admitted. "But no more. Meldron has made certain that I can no longer press that claim."

"What do you here, lord?" another asked.

"We came seeking refuge and will stay to build a fortress," replied Llew, and quickly explained about making alliance with the Galanae in the south.

"Then you will require men to help you," the Rhewtani champion stated firmly. "We will stay, if you will have us."

The man's words amounted to a pledge. And as he spoke my inner vision quickened. There was a rustling of clothing as the warriors rose one by one to address us. "I am Drustwn," said a low, solemn voice. I saw a thick-necked man of somber mien, self-possessed and confident.

"I am Emyr Lydaw," said another, and in my mind's eye I saw a fair-haired man with a huge copper carynx slung over his shoulder on a wide brown leather strap.

"I am Niall," said the third in a light voice. I saw a dark warrior with quick, clever eyes and a mouth ready to laugh.

"I am Garanaw," the fourth man said in a voice to strike sparks from steel: a man of restless vitality, wide-shouldered and strong, with red-brown hair and beard.

"I am Alun Tringad," said the fifth; his voice was lively and full-spirited. Into my mind came the image of a lean, long-limbed man with a high, noble brow and blue eyes, as eager for a fight as for amusement.

"And I am Bran Bresal," the leader said, pride in his men making his tone expansive. He came before my inner eye as a big man with long dark hair and beard neatly braided, black hair thick on his arms and the backs of his hands. He gazed at Llew with steady black eyes. "We beg the freedom of your hearth, lord," he said, spreading his arms to include his men.

I stepped forward and replied, raising my hand over my head, "Your coming has been foretold, and your welcome three times granted. May it be well to you with us, and may it be well to us with you. May you find among us all you seek." I lowered my hand. "I would summon the welcome cup, but there is no cup, and no ale with which to fill it."

"Your welcome is refreshment enough to us," Bran Bresal said. "You will not find us burdensome guests. We mean to do our share—"

"More than our share!" one of the men put in—Drustwn, I think.

"Yes, more than our share," Bran continued. "Where there is work, that is where you will find us."

"We do thank you," replied Llew. "But work can wait; rest now and take your ease. You will be tired from your journey."

Bran answered, "Tired, yes, and dusty, too. A bath would be a blessing, lord."

"Then that you shall have," Llew said. "Rhoedd has soap, and he will show you where we bathe."

The six warriors walked down to the lake with Rhoedd, leaving Llew and me to ourselves for a time. "Well?" I said when they had gone. "Do you accept the truth of the prophecy now?"

"Is there nothing you do not know?" he asked.

"Answer me," I insisted." Will you trust the path before you?"

"That I will do, brother," Llew replied, and added. "But I want something from you in return."

"Name the thing you desire, and I will give it if I can."

"There is to be no more talk of kingship."

"Llew, that is—"

"I mean it, Tegid. No more—understand?"

I thought best to let the matter rest there for the time being and did not press it further. He had taken the first step on the path; that was enough for now.

"Very well," I agreed. "I will speak no more of kingship."

"The Ravens," Llew muttered softly. "Who would have guessed it?"

"Listen!" I said.

We paused, and the sound that had caught my ear—at first broken and uncertain—resolved itself into song: the warriors had begun to sing as they made their way down to the lake.

"Happy shall be Caledon," I said. "The Flight of Ravens will flock to her many-shadowed glens—"

"And ravensong shall be her song." Llew finished the phrase. Indeed, as they reached the lakeshore their voices echoed strong and fine in the still evening air, filling the glen with a bold new sound. "They sing well, these Ravens."

Llew and I joined the men at the lake; after they finished bathing, Llew showed them where we would build the fortress. They were captivated by the idea of the crannog and pledged themselves to its construction. I believe they would have begun building it right then and there if I had not pointed out that we had no tools with which to begin.

Happily, that lack did not hinder us for long. The first of Cynan's supplies arrived three days later, led by Cynan himself and accompanied by a party numbering more than twenty. He brought eight ox-drawn wagons of tools, provisions and supplies; he also brought seven horses—five mares and two stallions to begin a herd—and four hunting dogs with which to breed a pack. Of the working party, eleven were builders, some of whom had brought their wives and children.

"They are to stay with you here until the fortress is built," Cynan explained when we had finished our greetings. "I told my father of your plans. He called it a glorious scheme—'That is a fine and glorious scheme!' says Cynfarch; and he has vowed to do all to sustain you until you are able to provide for yourself. He is eager to secure your goodwill and wishes to establish a strong ally in the north." He paused as Bran approached. "And it looks to me as if that day will be soon upon us."

"This is Bran Bresal," Llew said, "leader of the Ravens. They are staying to help us build Dinas Dwr."

I noticed that Llew neglected to mention the fact that Bran and his men were Rhewtani. "Let Cynan get to know them first," he explained later. "Why borrow trouble?" In this, I considered, Llew showed a subtle discretion.

Cynan and Bran exchanged greetings, whereupon Cynan called for the bowl, saying, "Let us drink to new friends and glorious schemes!"

"Cynan, you are a wonder," laughed Llew. "I would gladly summon the welcome bowl for you, but we have no ale, as you know."

"Do you not?" mused Cynan. "How is it that I see a vat foaming at your hearth?"

The silver-torced prince had brought his own ale vat and had instructed his men to install it at the hearth. Even as Cynan spoke, I heard the plunge of the cup as the bowl was filled. "To us!" cried Cynan, *"Báncaraid gu bráth!"*

"Sláinte mór!" we called in answer, as the frothy bowl was passed from hand to hand.

That night we ate well and, as the fire leaped high, I sang the

Battle of the Trees: a song of assembly and common cause, a song to stir men to action. The next morning, work began.

The builders assembled their tools and supplies on the meadow above the place I had chosen in the lake. Llew, Cynan and I discussed our plan with the head of the workmen—a man named Derfal, who was King Cynfarch's master-builder. While we talked, his men cleared the ground for some huts. The warriors, meanwhile, were put to work felling trees for timber—for the huts and also for boats. We would require six or eight sturdy, wide-hulled craft to carry stones and timber to the building site in the water.

The first days saw little more by way of activity than oxen hauling logs from the forest to the meadow. Then the builders' huts were quickly raised, and the boats began to take shape. As the finished boats took to the water, and the construction work began in earnest, our once-serene forest camp became a hub of noisy bustle and cheerful turmoil.

From morning to night the forest rang with axe-blows and the lowing of oxen. The camp bubbled to women's voices as they set about baking bread and roasting meat to feed the ever-famished workers. The lakeshore echoed to the laughter of children and the barking of dogs. The air shimmered with eager sound; a rainbow of joy spread over the glen. I walked here and there, listening to all, and it seemed to me gladness itself. Happy Caledon, I thought.

Long timber pillars were prepared, five carefully chosen oak boles, tapered and shaped, and then five more. With great heed and greater labor, these were floated to the site in the center of the lake and driven into the mud of the lake bottom so that their tops protruded above the surface. Then the builders and their helpers plied their boats ceaselessly, ferrying endless loads of stone from the lakeshore to the site. The stones were tumbled around each of the oak pilings, securing them in a thick bed of stone.

The five pilings were joined together with the five remaining logs, which were lashed to the portion of the pillar extending above the water, forming a five-sided ring in the water. Lastly, a solid webwork of oak branches was woven between the five sides of the ring. This became a platform which was covered first with stone and then earth. Upon this earth-covered platform the first round timber dwellings would be erected.

To this crannog would be added another, and then another, and more—until there were a score of small crannogs, all joined together by bridges and walkways, and circled about by stout timber walls. No sooner was the first crannog finished than the second was begun.

All this took place beneath Llew's watchful gaze. He could always be found with the builders, laboring alongside them by day, and head to head with Derfal at night, discussing the next day's work. Cynan, too, enjoyed himself enormously. Indeed, he looked upon the creation of Dinas Dwr as if it were his own undertaking. I think it was the first time he had had real work to do, work of substance and importance. Certainly, his father was an able ruler, and not the kind of man to place overmuch confidence in those around him; Cynan could not have many tasks of consequence to occupy himself in his father's house. Thus, Llew's venture became as much his own, and he gave himself to it as only Cynan could.

Maffar passed in a haze of sweat and strain. Rhylla, the Season of Seedfall, arrived as a welcome relief with its cooler days and nights. We aimed to work as long as the weather held good, and there were yet many fine days before Sollen's ice and wind would put an end to our activities.

Cynan, who had stayed as long as he could, announced his return to the south. "Harvest will begin soon and I will be needed to collect the king's tribute," he explained. "But I will return before the snow with provisions enough to see you through Sollen."

"You are a friend and brother," Llew told him, as Cynan and his companions mounted to their saddled horses; Cynan was taking four warriors with him, but the rest would stay. "Wait until the weather clears to return. I am certain we can survive until Gyd on what you brought the first time."

Cynan dismissed the offer without comment. "And I will bring word of the world beyond this glen of yours," he said.

"Go then," Llew replied, "and fare well. Return when you may."

When Cynan had gone, we walked down to the lake. I heard the dull chunk of the incessant axes as the builders chipped and shaped the timbers. I heard the slow earth-tread of the oxen as they dragged the logs to the wood yard. I heard the splashing of the children as they played at the water's edge.

We sat on the stones among pine-scented woodshavings, and considered all that had been accomplished: two crannogs finished—the first with two large dwellings and a storehouse—and a third begun; a cattle pen on the meadow for the oxen and horses; two builders' huts for tools and supplies, and four ample dwellings on the lakeshore. It was a good beginning.

"We have done well," Llew said. "It is looking like something now. I wish you could see it, Tegid."

"But I have seen it," I told him. "I have seen it all."

"As it will be, perhaps. But—"

"Yes, as it will be—and as it is." I touched my fingertips to my forehead. "In the time we have been here my gift has been growing."

"Truly?"

"It comes as it will—like the awen—I cannot command it. Sometimes it comes of its own, but a word will often call it forth. Or a sound. I never know when it will awaken. Yet each time I seem to see more."

Rhylla's crisp nights brought the mists from the lake and sharp, golden days set aflame by the sun's dying light. But the shining days dwindled and passed to grey, like fire to ash—like the Samhain fire that marks the year's turning: so bright and fierce as it flares from the hilltop, holding the trouble-fraught night at bay with brave light. But the fire dwindles to grey ash in the end—grey days of rain, endless until the creeping darkness gathers them and bears them away.

After Samhain, I often scented winter in the air. The coats of the horses and oxen grew soft, thick and long. The warriors hunted, fished, and chopped wood for the season of snows. The women preserved the meat—smoking some and salting the rest; they baked the hard black bread that would keep us through the winter. The children covered their sunbrowned limbs with warm woollen cloaks and leggings. The builders rubbed grease on their tools at night and wrapped them away in the lakeshore huts to keep them from rusting.

We moved from our camp among the trees to the dwellings on the lakeshore. There were fewer than thirty of us, so the four big dwellings on the lakeshore housed us in comfort... until the first of the refuge-seekers arrived.

18

The Challenge

Cynan returned the first moon after Samhain, bringing with him
seven warriors and five wagons loaded with supplies—food grain
and seed: oats, barley, and rye—and some luxuries: honey, salt and
herbs, woven cloth, and tanned leather. He also brought new spears,
and swords and shields enough for all the warriors. And, as if to make
certain we would not become complacent in our surfeit of riches, he
also brought with him thirty weary Eothaeli—starving, footsore
survivors of a tribe who had resisted Meldron's demands for
hostages and tribute and saw their king, warband, and kinsmen
slaughtered, their caer burned down around them, and all their cattle
driven off.

"I did not know what else to do with them," a mildly confounded
Cynan explained. "They were wandering lost on the moors. Cold and
hungry . . . bairns and all—with nowhere to go."

"You did right," Llew said.

"No weapons, no provisions—they would have frozen soon
enough," Cynan continued. "If I had reckoned on them, I would have
brought more grain. As it is, I cannot—"

"Never fret, brother," Llew assured him quickly. "It is for them,
and those like them, that we build Dinas Dwr. Bring them in, I say."

The Eothaeli stood apart, uncertain of their reception. Llew,

Cynan and I spoke to them—eight men, fifteen women, and the rest children, several babes in arms. Llew told them they had nothing to fear: they would be given food and clothing, they would be cared for, and, if they chose to, they could stay. Still they were reluctant to believe their good fortune.

A baby cried out—a small, squalling keen—and was quickly hushed by its mother. The sound kindled my inner eye and I saw a bedraggled clump of exhausted clansmen, wary and uneasy, fear peering out of their dull eyes. Foremost among them stood a gaunt, flint-faced man with his arm wrapped in a filthy blood-soaked rag, who appeared to be the leader of the group—all that was left of three family tribes. "It is not right that we should be treated shamefully. We are not outcasts," the gaunt man answered, his voice swelling with indignation. "We were attacked without provocation; our stronghold was destroyed, our people murdered, and our cattle driven off. We escaped death—but even death is better to us than disgrace."

"You are welcome here," Llew told him. "Where is the disgrace in that? Unless you believe our hospitality beneath your dignity."

"We are Eothaeli," the man informed Llew icily. "We are not an unimportant people, to be treated no better than cattle."

Llew leaned close and touched me lightly on the arm. "You tell him, Tegid. I am beginning to repeat myself."

The Eothaeli are a self-reliant tribe. They live—or once did—in the south of Llogres, clinging stubbornly to their rocky coasts with the tenacity of limpets. While they are known to be fiercely protective of their small, tight-knit clans, they are not known to possess great wealth in gold or cattle, nor uncommon skill in battle. What Meldron hoped to gain by attacking them, I could not guess. A few ships, perhaps, and some skinny cows.

The Eothaeli had begun grumbling darkly among themselves. I raised my staff and struck it sharply against the ground. "Listen, slow of wit!" I declared abruptly. "Hear the Chief Bard of Prydain!"

That silenced them. They did not dare mutter against a bard. Llew had tried reassurance; I decided on a more direct approach.

"Shame! Are you such ill-mannered and thankless guests that you reject the gift of friendship offered to you? You come lorn and empty-handed to us, but we do not turn you away. The warmth of our hearth is yours if you will accept it. Why do you stand there like captives of the hostage pit?"

I raised my staff, pointed at the head man and demanded: "What is your name?"

"Iollan," the gaunt man replied curtly, and then clamped his mouth shut.

"Hear me then, Iollan of the Eothaeli. Follow your own wisdom. We have offered you our welcome. It remains for you to accept it or decline. The choice is yours. If you stay, you will be treated fairly. If you leave, however, you go as you came: alone and unaided."

Iollan frowned but said nothing.

"Stubborn fool," Cynan whispered.

"Leave them to think about it," Llew said, turning away.

Cynan and I followed, but we had not walked ten paces when the head man called out, "We accept your offer of rest and food. We will stay—but only until we are strong enough to move on."

Llew turned back. "Very well. You are free to do as you please. We make no demands of you."

We led them to the meadow dwellings then, and arranged lodging for them. I thought to give them a house of their own, but Llew advised against it. "No, let them be dispersed among us—they will sooner become a part of life here. No one should feel like a stranger in Dinas Dwr."

Accordingly, we scattered the refugees among us, making room for a few of them in each house. In one day we had doubled our number, and the four houses were no longer as comfortable as before. But when the icy winds howled in the roof-trees at night we would be that much warmer for the nearness of our companions.

Sollen came on cold and wet, but not unbearable to us. Our houses were snug, the fires brisk and bright. Many a night we crowded together in the largest house and I took up my harp and sang. I sang the songs that have been sung since the beginning of this worlds-realm. I sang the *Tale of Rhiannon's Birds,* and *Mathonwy's Fountain;* I sang *Manawyddan and the Tylwyth Teg,* and *Cwn Annwn,* and the *Tale of Arianrhod's Silver Wheel,* and many, many others. I sang the cold Sollen away, and the days grew gradually longer.

By the time Gyd had coaxed the young green shoots from the land, the refugees among us no longer talked of leaving. They were one with us; and their defiance—born of pride and fear—had been replaced by an equally adamant resolve to shoulder the weight of work required to enlarge the settlement. They were eager to repay the kindness we had shown them, and their gratitude took the form of back-breaking labor: clearing the flat valley floor for crops, rowing the endless boatloads of stone for the crannog pilings, tending the oxen and horses, chopping wood, plowing ground, cooking, herding, tending.

Wherever there was a task to be done, one of the Eothaeli was there to do it, cheerfully, tirelessly, and with good grace. They worked harder than slaves. Indeed, had we made slaves of them we would never have imposed such labor as they undertook of themselves.

"These people are not like us, Cynan," Llew declared one balmy day, as he paused to look out over fresh-plowed fields. "I have never seen a people so eager to weary themselves in working. They humble us with their diligence."

"Then we must work harder," Cynan replied. "It is not fitting for the noble clans of Caledon to be surpassed by anyone."

Alun Tringad, standing nearby, heard this and announced loudly, "Do not think to surpass the Eothaeli unless you mean to far outdistance the Rhewtani as well—and that cannot be done."

Cynan drew himself up to meet the Rhewtani bluster. "If the men of Llogres were as hardworking as they are boastful, I might believe you. As it is, I have seen nothing to discourage me."

"Have you not, Cynan Machae?" retorted Alun. "Then open your eyes, man! Did that field plow itself? Did that wood chop itself? Did the logs lie down and roll themselves to the lake?"

"I believe I will sooner see a field plow itself, and wood chop itself, and logs lie down and roll themselves to the lake than see a plow, or axe, or ox goad in your hand, Alun Tringad!"

Others heard this exchange and stopped to look on; they laughed out loud at Cynan's reply. Someone called to Alun, encouraging him to make Cynan swallow his words.

"Brother, you have cut me to the heart with your rash talk," Alun avowed, his tone grave with the alleged seriousness of his wound. "I see there is only one way to save my honor. I will match a day of my work against a day of yours, and you will rue your hasty words."

"Unless you intend to talk me into submission," Cynan replied, "I will match you a day's work, and we will see who is the better man." He turned to me. "Tomorrow we will both plow, and chop wood, and haul timber. From sunrise to sunset we will work. And you will judge between us who has done more."

"Is this agreeable to you, Alun?" I asked.

"More than agreeable," the light-hearted Alun replied. "If you had said seven sunrises and seven sunsets—or even seventy-seven!—I would think it no hardship. Still, one day will be enough. For I would not wish to fatigue Cynan overmuch—I know how he treasures his repose."

Cynan's reply was thorny sharp. "I esteem your thoughtfulness, Alun Tringad, but you need have no qualms for me. Though I plow ten hides of land, I will still have ample time to rest while you strive to hitch the oxen!"

"So be it!" I shouted. "Tomorrow we will all watch this marvel. And we shall see who is worthy to stand beside the Eothaeli."

That night, as we sat at our supper, wagers were laid as to which would better the other. The Rhewtani were loud in favor of Alun, and the Galanae supported Cynan. Both groups clustered around their champions, encouraging them with high-sounding words and lofty praise. I noticed that, although the Eothaeli did not wager with the others, they entered into the fun all the same, lauding first Cynan and then Alun as the mood took them.

Cynan and Alun slept well that night. They awakened the next morning at dawn and went out to the oxpen to yoke their teams and hitch their beasts to the plow. Everyone followed, laughing and calling encouragement to one or the other of the chosen champions. Children scampered ahead, skipping in the still, clear air, making the valley echo to their happy whoops and shrieks.

Shouting good-natured derision at one another, the opponents took up their yokes and the contest began. Cynan succeeded in getting his team hitched before Alun had even yoked the first of his oxen. As he led his team from the pen, Cynan called over his shoulder to Alun, "Get used to seeing the back of me, brother. It is the only view you will enjoy all day!"

"Your backside is not a sight to be savored, Cynan Machae! Still, it is not a view I will be seeing—save when you bend over to kiss my feet in surrender."

Cynan left the cattle enclosure chuckling. He led his pair of oxen to an expanse of ground that had been cleared for plowing the day before; he set the blade of his plow deep in the untilled soil and took up the willow switch.

"Hie! Up! Hie!" he cried, and I heard the snap of the willow wand, and the soft, sighing groan as the plow carved the ground. I smelled the rich soil-scent of good black earth and heard the low grunt of an ox. At this, my inner eye awoke. I saw the oxen bend their necks and lower their heads. The plow shuddered forward; Cynan, holding to the haft, forced the blade down with his weight as the oxen dragged it over the grass. A black scar appeared amidst the green as the iron blade passed.

Cynan drove a straight, deep furrow to the end of the cleared field. He turned the oxen and started back to the cheers of the gathered throng. He finished the second furrow as Alun, having hitched his team, passed by on his way to begin plowing. "Take your ease, friend Alun," Cynan called, "for this field will soon be finished."

"Plow on, Cynan Machae," Alun replied happily. "And while you work your first field, I will finish two more."

Everyone laughed, but those backing Cynan began pressing the others to increase their wagers. Alun's supporters responded with defiance, and new wagers were quickly laid.

Alun reached the place where he meant to start; he set the plowshare and walked to the head of his team. "Beautiful beasts!" he called, loudly enough for all to hear. "Look at all this excellent ground before you. Look at the fair blue sky, and the red-rising sun. It is a good day to plow. You will perform wonders this day. Come, let us show these lazy laggards how to prepare a field!"

He then stooped and picked up a clod of dirt, crumbled it in his hands and rubbed the earth on the snouts of the oxen. Some of those looking on laughed, and someone cried, "Alun, do you mean them to eat a furrow through the field?"

The cocky Raven made no answer, but stepped close and whispered into the ears of the oxen, then took his place behind the plow. He did not shout, or use a switch, but merely clucked his tongue. "Tch! Tch!" he coaxed.

At this gentle command, the beasts lumbered forward. The plow smoothly sliced the earth and Alun Tringad walked behind, clucking gently and crooning soft endearments to his team. In this way he reached the end of the field, turned, and started back—all with much less effort than anyone would have believed. And certainly less strain than Cynan endured.

Alun's team pulled steadily, slicing through the thick turf and laying open one straight, deep furrow after another. Cynan, on the other hand, wrestled his way to the end of another furrow, turned his team, and, with willow switch snapping, began struggling back. The plow in Cynan's hand dragged and jerked as the blade struck stones; Cynan's broad shoulders bunched and bulged as he battled the plow and team. And it seemed to me that he pressed too hard—as if he would force the share through the soil with his own strength—and the earth resisted.

Alun, sweetly coaxing and cajoling, seemed to ease the blade through the yielding earth. His team pulled evenly and cleanly. Little by little, they began to gain on Cynan's team.

Furrow after furrow they plowed. The rich soil rolled from the plowshares in long, unbroken black curls. Birds gathered to hop among the new-cut ridges. The sun rose higher and the day grew bright and warm. Cynan saw his lead shrinking and redoubled his efforts. He shouted and slashed with the willow wand, driving his oxen harder and harder. The stalwart beasts lowered their heads until their noses almost touched the ground; their great muscled bodies heaved against the wooden yoke, hauling the unwilling plow forward.

For all his strength and struggle, Cynan could not prevent Alun's team from drawing even. Step by step, Alun's gently-persuaded pair matched Cynan's hard-striving team . . . and then passed it.

Alun's supporters shouted aloud as the last furrow was completed and Alun unhitched the plow; he led his team away from the fresh-tilled square of earth, calling and waving cheerfully to all. Cynan, jaw set, brow lowered, finished his field, released his team, and hastened to catch Alun, who was already disappearing into the forest, axe in hand, a stream of followers trailing behind him down the slope.

"The only work accomplished today will be done by Cynan and Alun," I observed, as the stragglers hurried away to join Cynan.

"Give them the day," Llew replied. "They have earned it." He grew reflective. "In my world," he said slowly, "people are granted a day of rest from their labors—one day in every seven. In past times it was a jealously guarded gift, though now it is no longer recognized as such."

"One day in seven," I replied, considering the idea. "It is an uncommon practice, but not unknown. There are bards who have asserted such notions from time to time, and kings have so decreed for their people."

"Then let us make such a decree."

"So be it! One day in seven the people of Dinas Dwr will rest from their labors," I agreed.

"Good, we will tell the others," Llew said. "But not yet. Let us join Cynan first, and rouse him to victory."

Cynan had paused long enough to choose a good stout axe from the storehouse on the lakeshore. We joined him as, ox goad in one hand and axe in the other, he drove the oxen along the lakeshore path leading to the forest.

"Well done, Cynan," Llew told him, and could not resist adding: "Still, I thought you would finish well ahead of Alun."

"And I thought I would never finish at all. That was the hardest ground I have ever put plow to. Did you see the size of those stones? Boulders! And these oxen are the most stubborn beasts alive!"

"Do not worry, brother," Llew said. "You will catch him soon enough. Alun is no match for you with an axe!"

"Am I worried by the likes of Alun Tringad?" Cynan snorted. "Let him chop all he likes, I will dazzle him. Give him fifty strokes to one of mine, and I will still fell more trees!"

By the time we reached the forest clearing where the workers had been cutting timber for the crannogs, Alun had managed a fair beginning. He had one large pine tree leaning and about to fall. The onlookers stood in the clearing, shouting their approval at each stroke.

Cynan chose a likely tree, spat on his hands, took up the axe, and with easy, rhythmic stokes began to chop. His followers called encouragement, and the clearing soon rang with the chunk and thunk of axes on tall timber and the sound of cheering voices.

Alun was first to fell his tree—much to the delight of the onlookers, who raised a clamor of triumph. He wasted not a moment, but leapt to the task of trimming the upper branches of the pine. As soon as he had the largest limbs cleaned away, he cut off the top of the tree and attached one end of a chain to the log and the other end to the iron ring of the yoke.

Then, with a cluck of his tongue, he urged the oxen forward a few steps. The log rolled over, and Alun quickly halted his team; he returned to the tree and finished trimming away the rest of the branches. Hastening to the head of his team, he began dragging the log from the clearing to the acclaim of his supporters.

"Worry not, Cynan," he called as he passed. "I will leave you some trees to cut—the small ones."

"Take no thought for me, Alun Tringad," Cynan replied through clenched teeth. He swung the axe hard and the blade bit deep. Already there was a goodly pile of woodchips at his feet. "It is Cynan himself that will be awaiting you with a cup in his hand when you finish."

"Would you care to wager whose hand holds that cup, brother?" Alun paused to inquire.

Cynan swung the axe hard. Another thick chip flew from the cut. "People will call me thief for taking your treasure," he replied.

"Let them call you what they like," Alun said. "Two gold armbands for your silver torc—hey?"

Some of those standing near who knew Cynan murmured to one another. Cynan's blue eyes darkened and his smile froze. "Your gold is not worth a tenth of my torc," he told Alun flatly.

"Three gold armbands then."

"Seven," Cynan countered, moustache twitching.

"Four."

"Five at least," demanded Cynan. "And two rings!"

"Done!" Alun cried, and then turned to his team. "Tch! Tch!" he clucked. The oxen lurched forward, dragging the log with them.

Cynan returned to his work, and if he had labored with determination, now he toiled with a vengeance—as well he would. His face flared and seemed to set his red hair alight; he bristled head to toe.

"I fear Alun has sealed his fate," observed Llew at this exchange. "Cynan might have allowed Alun to better him, but he will never let that torc go."

To the sound of Cynan's ringing axe, Llew told me how he and Cynan had become friends at Scatha's school for warriors. "It only happened at all because of that torc," Llew said. "He valued it higher than his life then, and but little lower now, I think." He chuckled at the memory. "He was unbearable! Haughty, pompous...I tell you the truth, Tegid, the sun never set on his vanity."

There came a loud crack and a long, low groan as the tree tilted and then crashed to the ground. Cynan was on it instantly, chopping away the limbs and branches. As his supporters shouted encouragement, he hitched the oxen to the trunk, rolled it, and finished cleaning the log, cutting off the treetop even as the oxen began dragging it away.

Alun returned to the clearing while Cynan was away and began chopping at another tree. But very soon the sound of Alun's axe was joined by that of Cynan, who had returned to the clearing on the run. Alun did not know the tempest he had loosed, but he was soon to learn. For the next tree to fall was Cynan's; he had cleaned the bole and topped it before Alun had felled his.

Those supporting Cynan raised a happy shout as the log was dragged away. Alun's supporters began exhorting their champion to speed, and the rhythm of Alun's axe quickened accordingly. The tree groaned under his blade and then fell. Soon he had cleaned and topped it, and the oxen were slowly dragging the log away.

The contest settled into an earnest pattern. First one and then the other felled, cleaned, topped and dragged a log from the clearing down to the lakeside—stopping only to swallow a few mouthfuls of water before hurrying on. The sun rose higher, spilling light over the treetops and into the clearing. The two rivals, dripping sweat from their exertion, stripped off their siarcs and hewed at the trees, standing to their work like the stalwart warriors they were. Cynan's torc flashed at his throat; the blue raven on Alun's arm appeared to soar as the muscles flexed beneath the flesh.

Wagers were doubled and then tripled—first one way and then the other, as first one challenger and then the other appeared to take the lead. Even the Eothaeli were drawn into the wagering this time, joining in the revel. Llew left my side to join the noisy onlookers, and I withdrew a little apart to sit on a pile of woodchips. I stretched my feet before me and leaned my back against a stump.

The forest clearing rang to the cheers of the crowd. Cheers became chants, as the people thrilled to the efforts of their chosen champions. The shouts of the people filled my ears, growing loud inside my head like the cries of a conquering warband. And in my mind's eye I saw Dinas Dwr, solid and strong, floating on the shining surface of the lake. I saw rich fields spreading across the valley, and wide hunting runs in the forests on the surrounding slopes of Druim Vran. I saw a courageous people rising up to claim a place among the great and powerful of this worlds-realm.

I roused myself from these musings to find myself alone. Sunlight no longer warmed the skin—the clearing was in shadow. I could hear, in the near distance, the voices of the people streaming down the hillside, following Alun and Cynan as they drove their ox-teams to the lakeshore where the logs they had cut were stacked. I made to rise, and felt someone grip my arm and pull me to my feet.

"I thought you had gone," Llew said. "Have you been asleep?"

"No," I replied. "But I have been dreaming."

"Well, come. The sun will set soon, and the winner will be declared. We do not want to miss that."

We hastened along the path to the lakeside where everyone had gathered to await the decision. Bran Bresal had taken it upon himself to address the crowd. "The trial undertaken this day was threefold: plowing, cutting wood, and hauling timber. From sunrise to sunset the trial was performed—" He paused as we came near to join the eager onlookers, and made to step aside for Llew.

"Please continue," Llew told him amiably. "You have made a good beginning.

But Bran would not, saying, "Lord, it is for you to judge between them. That is the agreement."

"Very well." Llew took his place, climbing up on the stack of logs. "The sun is going down; the work is ended," he said, his voice lifted in the dusk. "Two fields were plowed with an equal number of furrows each. Therefore, I judge the plowing to have been equal and even."

"Even!" Cynan shouted. "My field was all roots and rocks!" he cried in protest. "It was much the more difficult. The decision should go to me!"

"I began last, but finished first," countered Alun Tringad. "My field was just as difficult as his. The decision should go to me!"

The two men's supporters also raised their voices in protest. But

Llew held firm. "The trial entails the amount of labor performed—not its difficulty. The number of furrows is equal between them, therefore the labor was equal. We must look elsewhere for a way to settle the matter."

"Count the logs!" someone shouted. Immediately, the crowd took up the call: "The logs! The logs! The logs!"

Gradually, the call subsided. "Very well," Llew said, "the logs will decide the issue. Bran, you will count them."

Bran stepped to Cynan's logstack first, and began to count aloud, touching each log with his hand as he called out the number: "One...two...three...four...five..." The throng, silent, watched with bated breath as the total was tallied. "...nine...ten...eleven... Twelve! Cynan Machae has felled and stacked twelve trees!"

Instantly, Cynan's supporters gave out a great roar of approval. Cynan shouted something to Alun, but the words were lost amidst the noise. Llew, still standing on the stack of logs, motioned for silence. When the crowd grew still once more, he said, "Twelve logs for Cynan. Now we will count the timber in Alun's stack."

Bran moved to the second heap of logs. "One...two..." he began.

But how many logs Alun had felled was not discovered, for even as Bran stooped to the counting, there came the dreadful sound of the carynx—a long, loud blast of the battlehorn, falling from the ridgetop like the bellow of a mad bull, resounding across the lake and blaring through the glen.

19

Invasion

We turned as one to the ridgeway. The battlehorn sounded again, coursing through the hushed valley like a shiver of fear. At once my inward sight kindled to the image of a fiery sky, red and gold with the setting sun, and a battlehost emerging from the forest—some afoot and some on horseback: a hundred strong with weapons drawn. I saw their shields glint in the dying light. I saw their leader riding at the head of his warriors, surrounded by a mounted bodyguard.

Llew commanded the warriors to their weapons, and everyone else to flee to the crannogs. Although there were yet no timber walls, the people would be safer on the islands than in the houses on the shore. The Ravens flew to arm themselves from the huts, and everyone else surged towards the lake. Cynan ordered his warriors to bring horses, and three heartbeats later all was confusion as warriors rushed here and there, gathering spears and swords and throwing halters on horses. Men ran to launch the boats and women scurried, clutching babies; children bawled, and boats slid into the water.

"We will meet them on the meadow!" Cynan called, leaping into the saddle.

"Where the stream crosses the glen," Llew answered. "That will give people time to reach the stronghold."

Garanaw brought a sword to Llew and began strapping it to his hip. Llew sent him on his way. "Twenty against a hundred," Llew said as I joined him. "What do you think of our chances, Tegid?"

"I think it would be wise to wait and see who these men are and why they have come here," I replied.

He stopped jerking at the leather strap. "What have you seen?"

"Only what you have seen: warriors riding into our settlement. But they announce their coming with the carynx," I pointed out. "A strange thing to do when surprise would assure an easy defeat."

Llew returned to worrying the strap with his good hand. "It is meant to frighten us. They would rather we surrendered without a fight."

"Perhaps they mean to warn us instead."

Cynan returned for a final word. "It is a challenge—not a warning," he advised. "Take the battle to them, I say, before they have a chance to surround us."

"Fight or talk, it is for you to decide."

Llew hesitated, weighing the consequences of his decision. Cynan shifted uneasily. "We must take the fight to them," he insisted. "We are sorely outnumbered. We cannot allow them to surround us."

"Well? What will you do?" I asked.

"Cynan is right. They come with swords drawn. We must meet them."

"Yes!" replied Cynan. He jerked the reins hard. "Hie!" He kicked his heels against his mount's flanks. The horse galloped away.

Rhoedd came running, leading a roan stallion. He gave the reins into Llew's hand, cupped his hands for Llew's foot and boosted him into the saddle; next he held up a shield which Llew took upon his stumped arm; lastly he gave Llew a stout-hafted spear.

Bran Bresal, astride a spirited yellow mare, approached. "Will you ride with us, Lord Llew?"

"I will."

The battlehorn sounded its bull roar across the meadow. The horses stamped, tossing their heads and jigging sideways on the strand.

"Uphold us, Tegid," Llew said.

I raised my staff to him. "May your blade be swift and light. May your spear fly true."

Bran wheeled his horse; Llew urged his mount on and the two galloped away. I walked the shore to the place where the last people waited for the boats to return and take them to safety.

I heard rapid footsteps on the rocky strand and turned as Rhoedd, spear in hand, joined me. "I am to remain with you," he muttered, betraying his disappointment at having to stay behind and look after a blind bard.

"Fret not, Rhoedd," I said, seeking to soothe. "We will stay here where we can see what is happening."

He regarded me strangely. But I did not care to explain to him about my inner sight. The boats returned for the last of the passengers then, and one of the men called to us to hurry.

"Tell them to go on. We are staying."

Rhoedd waved them away, telling them that we would remain on the shore. Then he rejoined me, saying, "What will you do, lord?"

"Follow me." Taking my staff, I turned my back to the lake and began walking towards the meadow. Rhoedd walked at my right hand, casting furtive sidelong glances at me as he tried to discover how it was that I could see.

Llew, Bran and the Ravens advanced towards Druim Vran across the meadow. Cynan and the Galanae warband advanced a little south of the Raven Flight. The invaders made for the stream. They advanced slowly, mounted warriors at the fore, weapons at the ready. The last of them had cleared the forest.

"I make it two fifties and ten," I said.

Rhoedd made a rapid estimation. "Yes," he replied, glancing at me again.

The yellow glint of sunlight on metal flashed in my mind's eye, and the carynx sounded once more: loud as thunder, raw as a wound.

The foemen rushed forward with a shout. The horses drove across the stream and into the meadow, their hooves pounding the earth like a hollow drum.

The Ravens lashed their horses to speed. They charged headlong towards the invaders. Flying as one, and Llew with them, they swooped over the fresh-plowed ground, dirt thrown high from the horses' hooves. The swiftness of their charge stole the breath away. Like a well-thrown spear they flew, straight and true.

The onrushing enemy gathered itself, like a muscle contracting, bracing for the impact. Spears pricked sharp, gleaming deadly and cruel.

I halted, waiting for the clash.

At the last instant, Bran swerved the Ravens aside: away from those who now braced to receive them, and towards a new target. The advancing enemy saw the Ravens suddenly swing onto a new course and knew that death had caught them, for there was no time to prepare to meet the charge.

There came a keening scream, like that of an eagle diving to the kill. I wondered at the uncanny sound: sharp as a honed blade, piercing the ear and the heart. It was Bran and his warriors, their voices lifted in the terrible war cry of the Ravens.

The advancing line faltered. The invaders scattered. Horses stumbled, throwing their hapless riders. Footmen threw themselves to the ground to escape the onrushing hooves.

The center of the enemy line melted away before the Flight of Ravens. Cynan, who had begun his charge, saw the breech and aimed for it. Men who had barely escaped the Ravens now beheld another terror speeding towards them.

The footmen turned and ran back across the stream. The mounted warriors determined to stand their ground. They wheeled their horses and levelled their spears. They met. The ground seemed to tremble. I heard a crack like a tree-trunk splitting.

The enemy disappeared. The force of Cynan's charge swept them away.

"Hoo! Hoo!" Rhoedd cried, lofting his spear. "That has done it!"

The Raven's charge had been a knife-slash, Cynan's a spear-thrust completing the severing cut. With the center of their line gutted, the enemy battlechief sounded the retreat. They must regroup if they hoped to unite the two halves of the line.

But Bran had no intention of allowing them to reform the line. For even as the battlehorn bellowed out its signal, he was circling behind the enemy. Thus they turned to find themselves facing the swift-striking Ravens once more.

Those who stood against them were cut down. Those who ran fell beneath the hooves. The enemy advance halted as the line collapsed, its center shattered. Foemen fled across the stream, running for the shelter of the forest. The enemy battlechief strove to turn the rout. I saw him ordering his warband, vainly trying to gather them as the Ravens prepared for another strike.

The carynx sounded once and again. But it was Cynan who answered the call. The flame-haired firebrand levelled his spear and the Galanae warriors surged forward like a storm, cloaks flying, shields flashing.

I saw a lone figure ride out from the shelter of the wood on a piebald horse. My heart thudded in my chest like a clenched fist.

A groan escaped my lips. I staggered and clutched my staff to keep from falling. Rhoedd grasped my arm to steady me. "What is it? Are you ill?"

"Stop it!"

"What?"

I seized Rhoedd by the arm. "We must stop it!"

"Stop it—the battle?" he wondered, as I began running towards the stream. "Wait!"

I stumbled as I reached the plowed ground; I could not run fast enough. I shouted as I ran. "Hold! Hold! Llew! Hold!"

Perhaps the sight of a blind bard dashing madly across the field, floundering across the furrows, caught someone's notice. I do not know. But I heard a shout and Llew turned in the saddle; he did not see me, but his eyes scanned the meadow.

"Llew!" I cried.

He saw me running towards him, called something over his shoulder to Bran. I drew a deep breath and shouted with all my might: "Calbha!"

I think he heard me, for he halted and made to turn aside. "It is Calbha!" I shouted, pointing at the lone rider with my staff. "Calbha!" I began running again.

"What is it?" Rhoedd called after me.

"A mistake!" I cried, and together we raced for the stream.

A few swift steps carried us across the water. As we clambered onto dry land on the other side, I heard the long, shimmering blast of Emyr's carynx. Another blast halted the Ravens, who remained poised for the attack.

Llew galloped to meet me. "Tegid!" he shouted. "Are you certain?"

"It is Calbha!" I told him, pointing at the approaching rider with my staff. "His horse! Look at his horse! You have attacked a friend!"

He swivelled in the saddle and looked where I pointed. *"Clanna na cù!"* he cried. "What is he doing here?"

"Stop, Cynan!"

Llew jerked the reins so hard his horse reared and nearly fell backward as it wheeled. Llew slapped the beast across the withers and sped to head off Cynan's charge. Bran rode to meet him as he passed. Llew paused in his flight long enough to shout a word to the battlechief and then urged his mount to speed again. Bran shouted to Emyr, who began blowing the battlehorn for all he was worth.

I looked to where Cynan's warband was charging after the fleeing enemy. I glimpsed a flash of red hair and my inner vision dissolved into darkness. I was abruptly blind once more. "Rhoedd!" I shouted. "Where are you?"

"Here, Lord," came the reply close behind me.

"Rhoedd, I cannot see! Look and tell me what is happening."

"But, I thought—"

"Tell me, man! What is happening?" He hesitated. "Is Cynan still advancing?"

"Yes, lord, still advancing. No—wait! They are stopping!"

"Describe it, Rhoedd. Tell me everything—as you did before."

"Cynan has raised himself in the saddle; he turns this way and that. He is shouting something; I see his mouth move. He seems to be ordering the warband. They are listening to him ... and now ... Lord Cynan is moving forward alone. He is riding to meet Llew, I think—yes."

"What of the enemy rider? The one on the piebald stallion—what is he doing?"

"He has stopped. He sits his horse, waiting."

"What does he look like? Can you see?"

"No, lord, he is too far away."

"What else?"

"Now Llew and Cynan are coming together. Llew is making the sign of peace with his hand—he is signalling to his warband. The Galanae are halting, and Cynan is riding to meet Llew."

"What of Bran?"

"The Ravens are turning aside," Rhoedd answered after a moment. "They are riding to the fallen on the battleground." He turned back to Llew and Cynan. "The lords have reached the place where the stranger waits."

"Take me to them," I commanded, clutching his sleeve. "Lead me! Hurry!"

Rhoedd strode ahead and I held tight to his siarc. "They are riding to meet the stranger. Cynan carries his spear upright. The stranger waits for them."

The ground sloped upward, climbing to the ridge. Rhoedd paused. "An enemy warrior, fallen." He stooped to the body. "He is dead, lord."

We hurried on. I urged my guide to continue his description. "They are met. It seems that they are speaking to one another ..."

"Yes? ... Rhoedd?" He stopped in his tracks. "What is happening? Tell me—"

"I do not believe it, lord bard," he replied, his voice sharp with disbelief.

"Speak, man! What has happened?"

"The two of them—they are ... they—" he spluttered.

"Yes? Yes?"

"They extend their arms—they are embracing!"

Relief unclenched my heart. "Come, Rhoedd. Hurry."

Llew and the stranger had dismounted and were talking together when we reached the place. "Here, Tegid," Llew called, guiding me to him. I stepped towards the sound of his voice, and felt his stump brush my arm at the elbow.

"Hail, Calbha," I said. "If we had but known it was you, we would have spared you a fight—and the lives of good men."

"Your words are bitter to me, Tegid Tathal—not the less because they are true. I own the blame; the blood debt is mine alone." His remorse was genuine; he stood before us a stricken man. "I am sorry. Although I am a king without a realm or riches, on my honor, I will make redress by whatever means you deem acceptable."

"Calbha," Llew said, "do not speak of redress. We have suffered no lasting hurt today."

Cynan spoke up. "We lost not a single man—none injured, even."

"Look to the solace of your people," Llew told him. "You have born the loss, and we are sorry for our part in it."

"Lord Calbha," I said, "you are a very long way from home."

"I have no home," he muttered darkly. "I have no lands, no realm, no kingdom. My lands are stolen, my realm is forfeit, my people driven out." He paused, his voice cracking like a riven oak. "My queen...my wife is dead."

"Meldron attacked him," Llew explained, although I had already guessed what must have happened.

"Yes, Meldron attacked me—as he has attacked everyone else in Llogres," the Cruin king explained. "We held out as long as we could, but his forces are better armed and their numbers greater. Many have joined him. Those he has not put to the sword have alliances forced upon them. We resisted for a time, but it was useless."

"How did you know to come here?" I asked.

"We heard there was safe haven in the north, in Caledon."

"Then why did you come with the sword, man?" Cynan bawled in exasperation. *"Mo anam!"*

Calbha's answer was a groan. "Ahh...I was afraid...I acted rashly."

"Stupidly!" Rhoedd whispered. He had taken his place beside me.

Bran joined us then, and Llew acknowledged him. "Eight dead," the battlechief reported. "Six wounded—they are receiving aid now."

"The blood debt is mine alone," Calbha muttered. "I am ashamed."

"How many are with you?" Llew asked.

"Three hundred—not counting children."

"Three hundred!" Rhoedd repeated, astonished.

"Are they with you now?" asked Llew.

"Yes," Calbha answered. "They are waiting in the forest."

"Gather them and bring them to the lake. We will receive them there."

"What are we going to do with so many?" Rhoedd wondered aloud. "Three hundred—"

"Not Cruin only," Calbha hastened to add. "We met others on the way: Addani and Mereridi. They were without a lord and had no protection. There are also Mawrthoni, Catrini, and Neifioni wandering in the hills... we have seen them." He fell silent as the enormity of the calamity engulfed him. "All of Llogres is in upheaval—no man's hearth remains secure."

The Banfáith's prophecy came to mind: "Llogres shall be without a lord," I mused to myself.

"Mark me well." Calbha spoke in somber tone. "When Meldron has finished with Llogres, he will turn to Caledon. There is no end to his battle-lust. He means to rule all Albion."

So saying, the Cruin king remounted his horse and returned to the forest to summon his people. And the invasion of Dinas Dwr began.

20

Great Hound of Havoc

Calbha disappeared into the forest, and we returned to the lake to await the people's arrival. Soon they were streaming from among the trees. They came by scores; tribes and clans and families, survivors of Meldron's wanton depredations. Weary, travel-worn, exhausted, they came, dragging themselves miserably from hiding. But the setting sun lit their haggard faces and filled their eyes with light.

"Rhoedd is right," Bran remarked, watching the streams of refugees mingle to become a flood. "There are too many. How will we feed them?"

"The forest is full of game," Llew observed, "and the lake is full of fish. We will survive."

Cynan was not so certain. "They cannot stay here," he complained. "No—let me speak. I have been thinking, and it is clear that we do not have the means to support them."

"I have already told Calbha that they can stay," Llew replied.

"Clanna na cù," grumbled Cynan. "A day—two at most. Then they must move on. I do not like to say this, brother, but I will, because someone must: laudable your generosity may be, but it is also foolhardy."

"Finished?"

"Man, I am telling you, if they stay we will starve. It is as simple as that."

"And *if* we starve," Llew said firmly, "we will all starve together. Yes?"

Cynan drew breath to speak. I could not see him, but I imagined him shaking his head, or running his big hands through his wild red hair in irritation.

"It will be well, brother," Llew told him. I heard the light clap of a hand on a shoulder. "This is why we have established this place. Three hundred! Think of all the work we can do with so many pairs of hands. Why, Dinas Dwr will rise overnight!"

"If it does not sink under its own weight first," Cynan muttered.

Later, when we had settled the newcomers for the night—they were ranged in a score of camps along the lakeshore—we sat with a grimly silent Calbha and his bleak battlechiefs around the hearth on the crannog. We had retreated there to confer in peace without fear of being overheard. We ate bread and meat, and passed the cups from hand to hand while we waited for Calbha to tell us the thing we most wanted to hear—that which pierced him to the marrow to say.

The cup worked its quiet way, and at last Calbha's tongue was loosened. He began to speak more easily, and we to edge him closer to the matter at hand.

"Meldron has slaughtered the bards of Caledon and Llogres," I said. "In this he has surpassed even Lord Nudd, who slew only those of Prydain."

"He meant to kill us as well," Llew added. "As it is, I lost a hand to him, and Tegid lost his eyes."

"Meldron is mad," groaned Calbha. "He seizes the land and steals the cattle; what he cannot carry off, he burns. He cuts a wide swathe of destruction, leaving only ashes in his wake. I have seen the heads of warriors piled high as my chin, and hands heaped high as my belt. I have seen children with their tongues cut out..." He grew angry, and demanded: "What was their offense that they should be treated so?"

There was no answer to be made, and we offered none, but sipped our beer and listened to the soft flutter of the flames before us. "Tell us what happened," Llew said gently.

Calbha took a last swallow from the cup, wiped his moustache on the sleeve of his siarc, and began. "They came at us without warning. I had men riding the circuit of the land, but they were killed, I think; none of them ever returned. I had posted sentries. On the day you left us, I established a perpetual watch, or they would have overwhelmed us. As it is, I wish I had listened to you—if we had ridden against Meldron, as you suggested, we might have put an end to him before he grew so strong."

"How many warriors rode in his warband?" asked Bran.

"There were two hundred on horses, and three hundred on foot." Calbha paused and, in a voice spiked with rancor, added, "Most of the horsemen were Rhewtani. They and their lord rode under Meldron's command. I am sorry, but you asked."

"Where injustice is great," Bran replied, "all men must shoulder a portion of dishonor. I know well the burden I bear."

One of Calbha's lords said, "But do you know what it is to see your son battered to death beneath the hooves of charging Rhewtani warriors?" The man's voice was a wound, ragged and bloody.

"I am sorry," Bran Bresal said gently.

"We are all sorry," Calbha grumbled. He drank again, and then continued.

"We defended the gate and walls through the day—I was not fool enough to meet them on the battleground. They had the strength of numbers and I knew we had no hope against them on the field. But I thought we might hold them off. Our losses were light, we were well supplied, and they could not breach the walls no matter how many horses they had.

"We resisted this way for three days, and could have held out far longer. But Meldron attacked some of the smaller holdings and made the people prisoners. He brought these hostages to Blár Cadlys and began killing them before the gates. Even so, he was not content to murder them outright."

His voice became a croak. "He caused iron axle rods to be heated to glowing heat in a great fire. He took the fiery rods and extinguished them in the flesh of the captives. Some he pierced through the throat; some through the belly. The screams...the screams... Do you know what it is to die this way? Have you any idea what it sounds like?"

"What did you do then?" Llew asked gently.

"What could I do?" the Cruin king asked. "I could not allow my people to suffer so. I ordered the attack. We might all be killed—I knew and rued it well—but we would go down fighting."

Cynan commended the decision. "Better to die with honor like men, rather than allow yourselves to be slaughtered like beasts."

"No beast was ever slaughtered so shamefully," Calbha declared. "And do not think he was content to torture men alone. Women and children suffered, too."

"What did you do?" Llew asked.

"We attacked," spat one of Calbha's battlechiefs. *"Mór Cù* cut us down like saplings."

"Mór Cù?" Llew mused. "Why do you call him Great Hound?"

"This Meldron is like a mad dog," the man replied, "running over the land, devouring all in his path—a great hound of havoc."

"Our losses were heavy," Calbha told us. "We could not stand against them—there were too many and they meant to destroy us."

"How did you escape?"

"Dusk came upon us; it grew too dark to fight. That was a mercy. So I gathered all who could walk or ride and, under cover of darkness, we fled." Calbha paused; he was straining to keep his voice steady. "The Great Hound would not even allow us the dishonor of our escape. He pursued us through the night, hunting us by torchlight. They rode us down like animals and killed any who fell: the fortunate ones they stabbed with spears; the unfortunate were torn apart by dogs."

Calbha's voice had shrunk to a dry whisper. "My wife, my best beloved...she was not one of the fortunate."

The wind stirred on the lake. I heard the wavelets lapping at the timbers of the crannog. My heart was heavy with grief for Calbha's woe; it felt like a stone in my chest.

It was long before the Cruin king spoke again. "I do not know how anyone endured the night," he said, recovering some of his composure. "But by daybreak we straggled together and found that the Great Hound no longer pursued us. If he had not broken off pursuit, none of us would have survived." He swallowed hard.

"You came north," Llew said, to keep him talking.

"We came north. There was no safe place in Llogres any more. But I thought if we could lose ourselves in the empty hills of Caledon, we might escape. We travelled by night to avoid Meldron's scouts; we did this for many nights until we were well into Caledon. And by then we had found others—clans and tribes who had either escaped or had taken to the hills and glens rather than wait to be attacked and driven out."

When Calbha paused again, Llew asked, "How did you know to come here?"

"The Catrini and some of the others had heard of a place in the north of Caledon where we might find refuge. We planned to search for it."

"Man, then why did you attack us?" Cynan demanded. There was some resentment in the question, but more curiosity. "If it was refuge you sought, you have a strange way of seeking it."

Calbha's battlechiefs growled their disapproval of the question, considering it an affront to their king's dignity and respect. But Calbha silenced them with a word. "It was my mistake, and I rue it," he said. "I have dishonored myself and my people. Long will I bear the shame." He straightened; his voice became grave. "I claim *naud* of you."

The claim of naud was the most serious appeal for pardon and absolution that could be made, and only a king could grant it. Llew answered him with appropriate delicacy. "I hear your claim and would freely grant it, but I am not a king that you should seek naud of me. It was a mistake, brother. No one here condemns you."

"Men of my clan—my kinsmen!—lie cold beneath the turf tonight!" Calbha snapped. "The blood of those good men condemns me."

"Lord Calbha," I said, "we promised peace to you and offered war instead. It is no less our mistake, and no less our failing."

The Cruin king took his time answering. "Thank you, Tegid Tathal," he said at last, "but I know what I did. I saw the settlement here and I saw the horses, and I grew fearful of our reception. I was afraid and I attacked in fear. Nothing you say can change that." He paused, and added, "I lost hope."

"You are here now," Llew said. "It is over."

"It is over," Calbha agreed mournfully. "I am no longer worthy to be king."

"Say not so, lord!" wailed one of the Cruin chieftains. "Who else could have led us to safety?"

"Any coward would have served you there, Teirtu," Calbha answered.

"You are no coward, lord," the man declared.

"We are all cowards, Teirtu," Calbha answered softly, "else Meldron could never have grown so strong. We gave him through fear what we should have protected through courage."

We slept under the stars that night—and for a good many nights thereafter. We were a long time building enough shelter for our growing clan. And we would grow. As Calbha had warned, there were homeless tribes wandering the hills. Albion was in ferment; men were moving on the land, seeking safety and solace. The clans of southern Caledon and Llogres were as sheep driven before the ravening Hound. I little doubted they would find their way to Dinas Dwr, the safe haven of the north.

All that long Maffar, Season of Sun, they came. The Mawrthoni, Catrini, and Neifioni that Calbha had seen were first. Others followed: Dencani, Saranae, and Vynii from the southeast; Ffotlae and Marcanti from the fertile midlands; Iuchari from the eastern coast; and Goibnui, Taolentani, and Oirixeni from the high hills of northern Llogres.

We questioned every tribe and clan that came to us, and listened to their mournful tales. Each tale was the same: Meldron, Great

Hound of Havoc, raged through the land with murderous intent. Death and destruction rode with him, and desolation followed in his wake.

Many told us that they had heard of our northern refuge. When we asked them how they knew where to find us, all said that someone else had told them. Word spread on the wind, it seemed; men moving through the land heard the word and followed. We held council among ourselves to determine what we should do, for it seemed only a matter of time before word reached Meldron and he rode to destroy us.

"We cannot hide from him forever," Cynan said. "He will ride against us. But if we establish a line of beacons along the ridge, we can at least be forewarned of his approach."

This we did.

But in the end it was not a beacon fire which warned us of Meldron's progress. The alert came from the tribal remnant of a small clan on the eastern coast, five brothers and their dying mother, who brought news of ships full of warriors bound for Ynys Sci.

21

Assault on Sci

With my inner eye I saw them: three thirties of warriors, standing on the strand, watching the ships glide into the bay. A menacing line of dark clouds swept in low from the east; the wind whipped our cloaks. But the sheltered bay remained smooth as molten lead. I turned sightless eyes to the sky and saw a clear expanse of blue still gleaming above. I smelled rain on the air, and beyond the bay I heard the surge of waves on the rocky coastline.

Four ships, square-rigged and stout-masted, sailed nearer. The blood-red sails bellied in the wind as the low-riding vessels flew before the approaching tempest. Our horses, sensing the nearness of the storm, jerked and jigged, tossing their heads and hoofing the sand. Two men and four boys would herd them back to Dinas Dwr where Lord Calbha waited. We could not use horses where we were going, and, if we failed, Calbha would need them.

It was the evening of the third day since leaving Dinas Dwr. And the ships had sailed from southern Caledon to meet us.

"Three days' ride along the ridge will bring you to the coast here," Cynan had said, tapping the ground with a stick where he had scratched a few instructive lines. "This is where the ships will meet you." He tapped the ground again. "Four ships is all we have," he added, as if in warning.

"Four is enough," stated Llew firmly.

"We will not be able to take the horses."

"Horses would be no use to us," replied Llew.

"We are a small force against Meldron's host," Bran pointed out. "He has five hundred men at least—"

"If our observers are to be believed," said Calbha sceptically. "They could not agree how many ships they saw."

"Let Meldron take as many as he can haul with him," Llew replied with some force. "We cannot take more men than we have."

"But if they join battle with us on the field—" Calbha persisted. The king was protesting because it had been decided that he should stay behind to look after the people of Dinas Dwr.

Llew shook his head gently. "One day we will meet Meldron on the battlefield—and then we will want to match his forces. But not now. Superior numbers will avail Meldron nothing, nor would they help us." He rose, brushing dirt from his hands. "You will have your day of retribution, Calbha."

Thus the war council ended.

Cynan had departed immediately with four warriors, hastening to Dun Cruach in the south to fetch his father's ships. We spent the next days readying weapons and horses for the journey to the coast, waiting for the day of our departure, and salving Lord Calbha's bruised pride at not being included among the warband.

Three days later we set out at dawn, riding beside the long, glass-smooth lake through the silent glen. The thick-veiled darkness of my blindness was—occasionally, and without warning—illumined by blazing images of the world around me: men and horses moving through deep green valleys...silvery mist flowing down the slopes from the high ridgeway...sunlight bright on gleaming metal...red-cloaked warriors bearing round white shields...blue lake sparkling and bluer sky flecked with grey...twilight stealing swarthy across the sky vault, and stars burning like campfires on a vast darksome plain...

And I heard the keening cry of eagles soaring on the wind. I heard the soft plod of the horses' hooves on the track, and the light jingle of halter and tack. I heard the easy banter of the men, arming themselves with good humor for the confrontation ahead.

It was a risky plan—as any plan was destined to be, considering our woefully inferior position. Surprise was our sole advantage. Never again could we count on catching Meldron this way, not least because it would alert him to the fact that Llew and I were yet alive to trouble him. We had one chance, and one chance only. But perhaps, if all went well, one would be enough.

Llew knew the island well. His six years under Scatha's tutelage had prepared him for this undertaking. He knew where our ships could approach without being seen; he knew which hills and valleys would provide protection; he knew how the caer could be attacked to maximum effect. Our plan hung on Llew's intimate knowledge of Sci. And Cynan knew the island almost as well.

As we made our way along the ridge, I tried—as I had tried many times before—to see ahead a little, to draw aside the veil of the future for a glimpse of what we might expect when we encountered Meldron. But nothing came to me; neither foresight nor vision was granted, so I let it go. Knowledge would come when the Dagda bestowed it and not before. So be it!

Now we stood watching Cynfarch's ships enter the bay—one of the nameless thousands of inlets and coves the sea had carved out of the hard rock face of the northern headland. This place should have a name, I thought, listening to the wave-wash and the distant rumble of thunder on the rising wind: *Cuan Doneann,* Storm Bay.

Llew, who had been standing at the water's edge talking to Bran, approached, his footsteps sounding crisp on the pebbled strand. "I am liking that man more and more, Tegid," he said, taking his place beside me.

"He will be a good battlechief for you," I said. "The Flight of Ravens will soar under his command. And he will follow wherever you lead, brother."

He let the observation pass without comment. "Have you seen anything of Ynys Sci?" he asked instead.

"Nothing yet," I confessed. "Be assured I will tell you if anything comes to me."

"Do you think it is a fool's errand?"

"Yes," I replied. "But what of that? We cannot stand aside if there is even the slightest chance we can save them."

"I hope it is not already too late," muttered Llew gloomily.

"What do you wish me to say? Tell me and I will say it!" I spoke more fiercely than I felt, mostly to rout out the uncertainty I heard creeping into Llew's voice. Uncertainty, like doubt and hesitancy, is a form of fear.

"I wish the truth," replied Llew. "What do you think we will find?"

"You wish the truth? Then I will tell you the truth: I do not know. Until we arrive on Sci, we do not know what we will find!"

"Calm yourself, brother," Llew said, pricked. "I was only asking."

"But I will tell you something else," I said, relenting somewhat.

"What is that?"

"If we succeed, it will be long before Meldron dares attack anyone else. And that is worth daring, I think."

Thunder boomed out over the water, and we listened to the echo rolling along the headland. "It will be rough sailing," Llew said, after a moment.

"All the better. They will not think to look for anyone sailing out of the storm."

There came a shout from the beach. "Come," said Llew, "we can board now. We must not be seen to lag behind."

We walked to the water's edge and splashed our way to the ship—Llew with his spear and shield, I with my staff of ash. The men surged behind us, streaming to the ships and clambering aboard. The voyage would be rough, but the ships would fly like gulls before the breaking storm.

And we did fly! Though the sea heaved and rolled under us and the sails strained and masts groaned, the ships' sharp prows sliced the foaming waves, cleaving them with powerful strokes. That day, and through the endless, turbulent night, we braved the high sea swell.

Dawn brought us within sight of our destination: the shimmering silver-green promontories of Ynys Sci rising above the slate-grey sea. Yet we did not put in to land but lowered the sails and waited for nightfall. The sun seemed fettered to the sky, so slowly did it advance. While the ships pitched in the waves, the men slept fitfully or sat idly stropping the edges of their swords. Overhead the cloud-wrack raced, flying to meet the horizon.

At last, half-hidden in the ragged grey cloud-cloak, tatters streaming, the sun sank below the rim of the world to begin its journey through the nether realms. Darkness gathered, pooling in the east and spreading over the water. When we could no longer be seen from the island, Llew gave the signal and the sails were raised.

We approached Ynys Sci from the east and put in at a cove that Llew knew. The warriors slipped over the side and struggled to shore where they walked about on unsteady legs in the darkness. The surf ran heavy and the coast was treacherous—sheer seacliffs tumbling to shallow, rock-strewn bays—so, when the last man had come ashore, the ships withdrew once more. We assembled on the narrow strand and began threading our way up through the scree-filled clefts. Upon reaching the top, we pressed inland to reach our position before morning.

We went without benefit of torchlight and we went with speed; many a man stumbled over the difficult trail in the dark. Llew led, finding his way unerringly over the rough terrain: three columns of men, hastening through the night to reach the appointed place ahead of sunrise.

The rugged track gave way to long sloping hills, the sibilant whisper of feet through grass the only sound of our passing. Across the hills, across small streams, across the high-humped back of the island we marched, arriving at our destination in good time. While the men rested in the glen and waited for dawn, Llew, Cynan, Bran and I mounted to the hilltop where we could overlook Scatha's settlement: a handful of warriors' lodges and small dwellings—cookhouses, granaries, huts and stores—clustered around a large, high-roofed hall.

I sat with my back to the hillside while the others lay on their bellies, peering over the crest of the hill and waiting as daybreak gradually illumined the site below.

"He is there and no mistake," Bran said. "The practice yard is filled with horses. Close to two hundred I make it."

"*Clanna na cù!*" Cynan swore softly. "He is an arrogant hound. Let us take him now."

"Easy, brother," cautioned Llew. "Scatha and the others come first. Tangling with Meldron will not help them."

"But he is unsuspecting, and we are ready to fight. He cannot escape, nor can he bring more men than he already has. I say, take him now. We could defeat him."

"More likely we would die trying," Llew said. "Think, Cynan, they outman us five to one. They would cut us down where we stood."

"We will never have a better chance," grumbled Cynan.

"Look," said Llew, "I despise Meldron as much as any man here. But getting ourselves killed for spite will serve no good purpose. There are hundreds at Dinas Dwr depending upon our return. We will do only what we came here to do. Agreed?"

Cynan agreed reluctantly and said, "What if he has killed them already?"

"I see no signs of battle," Bran reported. "I do not think there has been any fighting here."

"Unless he murdered them without a fight," Cynan pointed out. "He would do that."

I rolled onto my side and joined the others. "Meldron came here seeking something," I offered. "And he is still here."

"So he does not have the thing he came here to get—is that what you are saying?" Cynan wondered aloud. "Then we have not come too late." I heard him shift on the ground. "Llew, we will...Llew?"

Llew did not answer. I heard a rustling movement beside me and the quick light tread of feet moving away. In my mind's eye I saw Llew rise and stride to the crest of the hill. Clutching his spear in his left fist, Llew raised the spear over his head in a gesture of silent defiance. Dawn's red-gold radiance broke over him so that he seemed to glow with a glimmer of the Hero Light. He stood for a moment, then turned away, walking slowly back down the hillside to his waiting warband.

"What are you thinking, brother?" I asked as I joined him. There was a long hesitation in which I saw him leaning his forehead against the spear shaft. "Llew?"

"I am thinking that I may face my friend today," he replied. "Simon—Siawn—was once my friend, my closest companion—we ate together, lived together . . . I never dreamed it would come to this. I tell you the truth, Tegid; I do not understand it."

"It is well to mourn the loss of a friend," I soothed. "Grieve then, but do not be deceived. Those men down there have grown wicked in their greed. Their iniquity stains all of Albion with the blood of the innocent they have slain. The evil they have worked has made them vile, and it must be stopped. This day is the day we begin to make an end of it."

Llew replied softly, "I know . . . I know—and I am sick with it. It feels like a knife in my gut, Tegid. Simon was my friend!"

"Weep for your friendship, but do not weep for Siawn Hy. Know this: he has been against you from the moment you came here. He has ever served himself alone. He and Meldron are rabid beasts and must be destroyed."

I heard footsteps behind us, and recognized Cynan's tread. Llew straightened. "It is time," Cynan said. "The ships will reach the bay soon. We must move into position."

"Go to your men," I told him. "We will join you."

"There is no time to—"

"Just a moment more, Cynan. Please."

"Very well." Cynan moved away.

"What is it?" Llew asked when he had gone.

"I have been thinking," I replied. "About the Singing Stones."

"Yes?"

"If Meldron has brought the stones to Ynys Sci, then we must try to get them back. It sickens me that Meldron holds the Song of Albion and uses it as he does. We must reclaim the stones and establish them in Dinas Dwr, where we can guard them."

Before Llew could reply, there came a shout from Bran, who had remained on the hilltop. "They are coming!"

"We have to go now, Tegid." He made to turn away, but I reached out and caught at the sleeve of his siarc. "What is it?" he said impatiently.

"The Singing Stones," I replied with some urgency. "We must recover them."

"Yes, yes," he agreed hastily, "if that is possible. But if all goes well we will not engage Meldron in battle. We may not have a chance to search for the stones—and anyway, he probably has not brought them here."

"He keeps them with him always."

"How do you know?"

"I know Meldron," I replied.

"Look, Tegid, this is no time to discuss it. You should have said something sooner. We have to go. The ships are entering the bay."

"But if the Singing Stones are on Ynys Sci?"

"Then we will get them if we can," Llew promised. "All right?"

"Very well," I relented, and we turned to join the others.

The warband was split into two divisions—one to follow Cynan, and the other to follow Bran. Llew and I would go with Bran to the settlement, while Cynan led his men to the bay below Scatha's caer.

At a sign from Bran we moved off. Llew knew just how close we could advance without being seen. The hills behind the caer would shield us most of the way, and nearer to the dwellings there were fields of tall grain through which we could advance unobserved.

Silently we went. The thick, damp turf muffled the sound of our approach, and we crept down the hillside to the barley field, our hearts thumping in our chests. We stooped and entered the field, moving among the rows, heads low, backs bent, the leaves rattling as we passed.

We crouched among the brittle stalks, the smell of damp earth and dry grain full in our nostrils; we listened for any sound of discovery. But no cry of alarm greeted our approach, so we settled at the edge of the field to wait.

Our ships had not been idle. Crewed only by two men each, the ships had sailed around the eastern promontory to the southern bay which served as Ynys Sci's only harbor. At dawn the ships would enter the bay, their sails black in the morning light, a forest of spears lashed upright to the sides.

We had but to wait until Meldron's sentries saw the ships and raised the alarm.

22

The Rescue

The shouts came first—muted and indistinct. This was the first alarm as one of the watchers on his circuit discovered our invading ships, and it was quickly answered by a nearer cry.

Most of Meldron's warband must have been camped outside the hall, for the response was immediate. There came a quick clatter as men snatched up sword, spear and shield, and then the tramp of running feet as they raced to the clifftops. A moment later, men poured from the hall and from the warriors' houses, racing to join their swordbrothers gathering above the bay.

"I hope we have not misjudged Meldron's vanity," whispered Llew.

"Difficult to misjudge that," I replied. "Listen!"

Even as I spoke, the great battlehorn, the carynx, sounded its dire bellow. "There!" Llew said. "Get on with it, Meldron. Let it begin."

Hunkering in the field, we waited. The battlehorn blared again, and as the blast resounded in the hills around us, it was joined by the neighing of horses and the excited shouts of men. My dark inner eye kindled to life and brought forth the image of ranks of horses, jittery on pickets ranged in the yard beside Scatha's hall, and men, cloaks flying, weapons flashing, rushing to their mounts.

"Do you see him?" I asked.

"No," Llew answered, glancing at me quickly. "Do you?"

I shook my head. "No. Meldron is not among them."

The riders massed in the yard. The carynx boomed its dreadful call once more, and I heard the hollow drumming of horses' hooves as they galloped away.

This is what we had been waiting for. At a silent signal from Bran, Niall crept from the cover of the barley stalks and flitted across the narrow distance from the field to the nearest building, which was a granary. He paused briefly, and then disappeared around the corner of the storehouse. A moment later, he reappeared and motioned us forward.

In groups of three or four we crossed the open ground between the field and the storehouse. The yard was empty, the horses gone; there were no warriors to be seen.

Bran signalled again, and a heartbeat later we were bolting across the empty yard to the hall. A swift scramble around the wall brought us to the doorway of the hall. Bran and Niall were first, Llew and I among the last. We ducked around the near corner of the hall and collided with those who had gone ahead.

They were standing flat-footed, staring at something.

"What is it?" Llew said, pushing his way to the front of the throng. "Why have you stopped?"

I followed at Llew's back; he stepped beside Bran and, like all the others, froze in his tracks. I put out my hand and grasped his shoulder. He half-turned to me, his features twisted in revulsion.

"Llew?"

My inward sight shifted to the source of his distress: row upon row of spears driven half-down into the ground; and on the standing point of each spear the head of a young boy. Meldron had murdered the warrior-Mabinogi of Scatha's school and spiked their heads before the hall in a hideous mockery of a warrior's assembly. Crows had been at the heads and hollow eye-pits regarded us accusingly.

Llew turned from the atrocity and moved towards the doorway. But Bran caught him by the arm and stayed him. He motioned for the Ravens to join him and darted into the hall, sword gripped tight in his hard hand, shield held high and ready.

The Ravens followed on Bran's heels, and others pressed through, storming into the hall as quickly as possible to confront those within.

But Meldron was not there, and the two warriors he had left behind were quickly subdued—two swift spearthrusts silenced them. We then turned our attention to their prisoner.

Lowering his spear, Llew knelt beside the naked body lying on the blood-stained hearth. "Boru?"

To my surprise the apparent corpse opened its eyes; its lips framed a faint smile. "Llew…" The voice was a husky rasp. "You came…"

"He is still alive. Bring water." I ordered, and Niall hurried away.

I knelt beside Llew as Bran began to cut the leather straps binding the man's hands and feet. He had been bound and tortured. Long strips of flesh had been sliced from his stomach, thighs and back. His hair was singed off, where his head had been held in the flames. One side of his body was charred where it had been roasted at the hearth.

"Boru—listen, if you can," Llew said. "We do not have much time before Meldron returns. Where is Scatha?"

The man struggled to speak but could not make the words heard. Niall returned with a cup of water. "Take the men outside and await us there," Llew told him, and turned his attention to Boru. Bran gently lifted Boru's head and Llew tilted the cup. The unfortunate Boru swallowed some water, gagged and choked. When the spasm passed, Bran lowered the head to the hearth once more.

"Scatha…she—" he coughed and the cough became a gasp for breath.

"Yes, Scatha," Llew whispered. "Where is she, Boru?"

"…I knew you would come back…ahh," Boru smiled again, a rictus of agony. A black tongue poked out between the cracked lips. Llew wet his fingers and dripped water onto Boru's tongue.

"Where is Scatha? And her daughters? Boru, do you know where they are?"

Boru fluttered leathery eyelids and his tortured body convulsed. The paroxysm released him and he sighed so deeply I thought his spirit had flown. But Llew held him yet a little longer. Placing his hand and wrist stump on either side of Boru's face, he leaned close and said, "You are the only one who can help us now. Tell me, Boru: is Scatha alive?"

The eyelids struggled open, the eyes fiercely bright. "Llew . . . you are here . . ."

"Where is Scatha—and her daughters, Boru? Are they here? Are they alive?"

Boru stiffened, black tongue straining at the words. "The caves . . . the sea caves . . ." he rasped, and I think that voice came from beyond death, for even as Boru uttered the words his eyes clouded and his muscles slackened; he released his hold on life and it sped from him.

"Go to your rest, brother," Llew told him softly, and lowered Boru's burned and battered head gently to the hearthstone.

"The sea caves," Bran said. "Do you know them?"

"Yes. There are caves on the west side of the island. We rode there sometimes."

"Is it far?"

"No," Llew said, "but we need horses if we are to reach the place before Meldron."

Bran made a quick inspection of the hall, returning ashen-faced.

Llew looked at him. "What have you found?"

By way of reply, the battlechief indicated that we were to follow him. He led us to Scatha's chamber at the far end of the hall. Govan lay on the sheepskins of the bedplace, her mantle pushed to her hips. She had been raped; and, when her attackers tired of that sport, they had cut her throat. Her skin was white as the fleece beneath her, save where her blood had pooled and thickened. Her head was skewed sideways, glassy eyes staring upward.

Llew groaned and sagged against me.

"The body is cold," Bran said softly. "She was dead before we came here."

Llew started forward. I gripped his arm and restrained him. "There is no time. Let us save the living if we can."

He shook his arm from my grasp, stepped to the bedplace. With a trembling hand he straightened Govan's legs, first the right and then the left, and then pulled her mantle down to cover them. He folded her arms across her breast, gently straightened her head, and brushed his fingertips over her eyes to close them. He paused for a moment, looking down on her, and when he stepped away again, she appeared as if she might have been sleeping—but for the blood and the vicious slash below her chin.

Without another word, he strode from the chamber and started towards the door of the hall. Bran caught him at the threshold. "One man would stand a better chance," he pointed out. "I will go."

"You do not know where the caves are," Llew said. "We will go together." He turned to Niall, who stood waiting just outside. "Take the men back to the beach and wait for the ships. We will join you there."

"How will you join us?" I asked. Our ships, spears bristling from the decks, had sailed into the bay to draw Meldron's warriors away from the hall. When the enemy arrived at the bay to challenge the spurious invasion, our ships were to continue on around the island; again, as if seeking a suitable landing place for warriors. Meldron, we hoped, would give chase, allowing us time to rescue the captives. Cynan's force was to wait in hiding until the enemy withdrew, and then they were to destroy Meldron's ships. Their tasks accomplished, both forces were to return to the place where we had come ashore; there we would meet our ships which had completed the circuit of the island.

It appeared now that Meldron would be drawn away from the bay, as we had planned—but in the same direction Llew must go to find Scatha and her daughters. We could not rescue them without being seen, and we could not risk being seen.

"You cannot cross the island in daylight—it is too dangerous and the distance is too great."

"We have no other choice," snapped Llew, moving out into the yard. He glanced to the bay and the smoke rising from the beach where Cynan had put Meldron's fleet to the torch. "Unless Cynan can be stopped."

We ran to the cliffs above the bay. Six ships rode low in the water, their sails aflame and their hulls stove in. Cynan and his men were gone; they had performed their duty and departed.

"Too late," Llew said. "We might have used one of those ships."

"Go to the caves and stay there. We will send a ship to you at dusk."

Bran and Llew left the bay at a run. I turned to the Ravens. "Niall, you will lead the men back to the cove to await the ships," I told them. "And you—Garanaw, Emyr, Alun and Drustwn—come with me."

Niall and the warriors departed, and the remaining Ravens accompanied me back to the hall. Garanaw and Drustwn lifted Boru's battered corpse and I removed my cloak; I spread it on the floor and Emyr and Alun wrapped the body in it. While Garanaw and Drustwn carried Boru's corpse from the hall, I led Emyr and Alun to Scatha's chamber. We wrapped Govan in a fleece from the bedplace and followed Garanaw and Drustwn from the hall and back through the barley field. On the hill above the caer, the Ravens hacked a shallow grave in the earth with their swords. We laid the bodies side by side in the grave and quickly replaced the turf.

I glanced towards the bay, but could not see it from where we stood. Neither could I see anything of Meldron's war host. I turned to the hills, dappled grey and green with cloud shadow sliding over them; the movement would mask our own. With that last glimpse, blindness descended upon me once again and darkness quenched the image.

We made our way back across the hills and down the cliffs to the rocky little cove where we had come ashore at dawn. We joined the rest of the warband and gathered on the shingle to wait. Drustwn found a dry rock on which to perch and we sat down together.

"Cynan should have come by now," Drustwn said, after a while. He rose to pace the strand impatiently.

The wind held steady off the sea, and the waves surged and

sighed on the rocks. We waited.

Drustwn returned to stand over me. "Something has gone wrong," he said. "They should have been here long ago."

At these words, an image came into my mind: a ship, passing slowly along the rock-bound coast. In the same instant, a shout came from the strand: "A ship! A ship is coming!"

Drustwn darted away. He ran a few steps up the shingle, returning at once. "It is one of Meldron's," he said.

I tried to hold the image of the ship, but it faded before I could see more. The warriors on the beach raised a defiant clamor as the ship entered the cove, and readied themselves to fight. Taking up my staff, I rose and called Drustwn to me. "Tell me what you see," I said.

Even as I spoke, the furore from the strand turned from defiance to shouts of welcome. "It is Cynan!" someone called.

"Yes! Yes, it is Cynan," Drustwn confirmed. "He has taken one of Meldron's ships." There came another shout from the water's edge as a second ship came into view. "Another ship! He has taken two!"

"Board the men," I told him. "Quickly! We may yet make good this rescue."

Drustwn ordered the men aboard, then took my arm and led me as we waded out to the nearest ship; he helped me climb over the side and called for the ship to head out to sea once more. Even as he swung himself over the side, the ships were being turned and poled into deeper water.

Cynan met us. "Where is Llew?"

"He has gone to find Scatha," I answered, and told him what we had found at the hall. There were boys of his own clan among the slaughtered of Scatha's school.

"I will kill Meldron," Cynan vowed when I finished. "I will tear out his black heart with my hands."

"How did you fare at the bay?"

"It could not have been better," Cynan replied. "The ships were close in—eight of them; these were the best. We had but to wait until our own ships left the bay and Meldron had gone in pursuit. We broke open the hulls and set fire to the sails." He slapped the rail with his hand. "All except these two. They are larger and faster than any of ours. I could not resist taking them."

"It is well," I said, and told him where Llew and Bran had gone.

At this, Cynan whirled and shouted orders to the helmsman to make for the western side of the island. "The Great Hound has swallowed the bait," he said, turning back to me. "It may be that in his haste to catch the ships he will not look behind him."

"And if he does?"

"Well," Cynan allowed slyly, "he will see but two of his own ships giving chase to the invaders. By the time he recalls that he ordered no pursuit, we will be out of his reach."

If the short voyage along the coast to the bay below Scatha's caer seemed long, the journey from the bay to the west side of Ynys Sci seemed everlasting. With every passing moment, my anxiety mounted. The closer we came, the more disturbed I grew. I sent my thoughts ranging far and wide that I might discover what disturbed me so. But nothing came to me, and I lapsed more deeply into a brooding apprehension.

Drustwn's shout brought me sharply to myself once more. "There! I see them! Here!" he shouted from the rail. "Llew! Bran! Here!"

At the Raven's call, the darkness faded and my inward sight returned. Clutching one of the mast ropes, Drustwn stood upon the rail, frantically waving his free hand. I turned sightless eyes towards the land and scanned the shoreline.

The seacrags were ragged with tumbled, jagged rock, and puckered with treacherous coves. Several of these were little more than holes in the rock, others held caves large enough to hide a boat. Floundering towards us through waist-deep water came Llew with Goewyn in his arms. Bran followed in his wake with Scatha close behind.

A cheer rose from the throats of those gathered at the rail. But the cheer died in the air, for on the cliff above the struggling figures there appeared a line of enemy warriors. Instantly, fifty or more began descending the rocks while those on the seacliff above hurled spears at the figures fleeing through the surf.

"Closer!" cried Cynan. The helmsman made some reply that I did not catch. Cynan disregarded him. "Closer!" he shouted, pounding the rail with his fists.

Spears flashed down from the clifftops, plunging into the sea. Cynan leaned over the rail as far as he could and cupped his hands to his mouth. "Swim!" he shouted, his voice booming across the water. "Swim for it!"

Spears fell from on high, arcing through the air, striking the surface of the water, falling all around. And now the first of the enemy had reached the strand and plunged into the water in headlong pursuit.

The warriors aboard ship began shouting encouragement to Llew and Bran. Llew, with Goewyn clasped to him, stumbled and went down, drenching them both. He rose again at once, renewed his hold on Goewyn, and lunged on.

"They will never make it!" shouted Cynan, his face red, big hands smacking the rail.

The words were hardly spoken when the ship lurched to one side with a hollow thump. The keel had struck a rock. Men leaped to the rail with long poles and began pushing, fighting to hold the ship away from the rock. At the first hint of this trouble, shouts rang from the clifftops. Some of the more impulsive foemen loosed their spears on us. The missiles fell short, but not by much.

Cynan threw a leg over the rail and leaped into the water. The Ravens dived into the waves behind him, and others of his warband followed. The first met Llew and helped him to carry Goewyn to the ship. The rest followed Cynan to meet the foemen splashing towards them. Bran saw his men coming to him, turned, and sent Scatha on to the ship.

Llew and Niall reached the ship and lifted Goewyn to the rail; she was quickly hauled aboard. Llew followed. I hurried to the place where Llew knelt beside her.

Goewyn was only half conscious. She lay in a sodden heap against the hull, her breath coming in quick, shallow gasps. One side of her face was swollen and discolored; there were red welts on her throat, and her arms and the palms of her hands were raked with scratches, as if she had fought her way through gorse.

Scatha reached the ship, raised her arms to the men waiting to receive her and was lifted aboard. Her hands and arms were scratched as well, but I could discern no other damage. She knelt beside Llew. Someone offered a cloak which she unfolded and put over Goewyn. "Go now. I will tend her," she told Llew.

He stood and turned to me. Before he could speak there came the loud, angry blare of the carynx from the cliffs above. "It is Meldron!" someone shouted. He had seen the ships and had broken off his pursuit of the invaders to return here. One quick look told him everything. The battlehorn sounded again and hundreds of warriors joined their swordbrothers swarming down the rocks.

"Get this ship turned!" Llew shouted.

The men strained against the poles and the prow swung slowly away from the cove.

Cynan and the Ravens engaged the foemen. Swords slashed, spears thrust, and the weapon-clash sounded sharp among the rocks. Images wheeled before my inner eye: sunlight flashing on shield boss and swordblade; red blood staining sea-green water; bodies floating, the swell tugging at lifeless limbs; white-frothed waves surging around the legs of the combatants...

The foemen raged on the clifftops. White gulls shrieked as they whirled in the blue air. Niall called for the warriors to break off the attack. At once Emyr sounded the carynx and Cynan raised his sword and turned back to the ship. A few moments later, the men aboard were leaning over the rails and pulling their kinsmen from the sea.

My inward vision flared with the image of a man on horseback, seething with black rage: Meldron—furious at seeing his ships stolen, grinding his teeth in frustration at having been tricked and seeing his enemies make good their escape.

And I saw something else—Siawn Hy, sitting easily in the saddle. He, like Meldron, was watching our ship withdrawing beyond their reach. But unlike Meldron he was not angry; he was smiling. And the smile he wore was cruelly cold, and brutal beyond belief. I saw him lean forward and speak a word to Meldron, who turned to regard Siawn closely.

The serpent Siawn spoke again, and Meldron's countenance lightened. He swivelled in the saddle and called something to his warband. When he turned back, Meldron's scowl of anger was gone and his features were calm once more; a cunning light gleamed in his narrow eyes.

And from out of the warband emerged a rider: broad-shouldered and tall in the saddle. On his head he wore a bronze war cap; his shield was long, his sword naked against his thigh. Even before I saw his face, I knew the man—I would have known him by the way he sat his horse.

Paladyr!

23

Escape

"Paladyr!" shouted Llew. "Tegid! It is Paladyr!"

"I have seen him," I replied, and with my inner eye saw Meldron turn to his champion. Paladyr wheeled his horse and retreated from the edge of the cliff.

"Where has he gone?" wondered Llew. "Can you see, Tegid?"

"No." I answered, sick fear coiling in the pit of my stomach.

Cynan, dripping water and blood from a cut on his upper arm, came to stand beside us. "Where are the others?" he asked.

"Boru is dead," Llew told him. "And all the warrior-school with him." He lowered his voice. "Govan is dead, too. But I do not think Scatha knows yet."

"What of Gwenllian?"

"I do not know," Llew answered. "Scatha said they were taken when she refused to join Meldron's warband. She and Goewyn were able to escape."

"Perhaps Gwenllian escaped as well," Cynan offered hopefully.

At Cynan's words, terror struck me like a blow from behind. I swayed on my feet, and put a hand to the rail to steady myself, pressing the other hand to my head.

Llew saw me and grabbed my arm to keep me from falling. "What is it?" When I did not reply at once, he shook me by the shoulder. "Tegid, what is wrong? What is it? What has happened?"

I opened my mouth to speak, but a groan escaped instead. The groan rose to a wail. I could not stop it, nor did I try.

"Look!" shouted Bran. Llew and Cynan turned to the clifftop. Paladyr had returned and now stood at the edge of the seacrag with something across his shoulder.

"What is it? What has he got?" demanded Cynan.

"No . . ." murmured Llew, his voice cracking with pain.

Paladyr shifted his burden to the ground and jerked it upright. Though I already knew what he held, my heart sank.

"Mo anam!" swore Cynan.

Llew muttered an oath between clenched teeth; Bran cursed Meldron and all who rode with him; Scatha looked on in mute horror: her daughter stood swaying on the cliff-edge with Meldron's champion.

On the cliff above us, Paladyr seized the neck of the Banfáith's mantle in his hands and ripped it to the ground. Her hands were bound together at the wrists, and she struggled feebly. Paladyr struck her in the face with his fist. Her head snapped back and her knees gave way. She fell against Paladyr.

"Gwenllian!" cried Scatha.

The others might look away, but I could not shut out the vision from my inward eye. Each action passed before that unblinking stare, and I wished for my blindness again.

Paladyr took Gwenllian in his arms and, with his enormous strength, slowly raised her above his head. She writhed in his grasp and kicked her legs, but he held her high and, stepping to the very edge of the seacliff, hurled her over.

Gwenllian's scream was cut short as her body struck the rocks. Her spine broke on impact, arms and legs splayed wildly. The body, white against the black, sea-slick rocks, paused, rolled, and then slid into the water, leaving behind a gleaming trail of crimson.

"Gwenllian!" Scatha shrieked, and the cry trailed off in a sob.

I pressed my hands to my head to keep out the hateful sight, but my inward eye shifted to the clifftop and I saw Paladyr gazing grimly down into the water. Meldron said something to his champion and he turned to reply to his lord. Then Paladyr stooped, gathered up his victim's cloak and held it up for us to see. He let it slip from his hands and fall into the sea. Meldron wheeled his mount and withdrew then, but not Siawn Hy. He sat on his horse gazing down at the ships. And when he saw that we were looking up at him, he smiled and slowly raised his spear in a impudent salute.

Then he, too, withdrew and I saw only the image of a woman's fair-formed body floating lifeless in the sea swell...milk-white flesh bruised and broken...dusky red hair drifting with the seaweed in the gentle currents...wide green eyes faded, lips parted, mouth open and full of water...

The image dissolved in darkness like a black mist and blindness reclaimed me.

Leaving the enemy to rant and rage on the seacliffs, we turned the stolen ships and set sail along the western coast of Ynys Sci. Towards dusk we sighted our own ships. At first they made to flee before us, but Meldron's ships were faster and as we caught them up they knew us. Working the ships close—hull to hull in the rolling swell—we transferred warriors to the lighter vessels and turned towards the mainland.

Llew settled Scatha and her daughter in the wind shelter before the mast and asked me to tell them what we had seen of Govan's death. I related the grim facts of her suffering and told of her burial. Goewyn clutched her cloak to her face and wept bitterly. For her part, Scatha bore her loss without tears and with great dignity.

"Thank you, Tegid Tathal," Scatha said, and then turned to comfort Goewyn. "Leave us now. Please."

The wind remained brisk and steady across the strait and we reached a protected inlet on the northern coast of Caledon with the dawn. We made landfall to rest and to assess the next part of our plan. When the men had been settled, Bran, Cynan, Llew and I gathered a little apart on a grassy knoll above the white sand beach. The sough of the tidewash on the beach made a most melancholy song.

"The blood debt is heavy, and Meldron will pay," Cynan declared bluntly. "It will be some time before he can leave that island. I say we should attack him now and destroy his support at the root."

"I agree," said Bran. "Strike now while his main strength is elsewhere. We may not have another chance like this again."

Cynan and Bran discussed the prudence of this course and Llew listened to their counsel. Then I felt Llew's brushing touch on my arm. "Well, Tegid? What do you say?"

"What is there to say that has not been said? We have delivered Meldron a hurtful blow. By all means, let us take the battle to him."

Llew heard the disapproval in my reply and asked, "What is the matter, Tegid? What is wrong?"

"Have I said that anything is wrong?"

"No, but I can tell." He nudged my arm with his wrist stump again. "What is it? Do not make us guess."

"The Singing Stones—" I began.

"Oh, yes," he said irritably. "What about them?"

"Attack Meldron's stronghold—well and good," I replied. "But it is wasted effort if we do not reclaim the stones."

"You said he carried them with him everywhere," Llew pointed out.

"I said I thought it likely. But since we could not search Sci, I think we should search his stronghold."

Bran interrupted this exchange, asking, "These singing stones you are talking about—they must be very valuable. Yet, I have never heard of them."

Cynan said, "Tell him, bard. I have heard the tale before, but I would hear it again."

I assented, pausing briefly to gather the words.

"Before the sun and moon and stars were set in their unchanging courses, before living creatures drew breath, from before the beginning of all that is or will be, the Song of Albion was sung. The Song upholds this worlds-realm, and by it all that exists is sustained. The Song is the chief treasure of this worlds-realm and not to be despoiled by small-souled creatures or unworthy servants."

Having begun, the words formed on my tongue of their own accord and flowed on in the song-style of bards:

"Meldryn Mawr, the Great King, like Prydain's mighty kings before him, defended the Song through the long ages of our clan's supremacy. Deep beneath the mountain fortress of high Findargad, Albion's Phantarch, High One, slept his enchanted sleep, secure behind the bulwark of a True King.

"But the Worm of fiery breath bit deep and corruption flowed from the bite. The kingship of Prydain sickened with rot and decay. Righteous sovereignty declined; the Defender faltered, and the enemies of the Song seized the day. The Phantarch was killed to silence the Song, but his strength was the strength of the Song of Albion itself, and his craft endured. Though the Phantarch, Bard of Bards, went down to death, the Song was saved."

Bran professed himself mystified as to how this could be. "That is what I wondered when I heard it, too," Cynan told him. "But just listen." To me he said, "Go on."

"You know the tale," I told him. "You tell it."

"Gladly," replied Cynan; I heard the zeal in his voice. "This is the way of it," he said. "With strong enchantments the Phantarch bound the Song to the very stones that killed him. Even as his life sped from him, the Wise One breathed the precious Song to the stones that became his tomb. He did this so that the Song of Albion would not be lost." He finished, saying, "Have I remembered it right?"

"Word for word," I replied.

"Forgive me," Bran said, "but there is something I do not understand. If Meldron sought to silence the Song, why does he hoard the Singing Stones? Would he not destroy them now that he has the chance?"

"You are perceptive, Bran," I remarked. "You have struck to the very heart of the matter."

"Enlighten me if you can," the battlechief said.

I began to make a reply, but Llew answered instead. "All this has come about by Siawn Hy," he said. "He is not of this world. He is a

stranger here, as I am. But unlike me, Simon—that is his name in my
world—did not believe in the power of the Song of Albion. He
thought that by silencing the Phantarch, he could usurp the power
for himself—at least, that is what he persuaded Meldron to do."

"Thus, for a time, the Song was silenced," I said. "Without the
Song to prevent its escape, the Cythrawl, Creature of the Pit, was
loosed. Chief Bard Ollathir, at the cost of his life, banished the
hellspawn—but not before it had summoned Lord Nudd, Prince of
Uffern, and his Demon Horde to wreak destruction on the people of
Prydain for daring to protect the Song. Through many bitter trials
we endured; and the ancient enemy was defeated before the gates of
Findargad."

Cynan could not keep silent any longer. "Llew performed the
Hero Feat upon the wall," he cried, and told how we had found the
Singing Stones and how, by inspiration of the Chief Bard's awen,
Llew had used them to save Albion. "And Nudd and the vile
Coranyid were driven back to Annwn."

"After the battle, we collected the fragments of the song-bearing
stones," Llew explained. "And Meldron took them."

"We did not know what he was planning at the time, or we would
not have allowed it," I said. "But Meldron had seen the power of the
stones and he thinks now to use that power to establish himself
Supreme King of Albion."

"Not while I live and breathe," Bran vowed. "I will never see him
High King."

"Nor I," added Cynan. "I say we shall not rest until we have freed
the Singing Stones from the Great Hound's grasp."

We talked of this and other things, and then Bran and Cynan
returned to their men. When they had gone, I said, "You did not say
what you think of attacking the Great Hound's stronghold: Cynan
spoke, and Bran, but you withheld your approval. Do you disagree?"

"No," he allowed, "the time is right. Meldron is stranded on Ynys
Sci—he will have his hands full repairing his ships."

"We can reclaim the stones and return to Dinas Dwr before he
floats a seaworthy hull," I said. "Why do you balk at that?"

"I do not balk, Tegid," he replied, bristling. "I just think that all this talk about the stones is ill-advised."

"How so?"

"We have enough to worry about without bringing the Singing Stones into it. Anyway, Meldron probably takes them with him wherever he goes—you said so yourself. It is a waste of time and nothing will come of it."

"Then why do you fear finding them?"

"Did I say I feared them?" he snapped. "Go ahead—look all you want if it will make you happy."

"Llew," I said, trying to soothe him. "It must be done. This will not be over until we have regained the Stones of Song and—"

"Tegid, this will not be over until Simon is back where he came from!"

He stormed away then, and stayed away from me the rest of the day. That night, as the campfires leapt high and bright, I sang *Pwyll, Prince of Prydain*, a worthy tale. Scatha and her daughter slept in one of the ships, and we slept under heaven's lights. We rose before dawn, and as the sun began its journey across the blue sky-vault, we began our voyage south to Prydain.

Maffar, Fairest of Seasons, blessed us with calm seas and steady winds. Our ships flew like gulls, skimming the glassy green seas. We camped in coves along the coast at night, and sailed through the long day following. We observed deserted habitations and unplowed fields along the coast, and occasionally someone would glimpse the flickering form of a wolf loping over the hills. Hawks, foxes, wildfowl and other creatures were sighted, but of human occupants we had no sign.

Prydain remained a wasteland. Meldron, instead of doing all in his power to revive the noble land of our people, had only deepened the desolation wrought by Nudd and the Coranyid. For he had spread devastation to the places hateful Nudd had never reached; now Llogres and Caledon bled beneath his cruel rapacity.

I wondered at this. Indeed, I had considered it long and often. Why had wicked Nudd attacked only Prydain? Why had Caledon and Llogres escaped untouched? Was Prydain somehow more vulnerable than the other two realms?

Perhaps the reason was something to do with the Phantarch and the Song. Or perhaps some other explanation remained to be discovered.

Nevertheless, the desolate land left me desolate as well. I felt the emptiness of all those empty hearths, and all those abandoned habitations. I felt the weight of sorrow for all Prydain's dead: unmourned, unburied, and unknown, save to the Dagda alone. As our voyage neared its end, I lapsed into a dolor as bleak as any I have known. The waste, the cruelty, the predation, anguish and distress could not be faced except through misery.

Scatha, in her sorrow, longed for some small comfort from me. But I could say nothing to her. How could I ease her loss when all of Prydain cried out to me for a healing word and I knew none to give? Before such terrible travail I stood mute. There was nothing I could say which would redeem the ruin, or lessen the loss.

Sorrow and be sad, deep grief is granted Albion in triple measure, the Banfáith had said. Ah, Gwenllian, your word was ever true.

24

Vale of Misery

"Let me do this," Cynan said. "I welcome it."

Llew was about to object yet again, but Bran spoke up. "The risk is great, but Cynan is right, it is just the sort of plan that will work."

"And if it fails?" Llew asked.

Bran shrugged. Cynan said, "Then you can attack the caer. But if it succeeds, we will have saved many lives."

Llew turned to me. "What do you think, Tegid?"

"Why take by force what we might achieve by stealth?" I turned to Cynan. "But do not go alone; take Rhoedd with you."

"Very well," Llew relented, "since there is no preventing you, you may as well go. We will await you here. If there is trouble, get out. You know the signal."

"I know, I know," Cynan assured him. "We have talked until even the horses know the signal. All will be well, brother. If the stones are there, I will find them."

Cynan and Rhoedd armed themselves and we bade farewell. Llew and Bran watched from hiding as the two made their way up to Caer Modornn. Inner sight was denied me, so I leaned on my staff and waited. The day was warm, the air still. I smelled the potent earthscent of leaf mould, rotting wood and damp soil. We had hidden ourselves in the shrubby seclusion of the river below Caer

Modornn—near enough to see without being seen—ten men only; the rest were camped a short distance away, well out of sight.

"They are at the gates," Bran reported in a little while. "The guards have challenged them. There are men on the wall."

"Cynan is talking to them," Llew said. "That is a good sign. He can talk the legs off a table."

"The gates are opening," Bran added. "There are men coming out—three...no, four men. That one—do you see him?" Bran asked Llew. "The dark one speaking to Cynan now—"

"I see him," Llew answered.

"That is Glessi. He is a Rhewtani chieftain—that is, he was once. He seems to have found a home with Meldron. I am not surprised; he was always slippery as an oiled snake."

"What is happening now?" I asked.

"They are still talking," Llew answered. "The one called Glessi seems to be thinking it over. He crosses his arms over his chest...he scratches his beard. He is making up his mind. Cynan is talking—I wish I could hear what he is saying." He paused and then added, "But whatever it is, it seems to be working. They are going into the caer. There!"

I heard a light slap of a hand on a shoulder or arm. "He has done it!" Llew said. "He is in."

"Now we wait," Bran replied. "I will take the first watch."

Llew rose and led me back to the river bank to sit with the Ravens. We settled among the hawthorn and willow scrub. Some dozed, others talked quietly. I sank once more into the dull reverie that had held me since coming ashore in Prydain six days ago.

A somber journey south along the western coast had brought us to Muir Glain, the wide, silver sweeping estuary east of ruined Sycharth where Meldryn Mawr had maintained his shipyards. In the time since I had last visited the place, thickets of briar and birch had grown where ships' hulls had been fashioned of strong oak. Nettlebeds flourished where woodchips once drifted deep as snow.

We sailed into the estuary and up the river as far as we could, and then anchored the ships where the water became too shallow. We established camp in a wooded glade and left the main body of our warband there. Taking forty with us, we moved deeper into the Vale of Modornn the next morning, leaving the rest behind to guard the ships.

Scatha was not of a heart to travel with us, so she remained behind to look after Goewyn, whose injuries required care. All that first day, and five days more, we followed the gleaming river north through the broad glen. When we came near the settlement, we left thirty men within hailing distance and then advanced to our position below the caer.

Meldron had determined to build his stronghold on the site of the old wooden caer which served northern Prydain. Caer Modornn was only ever used in times of war; it had never been a settlement. And, though I had once counselled Meldron against occupying it, I could see now why he insisted. A king interested in restoring Prydain would have been better served by a southern fortress open to the commerce of the sea.

But Meldron had loftier ambitions. The Great Hound of Havoc meant to have the whole Island of the Mighty. And Caer Modornn sat in a convenient position for a warband raiding into Llogres and Caledon. Oh, if I had known his intent—if I had known how deep was his treachery, and how great his greed, I would have destroyed him as one exterminates a vicious dog.

How many warriors slept in turf houses now because of him? How many women wept for their men at night? How many children cried for their mothers? If I had known what he had hidden in his heart, I would have slain him gladly. But, whether gladly or with profound regret, I should have killed him before he defiled the land with his corruption.

From our hiding place we had watched the caer and discussed our best approach to the problem of finding the Singing Stones. Cynan had argued for a simple but audacious deception: marching up to the gates and demanding the hospitality due to wandering warriors.

"They do not know me," he had said. "I will go alone with

Rhoedd. They will not take alarm at but two warriors at their gates. We are no threat to them."

"I do not like it," Llew had objected, thinking it foolhardy and reckless.

"But that is precisely why it will work, brother. They will never suspect our true purpose," Cynan had said. After more discussion, he had won his way. And now we waited.

The day faded slowly. I felt the cool nightbreath on my skin and heard the nightsong begin in the branches and undergrowth around me as dusk deepened to evening. Then I heard the light tread of footsteps and sat up.

"There is no sign," Bran said softly.

"I will take the next watch," said Llew. I heard the slight rustle of his clothing as he rose and started away.

Bran took Llew's place beside me and night thickened around us. "It will be dark soon," Bran said after a while. It came into my mind that he was looking at me, and it seemed to me that I felt the subtle shift of his eyes as his glance touched my face.

"Yes?" I asked. "What is it you are wanting to ask?"

He chuckled dryly. "You know I am staring at you," he said. "But how is it that you know?"

"Sometimes I imagine what is happening and I may be wrong," I told him. "But sometimes I see things in here," I touched my forehead with a fingertip, "and I see more than I could have imagined."

"As you did at Ynys Sci?" he asked.

"Yes," I said, and told him about meeting Gofannon in the sacred grove. "Since then," I said, "it seems that when sight is required, sight is granted. But it comes and goes as it will; I cannot command it."

We passed the early evening talking together. Niall came with bread and dried meat from our provisions. We ate and talked some more, and then Bran called Alun Tringad to take the next watch. I slept, but lightly, and the watchers alternated through the night.

I awakened to Emyr's urgent whisper. "The gate is open," he said. I rose at once. Bran was already on his feet.

"Wake the others—and tell Llew to join us." Bran told him. He hurried to the lookout place, and I followed. I heard the creak and snap of small twigs as Bran bent back the branches for a better look.

"What do you see?"

"The gate is—" he began, then said, "Someone is moving. They are coming this way."

"Is it Cynan?"

"I cannot see—it is too dark and he is too far away. But it must be. He is coming this way." He paused, then said, "No, it is Rhoedd, I think."

We waited, and but a few moments later heard rapid footsteps. "Here! This way!" whispered Bran sharply. "Where is Cynan?"

Rhoedd's voice answered him. "Lord Cynan will follow soon. He sent me ahead to open the gate and rouse everyone. We may have to move quickly when he comes."

"Why?" Llew asked, taking his place beside me. "What is he doing?"

"We found the place where the stones are kept. There is no guard, but there is a door and it is chained. He is going to break down the door and get them."

"He is mad! He will never be able to carry them alone," Llew said. "Someone will have to go up and help him."

There came a shout from the direction of the caer. A hound began barking with some ferocity, and more quickly took up the cry. And then we heard the night-shattering roar of the carynx.

"Well," grumbled Llew, "that has torn it!" I heard the whisper of his sword as he drew it. "We are in for it now. Get ready."

"Look!" said Bran. "Someone is coming. It is Cynan. He is free!"

But a moment later I heard the sound of footsteps pounding down the hill towards us. "Run for it!" he called as he came nearer. "They are after me!"

He did not say more, nor did he need to. For, even as he spoke, a great clamor issued from the direction of the caer: dogs barking, men shouting, weapons clattering.

"This way!" shouted Bran.

A hand seized my arm. "Follow me!" Llew said.

We ran to the river and plunged headlong into it. One way or another we floundered across and gathered on the far side. "They will search the thickets first," Bran said. "If we stay on this side we might lose them."

"Go north," I said.

"Our men are south," Rhoedd pointed out.

"Unless we want a battle on our hands, it would be better to lead them away from our men," I explained. "We can return by another way."

"We must get free first," said Alun. "Let us go while we can!"

"Where are the stones?" asked Llew.

"They were not there," Cynan said, catching his breath. "Meldron must have taken them with him."

"Are you certain?"

"Why do you think I smashed the box?" Cynan puffed.

"You smashed the box?"

"Of course," replied Cynan. "I had to make sure."

"Come on!" urged Bran. "Talk later!"

While the searchers beat the thickets behind us on the opposite side of the bank, we slipped into the brushy undergrowth and pushed our way north. At first it seemed as if we would elude them easily, but some of the searchers came across the river where the dogs picked up the scent and raised a howl.

Then it was a matter of outrunning them. Over rocks and under low trees we raced, branches whipping our faces and snatching our sleeves and cloaks. Bran led the way, setting a punishing pace, the sound of pursuit loud in our ears. Stumbling, falling, tripping over every root and rock, I blundered on. Llew and Garanaw ran beside me, hauling me upright when I fell, keeping me on my feet—all but carrying me along.

Gradually, the sounds behind us diminished as we outpaced our pursuers. When we came to a fording place, Bran led us back across the Modornn and we continued our flight on the other side. We crossed the river twice more for good measure, and dawn found us far north of the stronghold. We stopped to listen, and heard nothing.

"I think they have turned back," Cynan said. "We can rest now."

But Bran would not hear of it. "Not yet," he said, and led us to a high heathered bluff rising to the east some distance away; there we could watch the glen while we rested. We sat in the heather or lay on the rocks and waited for strength to return.

"Well," said Llew after a while, "must we pull it out of you? What happened back there?"

Cynan roused himself. "I wish you could have seen me," he said. "I was brilliant." He called to Rhoedd. "I was brilliant, was I not?"

"That you were, lord," Rhoedd replied. "Truly."

"Tell us your feat," prodded Alun Tringad, "so that we can properly appreciate this brilliance of yours."

"And then," put in Drustwn, "we can laud your achievement properly."

"Not that you need our help," added Emyr. "You seem more than able yourself."

Cynan drew himself up. "Listen to this," he said, "and prepare to be amazed."

"Get on with it!" cried Llew.

"Rhoedd and I went up to the caer together," he began. "We walk easy—two wayfaring warriors, who knows the difference, hey?"

"Yes, yes," said Alun, "we know all that. We saw you. Tell us what happened when you got inside."

"Rhoedd and I went up to the caer together," Cynan repeated firmly. "And here am I, thinking what I might say to the gatemen to get us inside the fortress. We are walking along and I am thinking—"

"We know this!" complained Alun. "They opened the gates and let you in. Then what happened?"

Cynan ignored him. "We are walking along and I am thinking. I say to Rhoedd, 'You know, Rhoedd, these men are used to lies. I suspect they are lied to from first light to last by Meldron and his brood.'

"'A most astute observation, Lord Cynan,' says Rhoedd to me. 'Most astute.'"

The Ravens groaned, but Cynan ignored them and continued. "'Therefore,' say I to Rhoedd, 'I will tell them the truth. I will tell them exactly what has happened to Meldron, and they will be so astonished they will ask us to come in and join them at table, just so that they can hear the tale.' So that is what I did.

"We are walking to the gate, see, and we are close now, and they spy us. 'Halt!' they call out from the wall. 'Who are you? What is your business here?' And so I tell them: 'I am Cynan ap Cynfarch and I have just come from Ynys Sci. I have word of your Lord Meldron.'"

"What did the gateman say?" asked Garanaw. The Ravens were warming to the tale.

"What does the gateman say?" chuckled Cynan, "He says, '*Our* Lord Meldron.' So I say, 'Man, are you telling me there is another Lord Meldron in this worlds-realm?' Did I not say it just like that, Rhoedd?"

"Just like that, lord," Rhoedd affirmed. "Word for word."

"Well, our man has to think about it for a moment, and then he calls for men—to help him think, I imagine. And we stand there bold as day, moving not so much as a hair. Then the gate opens and four of them come out to us. There is one with a great spreading moustache—"

"Glessi is his name," offered Bran.

"That is true," Cynan agreed. "Our Glessi frowns and smacks his chest and, 'What is this about Meldron?' he says, and, 'Who are you anyway?' Not fettered by manners is our man. So I tell him I bring tidings from his lord and he has no other choice than to welcome me properly. 'What do you want?' he says.

"'What do I want?' say I. 'I want a cool drink and a hot meal and a place at the hearth for my bed—that is what I want.' He frowns some more—our Glessi is a powerful frowner—and he says, 'Well, if you have come from Meldron, I suppose you had best come in.' And what do we do then, Rhoedd?"

"We march in proud as you please," Rhoedd answered brightly, relishing his part in the tale.

"Then what happened?" Llew asked.

"Well, they fetch the cups quick enough, and we drink and talk a while. 'What is it like in Sci?' they ask, and so I tell them: 'The weather is fine; the air is pleasant.' They say to me, 'Glad we are to hear it. But what of Meldron?' I say to them: 'Friends,' I say, 'you are fortunate indeed to be where you are, and not where your lord is tonight.'

"'How so?' they ask.

"'I tell you the truth,' I say, 'it is not good with Meldron in Sci. He has been attacked. Six of his ships have been wrecked and two stolen. Long he will be repairing even one of them to take him off that island.'"

"What do they say to that?" asked Niall.

"What do they say? They say, 'Terrible! Most unfortunate!' What do I say? I say to them, 'Aye, terrible it is. We escaped with our lives and came as soon as we could.' Cynan laughed, and the Ravens laughed with him. "They thanked us for telling them, did they not, Rhoedd?"

"That they did, Lord Cynan. That they did."

"Well, we eat our supper then, and drink some more—I make certain the cups keep moving, see—and all the time I am watching what they do and where they go. I tell them I have to pee and Rhoedd and I go outside. We walk around a little, but it is dark by this time and I do not see very much. But I do see a storehouse near the hall, and it has a door that is chained. When I go back, I pull Glessi aside and say, 'Meldron must have much treasure to fill so large a storehouse.'"

"You said that?" asked Bran.

"I did," declared Cynan. "And our Glessi is careless in his cups; he makes bold to boast. 'Treasure!' he cries. 'It is nothing less than the Song Stones of Albion. Most rare and powerful, they are, and most valuable. Their foremost virtue is invincibility in battle.' He tells me this, and more besides. Well, I have only to wait until they are asleep; then Rhoedd and I leave the hearth, slip out to the storehouse and get ourselves inside. And there is the box: wooden it is, and bound with iron bands and chains."

"What did you do?" asked Drustwn.

"Tell him, Rhoedd."

"Lord Cynan sent me to open the gate. He said, 'Rhoedd, I fear I must make a great noise. We must be ready to fly.' So I went to the gate and opened it and came to rouse you."

"I watch him from the door," Cynan continued. "And when he has the gate open, I take up the box. It is heavy, yes—but I am thinking it is not as heavy as it should be. I get it up in my arms and I take it outside and I heave it up high and hurl it against the water trough in the yard. Oh! the noise!"

"And then?" Llew demanded. "What did you see?"

"I see that the box has not broken. I must throw it again. So up it comes and down it goes, and—crash!—the box smashes into pieces. And here am I, on hands and knees, pawing through the splinters. And what do I find?"

"What *do* you find?" said Alun impatiently. "Get on with it, man."

But Cynan was not to be rushed. "I am looking for the Singing Stones. I am looking, but I am not seeing them. What am I seeing?"

"Cynan!" cried Llew. "Spit it out!"

"I am seeing sand," Cynan announced. "Nothing but clay and sand from the river bank—that is what I am seeing! The stones were not in the box. Here! See for yourself." I heard a movement and the light patter of sand poured upon stone.

"This is what was in the box?" Llew asked.

"Nothing else," Cynan assured him.

Llew took my hand and stretched it out, palm up. He filled my hand with a dry, gravelly substance. I lifted it to my face, sniffed it. It smelled of wood and soil. I shook it from my hand and touched a fingertip to my tongue: mud.

"That is my tale," Cynan concluded. "I would that it had a better end to it, but there it is."

"Perhaps they are hidden somewhere else," suggested Bran.

"No," I told him. "We will not find the stones at Caer Modornn. Let us return to the ships and go home."

"We cannot go back the way we came," said Llew. "We will have to go around the caer to the west."

"All the better," I said. "We will spy out the land and see how Prydain fares under Meldron's reign."

We bent our way west, away from the river and, once we were out of sight of the caer, we turned south and soon came to a settlement—although it was in truth no more than a handful of miserable mud-and-twig huts beside the turgid trickle of a shallow stream. Yet more than seventy people lived in the close-cluster of stinking hovels—Mertani clansmen whose king and nobles had been conquered and killed. Seventy ill-clothed and underfed wretches. In the guise of offering them sustenance, Meldron had made them slaves.

A starving dog barked as we entered the holding, alerting the inhabitants who emerged from the huts as we came near. At the yapping of the dog, my inner vision kindled and I saw the place we had come to. Half-naked children, barefoot and big-eyed, lurked behind their slump-shouldered parents. Everyone wore the grim, hollow look of people whose lives have become a burden they can no longer bear.

Cynan addressed the chief of the holding, a man named Ognw, who told how they were forced to work the fields but were denied the proceeds of their labor. "Meldron takes it all," he complained, the people muttering darkly behind him. "He gives us the leavings. Nothing more."

"Yet you can hunt in the woods," Bran pointed out. "There is no need to go hungry."

"Oh, aye, we are allowed to hunt," Ognw replied bitterly, "but we have no spears or knives."

"Why?" asked Cynan.

"Weapons are forbidden to us," the chief muttered. "Have you ever tried to bring down a stag with nothing but your two bare hands? Or a wild pig?"

"We get no meat," one of the onlookers volunteered. "We get only mouldy grain and sour curds."

A man with one eye described how the king sent warriors to seize the harvest even as it was gathered. "They say we will be given all the grain we need for the asking," the man said, scoffing. "We ask— oh, yes, we ask. But we receive spit." He spat on the ground.

"Two of our kinsmen went to the king for meat," Ognw added. "Three days later their bodies were brought to us for burial. They told us our kinsmen had been attacked by a wild animal."

"There was no wild animal," the one-eyed man said, "only Meldron."

"Meldron takes everything for himself," a woman told us. "He takes it all, and gives nothing back."

We left them and continued our circuit of the land. The nearer to Caer Modornn we came, the closer together the settlements became. At each holding we saw the same appalling hardship and squalor, and heard a similar tale of distress: the king's demands, the king's desires, the king's deceits fuelled their suffering. Meldron had turned the wide, generous Vale of Modornn into the Vale of Misery. The people groaned under the weight of their affliction.

As we listened to their desperate pleas, it became abundantly clear to me how Meldron had fared so well in his dealings with the kings of Llogres. Those weaker than himself he attacked; the stronger kings he wooed and won with lavish gifts and over-generous alliances and trade agreements. All this, to the hurt of the people.

Even the Llwyddi, Meldron's clansmen—and my own!—did not escape the torment of their cruel lord. The Llwyddi fared no better than the cattle they herded in the wooded hills. With my inward eye, I saw my own blood kin, and I no longer knew them!

"Tell us our crime," demanded one of the men, a kinsman who had served Meldryn Mawr faithfully, and had endured the horror of Nudd and the privations of Findargad. "Tell us what we have done to deserve this. Our cattle are treated better than we are—and if anyone dare touch them he must answer to Meldron."

A sunken-cheeked woman with a naked, sickly babe clinging to her breast stretched a hand towards us. "Please, lord, help us.

We are dying here."

Cynan turned to Llew. "Well, will you give the order, brother, or will I?"

"I will do it," Llew replied, "and gladly."

Llew turned to the Ravens. "Drustwn, Emyr, Alun," he called, "bring the cattle here. They will be slaughtered for meat. Garanaw and Niall, bring wood and prepare a fire." Then he told the people, "Today you will feast until you can hold no more."

But the people were horrified. "No!" they shrieked. "If Meldron finds out, he will kill us!"

"Meldron will not find out," Cynan assured them. "He is gone and will not soon return. And when he does you can tell him that Llew and Cynan killed the cattle to spite him."

The cattle were gathered in from the hills; the fire was kindled. Three cows were slaughtered, and the rest of the herd was driven to the surrounding settlements. At each place, cattle were killed to feed the people. Though they welcomed the meat, they still feared Meldron's wrath, and that cast a shadow of gloom over the feasting.

"We should not linger here any longer," Bran warned. "We have done all we can for them."

"Yet I would do more," Llew said. He turned to me. "Can we take them with us, do you think?"

"If they will come. But I do not think they will leave their hovels."

Cynan disputed this, saying, "Not leave? If you were slave to Meldron would you stay even a moment longer if someone offered you freedom?"

"Offer then," I replied.

This Cynan and Llew did; they made the offer of freedom to any and all who would take it. None would join us, however; all preferred to stay in their huts, wretched though they were—and they were loathly indeed. And though we argued long, we could not persuade them that we would not turn against them as Meldron had done. We could not make them see that it was life we offered, not the living death they knew.

Their refusal to leave their slavery saddened me more than

anything I had seen. My soul cried out in grief sharp-pointed as an enemy's blade. I could have wept for their stupidity. But Meldron had so cowed and confused them that they could no longer think or feel like human beings. They did not understand that we offered a return to freedom and dignity. How could they understand? These words had ceased to have any meaning for them.

We made the offer of freedom at the next small holding. Again we were rebuffed. Without so much as a word, the chief led us to the top of the hill behind the settlement where there stood a small cairn. We wondered at his manner, leading us there, but our approach sent a flurry of crows squawking into the air and we saw that the cairn was not stones heaped high, but a mound of skulls. Many had sun-dried flesh still clinging to them, and hanks of matted hair. The birds had been doing their work, however, and clean bone gleamed white and hard in the sun.

I was spared the sight, but I did not need to see it to feel the outrage of the act. Llew described it to me well enough, and then turned to the chief, "What happened here?" Llew asked gently.

"Meldron judged the harvest too small. He accused us of keeping some back," the man explained. "When he could not find the grain he said we had hidden, he began murdering the people. He left us this, so we would not forget."

"Man," said Cynan, "will you not come with us now?"

"And give Meldron another excuse to kill?" the man replied. "If he caught us, none would be left alive this time."

"You will be safe with us," Bran told him.

The man scoffed grimly. "There is no man safe as long as Meldron lives."

"This sickens my heart," Cynan declared. "Let us go from here."

Llew agreed reluctantly. "We can do nothing more for them, and to stay any longer will increase the danger to ourselves."

We left the Llwyddi settlement behind and camped in the woods a short distance away from Caer Modornn. As soon as it was daylight, we skirted the stronghold and made for the estuary where our ships waited. We joined our warband where we had left them,

and set out for the ships. Though the sun shone on us each day, it did
not warm us or lighten our spirits; Prydain had become bleak and
cheerless as a fen. The knowledge of Meldron's wickedness soured
our souls, so that even in bright daylight the trail seemed dark and
brooding.

We raised sail the moment we boarded, and left Prydain on the
outflowing tide. Sadly, we had achieved but little of what we had set
out to do. Gwenllian, Govan, Boru, and all the young of Scatha's
school were dead. The song-bearing stones were still beyond our
reach. Nevertheless, we had saved Scatha and Goewyn. And, truly,
we had dealt Meldron a blow which he would not soon forget.

That might have been reason enough to rejoice. Yet it was not
jubilation, but sorrow which accompanied our return to Caledon. Our
hearts were heavy-laden with the dead weight of misery we had
witnessed in Meldron's realm. Every man among us lamented the
distress of that tormented land, and every man, each in his own way,
vowed to avenge it.

25

Dinas Dwr

In Caledon, in the far-hidden north, the secret realm grew. An acorn sprouting, sinking its taproot deep, its slender wand of a trunk shooting up, branches forming, new leaves spreading in glossy clusters...a mountain oak. That was Dinas Dwr, an oak of the mountains; young and green, but growing strong. In far-hidden Caledon, in Dinas Dwr, we were becoming a people.

The toil was staggering: land cleared for crops; cattle bred for stock and raised for herds; dwellings built to house our growing population; ore dug from the hills for copper and iron for smiths to craft; children taught and warriors trained; craftsmen found to adorn our lives with beauty; chieftains raised up to lead.

We opened the land, adding hide to hide; we planted rye and barley and filled the storehouses—built more storehouses and filled those. Our cattle grew sleek and fat on the plentiful grass of the meadows; the herds increased. Among the hills we dug the ore-bearing rock; we smelted copper and iron, and even gold, for the craftsmen and smiths. The city on the water grew as our builders continually enlarged the crannogs in the lake. Chieftains arose, leaders who prized loyalty and justice; we gave them authority and were rewarded with fealty.

Ever and always, the storm of strife rumbled beyond the

protection of our high ridgewall. And trickling down from Druim Vran, like a dismal freshet, there flowed an unending stream of exiles. Each battle season brought more refugees seeking safe haven from the blood-tempest raging in the land. Thus we heard the tidings of the wider world, and those tidings were not good.

I knew that Meldron must have been scouring the land for some word of us. Indeed, sometimes, with suddenly-fired inner vision, I glimpsed, as through storm-gathered clouds, the angry face of the Great Hound himself. I saw his hateful eyes scanning far horizons, saw the bulge of his jaw as he set his teeth, and I knew that somewhere blood would flow and fire waste.

One day we would stand against him in battle. Whether that day was near or still far off, I could not say. But I began to feel that while we stayed in our hidden glen behind the high bulwark of Druim Vran, we were safe. Perhaps some power protected us here and kept us from Meldron's ever-searching eyes. Perhaps the Swift Sure Hand covered us with the *Llengel*, Mathonwy's cloak of concealment. Who can know? And though I continually searched through each revolution of the year's wheel, I saw no clearer sign.

Through this time, I served as Chief of Song to our many-tribed clan. I sang often, but always on the hallowed days. This was no hardship, but I grew uneasy as the seasons passed. For it seemed to me that, as the last of my kind, my position was perilous. If some accident befell me, or if we were attacked and I were cut down in battle, Albion's great and wonderful tales would be lost, the vast knowledge of our worlds-realm would vanish. I came to view myself as a rushlight in a drafty corner: an unchancy gust, a breath of errant wind, and the very spirit of our race would be snuffed out and lost evermore.

I did not like to think how much had already been lost with the destruction of the Learned Brotherhood. I was a bard—Chief Bard of the Island of the Mighty. If the decline which I feared could be halted and turned again to ascent, it was my duty to try.

It was in Gyd, when the warmth of the Sweet Season caressed the land, that I determined to establish a school of bards. I brooded long over this, and then took my plan to Llew. I met him one morning as he stood watching the gifted Garanaw instruct a willing handful of boys in spear handling.

"He is a marvel," Llew said of Garanaw. "If only you could see him, Tegid. Do you know what the boys are calling him now?" he asked. "Garanaw Braichir—Garanaw Long Arm. His spear-skill reminds me of Boru."

Scatha had begun her warriors' school anew the year before. She and Bran had chosen the most fit and able of the young boys to join the school, and she and the Ravens had begun instructing them.

"We will need warriors," Llew said. Although he spoke the words absently, I saw in my mind's eye the image of a smoke-clouded battleground. In the darkness and smoke it seemed to me that a battle was raging which I could not see. Whether this image was that of a present event, or one yet to come, I had no way of knowing.

"Yes, we will always need warriors," I answered, shaking off the image. "But we need bards, too. Perhaps even more than we need warriors."

"That is true." Though I could not see him, I sensed that he had turned to observe me; I felt his eyes on me. "Well, brother bard, speak it out. What is on your mind, Tegid?"

"Scatha and Bran are training young hands to swing our swords," I told him. "I must begin training young tongues to sing our songs. We need chieftains of battle, yes. But we need champions of song as well!"

"Calm yourself, brother," soothed Llew. "A school for bards—is that what you want? Just say so."

"I am saying it. And I intend to start at once. I have waited too long already."

"That is fine. Great."

We turned, then, and began walking towards the lake. There were more huts along the shore now; several craftsmen—a stonecarver, a bronze-smith and a woodworker—had established their huts among the first of the dwellings we had built on the shore.

"Dinas Dwr," Llew said, savoring the words. "It is happening,

Tegid. Warriors, bards, craftsmen, farmers—" Llew said, as we passed among the dwellings. "It is happening. Dinas Dwr is a realm unto itself."

"All it lacks is a king," I pointed out. Llew made no reply.

We walked a little farther and I heard the splash of oars as a boat from the crannog drew near to the shore. I felt Llew's attention shift as the craft touched the shingle. I heard the scrape of the wooden hull on the small stones and my inner vision kindled with the image of the boat's occupant: a woman dressed in a simple loose mantle of pale yellow, the color of sweet butter. Sunlight lit her hair, tinting it with the sun's own hue. Around her neck she wore a necklace of tiny gold discs, each disc bearing a fine blue stone.

"Greetings, Goewyn," I called, before she or Llew had spoken. I saw her smile readily as her eyes flicked quickly to Llew's face and back to me.

"Hello, Goewyn," Llew said, and I noted the flatness of his greeting.

"I do not think you are blind at all, Tegid Tathal," she told me brightly as she came to stand before me. "I think you do but feign blindness."

"How so?" I asked. "Why would I employ such an absurd ruse?"

"But it is not absurd at all," she insisted. "If a man thought to be blind could see in truth, he would see more than anyone else—for he would see how men truly regard him. Thinking him blind, men would not disguise their actions. He would see them as they are and know them for what they are. In the end, the blind man would be the wisest man of all."

"Shrewd indeed," I allowed. "But, alas, it is not so with me. Of that you may be assured."

"But I am not assured," she replied pleasantly. "Greetings, Llew, I thought to find you on the practice field with Garanaw."

"We have been watching him," Llew said. "But Garanaw needs no help from anyone—least of all a one-handed warrior."

His words were curt and his tone dismissive. Goewyn bade us farewell and went her way. I turned at once to Llew. "Why are you trying to drive her away?"

"What? Drive her away? I am not trying to drive her away."

"She loves you."

Llew laughed, but it was not a pleasant sound. "You have been standing in the sun too long. I like Goewyn; she is a joy to behold and to be with."

"Then why do you discourage her so?"

"Meddling bard, what are you talking about?" He said this amiably enough, but a sudden tightness in his voice betrayed him.

"Do you think she cares that one of your arms is a whit longer than the other? It is you she loves, not your right hand."

"You are talking nonsense."

"Or is it that she was abused by Meldron's wolves?"

"Who told you that?" he snapped.

"She did—last winter. She was a long time healing from the injuries she received at Meldron's hands. You rescued her; you saw her condition—she assumed you knew. She came to me and asked me if that was why you spurned her."

"Stop it, Tegid. You are embarrassing yourself."

"Am I?"

"Yes—you are."

I could feel the heat of his anger as he turned and stalked away, bristling. His denial had been as flat as it was forceful—proving that all I said was true. And the truth went deep into a wounded place within him.

I continued on my slow way around the lake. On the wooded slopes of the ridge I knew I would find a birch grove among the pines, which could serve as the first of many teaching places. As I walked, tapping the uneven ground before me with my staff, I ordered the ranks of the Learned Brotherhood in my mind, beginning with the lowest: the Mabinogi.

Those I chose would become *Cawganog* and *Cupanog,* and I would begin to train their minds to the Hero Feat of memory which is the bard's art. Perhaps I would discover one in whom the awen already glowed like an ember—that would be best. Anyone who could master the mental skills would become a Filidh, then a Brehon, then a Gwyddon, and, in time, Derwydd. From among the Derwyddi would be chosen the Penderwyddi, the Chief Bards, one for each of the three ancient realms of Albion. And one day, from among the Chief Bards of Prydain and Llogres and Caledon there would arise a Phantarch—the Chief of Chiefs, who, in his hidden chamber, sang the Song of Albion which upheld this worlds-realm.

The thought caused me to wonder: would there ever be a Phantarch again? Would the Song of Albion be sung again in Domhain Dorcha? Would the life-quickening Song shine again as a light within the Deep Dark?

I paused beside the lake. The sun warmed my face and neck; the breeze from the water lifted my hair; birdcry sounded clean and clear in my ears. In this protected place we were safe. Yet that safety could not long endure if the words of the Banfáith's prophecy were to hold true. And her prophecy had proven true through all things. So be it!

It was cool among the slim white birches. I stood motionless, the young branches lightly shifting over my head. The new leaves fluttered like feathers and, in my mind's eye, I saw the dappled light playing among the slender trunks and shifting over the thick, green grass of the copse. Here, I thought, is where we will begin. Here, in this grove, I will once more establish the bardship of Albion.

It was a mighty work stretching before me, a path with a far destination. Tomorrow I would begin; I would search out the young ones who would embark with me on the journey—through the oghams of trees, birds, and beasts; through lore of wood and water, of earth and air and stars; through all types of tales: those of the Anruth, and Nuath, and Eman, the Dindsenchas, and Cetals, Great Orations; through the *Bretha Nemed*, the Laws of Privilege and Sovereignty; through the Four Arts of Poetry, the Bardic Laws, and the *Taran Tafod*, the Secret Tongue; through all the sacred rites of our people. Perhaps I would find one in whom the *Imbas Forosnai*, the Light of Foresight, burned brightly—perhaps another Ollathir.

I lingered in the grove and performed a saining rite: I cut three

slender branches from three birches and plaited them end-to-end into
a leafy hoop. I took the hoop and rolled it in a sunwise circle around
the perimeter of the grove—three times around the grove, and then I
placed the hoop in the center of the grove. I brought out my pouch
which contained the Nawglan, and I poured a portion of the Sacred
Nine into the center of the birch hoop; I poured the Nawglan in the
triple-rayed shape of the *Gogyrven,* the Three Rays of Truth. As I did
this, I spoke the saining words:

> *In the steep path of our common calling,*
> > *Be it easy or uneasy to our flesh,*
> > *Be it bright or dark for us to follow,*
> > *Be it stony or smooth beneath our feet,*
> *Bestow, O Goodly-Wise, your perfect guidance;*
> > *Lest we fall, or into error stray.*

> *In the shelter of this grove,*
> > *Be to us our portion and our guide;*
> *Aird Righ, by authority of the Twelve:*
> > *The Wind of gusts and gales,*
> > *The Thunder of stormy billows,*
> > *The Ray of bright sunlight,*
> > *The Bear of seven battles,*
> > *The Eagle of the high rock,*
> > *The Boar of the forest,*
> > *The Salmon of the pool,*
> > *The Lake of the glen,*
> > *The Flowering of the heathered hill,*
> > *The Craft of the artisan,*
> > *The Word of the poet,*
> > *The Fire of thought in the wise.*

> *Who upholds the gorsedd, if not You?*
> *Who counts the ages of the world, if not You?*
> *Who commands the Wheel of Heaven, if not You?*
> *Who quickens life in the womb, if not You?*
> *Therefore, God of All Virtue and Power,*
> *Sain us and shield us with your Swift Sure Hand,*
> *Lead us in peace to our journey's end.*

So saying, I rose and left the grove, returning to the lake. As I emerged from the trees and proceeded along the shore path, I heard a light splash behind me. Thinking a fish or frog had jumped, I paid the sound no attention, and continued on, tapping my staff before me. But as I neared the first of the lakeside huts, I heard the sound again—a wet plunk at the water's edge.

I stopped. Turning slowly, I called out, "Come here!"

There came no response to my summons, but the sound of breathing reached my ear. "Come here," I said again. "I want to talk to you."

I heard the faintly dripping pat of a bare foot on a stone. "I am waiting," I said.

"How did you know I was there?" came the reply. The voice was clear and confident, bold, yet not without a pinch of respect; the speaker was a young boy.

"I will tell you that," I said, "if first you tell me why you were following me. Bargain?"

"Bargain," replied my young shadow.

"Very well."

The boy drew a deep breath, paused, and then said, "I followed you to see if you would sing." Before I could reply, he added, "Now you must tell."

"I knew you were behind me, because I heard you," I answered, and then turned away quickly and began tapping along the pebbled shingle.

The boy did not accept my answer. He scampered to my side, protesting, "But I was very quiet!"

"Yes," I agreed, "you were very quiet. But my ears have grown very long."

"They are not so long."

"Long enough to hear a noisy boy like you."

"I am not noisy!" my young companion complained. And then, without a pause to draw breath, he asked, "Does it hurt your eyes to be blind?"

"Once—at first. Not any more." I told him. "But I am not so blind as you might think."

"Then why do you tap all the time with your staff?" Though impertinent, he meant no disrespect.

"Why do you ask so many questions?"

"How will I find out anything unless I ask questions?" he demanded.

"Why do you want to hear me sing?"

"I am not the only one who asks so many questions," replied the boy under his breath.

I laughed, and he seemed to enjoy the fact that he had made me laugh. He skipped ahead of me a few paces and waited; I heard the plunk of pebbles tossed into the lake. "What is your name, boy?"

"I am Gwion Bach," he answered happily. "Like in the song."

"Which is your clan?"

"The Oirixeni of Llogres. But there are not so many of us as before," Gwion said. There was pride in his voice, but no sadness. Probably he was still too young to understand what had happened to his clan, or what it meant.

"Hail, Gwion Bach. I am Tegid Tathal."

"I know—you are Chief Bard," he said. "Everyone knows you."

"Why did you want to hear me sing?"

"I never heard a bard until I came here," he explained.

"And do you like what you hear?"

"I like the harp."

"What about the songs?"

"My mother sings better."

"Then maybe you should go back to your mother."

"She is not with us any more," he muttered. "She was killed when raiders burned our stronghold."

I stopped walking. "I am sorry, Gwion Bach. I was unwise to speak as I did just now."

"I understand," he replied. At the utterance of that simple affirmation, my inner vision kindled and I saw a boy with curly dark hair, slight, but nimble as a thought, with big dark eyes and a face which proclaimed every fleeting thought. Eight or nine summers, I guessed; not more. Yet he was intelligent and self-assured; his self-confidence would easily accommodate a boy twice his age.

"Tell me, Gwion Bach," I said, "would you like to learn the songs?"

He did not answer at once, but took his time considering. "Would I have a harp of my own?"

"If you mastered the art of playing it—yes, of course. But it is very difficult and you must try very hard."

"Then I will try," he answered, as if he were conferring an extravagant gift on me.

"Who is your father? I will ask him if he will allow me to teach you to be a bard."

"My father is Conn, but he was killed, too." His face fell as he remembered his grief.

"Who cares for you now?"

"Cleist," he replied simply, and without further explanation. "Are you seeing me now?"

His question took me aback. "Yes," I told him, "in a way. Sometimes I see things—not with my eyes, but inside my head."

He cocked his head to one side. "If you see me, what am I holding in my hand?"

"You are holding a silver branch," I told him. "A birch branch. You saw me cut them in the grove and plucked one for yourself."

At this he squeezed shut his eyes and put his thumb in the center of his forehead. After a moment, he opened his eyes once more and announced, "I cannot see you. Will you teach me how to do this?"

His small face was so earnest, so trusting, that I had to laugh again. "I will teach you better things than that, Gwion ap Conn."

"If Cleist agrees."

"Yes, if Cleist agrees."

We walked together among the huts, and Gwion led me to the house where he dwelt with several Oirixeni kinsmen. I would ask Cleist; we would discuss the matter in the proper way. All the same, I knew already that I had found my first Mabinog. Rather, he had found me.

26

Dead Water

Wasps droned in the shadowed grove, buzzing lazily in the midday heat. Gwion and his two companions—clever Iollo of the Taolentani, and shy, smiling Daned of the Saranae—sat on their birch log, peeling the papery bark and striving to remember the ogham of the trees. Eyelids closed, I drowsed, listening to the sing-song recitation of my three Mabinogi.

"Beith the birch," they said, *"Luis* the rowan, *Nuinn* the ash, *Fearn* the alder, *Saille* the willow, *Huath* ... the oak—"

"No. Wait. Stop." I said raising my head. "Huath the oak? Is that so?"

Silence for a moment, and then Daned ventured, "Huath is holly?"

"No, but you are closer. Think now. What is it?"

"Hawthorn?" wondered Iollo.

"Correct. Continue."

"Huath the hawthorn, *Duir* the oak," they began.

"From the beginning," I instructed. "Start again."

"Again?" Gwion objected. "it is too hot to think. And anyway, I am sick of trees. I want to talk about something else."

Another time I would have insisted they finish their recitation, but Gwion was right: it was too hot to think, too hot to move. Since

Alban Heruin, the Highest Light, the days had become oppressively hot. The sun poured down from a white sky like molten metal from a furnace, withering every green thing under heaven. The air lay heavy, stale and still: not a whisper of breeze rippled the lake, not a leaf stirred.

"Very well," I relented, "what would you like to talk about?"

"Fish," replied Gwion.

"Very well, recite the ogham of the fish," I suggested.

"Please, Penderwydd," Iollo said, "must we?"

I paused to consider, and Gwion saw his chance. "I want to know about the salmon," he said quickly.

Sensing a trap, I said, "Yes?"

"Well," he replied seriously, "why are there no salmon in our lake?"

"But you know the answer to that," I said. "Or should know."

"They are sea fish," offered Daned.

"Yes."

"But we had salmon in our river in Llogres," Gwion persisted. "And we were far from the sea."

"Iollo," I said, "what is the principal difference between the river and the sea?"

"Rivers and streams are sweet water; the sea is salty." He thought for a moment. "How is it then that salmon is found in a river?"

"How indeed?"

Gwion sensed the discussion going astray. He tried to steer it back on course. "But why are there no salmon in our lake?"

"Our lake does not join a river," Iollo explained, "so the salmon cannot get in."

"There is a river," Gwion insisted. "It is on the other side of Druim Vran. And it goes under the hill and comes into the lake."

"Is this so, Penderwydd?" Daned wanted to know.

"It is so," I told him.

"I will show him," Gwion offered, jumping up—a little too readily, I thought. "Shall I, Penderwydd?"

I hesitated. Gwion held his breath. Sitting on my turf mound, staff across my knees, I remembered another hot, lazy day in another green-shadowed grove—a day when I sat on such a log, stupid with torpor, struggling to recall some elusive scrap of a fact, desperate for sleep and for Ollathir's approval.

"Oh, very well," I relented. "Let us discover the answer to this riddle. To the lake! Lead the way, Gwion!"

Gwion leaped ahead. "I hear and obey, Wise One."

"Then go!" They charged from the grove in a rush and raced down the path to the lake. The birch leaves were still quivering to their cries of wild relief when I heard the running footsteps of one returning. Two heartbeats later I felt two slim arms snake round my waist and a sweaty head press against my stomach. Gwion did not say a word, but his hug was eloquence itself. I ran my fingers through his sweat-damp hair, and he darted away again.

Taking up my staff, I made my way down the well-travelled slope from the grove to the lake. I paused for a moment on the trail to stand in the harsh sunlight: I could feel it like a flame on my face and arms. The heat drained both strength and will alike; it seemed a most unnatural thing.

As I stood contemplating, I heard a shout from the lake and an answering splash as one of my boys plunged into the water. My inner vision flared at the sound, and I beheld the image of another young face—female, this one, gaunt with hunger, and pale with exhaustion beneath the dirt and sweat, but straight-browed, clear eyes alight with fierce determination. I knew the face; I had seen it before...

"Penderwydd!" shouted Gwion. "Come swimming with us!"

I made my way to the lakeshore and sat down on the rocks. I removed my siarc and buskins, and stood. The cool water on my hot feet soothed me wonderfully. Gwion saw me standing to my ankles in the water and loudly urged me to come in.

Why not? I shed my breecs and waded in. The water was a mercy. I sank to my neck, feeling the round stones like cool lumps beneath me. "Here! Over here, Wise Master," my Mabinogi cried.

I dived under the water and swam to the sound of their voices.

Soon we were sporting in the water, our voices ringing in the still, dead air. In moments, our cries were answered by others—wild, exuberant, happy: the shouts of the boy warriors as they ran to the cool water. Garanaw, following our example, was allowing his noisy brood a swim.

We moved further from the shore to allow room for the warrior-Mabinogi. "It is cooler here!" shouted Iollo.

"Watch this!" Gwion called.

I heard a splash as he dived. A moment later he surfaced again, spitting water in a high arc. "It is cold down there," he reported.

"I can stay under longer than that!" declared Daned, and the challenge was taken up by the others. All three began diving to the bottom of the lake where they clung to the stones to keep from bobbing to the surface too soon. This went on for some time, and I contented myself with floating idly on the surface until Gwion's shout brought me back to their game.

"Penderwydd! I have found something! Penderwydd!"

I swam to the sound of his voice. "What is it, Gwion?"

"Here," he said. The water was not too deep for me, so I stood, and he placed a metal object in my hands. "I thought it was a stone," he said.

I turned the object in my hands, feeling the sides and rim. Iollo and Daned swam close. "A bowl!" Iollo said. "Where did you find that?"

"In the water," Gwion told him. "Down there."

"Lord Llew found a cauldron in the lake when we first came here," I told them.

"How did it get there?" Daned wanted to know.

"There have been people in this region before," I answered. I felt the patterned sides of the bowl, slick on one side where the water moss had grown like otter's fur.

"I am going to find one too!" Iollo announced.

The diving began in earnest then. And I thought they would drown themselves trying to outdo one another in finding another treasure. I thought it unlikely that anything of great value would be found, and indeed, nothing was found at all until—

"Penderwydd!" shouted Iollo. "Here! I've found something—and it is silver!"

He splashed his way to me and I held out my hands. "What is it?" he wanted to know.

"You can see it, at least. Can you not tell?"

He put the object into my hand. My fingers played over the odd shape: small and flat, the metal smooth, although there seemed to be some scratches or an incised design on the surface.

"It looks like a fish," Gwion volunteered. "But it is flat and there is no tail or fins."

"There is writing," added Daned. "Here." I felt a small hand take my finger and press it down on the shape.

"Do you not know what this is?" I asked. "Have you never seen one?"

"It looks like a leaf," said Gwion.

"It is a leaf," I replied.

"Made of silver?" Iollo said. "Then it is very valuable."

"Yes, and more," I said. "It is an offering made to the god of this place: a birch leaf made of silver to honor the lord of the grove."

The discovery of the silver leaf-offering spurred them on with renewed vigor, and it was not long before the young warriors had heard about the find and joined in the hunt. I left them to it and retreated to the shore. I climbed from the lake and lay down on the rocks to let the sun dry me.

"Tegid! There you are at last!"

"Yes, Drustwn, here I am." I sat up slowly.

"Llew sent me to bring you," the dusky Raven said.

I heard the stirring of anxiety in his tone and asked, "What has happened?"

"A rider has come from Dun Cruach. Llew asked me to find you. Bran and Calbha are with him."

"We will go more quickly if you lead me," I said, already pulling on my clothes. I dressed and took up my staff. Drustwn led me along the lakeside, handed me into a boat and, with a heave of his broad shoulders, pushed the craft away from the shingle. In the same motion, he leapt into the boat and, taking up the oar, began to propel us across the water towards the crannog.

Our floating city had grown, keeping pace with our increasing numbers. The crannog now resembled an island with shrubs and trees among the tight-clustered dwellings; berry thickets lined the earth rampart outside the surrounding timber wall. A gaggle of young girls were fishing from the edge of the landing; I heard the splash as they dangled their feet in the water. Their happy chatter fell on the ear like birdsong.

Drustwn scrambled from the boat as it touched the landing. I felt his hand upon my arm as I rose, and he did not release me until my feet were firmly on the rough planks. We hastened through the open gates into the first of many interconnecting yards, through that to another, and another beyond, to where the hall stood on its raised platform of earth and stone.

I smelled the scent of stale smoke as we passed through the open doors, and heard the soft mumble of voices at the far end of the hall where Llew and the others had gathered.

The rider, whoever he was, smelled of horse and sweat. He gulped at the ale in his cup, guzzling it down as only a very thirsty man can. Llew touched my shoulder with the stump of his right arm as I came to stand beside him—that touch had become his habitual gesture. When there were others in council with him, he wanted me at his side. And he always brushed my shoulder—as if to assure the blind man of his place. But it was more to assure himself, I think.

"Ah, here is Tegid now," Llew said. "I am sorry to intrude on your teaching, but I thought you would want to hear this."

"Greetings, Tegid," said the messenger.

"Greetings, Rhoedd," I answered, recognizing the voice at once. "You have ridden hard. Your message must hold some urgency."

"Drain your cup," Llew told him, "and then you can tell us."

Rhoedd swallowed the last of the welcome cup and drew a deep breath. "Ah, thank you, Lord Llew. Never have I tasted a better draught, nor needed one more."

At these words I saw within my mind a rush-fringed pool, still—unnaturally so. It lay glimmering darkly beneath a hazy sun; no breath of wind touched the turgid surface, no bird stirred among the dry rush leaves. Dead water, lifeless and silent. As I gazed upon the vision given me, I saw the rotting skeleton of a sheep sinking into the mire at the water's edge of this dead pool.

"Fill his cup again," I instructed. "He has had nothing to drink for three days."

"Is this so?" asked Llew.

"Yes, lord, it is so," Rhoedd said, and I heard the splash of ale in his offered cup. "I had water enough for only two days."

Rhoedd drank again, gratefully. We waited while he gulped down the sweet, brown liquid. "Again, I thank you," Rhoedd said when he had drunk his fill. "I am come from Cynan, who sends his greetings."

"His greetings?" Bran wondered.

"Man, you have ridden the hooves off your horse to bring greetings from Cynan Machae?" Calbha asked bluntly.

"Greetings," Rhoedd replied stiffly, "and a warning. The warning is this: protect your water."

Surprised by Rhoedd's words, it was a moment before the others could speak. But I had seen the vision of the dead pool. "Poison," I said.

"That is the truth of it," Rhoedd said. "Our water has been poisoned. It is tainted and any who drink it become sick. Some have died."

"Poisoned water," Calbha sympathized, his voice grave. "It is a cruel thing."

"Where else has this happened?" Llew asked.

"In all the Galanae holdings it is the same," Rhoedd said. "It is not known how far the corruption has spread—that is why I did not stop to drink on my way here."

"But our water is good," Drustwn said. "Could you not see that?"

"I will tell you what I have seen," Rhoedd replied. "I have seen the babies writhing as they die; and I have seen their mothers wailing in the night. I have seen strong men lose control of their bowels and collapse in their own filth; and I have seen children made blind with fever. That is what I have seen. The taint has spread far—I did not know how far. I dared not trust the water I found along the way."

"Well, you may drink your fill without fear," Bran told him. "There is no taint here."

"What is to be done?" asked Llew. "What aid can we give to Dun Cruach? Can we bring water?"

"King Cynfarch asks no aid," Rhoedd said. "He only thought to alert you to the danger."

"All the same," Llew said, "we will go to him. And we will bring with us as much water as we can carry."

"We cannot carry much," Bran pointed out.

"We can take enough to allow them to travel here," said Llew. "We will leave as soon as vats can be prepared."

Although I counselled otherwise, it was decided that we should carry water to Dun Cruach and bring the people to Dinas Dwr. The decision did not sit well with me. I did not begrudge Cynan the water—far from it! Nor did I object to Llew's desire to help. But the thought of leaving Dinas Dwr made me uneasy and anxious.

Llew wanted to know why I felt this way. "I do not think it wise for us to leave Dinas Dwr," was all I could tell him.

The next two days the wagons were prepared which would carry the water, and the vessels filled. The night before we were to set forth from Dinas Dwr, I waited until Llew had quitted the hall and then went to his lodgings. "We must not ride out tomorrow," I told him as I entered. "It is not safe to leave Druim Vran at this time."

"Welcome, Tegid. What is on your mind?"

"Did you hear what I said?"

"I heard you. And I have been expecting you all day." I heard the soft tread of his feet on the stones as he moved to the table across the room. There he took up a jar, for I heard the light splash of liquid as he poured the cups. He turned to me, and I felt the brushing touch of his stump against my hand. "Here," he said, "sit down and talk to me."

He lowered himself to a calfskin on the floor and I sat down facing him, placing my staff at my feet. Llew took up his cup. *"Sláinte!"* he said.

"Sláinte môr," I replied, raising my cup. He touched the rim of his cup to mine and we drank. The ale was warm and stale; it tasted sour in my mouth.

"Now then, what is troubling you?" he asked after a moment. "You have begun your school for bards. You have said that we are safe here; the glen is secure."

"The glen is secure. No harm can befall us here," I replied. "That is why we must not leave this place."

"I do not understand, Tegid. We sailed to Ynys Sci, and even rode into Meldron's stronghold. You said nothing about staying here then. Correct me if I am wrong, but you urged us to action."

"That was different."

"How?" he demanded. "How is it different? I want to know."

I felt my stomach tightening. How could I explain to him that which I could not explain to myself? I said, "We took Meldron unawares. That will not happen again."

"That is no reason."

"Meldron must know we are hidden somewhere in Caledon. He is searching for us even now. If we leave, he will find us and we are not yet strong enough to face him in battle."

"You surprise me, Tegid. We are only taking water to Dun Cruach, not riding to challenge Meldron face-to-face. Anyway, it is the least we can do for them—after all Cynan and his father have done for us."

"I do not question our debt to Lord Cynfarch and his son. You are right to feel the way you do. But we cannot leave the valley now."

"But now is when they need the water," Llew insisted, gently, but with growing agitation. "Now—not next Lugnasadh or whenever."

"If we leave Dinas Dwr, there will be trouble," I told him flatly.

"Trouble," he said slowly. "What sort of trouble?"

"I cannot say," I admitted. "Disaster."

"Disaster," he repeated. "Have you seen this disaster?"

"No," I confessed. "But I feel it in my bones."

"It is too hot to argue about this, Tegid," he said, and my inward eye awakened at the words.

I saw dust billowing in dun-colored clouds from a parched land, borne aloft on wild winds. The sun did not shine, but hung in a brown sky with a dim yellow pallor. And no living thing did I see in the sky or on the ground. The words of the Banfáith's prophecy came to me. *"The Dust of the Ancients will rise on the clouds;"* I intoned softly, *"the essence of Albion is scattered and torn among contending winds."*

Llew was silent for a moment. "Meaning?" he asked at last.

"Meldron's reign is defiled," I told Llew, "his desecration has begun to corrupt the land itself. His unrighteous kingship is the abomination which walks the land, poisoning it, killing it. And worse is to follow."

He was silent again. I took up my cup, drank, and then replaced it on the floor.

"In the Day of Strife, root and branch shall change places, and the newness of the thing shall pass for a wonder," I recited.

"Well? Enlighten me," he said wearily.

"Root and branch have changed places, you see? In Meldron, king and kingship have changed places."

"I am sorry, Tegid—it is late; I am tired—I do not understand."

"The words of the prophecy—"

"I know, I know, the prophecy—yes. What does it mean?"

"Sovereignty, Llew. Meldron has seized the power that only the bards hold. He made himself king and now claims sovereignty. He has reversed the order."

"And this has poisoned the water?" Llew asked, straining to understand. "Actually poisoned it?"

"So I believe. How long do you think such brazen evil can reign in this worlds-realm without poisoning the very land itself?" I said. "The land is alive. It draws its life from the people who work it, just as they draw their life from the king. If corruption taints the king, the people suffer—yes, and eventually, the land will suffer as well. That is the way of it."

"This is Simon's doing," he said, using Siawn Hy's former name. "All of this has come about through him. It was Simon who told Meldron that kingship could be taken by force. And Albion is dying because of it."

He did not wait for me to reply. "If I had done what I came here to do, none of this would have happened."

"It is pointless to talk this way," I told him. "We do only what we know to do, we do what we can."

"All the more reason to help Cynan now," he retorted.

There was no changing his mind. I had said what I came to say, and it had not moved him. "Very well," I said. "We will go. We will take water to Dun Cruach, and we will brave the consequences."

"Whatever you say, brother," Llew agreed amiably. "What about your Mabinogi?"

"Goewyn will look after them."

"Then it is settled. We leave at dawn."

We parted and I left him to his rest. I was too angry and overwrought to sleep that night; and the air was too still and warm.

27

The Giant's Stone

I held vigil in my grove, sitting naked on my turf mound, feeling the heat of the night on my skin—listening to the unnatural stillness, seeking with my inner sight that which I once might have sought in the Seeing Bowl. I searched the many-shadowed pathways of the future for the source of my foreboding. My inward eye brought forth many images—all of them desolate and disheartening: starving children with wasted limbs and protruding bellies, bloated cattle lying dead in poisoned streams, silent settlements, withered crops, crows holding court upon the gleaming ribcages of the hapless dead...

It seemed to me that oppression lay like a stifling hide upon the land, thick, heavy, dense and vast: a rotting hide, putrid with decay, suffocating all beneath it.

I rose heavy-hearted, pulled on my clothes and walked down the pathway to the lakeside where the horses and wagons were ready and waiting our departure. Goewyn was among the few gathered to see us away.

"Farewell, Tegid. Worry for nothing while you are gone—I will care for the Mabinogi," she said, grasping my hands. Her hands were warm as they pressed mine.

"Thank you, Goewyn."

"You are troubled. What is the matter?" She did not release my hands, but held them more tightly. "What have you seen?"

"Nothing . . . I do not know—nothing good," I told her. "If it were left to me, we would not leave here at all."

She leaned close and I felt her warm breath on my cheek as she kissed me. "May you journey in peace and return to us in safety," she said.

Llew and Bran approached just then, leading their horses. Goewyn bade them farewell, and, as Llew made no kindly remark, she departed.

"You and Alun lead the wagons," Llew said, turning to Bran. "I will ride behind with Tegid and Rhoedd and the others."

We mounted our horses and the signal was given. I heard the creak and grate of wooden wheels on the shingle as the wagons began trundling slowly along the lakeshore towards the ridge. We waited until the last cart passed before taking our places at the end.

In all, there were six high-sided wains filled with skins and vats of fresh water accompanied by ten warriors, led by Bran and two Ravens. The rest of our Ravenflight were to stay behind and guard Dinas Dwr under the command of Calbha and Scatha.

Though the sun was newly risen, the air was already hot. We followed the groaning wagons up the slope of Druim Vran, then carefully, and with great difficulty, down the steep face of the ridgewall. By the time we reached the glen on the other side we were all sweating and exhausted, and the journey had only begun.

We followed the river as it bent east and south. Our two Ravens, Alun Tringad and Drustwn, rode well ahead to scout the way lest we encounter any of Meldron's spies. We met no one, however. Neither did we see any sign that Meldron's blight had yet invaded northern Caledon. The rivers and springs ran clean and pure; the lakes appeared fresh. Even so, owing to Rhoedd's warning, we drank nothing from any source along the way.

The first two days of our journey, I remained alert to every sound and every scent—searching, I think, for some sign, however faint, of the doom I felt looming nearer with every step away from Dinas Dwr.

Still we journeyed on without hindrance, yet my fears remained as acute as ever.

After three days, we left the riverway and joined Sarn Cathmail, the old high track which joins the dark northern forests with the heathered hill-lands of the south. Our scouts ranged further ahead as the land opened; and, though they proceeded with all caution, they saw no one. Thus we travelled on—and my foreboding grew.

And then, at midday on the fourth day, we came in sight of the way-stone which marks Sarn Cathmail at its mid-point. *Carreg Cawr,* the Giant's Stone, is an enormous blue-black slab which towers three times man-height over the raised stone-paved trackway. Like other such stones, it is carved with saining symbols which guard the road and those who travel upon it.

"One day more, I think," Llew said. "We are doing well despite the heat. It is very dry here—the grass is brown."

As he spoke, my inner vision kindled and I saw the long, slate-colored road stretching before us across a grassy plain surrounded by low hills under a white, barren sky. I saw the loaded wagons lurching and bumping over the track and, rising above, Carreg Cawr, black in strong sunlight.

The scouts had passed the Giant's Stone and had ridden on ahead. Indeed, there was nothing to prevent them. Bran and the warriors passed by, and then, one by one, the wagons reached the stone and rumbled on. But, as I neared the stone, the foreboding which had ridden with me since before our beginning grew to a palpable discomfort of dread.

Drawing near to the stone, I reined my horse to a halt. Llew travelled on a few paces and stopped, almost directly beneath the great hulking stone. He gazed at it, tracing the ancient symbols with his eyes. "The symbols," he called back to me. "Can you read them?"

"I can," I replied curtly. "They are tokens of protection. They hallow the sarn."

"I know that," he said testily, "I mean, what do they say?"

Without waiting for an answer, he turned in the saddle, lifted the reins, and urged his horse forward once more. I sat for a moment, listening. I heard only the wind fitfully winnowing the long grass of the smooth hills and, far-off, the shriek of a hawk. And then I heard Llew cry out.

His shout was more surprise than pain. I glimpsed a shadow flicker behind the Giant's Stone as Llew whirled in the saddle. "What was that? Did you hear anything?"

"No."

"Something hit me just now. It felt like a rock—right in the back. I could have—"

"Shh! Listen!"

Llew lapsed into silence and I heard a slight scratching sound coming from the Giant's Stone. Then I heard a dull clink—as of the links of an iron chain; and then... nothing.

"There is someone lurking behind the Giant's Stone," I told Llew, who armed himself instantly, drawing his spear from beneath his saddle.

He turned his mount towards the stone. "Come out," he called. "We know you are hiding there. Come out at once."

We waited. No answer came. Llew made to speak again, but I restrained him with a wave of my hand. "Hear me," I called towards the stone. "It is the Chief Bard of Albion who speaks to you now. I demand that you show yourself at once. You will not be harmed."

A moment passed in silence. Then I heard the soft, slow, stealthy tread of someone moving in the long, dry grass at the base of the Giant's Stone.

A slight figure appeared, wearing the remains of a ragged siarc and a green cloak. And beside the mysterious person walked an enormous, slate-grey hound with a distinctive streak of white across the shoulder. I knew who it was, even before Llew shouted: "Ffand!"

He vaulted from the saddle and ran to the ragged girl. The dog barked and was silenced with a simple, "Twrch!"

"Ffand!" cried Llew. "Ah, brave Ffand!" he caught her up in an embrace that lifted her off her feet. She laughed as he kissed her on a dirty cheek. "What are you doing here—way out here alone?" he asked, releasing her.

"But I am not alone," Ffand replied. "Twrch is with me." She patted the dog's back, which came even to her hip.

"Twrch!" Llew reached his good hand towards the dog.

Twrch stretched his neck and sniffed Llew's hand. Did he recognize the scent of his old master? Yes, indeed; for the great beast began barking and immediately leaped up—placing a huge paw on each of Llew's shoulders—and then proceeded to lick his face. Llew held the dog's head with his good hand, stroking the animal's neck with his stump, and Twrch licked that, too. "Quiet! Quiet, Twrch!" Llew gazed at Ffand. "What are you doing here?" he asked again. "How did you get here?"

"I have been looking for you," Ffand said.

"Looking for me?" wondered Llew, bemused.

"They say that Llew raises a kingdom in the north. And Meldron searches the north. So I have come north to find you," Ffand explained.

"Very sensible," Llew assured her.

"You said you would come for the dog," Ffand told him crossly. "You came, but you did not wait for us." Her tone accused him, and then instantly relented. "So we decided to come to you."

"Wait for you? What do you mean?"

"When you came to Caer Modornn."

I dismounted and walked to where they stood. "It is true that we came to Caer Modornn, but we did not see you, Ffand."

"You forgot about me," she said indignantly.

"Yes," Llew admitted. "I am sorry. If I had known you were waiting for us, we would never have left without you."

"And I would not have to throw rocks at you," she said, and my inner sight flared with the image of a fine young woman with long brown hair and large brown eyes; her skin was lightly tinted from the sun. She had obviously travelled a very great distance, yet she appeared healthy and strong, if a little tattered and thin.

She had grown in the time since I had last seen her, although she still had much of the child about her. Lithe in her movements and manner, she seemed as wily as a creature of the wood. Indeed, she told us how she had been living in the years since she had rescued us.

There was never enough food, so she and Twrch had taken to the woods to fend for themselves. They spent most of the time hunting, bringing back whatever they could catch to share with the holding. "Even a hare or a squirrel," she said. "It was the only meat we could get."

"Ffand," said Llew, "you are a wonder. Are you hungry?"

"More thirsty than hungry," she replied. "The water is bad hereabouts."

I returned to my mount, and the food bag tied behind my saddle. I brought out a portion of hard cheese and some of the small barley loaves we carried. These were accepted gratefully. Then I gave her my water skin, which she all but drained before offering the rest to Twrch; the dog drank what was left, and then licked the skin.

Ffand broke one of the loaves and began to eat at once. As I suspected, she was ravenous. The dog sat beside her, licking its chops but not otherwise complaining.

"I do not wonder that Meldron fears you so much," she said, breaking a loaf in half and stuffing it into her mouth.

"How do you know that Meldron fears us?" I asked.

"Ever since you came to Caer Modornn," she said, chewing happily, "Meldron has been searching for you. There is no one in all Albion who has not been questioned by Meldron's Wolf Pack: Where is the cripple Llew? Where is blind Tegid?" She swallowed and said, "He has vowed to destroy you. He has said that anyone who finds you will be granted lands and wealth—much wealth."

"So," said Llew, "you have come looking for me."

Ffand took his jest seriously. "Not for him! Never for Meldron!" she gasped, suddenly horrified that he should think that of her. "I came to warn you and to bring Twrch. He is a good dog—I trained him myself—and every king should have a good dog."

"And I thank you, Ffand," Llew replied warmly. "I could use a good dog—even though I am no longer a king. It seems that once again, I am in your debt."

The last of the wagons had disappeared over a rise of hill. "We must go now," I said. I turned my head and cast my inward eye towards the way-stone. "We should not linger here any longer."

"Tegid is right, we should rejoin the others."

"Come, Ffand, you can ride with me until we reach the wagons." I walked to my horse, swung myself into the saddle, and let down my hand for her.

She looked up at me curiously and bit her lip. "Can you see me?" she wondered.

"Yes," I answered without explaining, "so stop gawking and give me your arm."

I pulled her up behind me on the horse; Llew remounted, and we continued on our way. Twrch trotted along between us, first beside Llew, and then beside Ffand and me—as if he would happily divide his presence between two masters.

Before my inward vision darkened once more, I glimpsed the great hound, head lifted high to scent the wind, long legs loping gracefully along beside Llew as if he had always enjoyed the easy pleasure of a noble position.

Then the image faded and darkness reclaimed my sight. I was left to muse on the meaning of what had taken place. Ffand's appearance was no threat to us, certainly. All the same, my feelings of dread were equally certain—and indeed, had not abated. I still felt deep foreboding in my bones. The Giant's Stone still loomed over the trackway, a dark, brooding bulk, but we passed by unharmed.

It seemed to me then that I felt a peculiar pulse in my stomach and chest. And then the sound reached me: something heavy moving, slowly, ponderously—the sound of large millstones grinding. I pulled on the reins and turned my mount on the road.

"Ffand," I said urgently. "Look at the way-stone—the Giant's Stone—look at it and tell me what is happening. What do you see?"

"I do not—"

"Quickly, girl! Tell me what you see!"

My shouting alerted Llew, who halted and called back to me. "What is it, Tegid?"

"I see the stone," Ffand told me. "I see nothing else. It is just..."

She paused. "What was that?"

"Did you see something?"

"No, I felt something—here in my stomach."

The horse grew skittish; it whinnied and stepped sideways. "Keep your eyes on the stone," I told her. "Do not look away. Tell me all you see."

"Well," she began once more, "it is just there. As I said, it is—" She gasped. "Look!"

"What? Ffand! Tell me what is happening!"

"Tegid!" Llew shouted, and I heard the sharp clatter and chop of iron-clad hooves on stone as his horse shied and reared.

My horse tossed its head and neighed in fright. I wound the rein around my hand and held it taut. Ffand gripped tight to my cloak.

"Speak, girl!"

Llew clattered to a halt beside us. "The stone is moving," he said. "Trembling, or vibrating very slowly. And the ground around it is splitting."

I heard a sound like that of a tree stump groaning as it is uprooted . . . and then silence. "What else? Is there anything else?"

"No," replied Llew after a moment. "It has stopped now."

I heard another deep rumble and realized that the sound was coming from Twrch; the dog growled softly, a note of menace low in his throat. "Quiet, Twrch," Ffand scolded.

I heard the keen of a bird . . . no, a whistle—it was a signal; someone was signalling with a whistle . . .

Twrch barked. I heard a scrabble of claws on the paving stones, and Ffand shouted, "Twrch! Come back!"

"Tell me what is happening!" I cried. "I cannot see it!"

"The dog," Llew said. "Twrch is running towards the stone. I do not see—"

"Look!" cried Ffand. I could feel her slender body trembling with excitement. "There is something . . ."

"Tell me! Tell me!"

Llew answered. "It is an animal. A fox, I think. No, its legs are too short and its head is too big. Maybe a badger . . ." He paused. "No, it is too far away—I cannot quite see what it is. But it has come out from the base of the stone."

Twrch barked again. The sound was further away.

"Now the animal has seen Twrch. It is running away."

"Which way?"

"It is running at an angle to us away from the stone. Twrch is chasing it. He is going to catch it—"

"Twrch!" Ffand screamed from her place behind me. "No!"

She hooked an arm around my waist, bent sideways, and slipped off the horse. I heard her buskins slap the paving stones as she raced after the dog, shouting, "Twrch! Stop! Come back!"

In the middle distance, I heard Twrch bay as he closed on the animal. I heard a snarling growl as the other beast turned to defend itself. The snarl became a frightened yelp—abruptly cut off. Even at a distance I heard the snap of its neck as the great hound seized the hapless creature and shook the life from it.

"Well," Llew said, "that is that. Whatever it was, Twrch killed it. Come, we will see what it was."

We left the sarn and rode a short way out onto the turfy plain to the place where Ffand stood holding the straining hound by his chain-link collar. Twrch barked eagerly as we dismounted, pleased with his kill.

"No." Llew groaned. "Oh, please, no . . ."

"What is it?" asked Ffand, her voice rising on a puzzled note. I could tell she was staring at the dead thing lying in the grass before her and was mystified by what she saw.

"Do you know this creature, Llew?" I asked.

"It is a dog—a kind of dog," he answered, in a tone of misgiving and regret.

28

Dyn Dythri

"A dog? Are you sure?" asked Ffand.

"A corgi, I think."

At his utterance of the odd word, my inner vision flickered to life with the image of a strange, short-legged creature with a dense coat of mottled red, yellow, and brown. It had a big head with fox-like ears, and a short muzzle; its body was thick, stout and tailless. A curious beast, it appeared half-fox and half-badger, but with the grace and virtue of neither.

The image faded, but not before I had glimpsed Llew's anxious glance towards the Giant's Stone.

"I think we should go," he said uneasily.

Even as we were climbing into our saddles once more, we heard the hollow grinding of the trembling stone and felt the deep earth-pulse in our entrails. The ground shivered beneath my feet. The horses whinnied. I held tightly to the reins to control the animal as the uncanny sound grew louder, and the deep, rhythmic throbbing grew stronger.

Twrch growled and ran towards the Giant's Stone. Ffand shouted, and dashed after him. And Llew, in the saddle now, lashed his mount forward to catch her, shouting, "Ffand! Wait!"

My mount reared beneath me. I pulled his head down hard to

keep him from bucking and bolting.

The deep trembling stopped.

"Hold him, Ffand!" shouted Llew.

My inner eye remained dark, and I cursed my lack of sight. "What is happening?" I cried, following him. "Tell me!"

"A hole—a passage has opened beneath the stone," he told me. "I saw something moving. It is gone now, but I think it was a person."

He dismounted and thrust the reins into my hands. "Hold these!" he said. "Twrch will tear him to pieces."

Before I could reply, Twrch began barking wildly again. Ffand shouted, scolding him. But the dog did not heed her. In almost the same instant, I heard a shout from the direction of the stone—a human voice, that of a man. The voice called again, speaking a word I did not know.

Llew shouted at Twrch to quiet him. "Hold him, Ffand!" he commanded. "Whatever happens, do not let him go."

I heard another shout in the odd tongue, and an answering call. Llew shouted something I did not understand. And then—"Tegid, get down!" he shouted.

In the same instant, the air convulsed with quick thunder. I felt the pressure of the sound on my skin. Something flew past my ear, whizzing as it went.

"Twrch!" Llew shouted. "No!"

The sharp thunder cracked again. Ffand shrieked. Twrch's growl became brutal and fierce, a lethal warning. Llew shouted to stop him.

"Twrch!" Llew cried, his voice tight, frantic. "Twrch, no! Stop him, Ffand!"

A third thunderclap shattered the air. I heard a man scream.

And then I heard Twrch growling and Llew shouting. I ran towards the sound. "Llew!"

"Twrch!" Llew bellowed.

"Llew! What is happening?"

My ears buzzed and my head ached from the sound. I smelled sour smoke in the air. Llew was yelling at Twrch to stop. Then all went very still and quiet. Twrch growled softly, as if gnawing a bone.

Llew murmured something that sounded like, "He has done it."

I moved quickly to where Llew stood. "What has happened?"

"It is a man, a stranger—Dyn Dythr," he said, indicating that the stranger was from his own world. "He had a gun—a weapon."

"A weapon made that sound?"

"It did." His voice still shook with excitement and alarm. "He was frightened. He started shooting at us—"

"Shooting?"

"Sorry—using the weapon, I mean—he started to attack us with the weapon. Twrch killed him."

"That is too bad. The stranger showed an uncommon lack of prudence."

"You can say that again," agreed Llew sourly. "He was stupid to—"

Before he could finish, I heard a scratching sound coming from the direction of the Carreg Cawr; Llew tensed. *"Clanna na cù!* There are more!" He darted forward to seize the dog. "Twrch! Stay, Twrch!"

To me he called, "Do not move, Tegid. I will speak to them."

"How many have come?"

"There are two," he said. "No—wait...three. There is another one coming out now..." He paused, and then I heard him shout a strange word: "Nettles!"

"Nettles!"

This peculiar utterance awakened my inward eye. The darkness thinned and brightened and I saw that a cavern hole had opened at the base of the Giant's Stone. Standing before this hole were three frightened men, slight of stature and dressed in the curious drab clothing of strangers; their hair was cut close to the scalp, revealing skin of an unhealthy yellow-grey pallor. Clearly, the light of life did not burn brightly in them.

The Dyn Dythri stood hunched together, their hands to their faces, tears streaming from their weak eyes. When at last they dared peer out from behind their fingers once more, they gaped at us, hands hovering at their pallid faces, as if their eyes hurt. Their mouths were slack with surprise; their wasted limbs trembled. These cowering strangers were dull, spiritless creatures indeed.

"Nettles!" Llew cried again. One of the men started, and I realized the peculiar word was his name. He was smaller than the others, round-faced, with a sparse mist of silvery hair on his head like cloud wafting round a barren mountaintop. On his face glinted a singular ornament: two round crystals bound by metal rings joined together with thin silver bands.

The man, eyes wide behind the crystals, regarded Llew for a moment, and then smiled with recognition. One of those with him, still quaking at the sight of us, muttered something and I realized I had heard the rough speech before: it was the tongue Llew spoke when he came to us. And it marked these visitors as members of his clan.

"Tegid! It is Nettles—Professor Nettleton. I told you about him, remember?" Llew turned and approached the small man. The two looking on shrank even further into themselves—as if they would disappear completely.

Llew said, *"Mo anam,* Nettles! What are you doing here? You should not have come." He spoke to the small man, who merely gazed blankly at him, his smile thin and uncertain. Then Llew, remembering his former tongue, said something to the man, who replied. They talked together for a moment. Llew looked at the two other men, who cringed from his glance, then pulled the small man to where I stood.

"This is Nettles. He is the nearest thing to a bard that we have in our world. He is the one who helped me."

"I remember," I replied. My inner sight held his image before me, and I saw that despite his frailty and ugliness, his eyes gleamed with the bright intelligence of a keen and sagacious mind.

With much halting and stammering, the two spoke together, and I turned my attention to the other two who still stood shuddering beneath the stone. They had seen the man Twrch killed—the body lay face down a few paces from them—and were shaken by it.

One of the men—a hands-breadth or so taller than the other—wore the air of a leader. He stepped hesitantly towards the body.

Twrch growled, his hackles rising. The man immediately stepped back. Twrch subsided.

The small man glanced at the body, and then said something to Llew, who answered him in his own tongue. They talked a moment, and then Llew said to me, "I told him what happened. I asked if they carried any more—um, weapons. He does not know."

Llew's eyes narrowed as he glanced at the two men standing before the stone. "This is a disaster, brother," he declared bluntly. "You know how much trouble Simon has caused here—these men are worse. I have seen them before, but they do not recognize me. The tall one—Weston—is the leader. Twrch killed one of his men."

In his clumsy tongue, Llew addressed the small man Nettles, then said to me: "They must be watched, and returned to their own world as soon as possible. Nettles agrees; he tried to stop them," Llew explained. "He has prevented them from coming for a long time. But they got lucky today—or rather, unlucky."

I did not fully understand what Llew was saying—though I knew he was referring to the arrival of the strangers. He was angry and wanted them to go back—that I understood.

After a moment, Llew and the small man walked to the place where the others waited. The two strangers cringed at Llew's approach—as well they might. For, though he had but one good hand, he could have slain either of them with a single blow.

Seeing him before them reminded me how much Llew had changed. His shoulders were wide and his back broad, his arms corded with muscle, his legs long and strong. As the Giant's Stone soared above him, so he towered above the frail creatures cringing beneath it.

He stepped before them, and I saw in my mind's eye their craven faces pinched with fear; I heard them speaking in their uncouth tongue with the one called Nettles.

Llew returned to me. "Nettles is telling them what is to—" He halted, turning around quickly. "Wait! Where is Ffand?"

Suddenly, Llew was racing away. "She is hit!" he shouted. "That idiot has shot Ffand!"

"What?"

"Over here, Tegid! Hurry!"

She lay crumpled on the ground—little more than a cloak flung on the grass, it seemed. A deep red stain spread slowly over her side.

"She is bleeding. It is bad, Tegid." He gently probed the wound with the fingers of his good hand. "The bullet—" he said, "I think it went through. The wound is clean, but she is bleeding badly."

I tore a strip of cloth from the edge of her cloak, folded it and pressed it to the injury. "We will bind the wound," I said. "That is all we can do until we reach Dun Cruach."

Llew held the folded cloth to the wound while I bound it with another strip torn from her cloak, tying the knot tightly over the injury to hold the cloth in place.

"I hope that serves until we get to Dun Cruach. You must take her to the wagons, Tegid. I will deal with these—these intruders," he spoke the last of these words through clenched teeth. "Can you see?"

"Well enough." I stooped to gather Ffand in my arms, and heard behind me the sound of horses approaching: Bran and Alun had arrived. The sudden appearance of these two Ravens, with their blue markings, armbands, spears, and shields, alarmed the strangers anew. They cowered close to the Giant's Stone, watching the warriors with wide, fearful eyes.

"We heard a strange noise," Bran explained, eyeing the strangers, "and thought to discover what had happened to you."

Alun regarded the strangers with a frown. "Dyn Dythri," he muttered.

"Fret not, Alun," Llew said coldly. "They are not staying long. They are going back where they came from as soon as possible."

"Will you do it now?" asked Alun, regarding the Giant's Stone. "Here?"

"No," Llew told him. "The portal—the gate is closed now. We must find another place to send them back." He indicated the strangers cringing in the shadow of the stone. "Take them to the wagons, Alun." To Bran, he said, "You take Ffand. Make a comfortable place for her. Tegid and I will follow—we have something to do first."

I raised Ffand in my arms and gave her to Bran, who took the unconscious girl on the saddle before him, turned his horse and started back. Alun, spear in hand, rode to where the strangers stood gawking. A quick gesture with the point of a spear was all it took to get them moving. They started off along Sarn Cathmail; we waited until they were out of sight behind the hill and then proceeded to bury the dead stranger in the shadow of Carreg Cawr.

Llew cut the turf with his sword and rolled back the grass. He chopped at the earth with his knife, then we scooped out the loose soil with our hands; Twrch helped dig. When we had made a shallow grave, Llew went to where the body lay. He searched in the grass for a moment before finding what he was looking for. He stooped and picked up an odd object: small, square, with a short, protruding shaft; it was blue-black in color, but with a metallic sheen on its surface.

"It is the weapon—a gun," he explained. The object did not look large or powerful enough to do any harm, let alone make the shattering sound we had heard. Llew broke the thing open and shook out several tiny seed-like things. He picked them up.

"Bullets," he said, and put the tip of one in his mouth. He bit the tip off, spat it out, and poured out a black powder from the bronze husk that remained. He repeated the process with each of the objects, and then tossed the gun into the grave. "There," he said with grim satisfaction, "that has fired its last shot."

We dragged the stranger's body to the grave and rolled him into it. The man's throat was savaged; blood soaked the front of his thin siarc. Twrch watched us silently as we replaced the soil and turf.

We returned to our horses then, and started off once more, hastening to the wagons to rejoin our companions. That night we camped in the heather beside Sarn Cathmail. We held vigil over the Dyn Dythri, lest they escape, and the next day we continued on our way. Gradually, the land began to change: the ground, already dry, was cracked and baked hard by the sun; what little grass remained was thin and bleached white. The heather was brown and the sky a filthy yellow with windborn dust.

The scouts returned with the report that the streams and marsh springs ahead were tainted. A short while later we came to a small, dead lake. The water was putrid, and a black scum floated on the surface. Flies swarmed in clouds along the strand where dead fish bloated in the sun.

We rode on, passing streams and pools and lakes of various sizes and at each place the water was black and noxious, the banks rimed with a foul, ocher frost; all the plants on the water marges were withered, brown and dry. Here and there, the bones of poisoned animals glimmered dully in the sun and, nearby, the carcasses of scavenging birds.

We journeyed through a still and silent land. But its silence was pestilence, and its stillness the quiescence of death. The air stank of sickness, rot and corruption. The heat and stench combined to assault us cruelly. Our eyes stung and our stomachs churned; we reeled with nausea in our saddles. Even the horses were sickened by the foul air: foam dripped from their mouths, their muscles jerked and twitched, and they would not eat.

"It is worse," Rhoedd muttered gloomily. "Worse than when I left. Now the air is bad as well; it did not smell like this when I was here before."

"Given time," Bran observed, "all corpses stink."

Rhoedd had warned us, but the reality was worse than anything he could have said. For, under that dismal yellow sky the land appeared beyond remedy. And with each step the stain deepened. The mysterious taint had penetrated deep, seeping outward, silently spreading its poison throughout Albion.

29

Blight

The weight of the wagons prevented us from travelling more swiftly, or we might have reached Dun Cruach sooner. As it was, we endured two more days of fierce heat with the stink of death in our nostrils, breathing dust and decay at every step.

The sun seemed to singe the sky and turn the ground to ash. I was spared the eye-withering light, but the stagnant, unmoving air lay on my lungs like wool making each breath a lingering misery. We rode without speaking, heads down, disheartened by the pitiless blight.

The ride provided by the wagons was too rough and jarring, so we took it in turns to carry Ffand. She weighed nothing, and regained awareness infrequently. We gave her to drink and bathed her face and neck with cool cloths to make her comfortable, but her wound was severe and I did not think she could endure much longer.

We reached Dun Cruach at dusk—heat-dazed on stumbling horses, and numb with the rigors of the journey. But the sight of the stronghold with its people streaming forth from the gates to welcome us lifted our hearts. They saw the vats and ran to them. Within moments the wagons were aswarm and the still air shivered with squeals of joy and shouts of gladness. Ffand, cradled in the saddle before me, stirred at the sound but did not awaken.

Cynan's voice rose above the rest. "Welcome, brothers!" he called, hailing us happily. "Never were guests more welcome in Dun Cruach. All the same, you will get no welcome cup. We drank the last of the ale yesterday."

"Greetings, Cynan," said Llew, climbing down from the saddle. "We came as quickly as we could."

"And none too soon," Cynan replied. I heard a muffled slap as Cynan delivered his customary clap upon Llew's shoulder, then, as I still sat my horse, I felt him grip my knee. "Thank you, my friends. We will not forget this."

"It is but a small repayment for all you have done for us," Llew told him.

"Who is with you, Tegid?" Cynan asked. "Do not tell me you have taken a bride."

"This is Ffand," I told him. "We found her on the way."

"She is the one who helped us escape from Meldron at Sycharth," Llew told him.

"Oh?" Cynan said.

"And she is wounded," Llew told him. Before he could say more, Bran and Alun came to where we were standing to ask what should be done with the strangers. "Bring them to me," Llew ordered.

"Dyn Dythri among us?" Cynan wondered. He must have turned his gaze to the wagons where Bran and Alun were unloading our prisoners. He paused, taking in their strangeness. "You have seen fit to bind them," he remarked.

"It seemed best," Llew replied. "They are enemies. One of them wounded Ffand—he is dead," Llew said, and told him how we had captured the intruders. "We will send them back to their own world as soon as possible. Until then, we must make certain they do not escape." He paused, and added, "Although the one with hair like lambswool—he is a friend."

"An odd way to oblige a friend. Yet, if that is the way of it—I will have a storeroom readied to receive them. My father has never used a hostage pit." He called instructions to Bran and Alun, then turned and urged us to join him in the hall. "It is too hot to stand in the sun like this. It is cooler inside."

Cynan called to some of his people, commanding them to take Ffand, to dress her wound and make a place for her to rest. "I will attend her soon," I said, passing her to their care.

We went into the hall to greet Cynfarch. The king welcomed us stiffly, almost angrily, then turned away and began ordering men to ration out the water.

"It is hard for him to accept your help," Cynan explained. "This came upon us so quickly—there was no warning. We have lost many to the poison. We tried digging new wells, but it is so dry—"

"We have come to take you back to Dinas Dwr," Llew said. "The water we brought will serve to get us there. How soon can you be ready to travel?"

Cynan paused. "We can leave at once," he answered, "but I do not think Cynfarch will go."

"We will talk to him."

"By all means," Cynan agreed. "But do not expect to change his mind. It was all I could do to get him to send Rhoedd—and then he would not allow me to ask your aid. My father can be very stubborn."

"Perhaps he will change his mind now that we are here," Llew suggested.

"Perhaps," Cynan allowed. "Let me speak to him again after supper."

It was a dismal meal we had that night. Cynfarch, embarrassed by his inability to feast us properly, sat frowning and silent in his chair, a grim companion. The people, though glad for the water, could not surmount their lord's melancholy. In the midst of a wasted land, Dun Cruach had become a cheerless and desperate place.

"It is worse than I thought," Llew whispered, when we were at last able to withdraw from the table. We stood outside the hall, but the air was still hot with no breath of wind to freshen it.

"We should not have come," I told him.

"They would have died without the water," Llew observed sourly.

Cynan joined us. He saw Llew's expression and said, "If you are plotting Meldron's demise, I am your man."

"Have you told Cynfarch yet? We dare not linger here any longer than necessary."

"I told him," Cynan replied sullenly. "My father would die before losing his realm."

"His realm is lost already!" hissed Llew. "His life is forfeit next."

"Do you think he does not know this?"

Silence intervened for a moment. The two stood looking at one another; I could feel them tense and angry in the heat.

"Would he do it for the sake of his people?" I asked.

"For them, aye, but for no other reason."

"Then we must make him see that if we stay even one day more, the people will die."

"Easy to say, difficult to do," Cynan retorted. After a moment he added, "My father thinks the rain will come and the blight will end. He is deluded, and I tell him so. But he will not listen."

"We should talk to him now," Llew suggested, "and settle the matter once and for all."

"It is late, and he is in no mood to talk," Cynan said. "Better to leave it till morning."

We lapsed into silence once more, uneasy and ill-tempered in one another's company. The quiet grew strained and awkward; we were all thinking of the task ahead and whether to approach Cynfarch now, or wait until morning. Rhoedd saved us from having to decide—he appeared just then to say that Cynfarch wished to see the intruders. "The king desires them to be brought before him at once," Rhoedd told us.

Llew hesitated. "Very well," he said slowly. I could tell he did not care for the notion of allowing the strangers even a momentary glimpse of freedom. "Bring them." They turned to go back into the hall. "Coming, Tegid?"

"In a while," I answered. "I will see to Ffand first."

Cynan called one of the women from the hall to lead me, and I followed her to a nearby dwelling. "She is here," the woman said, and my inner eye awakened at her voice. I saw Ffand asleep on a soft bed of fleeces; a woman sat beside her, tending a glowing rushlight. As the room was warm, she was bare beneath a thin yellow covering. The women had used precious water to wash her and had bound the wound with clean cloth. They had combed Ffand's hair and braided it.

I knelt beside her and spoke her name. "Ffand. It is Tegid. Can you hear me?" I touched her small bare shoulder. "Can you hear me, Ffand?"

She stirred and her eyelids opened slowly. "This is not Llew's fortress," she informed me in a voice thin as spider's silk.

"No, it is not. This is Dun Cruach, the settlement of our allies, Cynan Machae and his father, King Cynfarch."

"Oh," she sighed, much relieved.

"Did you think it was Dinas Dwr?"

"They say that Dinas Dwr is an enchanted fortress with walls of glass so that it cannot be seen," she whispered. "That is why Meldron cannot find it. And I did *not* think that this was Dinas Dwr." Her disdain was profound. She closed her eyes again as if to shut out an offensive sight.

"How do you feel, Ffand? Does it hurt?" She shook her head slightly. "Are you hungry?"

Her eyes flickered open once more. "Was he Nudd's man?"

"Who?"

"The stranger," she said, her voice growing softer still. "Was that why he was hiding under the Giant's Stone?"

I considered this for a moment. "Yes," I told her. "He was Nudd's man. That is why he was hiding under the stone."

"Then I am glad Twrch killed him." She swallowed; the muscles of her throat worked but her mouth was dry. I lifted her head and took up the cup. She drank a mouthful and refused more.

I rose. "I will look in on her again in a while," I said. "Bring me word if she wakes again before then."

The women nodded and resumed their vigil, and I returned to the hall. My inward eye remained watchful, and so I entered to see the strangers, standing before Cynfarch, each with a warrior gripping his arm. The strangers blinked and gaped at the host gathered around them. I took my place beside Llew, who stood a little to one side watching.

Cynfarch, a commanding presence on any occasion, sat like proud authority in his chair. He gazed upon the strangers with cold curiosity, then raised his hand and beckoned the tall stranger forward. He swallowed hard and raised his hands in entreaty, whining pitifully in his disgusting tongue. Even without knowing the words, I could see that the wretch was pleading for his miserable life.

"Rhoi taw!" Cynan cautioned. His meaning was clear enough, for the man clamped his mouth shut with a whimper. "Noble Father," Cynan said, turning back to the king, "I have brought the Dyn Dythri before you as you have commanded. Look upon them, lord, and know that they are not of our kind."

"That I can readily see," Cynfarch replied. "I would know why they have come here."

"I will ask them," Cynan offered, "but I do not think they can speak our tongue."

"That may be," the king replied. "Yet a man must answer for himself if he can. Ask them."

With that, Cynan turned to the man called Weston and demanded, "What is your name, stranger? And why have you come here?"

The stranger stiffened at Cynan's address. He made a mewing sound and gestured helplessly. Some of those looking on laughed, but it was an uneasy laughter and died as it was given breath. The other stranger cringed, his eyes wide with terror.

Cynan turned back to his father. "It appears that the stranger does not possess the understanding, lord."

"I do not wonder, to look at him," the king mused. "Still, I would learn why he and those with him have come. Is there anyone who can speak for him?"

"That I will soon determine," Cynan said, and stepped to where Llew and I waited. "Well, brother? Do you wish to speak for him?"

"Nothing good can come of this," Llew muttered, stepping forward. Ignoring the man Weston, he summoned the small, white-haired stranger to join him.

"This man is called Nettles," Llew told the king. "I know him; he is my friend. He is very like a bard and can be trusted to speak the truth. In this he is not like the others." Llew motioned for the man to move beside him and placed his good hand on the small man's narrow shoulder. "He is honorable—a man of great wisdom and learning. He has fought to prevent those with him from coming here, and will uphold your judgment in this matter." He paused, regarding the small man with affection. "I am able to understand his speech. Ask him what you will, I am prepared to speak for him."

"That is well," replied the king. "I would know why they have come to our world, and what they intend."

To the amazement of those gathered in the hall, the snowy-haired man answered without hesitation in a tongue very like our own, though I could make nothing of it. "What is he saying?" I asked Llew, who was smiling grimly as he watched the small man.

"I have no idea," he replied. "He is speaking a tongue called Gaelic."

"You told him to do this?"

"No," he answered, "it was his own idea. He thought it might be useful."

Before he could explain further, the king said, "He speaks forthrightly, this one. What did he say?"

"Allow me to speak with him, noble lord," Llew said to Cynfarch. Llew turned to the small man beside him and they spoke together. Weston and the other stranger stared at them in amazement.

Then the small man spoke out in a bold voice. When he had finished, Llew spoke in turn. "Great King," Llew said, "he says that they have come here from a place beyond this worlds-realm. He says that he is not lying when he tells you that the men with him are not good men. They have long striven to gain entrance to Albion and have at last succeeded, as you see."

Llew put his head close to his friend's and they spoke together in low voices. Weston strained forward to hear what they said, but the guard beside him gripped his arm and pulled him back.

Nettles spoke again, and Llew continued, "Do not be deceived. Though they may appear to you weak and insignificant, they bring with them a terrible power and malice to corrupt and defile. They have little knowledge of what they do, and yet that little serves no good intent. It is well that they have been made prisoners, for they are not to be trusted."

The king listened to this gravely, and then turned his attention once more to Weston. The stranger trembled under Cynfarch's stern gaze, sweat trickling down the side of his head and neck. When at last he could abide the king's stare no longer, he flung out his hands towards Nettles and bleated at him in his odious tongue.

Llew and Nettles conferred. "This man is called Weston," Llew said to the king. "He is demanding to know why he is being held prisoner. He says that you have no right to treat him this way, and commands you to release him at once."

The stranger's demands infuriated the king, who made up his mind about the Dyn Dythri at once. "The stranger's ignorance is plain," Cynfarch said, his voice a menacing rumble. "Does he not know that I am a king? And as justice is my duty, so its exercise is my right. Does he fail to understand this?"

"I believe he owns no man king, lord," Llew offered. "I think I can say with certainty that these strangers neither esteem nor regard sovereignty—whether among themselves or among others."

Cynfarch's blue eyes narrowed. "That also is plain to see. No intelligent man comes before a sovereign lord with demands who has not first won that right through fealty and service."

"Father," Cynan put in, "Llew has counselled that these strangers should be returned to their own world as soon as possible."

"Is this so?" Cynfarch looked at Llew.

"It is so, lord," replied Llew. "The Chief Bard knows how it may be accomplished."

"Then let it be done as you think best," the king said. "If banishing the Dyn Dythri to their own realm will keep us from harm and cause them no hurt, so be it." He raised his hand to the guards, "Take them away. I will hear no more."

The strangers were removed at once, Weston still protesting noisily as the warriors dragged him from the hall. The king shook his head slowly, a scowl on his face. The uncouth behavior of the strangers had embarrassed him.

Llew, recognizing his chance, said, "Lord Cynfarch, you have seen how matters stand. The water is poisoned; arrogant strangers invade Albion with impunity; Meldron roams Caledon destroying all who raise arms against him."

"These are very bad times," the king agreed.

"And there are worse to come," Llew said. "But at Dinas Dwr there is water enough for all, and food; and we are safe behind Druim Vran. I invite you to come with us to safety in the north—at least until Meldron is defeated."

"But how will Meldron be defeated," demanded Cynfarch, "if no one will stand against him?"

"We will stand against Meldron," Llew assured him. "When the time comes to stand, you will not find us slow to take up our weapons. We have brought water; it is enough to last until we reach Dinas Dwr. But we cannot wait. We must leave here at once."

The king considered this. "I hear what you say," Cynfarch replied. "I will give you my decision in the morning."

Llew seemed inclined to press the matter further, but I knew that would only harden Cynfarch's judgment. I spoke up, saying, "We will await your decision, lord."

Cynfarch withdrew to his chamber then, and the people went to their sleeping places, leaving Llew, Cynan, Bran and myself to talk together alone. "How can he refuse?" Llew wondered. "There is no water. You cannot stay here any longer."

"Yet we cannot go from here unless the king agrees," Cynan said. "That is the way of it. We will have to wait until tomorrow for his decision."

"Well then," put in Bran, "I am going to bed." He rose, and I heard his footsteps move away to a corner of the hall where he might lie down on a calfskin on the straw-covered floor.

"That is good sense," Cynan said. "Come, I will show you to your beds."

We rose and moved to the door of the hall. Upon stepping outside, however, we were met by one of the women watching over Ffand. "Lord Bard," she said, addressing me, "you must come at once. The child is calling for you."

The three of us went in to Ffand together. As we entered the rushlit room, I heard the woman with her say, "Here is the bard, child. Llew is with him."

At these words my inward vision quickened, and I saw the slender form of the girl lying in the bed, her skin pale in dimly glowing light. "Tegid?" she said.

"Here, child," I said, kneeling beside the bed. "I am here, Ffand."

"I am cold," she said. Her voice was a wisp with hardly a breath behind it.

The hut was uncomfortably close; the air stale. Yet she trembled with a chill. "Bring another cloak," I told one of the women.

Llew knelt beside me. "Does it hurt, Ffand?"

She gulped a breath. "No," she said. "But I am so cold . . . so cold."

"What did you want to tell me?" I asked.

It was a moment before she spoke again. "Where is Twrch?" she asked.

"He is outside. He is waiting for you. He has not left the door all day."

"Do you want me to bring him?" Llew asked.

She shook her head—the feeblest of movements. "He will get into trouble without me," she whispered.

"Ffand," Llew said, "you will get better. You will be able to look after him again soon."

"Take care of him," the girl said, her voice growing weaker. "He is all I have."

"Ffand, listen—" Llew began. He took her hand. "Ffand?"

But her spirit had already flown. Without so much as a shudder or sigh, Ffand was dead.

Llew sat holding her hand for a moment, then leaned over her and kissed her forehead. He rose quickly and went outside. The woman had returned with the cloak. Together we unfolded it and spread it over Ffand's body. Then I went out to the others.

"—and then get Bran and Alun," Llew was saying. "I will get the horses."

Cynan dashed away, and Llew turned on me. "The Dyn Dythri go back tonight! I will make sure of that." he said angrily.

"But we must—"

"Tonight!" Llew shouted, darting away. "And you are coming with us, Tegid!"

30

Where Two Roads Cross

The heat of the day had dwindled to a sultry swelter; even in the deepness of the night there was no comfort to be found. Yet, we pressed briskly on: Llew, myself, and four of Cynan's warriors riding guard on the strangers who travelled in two of Cynfarch's chariots. Cynan rode just ahead with a torch, scouting the way; Bran and Alun rode behind.

Our destination was the place where Sarn Cathmail, our trail from the north, crossed the track that led west into the central hills of Caledon—a crossroads. According to Cynan this crossroads was surmounted by a mound with a birch grove at its summit. It was a holy and sacred place, and it was from here that we intended to send the Dyn Dythri back to their own world.

Llew remained insistent that the strangers should be returned at once, and there seemed no reason to gainsay him. So we set out, hoping to reach the crossroads at dawn and the time-between-times, when the door between the worlds would stand open for a moment at that holy place.

The night was against us; with no moon to light our way, the journey had taken far longer than we had foreseen. Now we were trying to make what haste we could to reach the place in time.

"It is uncanny," Cynan muttered. "I know the land hereabouts.

We must have ridden past the mound in the dark." He paused, reining his horse to a halt, and turning to me. "Maybe we should turn back."

From out of the darkness, Llew answered him. "No," he replied tersely, drawing even with us. "We would have seen something of the hill trail—even in the dark. We will go on."

"Seen something!" protested Cynan. "I cannot see my hand in front of my face, let alone see the track ahead."

Llew remained adamant. "We go on, Cynan. I will not suffer them to remain in Albion even one more day."

Cynan sighed, but urged his horse to a swifter pace.

Whether bright midday or blackest night—it was all the same to me. My inward eye remained blind. Seeing nothing, I listened, alert to any sound that reached me through the still night air: Twrch padding softly, occasionally snuffling the path; the flutter of the torch, the clop of the horses and the creak of chariot wheels. Once I heard a bird, startled by our passage, give out a sharp cry as it took wing, its call a disembodied shriek dwindling into the formless void.

After a time, we descended a long hill-slope into a valley. Cynan halted to determine our location. The chariots bumped to a stop behind us. "I cannot see a thing," Cynan complained. "Tegid would have a better chance of finding the crossroads in the dark."

"We cannot have gone far wrong," suggested Llew. "Do you know this valley?"

"I do not," Cynan told him, his voice edgy with frustration.

"But you must have some idea where we are," persisted Llew.

"I might if I could see," Cynan snapped.

Llew was quiet for a time. The torch crackled—Cynan's frustration made audible.

"Well?" asked Cynan.

"We go on," he said. "This path may lead to Sarn Cathmail—"

"It might," Cynan agreed sourly, adding, "then again it might not."

Llew clicked his tongue and urged his horse on. I heard the sigh of leather and the creak of the wheels as the chariots started forward once more. I fell into line and followed the others, wishing my inner vision would awaken and reveal some feature of the land to me. But I proceeded, like those with me, in darkness.

It seemed to me a long time that we rode without finding the track or the mound. No one spoke; there was no other sound but the beat of the horses' hooves and the occasional bump of the wheels. I must have dozed in the saddle without realizing, for the next thing I knew we were scrambling over the low hump of a hill and I heard someone say, "It is growing light in the east." And at almost the same instant, Cynan shouted, "There it is!"

I shook myself fully awake. "There is the mound," Cynan was saying. "You can just make it out to the south."

"How far?" I asked, reining in beside Llew.

"Not far," he answered. "If we hurry, we will just make it in time." He snapped the reins. "Ride!"

A heartbeat later we were all racing headlong towards the mound in the thinning gloom. I followed the sound of the hoofbeats, and arrived just behind Llew. "Sarn Cathmail!" he shouted, leaping from the saddle. He ran to my horse and put a hand on the bridle as I halted the animal. "Hurry, Tegid. There is not much time."

I slid from my mount, snatching my staff from behind the saddle as my feet touched the ground. "Take me to where the two roads cross."

Llew led me to the place where a well-worn track skirted the mound and crossed Sarn Cathmail; there, taking my staff, I raised the wood to the four quarters, invoking the virtue of each in turn so that the crossroads would be established as a sacred center. Then I ran to the eastern quarter whence comes the obscuring darkness. I touched the end of my staff to the ground at this place and began inscribing a circle on the ground, uttering the quickening words of the Taran Tafod.

"Modrwy a Nerth ... Noddi Modrwy ... Noddi Nerth ... Modrwy Noddi ... Drysi ... Drysi ... Drysi Noddi ... Drysi Nerth ... Drysi Modrwy ..." I repeated once and again—and I felt the awen, kindled by the words, leap like a flame within me. My tongue seemed touched

with fire, and the words of the Dark Tongue flew away like sparks into the dwindling darkness.

I continued repeating the words until I finished in the place I had begun, enclosing the crossroads within the all-encircling ring. And, as the tip of my staff joined the two ends of the circle, I felt the hair on my arms prickle and rise; my skin tingled with the surge of the power flowing around me.

"Bring the Dyn Dythri," I called, and I heard the quick tread of feet as they approached.

"Do you see the circle I have marked on the ground?" I asked. "Let that serve to guide you. Cynan, take two men and, with a stranger beside each of you, walk the circle three times sunwise," I instructed, making the motion with my hand.

"Now?" asked Cynan.

"Yes, now. Quickly."

Cynan called Bran and Alun to take charge of the other two strangers, and they began treading the circle I had inscribed. When they had finished, I said, "Now take the strangers to the center, where the two roads cross. Hurry!"

"It is done," reported Bran a few moments later. "What would you have us do now?"

"Unbind them so that they do no injury to themselves," I directed.

Upon finishing this task, Cynan said, "It is done."

"Leave them where they stand, and take your place with us outside the ring," I answered. "Keep your spears at the ready."

The men obeyed, whereupon Llew asked, "And now?"

"And now we wait."

"What will happen?" asked Bran.

"That you will soon discover," I replied. " Tell me what you see."

We waited. I listened carefully, and heard only the sound of the men's breathing.

After a while, Cynan complained, "Nothing is happening."

"Just wait," Llew told him.

"But it is almost daybreak, and—"

"Quiet!"

At this exchange, one of the strangers shifted—I heard his feet on the paving stones. Alun Tringad gasped, "Did you see?"

"What?" Llew asked. "I saw nothing."

Cynan grew excited. "Look!" he said. I felt him grip my arm in his excitement. "Something is happening!"

Twrch barked sharply.

"Tell me what you see. Describe it!"

"I see water! It looks like water—as if they are covered with water," he said.

"Are they sinking into the water?" I asked.

"No, they are as before; they have not moved," Llew told me. "But they are changing shape—rippling. They appear as a reflection in water."

I grasped then what he meant. It was the time-between-times. The Dyn Dythri stood on the threshold, but they must be driven across and into their own world.

"That is well," I said. "Now, Cynan—you and your men take your spears and raise them. At my sign, all of you shout at once: rush at the strangers as if you would chase them. But do not go into the circle yourselves. Do you understand?"

"Yes," he said and called to the guards to ready themselves for a feinting charge.

"Hurry!" cried Llew.

I raised my staff high and brought it down quickly. "Now!"

With a wild shout, Cynan and the warriors leapt at the strangers. I heard a confused cry, and the sound of someone stumbling and falling with a grunt. "What is happening?"

"It is—they are going," Llew told me. "They are crossing over. One of them is gone already—I cannot see him. He has disappeared! And now Weston is going...he is—" Llew broke off.

"What is it? Llew?"

He made no answer, but I felt him start forward. "No! Llew, come back!"

"Nettles!" he cried. "Wait!"

I thrust out my hand and caught the trailing edge of his cloak as he darted forward. "Llew! Stop!"

I held tight to his cloak. He struggled forward. "Let me go!"

"Llew! Stay!"

Twrch barked wildly.

Llew shrugged off the cloak and rushed forward into the circle. Cynan called him back. Bran shouted . . . but he was gone.

We stood in stunned silence. The three strangers had vanished— and Llew with them.

"Why did he go?" asked Cynan, when he found his tongue.

"I do not know. Perhaps he saw something . . ."

"What? I do not understand. Why would he leave us?"

"I cannot say."

We waited in the awkward stillness after the tumult of the moment. The breeze lifted as the sun rose. Cynan touched my arm gently. "I think we should go from here." Regret and shock made his voice sound strange in my ear.

"Yes," I agreed.

When I made no move, he touched me again. "Soon," he said. "It is growing light."

"We will leave soon."

He called to his men and they began moving towards the horses and chariots. I stood alone, struggling still to comprehend what had happened. I heard hooves on the road behind me; Bran, mounted, led my horse to me and pressed the reins into my hand.

"Come," he said. "He is gone."

Clutching my staff, I raised myself slowly into the saddle. My companions were already moving away. I could hear the hollow clop of hooves on the road, and the slight grumble of the chariot wheels. I paused, hoping that my inward sight would awaken and I would see something . . . but my inward eye remained dark. So I lifted the reins, and turned my horse to follow the others.

Even as I turned, I heard Twrch whine softly—a plaintive cry for his missing master. I did not need to see him to know that the hound still stood gazing at the place where he had seen Llew disappear; he had not moved.

I whistled to him softly. When he did not respond, I called him. "Come, Twrch."

But the dog did not move.

"Twrch!" I called more sharply. "Come, boy!"

When the hound refused my command, I wheeled the horse and returned to the crossroads. I dismounted and, guided by his whine, laid my hands on the hound, grasped his chain-link collar and pulled. The dog paid no heed to my effort; and, though his forefeet were lifted from the ground, Twrch remained firmly planted on the road.

"Twrch! Come!" I jerked the iron links hard. The stubborn animal did not give ground. I jerked the collar again; the dog yelped in pain, but did not budge. "Twrch!"

I did not like hurting him, but I could not shift the beast. Yet I could not leave him there. I would need a rope to drag him away. I turned and called to Cynan. Twrch barked.

I turned back and stooped to the dog, stretching my hand towards his collar. The canny beast must have sensed my intent, for he dodged to the side before I could lay hold of him again. "Twrch! Stop it! Come, boy."

I lurched forward, tripped on a paving stone, and fell to my knees. The staff flew from my hands. I caught the hound by a handful of fur and held on. Fumbling for the dog's collar with the other hand, I struggled to my feet. Twrch barked again, loudly, furiously, and bounded forward, dragging me with him.

I fell onto the road and the dog twisted and broke free. "Twrch!" I called, scrambling to my feet. "Here, boy! Come, Twrch!"

I stepped forward. Twrch barked sharply—once, twice... The sound seemed to come from a great distance. And then all I heard was the sound of my own footsteps upon the crossroad stones.

I squatted down and began patting the road around me for my staff. I heard a sound like that of a rush of air, but I felt nothing. Instinctively, I thrust out my hands.

My flailing arm connected with a living body.

I struck out again. To my surprise the body collapsed and

toppled over me, sending me once more sprawling onto the road. I fought my attacker, swinging my arms and kicking my legs—landing blows by chance.

"Tegid!" someone cried. I swung my fist towards the sound. A hand seized my wrist in mid-air and held it. "Tegid! Stop it, Tegid!"

The voice was Llew's. And it was Llew who stood over me.

"Llew! You came back."

He released my hand, then sank to his knees beside me, panting. He was so out of breath that it was some time before he could speak normally. I seized and shook him.

"Llew! What are you doing? Why did you leave?"

"Here, help me," Llew said. "Nettles—"

Only then did I realize what he had done. "Nettles is with you?"

"Y-yes," replied Llew, gulping air. "I went—after him...I brought him back with me..."

Bran appeared beside me. He caught me by the arm and pulled me to my feet. "What has happened?" he asked, as mystified by Llew's sudden reappearance as by his equally abrupt departure.

"He has crossed the swordbridge between the worlds to bring the stranger back."

"Why?"

"I do not know."

"Where is Twrch?" Bran asked.

"The dog followed his master," I replied. "But, unlike Llew, he did not return."

"Twrch followed me?" Llew wondered.

"Yes," I told him, harshly—for I was angry with him. "I tried to prevent it, but I could not hold him back. Twrch is gone. And I do not think he will find his way back to us."

The sound of iron hooves striking the paving stones clattered behind us and, with a shout, Cynan threw himself upon us—as if to disentangle two combatants—seizing us in his hands and pulling us apart.

"Peace!" Bran cried. "Cynan, peace! It is Llew!"

"Llew!" Cynan hauled Llew to his feet.

The sun was well risen now—I could feel the warmth of its rays full on my face. To Cynan I said, "Can you find your way home, do you think?"

"I found the way here in the dark, did I not?" Cynan sniffed scornfully.

"Then lead the way. We should be gone from here."

Cynan called for Llew's horse to be brought, and I turned to where Llew stooped over Nettles' slight body. He was speaking to the small man in their rough tongue, but straightened when I touched him. "He is well. He can ride in one of the chariots."

"And you?"

"I am unharmed," he said, placing a hand on my shoulder. "I am sorry, Tegid. I would have warned you, but I thought of it too late."

Nettles uttered something in his broken speech and Llew answered him. To me he said, "I had to do it, Tegid. They would have murdered him. Weston would have killed Nettles when they got back. Besides, I think we will need him with us. He knows much that can help us."

"Very well," I said. "No doubt it is for the best. Come—"

"We will have to teach him the language—you can do that, Tegid. You taught me, after all. And Nettles will be quick to learn— he already knows a very great deal. As I say—"

"Say no more now," I urged. "In truth, I am not against you in this. We will talk later. But we should go."

The sound of the chariots rumbling over the stones of the sarn made a dull thunder in our ears as they returned—which is why we did not hear the enemy riders until they were almost upon us.

31

Trafferth

"Ride! All of you!" Cynan shouted. I heard the grating ring of a sword unsheathed. "Away! I will meet them!"

"How many are there?" I called.

"Twenty, I think," Llew said. "Maybe more. I cannot tell."

"Go!" urged Cynan.

"We stand together," Llew said. Bran and Alun backed Llew's decision, and the warriors voiced their acclaim. "But," Llew added, "it is two of them to every one of us. What do you suggest?"

"We have chariots," Cynan pointed out. "We can do a great deal of damage with those. I will take one, let Bran drive the other."

"Right," Llew said. He spoke a quick command to Bran, and then turned to me. "Tegid, take Nettles with you. Remain on the road. We will join you when we can."

"I am staying," I said.

"You could get away—"

"I am staying."

Llew did not have time to argue. "Stay then," he said. I heard the slap of leather across a horse's withers and a confusion of men's voices shouting orders, hooves clattering on the paving stones, and the cries of the enemy warriors as they drew nearer.

Someone ran to me. "Hold our horses," said Alun Tringad,

pressing the reins into my hand and racing away again.

"Follow me!" Cynan shouted. "Hie! Hie-yah!"

The hammer-sharp ring of iron-shod hooves sounded on the sarn as the warriors swept past. My inward eye awakened instantly at the noise, and I saw before me the level road and two chariots on it. Cynan drove the first, speeding towards a tight-clustered warband of twenty or more enemy warriors. Bran stood in the second chariot to the left of Cynan and Alun drove it, matching Cynan for pace. Llew rode to Cynan's right, with the remaining warriors around him.

A voice spoke beside me. *"Trafferth?"*

I glanced down to see Nettles looking up at me. He repeated the word again. "Trafferth?"

He was trying to speak to me in our tongue. Although his utterance was rough, I understood his meaning. "Yes," I told him, "trouble."

I do not know if he understood me, but he nodded and turned his eyes back to the battle. My inner sight shifted and I saw the two lines hurtling towards one another—but I viewed it from high, high above with the eye of a soaring hawk:

I saw the sleek necks of the horses straining towards the clash, heads thrusting, nostrils flared, flecks of foam streaming from their mouths. I saw Cynan, red hair like a firebrand above gleaming shoulders, muscles bunched as he drove the chariot, a bundle of spears ready to hand; Llew, sword at his side, spear lofted high; and Bran standing like an oak in the center of the second chariot, three spears in his hand, while Alun, head down, reins gathered in his fists, shouted hearty encouragement to his team. I saw the warriors, fierce in the fight, sword and spear in hand, blades keen, spearpoints glinting hard and sharp in bright morning light. The legs of the horses blurred with speed, stretching and gathering, hooves pounding—a dull thunder on the earth.

The enemy swept ever nearer, spreading in a wide arc to surround and contain the battle with their superior numbers. They held spears and long shields; their horses wore chestplates and leggings of bronze, and long-horned headpieces. Several of the

warriors wore horned warcaps, and one of them carried a carynx
curving from waist to shoulder like an enormous serpent. Their faces
were hard: fierce determination burned in their narrowed eyes. From
the look of them, they were members of Meldron's Wolf Pack—which
meant that the Great Hound must be very close at hand.

The two battle lines swept closer. I braced myself inwardly for
the clash, gritting my teeth.

Cynan and Alun drove for the center of the enemy line and
severed it as enemy warriors scattered on either side—avoiding the
chariots and fixing on the mounted warriors instead. But Llew and
the others remained well behind, so that the enemy could not take
them head on and blunt the attack.

The chariots slewed around, swinging out behind the turning
horses, flinging dust clouds high. The enemy line, divided like a
severed snake, curled in upon itself as the two separate halves drew
together. It was then that the mounted warriors struck.

Breaking from behind Cynan, the horsemen drove into the
churning enemy straight and swift as a thrown spear. The ground
trembled under the clash; horses were lifted off their feet and thrown
screaming onto their sides. Spears splintered and broke. Swords
flashed.

Cynan and Alun drove their chariots into the fray, striking in
from the flank. The enemy surged backwards like a retreating wave
in their haste to make way for the speeding chariots. Men shrieked
and horses collided.

Bran, upright, arm high, hurled a spear into the chaos. With the
force of the chariot behind the throw, I saw an attacking foeman
lifted clean from the saddle as the spear split his shield and pierced
him through.

Cynan sped through the enemy ranks like a mad bull charging
through a fog. Warriors howled as they fled before him. Head high,
bellowing wildly, spear quick and deadly in his hand, his challenge
loud in their ears, he raked them with his spear as he passed. I saw
more than one man fall beneath his wheels.

In the space of but a few heartbeats, the enemy line was shattered and their warriors dispersed. Whereupon, the chariots spun as one and charged into the second half of the enemy warband, which had turned and gathered itself for a charge. Again, the speed with which the chariots moved and the ferocity of Cynan and Bran's attack could not be endured.

The chariots struck to the heart of the advancing foe—struck, disappeared in the confusion of rearing horses and striving bodies, and then appeared again on the other side, where they halted, turned and prepared to strike again. The dust cleared. Five men lay on the ground, three horses thrashed in the dust, and five mounted warriors spun in rattled disorder.

Llew and the others made quick work of them. I saw the sun-glint of slashing blades, and then five horses running riderless along the sarn. I glanced down at Nettles: he was kneeling in the dust with his hands over his eyes, his shoulders trembling.

The remaining enemy gathered for a final charge. Cynan and Alun drew their chariots together side by side. Cynan raised a spear and shouted, lashing his team to speed. The horses reared and plunged forward, eager under his urging. Alun gave a long, whooping cry and his team burst forth as if hurled from a sling. Llew and the others turned and joined the chariots in mid-flight, spears slicing the air as they came.

This was too much for the enemy. The charge faltered and dissipated as the foemen broke ranks and fled before the onslaught. Away they flew, racing back the way they had come. Of the twenty that had attacked, only six remained. Llew and the warriors gave chase, hurling spears after the fleeing enemy. But the spears fell short and the six got away.

Cynan loosed a whoop of triumph then, leaped from his still-moving chariot and, with a quick chop of his sword, struck the head from the nearest dead foeman. He took up the man's spear, spiked the head upon it, and then planted the spear in the ground.

Overcome with joy and relief, I raised my voice in a victory chant, loud with exaltation—as if to make the distant hills ring with my defiant song. I turned to Nettles. "It is over! We have defeated them!"

He lowered his hands and blinked at me; he did not understand, but no matter. *"Gorfoleddu!"* I told him. "Rejoice!"

The small white-haired man smiled. "Gorfoleddu," he repeated, saying it twice more to himself and nodding.

Bran and Alun were first to return. Llew and the mounted warriors followed close behind, and Cynan after them, complaining: "We should pursue them," he said. "They will tell Meldron."

"We were fortunate this time," Bran said. "They were not prepared for the chariots. It will not be so again."

"All the more reason to finish what we started," Cynan argued.

"Bran is right," I said. "It may be that Meldron's whole war host is camped just over the hill. We should return to Dun Cruach while we have the chance."

Cynan remained unconvinced. "Let them summon the Great Hound himself. I am not afraid."

"There will be other battles," Llew said. "Let us take the victory we have been given and leave the fighting for another day. There are people waiting for us, brother. Lead us home."

We remounted, turned our horses, and hastened away. I could follow Llew's lead and, even with Nettles behind me, had no difficulty keeping up. The chariots rumbled over the sarn and we made for Dun Cruach. The day waxed hot and sticky, but Cynan pushed a steady pace over the dry, withered hills, and we arrived at Dun Cruach as the sun dwindled to a dull, white cinder hanging just above the western horizon.

Upon our arrival, I discovered that Ffand had been buried earlier that day. "It is so hot," explained the woman who had cared for her, "burial could not wait—and I did not know when you might return. Are you displeased, lord?"

She meant no rebuke, but her words stung me. "No," I told her, "you have done well. I should have attended her myself."

She led Llew and me to the burial place: a small square of earth in the shadow of the hall. "It is cooler here," the woman said. "It is the best place I could find."

I thanked her and she left us. Llew was silent for a long time, gazing at the fresh-turned earth. "You see how it is," he said at last. "We strangers do not belong here, Tegid. We cannot stay—we can never stay."

After an early supper, Cynan recounted the events of the day over cups of water in Cynfarch's hall. Those of our party who had remained at the caer, to oversee preparations for our return journey north, noisily expressed their annoyance at missing the excitement. And we were made to tell and retell the tale so that all could share it anew. In consequence, the night was deep around us before we found opportunity to speak to Cynfarch.

"Lord Cynfarch," Llew said, standing to address the king. "It is good to sit with you tonight and to recount our victory for you. But I am reminded that we have lost a day already and we still await your decision. Will you go with us to Dinas Dwr?"

The king frowned. "I have decided..." he said tersely.

Llew remained silent, awaiting Cynfarch's decision. But the king's word never came. For at that moment we heard the cry of the watchman on the wall. An instant later, the short, sharp blast of the battlehorn raised the alarm.

The cry of alarm awakened my inner sight. I saw the timber wall before me...warriors tense in the moonlight, edged in silver...stars hard and bright in a deep dark sky...the door of the hall flung wide, and warriors tumbling out into a pale yellow square of light...

I ran with the others to the wall and mounted the rampart. I saw the darkling land...empty—but for the faint glimmer of a single campfire in the distance. I turned to the warrior who had sounded the alarm, and opened my mouth to speak. But, even as I turned, I caught a winking movement in the dark: another fire.

The warrior raised his arm and pointed across the black distance. I looked where his finger led me, and saw that second glimmering flicker break into a cluster of several lights. Those clusters separated further, becoming a long string of lights.

Bran appeared at my side. "What is it?"

"It is Meldron," I replied. "He has found us."

Suddenly, the wall was swarming with warriors. Llew and

Cynan stood beside me to watch the silent, glimmering lights forming and spreading across the plain. There were scores of flickering shimmers now, quivering barbs of light, and more with every breath.

"So, he thinks to strike at night," Cynan remarked. "Let him come. We will prepare a welcome for him he will long regret."

Llew said nothing. He stared into the darkness as if trying to peel it away; his face was rigid with concentration, his eyes narrowed, brows knit together. His jaw muscles bulged.

I was more distressed by his expression than by the sight of Meldron's gathering host. "Llew?" I touched his arm; it was like touching the exposed root of a tree. The sensation unnerved me. "Llew!"

He turned his face to mine. His eyes glittered strangely in the moonlight—staring at me, but not seeing me.

"Speak to me, Llew," I said, laying my hand to his unnaturally rigid arm. "What do you see?"

He opened his mouth slowly . . . It was then that I saw the tiny flecks of foam at the corner of his mouth, and knew! My heart quickened within me. I knew what it was that gripped him. I knew—and the knowledge brought both hope and fear. For I had seen it before, and I knew its source.

Cynan, too, had witnessed the change in Llew. "What is happening?" he asked. "Tegid! What is wrong?"

Llew began to shudder. He reached towards me, clawing at me with his good hand. Cynan gripped his arms and struggled to restrain them. "Tegid! Help me! I cannot hold him!"

32

Firestorm

Cynan threw his arms around Llew's shoulders and held him in a wrestler's grip. Llew's eyes fluttered in his head. From his gaping mouth came a cry—keen and loud and fierce—like that of a hunting wolf, or a soaring eagle. He raised his arms and shrugged Cynan aside, flinging him away as if he were no more than a shred of rag clinging to his back.

In the same motion, Llew leaped from the rampart and ran across the yard towards the hall. Cynan rolled to his feet and made to rush after him, but I stayed him, saying, "Wait! Do not prevent him. He cannot hear you, and you might come to harm."

"What is wrong with him, Tegid?" Cynan demanded as Llew disappeared into the hall. He turned on me. *"Saethu du!* What is it?"

"Watch!" I said and, even as I spoke, Llew burst forth from the hall once more—carrying a firebrand in his good hand, and a leather cask under his other arm. He paused at the gate, pushed against it, and squeezed through.

"Clanna na cù," said Cynan.

"Go," I told him. "Gather your men and make ready to follow him." Cynan stared at me, aghast.

"Hurry, man!"

Cynan spun away, shouting commands to the warriors standing

near. He leaped from the rampart to the yard below and called for his weapons. His words were still resounding in the air when the battlehorn sounded. The warriors turned as one and flew from the rampart to the hall. Out of the turmoil emerged the figure of Bran Bresal, spear in hand and shield on his arm.

"Bran!" I cried. "Here!" A moment later the warrior chief stood below me. "Follow Llew, but lay no hand to him. Whatever he tells you to do—do it! Do not prevent him!"

He raised his spear in salute and darted away. I realized I need not have cautioned him. Bran would obey willingly and without question any command Llew would utter.

I turned once more to see Meldron's war host, closer—the light of hundreds of burning torches, flaming bright, spreading across the plain—and Llew, firebrand high, flying to meet the foemen.

The yard below me was a roiling mass of confusion: warriors swarming, voices calling, horses moving in the moon-dim light, weapons gleaming. The gate swung open and Bran dashed out a moment later, torch in hand.

He ran to join Llew, and I watched their twin trail of flame recede until they reached a place well away from the wall, whereupon Llew stopped and drove his torch into the ground. He heaved the leather container to his shoulder and began walking slowly backwards.

Cynan, armed and ready for battle, rejoined me on the wall. "What is he doing?" he asked. "Is he mad?"

"No," I told him. "Now gather your men and be ready."

Cynan sprang away again, and I turned back to observe Llew. He stopped pacing and stood for a moment on his measured spot, then he hastened to the place where he had planted his burning brand. Still holding the leather cask on his shoulder, he now began walking backwards in the opposite direction. I watched him, and it came to me what he was doing.

"Cynan!" I shouted, turning from the wall. "Cynan! Bring the king!"

Cynan stood in the center of the yard, ordering his men. Horses had been saddled and stable hands ran to bring them to the warriors.

He snatched the reins from a running youth. "Cynan!" I cried. "Where is Cynfarch?"

"He is readying his chariot," Cynan called. "He will ride before us into battle."

"Send someone to bring him to the wall. I must speak to him at once. Hurry!"

Cynan laid his hand on the warrior nearest him, nodded, and the man disappeared into the tumult of the yard. "You come, too," I shouted to him.

I felt the presence of someone behind me. I turned to see the stranger Nettles standing with me on the wall. He raised his arm and pointed out upon the plain. Where before there had been hundreds of gleaming torches, a thousand now burned. And I heard a sound like far-off thunder rumbling across the plain as the sparkling lights drew ever nearer.

Llew threw aside the leather cask and ran to snatch up his torch. Bran stood by him, but Llew seemed not to see him; seizing the torch, he held it to the ground. Instantly, flames leaped high and sped away from him on either side, tracing a wide arc through the dry grass.

Cynfarch, gripping an upright sword, called to me from the yard below. At that moment there came a sound like the rush of a roaring wind and the yard shimmered in flickering light. Through the open gate the king saw a curtain of flame leaping high into the night sky. Cynfarch took one look at the spectacle before him and demanded, "What is he doing?"

"He is preparing a way for us," I replied. "We must make ready our departure."

"Departure?" The king's mouth writhed and he drew breath to condemn the suggestion with scorn.

"We are leaving," I told him. "Behold!" I stretched my hand towards the shimmering flames. "Llew has set a shield before us."

"What has he done?" Cynfarch roared.

"A fire-shield!" Cynan cried.

"Summon him!" the king shouted. "He has defied my authority."

"The Penderwydd's awen is upon him," I told the king. "He hears only the voice of the Swift Sure Hand. Summon him, by all means, but I do not think he will obey you."

Llew stood outlined against the firelight, his hand raised over his head, palm outward, in the attitude of a beseeching bard. His image shifted in the shimmering light, making it appear that he was dancing before the fire.

Higher and higher the flames leaped as the fire streaked through the dead dry grass. The heat generated a fire-wind which whipped the flames yet higher and hotter.

Bran, spear upraised, turned to the wall and motioned the warband forth. Instantly—as if they had been waiting for this signal all their lives—the warriors raced from the fortress to join Llew. Lofting torches gathered from hall and storehouse, they ran out through the gates and joined Llew at the fireline. The shouts of the warriors and the rising voice of the flames—fire joined to fire as the warriors ignited fresh blazes—grew to fill the night.

"Cynfarch!" I called. "The matter has been decided. Gather your people and your cattle, and what treasures you can carry. Make ready to leave, and look your last upon this place."

King Cynfarch's face darkened with rage. But Cynan, eyes alight with the blaze, clapped a hand to his father's shoulder and said, "Your anger cannot stand against his deed. Let us be fearless men, wise in our strength. Let us use Llew's shield of fire to cover us while we depart."

"While we *flee!*" the king shouted angrily. "He cannot do this! He has no authority over me or my people!"

"It is not by Llew's authority that this has come about," I answered, "but by the authority of One who commands fire and wind. If you can make the wind and the flames obey you, then do so. Otherwise, I suggest we prepare to leave while we may."

Cynfarch spun on his heel and hurried to the hall. I turned back to see that the flames had become a towering wall of blazing fire, a great, rippling sail, billowing outward in the heat-incited wind. Cynfarch's warriors completed the task Llew had begun. Streaks of fire coursed through the dry grass, igniting great swathes which raced before the rising wind.

"Come," I said to Nettles. "It is time to go." The small man turned from the blaze and followed me without a word.

We withdrew from the wall, and joined the uproar taking place in the yard as people scurried to retrieve their treasured possessions from the hall and from their houses. Ten or more wains stood in the yard: four in which we had brought water, with the vats still on them; the rest were quickly filled to overflowing with the wealth of the clan.

Cynfarch appeared in his chariot and took his place at the head of his people. Cynan, on horseback, shouted orders. A man came running with my horse. I took the reins and dismissed the man to join his family, then mounted and helped Nettles to a place behind me— and not a moment too soon. There came a rush from the far corner of the yard and suddenly we were engulfed and surrounded by frightened cattle, bawling and bellowing at the sight of the towering flames.

King Cynfarch in his chariot, his driver beside him, raised the curving carynx to his lips and gave a sharp blast. Two hundred people moved as one body towards the gates. The king led us out onto the firelit plain.

I paused outside the gates to wait with Cynan until all were away. The families passed through first, hastening off along the firewall after the king's chariot. Next came the cowherds who drove the pigs and cattle—the sheep would follow of themselves—and lastly, the wagons laden high with the tribe's treasure.

Cynan turned his face to the fire. The horse beneath him shied and twitched, tossing its head. "Look at it!" he said, lifting his voice above the flame-roar. "The flames are drawing the wind!"

The intense heat of the fire created a gale all its own, gusting wildly, whipping the flames, driving them higher and faster: a raging torrent of flames.

"Choke on that, Meldron! Ha!" Cynan exclaimed. "Llew has bested you again."

"Where is Llew?" I shouted.

"I do not see him!" Cynan answered, searching the rippling,

shifting fire. "Nor Bran!"

I scanned the withering flame-bright wall with the sight of my inward eye for some sign of Llew. Then Nettles tapped me on the shoulder and pointed towards the leading edge of the fire. I saw Llew, body glistening from the heat, astride a galloping horse speeding along the shimmering wall. He seemed a creature of the storm, oblivious to the flames swirling around him. Bran followed a little distance behind him. And the warriors, mounted now, raced with their torches all along the blazing border, pausing in the gaps to kindle new fires and then racing on.

"There!" I shouted. "He goes before us."

Llew disappeared again in the swirling smoke and jutting flames, and we looked to the task at hand. King Cynfarch led the people out upon the charred and smoking plain, then turned to the north, moving away from the inferno. We followed behind with the wagons; Llew and the warriors ranged ahead keeping the shielding flames between us and the enemy, feeding the firestorm afresh.

All the next day we journeyed north unseen, through a foul haze of smoke that darkened the sky and cloaked the sun. Black ash fell in a filthy rain over us. We pulled our mantles over our heads and plodded on. With every step, I expected Meldron and his war host to emerge from the murk and cut off our escape.

But no enemy riders appeared; not the dull glint of a spearpoint did we see, nor did we hear the rumble of horses' hooves. Still I looked for the trap.

Day followed day, and each dawn the sun rose hotter and more fierce than the last. The land, already dry and hard as fired clay, cracked like a loaf baked too long in the oven. Dust clouded thick where the people walked. The heat became stifling. We rested from first light to last, and travelled through the night—hoping to elude both the heat and Meldron's war host, who could surely track us by our footprints in the dust.

It was not until we began the long ascent into the northern hills that I began to hope that we might yet elude the foe—not until I felt the land begin to rise towards Druim Vran that I thought we had truly done so.

After the frenzy of the awen, Llew remained subdued. Bran rode with him, but he spoke to no one and rode with his head down, his body bent forward in the saddle as if in pain. I tried to rouse him, but could not—he even spurned Nettles.

The small stranger rode with me; he became my constant companion, my shadow. I began teaching him our tongue, and soon grew to respect his agile mind—the speed with which he mastered the most difficult expressions. Indeed, before we reached Druim Vran, we could converse in simple words. I found him an amiable companion, willing and eager.

That was the only good thing to come out of the journey. As for the rest, I remained wary and ill-humored—and I was not the only one. Despite Llew's brilliant diversion, Cynan also feared we had eluded Meldron too easily, and the thought did not sit well with him. We stood together beside our horses as the last wagon and the last of the sheep crested the hump of Druim Vran and began the descent to our hidden lake fortress.

"Well, brother," he said, "you may call me a fool for fretting, but I am still uneasy." He turned away from me as he spoke; and though I could not see him, I knew he was looking at the trail behind us, watching for Meldron to appear.

"You were happy enough to leave Dun Cruach," I pointed out.

"Oh, aye," he agreed sourly. "That was well done. And necessary, I grant you that. We had no other hope. Still—" he paused, looking down the trail again, "it is one thing to leave, and another to arrive safely. Am I right?"

"Even so, we have arrived safely."

"Have we? I do not hear your tongue awag in reassurance, eh?" He paused, then growled, "I am listening, bard, but I hear nothing."

"I make no secret of my fear. And you are welcome to share it, Cynan Machae. I considered this journey ill-advised; I warned against it from the start. And though we stand once more within the protection of our high ridge, I feel no safety here. I tell you the truth, the deed is far from finished."

Even as I spoke the words, I heard the hollow sound of my own despair. Why? Cynan was right to question it. I had been against leaving Dinas Dwr, but the undertaking had ended well. So why did I still feel the chill of foreboding in my bones? Was all as peaceful as it seemed in our hidden realm, or did some fresh disaster await discovery?

Shouts of greeting reached us then, echoing up from the lake, as the people hastened to welcome us home. Cynan remounted his horse. "Come, or we will miss our greeting."

I listened to the joyful shouts, hearing in the sound not welcome only, but something else as well—an elusive note. What? Was the greeting a little too ardent, the welcome too exuberant? Or had I been so long expecting the worst that I could not recognize happiness when I heard it?

Cynan saw my hesitation. "Why do you delay?"

"It is nothing," I told him, snatching up the reins and lifting myself to the saddle once more. "Let us join the celebration." I snapped the reins and started down the steep trail.

"Tegid," he called after me, "is something wrong?"

His question did not remain unanswered, for we had ridden but half-way to the lake when we caught the unmistakable stench of death in our nostrils.

My horse halted, refusing to proceed. But I struck him across the withers with the reins and urged him to speed. Cynan shouted behind me to wait. I did not heed him but flew headlong down the trail to the lake.

33

The Word Already Spoken

I realized well before I reached Dinas Dwr what was wrong. A man does not need eyes in his head to recognize the stink of rotting fish—even the dullest of noses will do. The stench grew stronger as I drew nearer the lake, becoming more fierce and virulent with every step.

By the time I arrived, the crowd had quieted. I pushed through the curiously reticent assembly, and found Llew standing on the shingle, stunned. "You warned me, Tegid," he muttered. "But I would not listen."

The sound of his voice roused my inward sight. I saw our shining lake dead, its clear water turbid with poisonous scum—like the eye of a corpse long dead, or the once-bright surface of a silver mirror now tarnished and corroded. The shore was strewn with dying vegetation, wilted and reeking in the hot sun. From one side to the other, the lake was defiled with the bloated remains of fish and water fowl. The surface seemed to quiver, gurgling gently as bubbles formed and burst, releasing evil-smelling vapor to foul the air. The whole valley stank.

Bran, standing near, gazed upon the tainted lake and said, "The poison has touched Dinas Dwr at last. And now there is no safety anywhere in this worlds-realm."

Scatha and Goewyn came to us. The women greeted us warmly

and kissed us. I saw that Goewyn took her place beside Llew and remained there; she said little, but her eyes never left him. Despite her nearness, Llew had not a word to spare for her. Neither did he look at her—if he had, he would have seen how his lack of regard cut at her heart.

Noting soot and ash amidst the dust on our clothes, Scatha surmised that we had come through fire, and Alun spoke up boldly to praise Llew, telling all gathered near about the Hero Feat of the fire-shield.

"Would that I had been there to see it," Scatha replied, and the Ravens echoed her, trying to cheer us. Yet despite all, their welcome remained somber, for they were no less dismayed than we by the horror.

"It is a wretched homecoming," Goewyn said. She stretched a hand half-heartedly towards the lake. "I am sorry you had to find it so."

Llew looked around at those gathered near. "Where is Calbha?"

"He is searching for water. He took six with him, and they have been gone four days," Scatha answered. "Our supplies are very low."

"We have left the crannog," Goewyn said awkwardly.

Scatha added, "We thought it best—until the plague is over."

"No doubt that is best." Llew gazed out across the lake with an expression of grief. Tears glazed his eyes; he blinked and they spilled from his lids and started down his cheeks. He brushed them away quickly with the stump of his arm. "If I had been here..." he muttered, and then turned his back on his city in the lake.

As Goewyn said, the people had moved from the crannog to a camp at the end of the glen, hard against the ridge—as far from the lake as possible in the valley. Even so, it was not far enough. The stink of the dead lake under the blistering sun assailed us with undiminished vigor.

Cynfarch and his people settled among us, bewildered and forlorn. It seemed to them that they had fled to a worse fate than they left behind. Cynfarch, much disheartened, rumbled restless through the Galanae encampment like a storm waiting to break. To his credit, he held his tongue and kept his misgivings to himself.

Two days passed and the sullen sun blazed ever hotter. We measured the water and apportioned it carefully, awaiting some word or sign from Calbha. But there was none.

Neither was there any respite from the stench of the lake. The searing sun and withering heat served to increase the rot and decay, making the once-clean, cold water a festering, putrid, bubbling stew. My Mabinogi came to me, wanting to proceed with their learning, but we could not abide the heat and stink; even our shaded grove offered no escape. I abandoned the teaching, saying, "We will begin afresh when this blight is over. Go back to your kinsmen and do what you can to help them."

Gwion took it hard, so I gave him my harp, saying, "Keep this well-tuned, Gwion Bach. If you are ever to be a Filidh you must learn the proper care of a harp."

"Summon me when you will, Penderwydd," Gwion vowed. "Day or night you will find this harp ready to your touch."

The boy dashed away—he could not wait to try the harp. I turned to Nettles, who had accompanied me to the grove. "It was but a small thing," I said.

"But it—ah, restored his spirit," he observed, hesitating only slightly over the words.

"Would that I could do as much for the rest of Dinas Dwr," I replied.

By day the scent of death assaulted us; by night the children cried in thirst and fever. Food was prepared and served, but it went uneaten. With the foulness in the air drawn into our mouths at every breath, no one could stomach a bite. The heat and stench sapped both strength and will; we moved in a torpor, dazed by the enormity of our misfortune, and daunted by our own inability to overcome it. Here was an enemy we could not fight, much less conquer.

At dusk on the second day, Llew sought my council. "Something must be done, Tegid. Follow me." He led me away from the camp to a place where we could speak without being overheard. We sat together side by side on a rock below a cliff-face of the ridge. The rock was still warm from the day's heat, and black flies swarmed in the evening air. "Calbha has not returned, and the little water we have left will soon be gone."

"How many days?"

"Three or four days, five at most—if we are stinting."

A mouthful of water a day for man and beast, two for the children...how could we be more stinting than that? I wondered.

"I do not think Calbha will return in time," Llew continued, "if he returns at all."

"What would you have me do?"

Llew considered, and I heard the buzz of insects rising as the heat of day ebbed somewhat. The sound was dry and dusty as the hard-baked earth itself.

"I do not know," he said, his voice sinking into despair. "There is nothing anyone can do." After a moment he added ruefully, "I should not have left."

I wondered at these words. It was true: he should not have left Dinas Dwr; I had told him as much in my warning. But the way he said it...the way he said it sparked in me a peculiar feeling: as if a current flowed beneath my feet, a mighty stream, a river cataract rushing below the crust of earth beneath us. I imagined that I could feel this hidden power seeping up through the rock on which I sat.

"You knew this would happen, Tegid," Llew continued. "You said there would be disaster. Well, you were right."

"What do you mean?"

"This would not have happened if I had stayed," Llew replied bluntly.

Again I felt the hidden power surge, trembling in the very earth and air around us. *This would not have happened if I had stayed*... He knew! He felt it, too. But why?

Why would remaining in Dinas Dwr have changed anything—unless Llew's presence itself exerted some power over the evil rampant in the land? He possessed Ollathir's awen. The awen of the

Chief Bard of Albion could be a potent and powerful weapon—he had shown it in the inspired creation of the firestorm. Was that it? Or was there something else?

"Llew, what are you saying?" I asked.

"I should have listened to you," he replied dully. "There. I have said it. Do not make me say it again."

"That is not what I meant," I told him. "Why do you think your presence would have prevented the blight from poisoning the lake?"

He shifted on the rock beside me. "Who knows?" he replied angrily. "What do you want from me?"

"It is said that the True King in his kingdom holds the power to protect and preserve. Is this why you feel your presence would have made a difference?"

"You have all the answers," he replied tartly. "Then answer me this—" I heard the slap of skin on skin as he struck his upraised stump with his open palm. "I am maimed, Tegid. Remember?"

He stalked away then, leaving me no wiser than before—except in this respect: I knew now that some great and powerful force lay hidden close to hand, like a sword sheathed against the Day of Strife. It remained for me to discover how it could be raised. If I could do that...

But first I must find it.

I drew up my legs, crossed them, and settled myself on the rock. I breathed deeply and exhaled—once...twice...three times—clearing my thoughts, putting fear and anxiety far from me, emptying my heart of all but the desire to penetrate the mystery. When I was completely calm and content, completely at peace, I took three purifying breaths and recited an invocation:

> All praise to the Swift Sure Hand
>   for his deliverance at need;
> All praise to the Word-Giver,
>   for Truth's Three Pillars;
> All praise to the Living Light,
>   for Wisdom's holy fire!

Attend me now, Great Guide, and lead me in your ways. For,
wide is the world, and tangled the paths by which a man must go.
And I am so easily led astray.

Here am I upon my rock, and here I stay:
    I will be unmoved until you, Unmoved Mover,
        move in me;
    I will keep silent until you, Living Word,
        speak to me;
    In darkness will I sit until you, Light of Life,
        illumine me.

Grant me now, Gifting Giver, three things I seek:
    Knowledge of the thing I do not know;
    Wisdom to understand it;
    Truth to discern it rightly.

And then, calm within myself, silent, expectant, I rested my
hands on my knees and waited. Peace...peace. I listened and waited.
I waited...peace...

The air, still and heavy as a cloak, held all the sounds of the
valley as if transfixed in amber. I heard, a small distance away, the
muted speech of mothers coaxing their children to sleep. I heard the
whimper of a dog, the lowing of a cow, and the twitter of swifts as
they returned to their nests in the cliff-face above me. I heard the
sound of the world sinking into darkness, a hush like an exhalation,
a sigh of gratitude for escape from the hateful day's hurts and
harms.

I shut my ears to these sounds and listened inwardly...
peace...peace...peace...

I heard the sound of my own heart beating regular and slow. I
heard the sound of my own voice falling like a flung stone into the
silence of a well. I heard my plea for knowledge and wisdom echo in
the rippling depths.

The echo ceased, swallowed in the depths. And in reply, I heard
the voice of Ollathir, Chief Bard, Wise Leader and friend, now
departed:

"Why speak a word that is already spoken?" Ollathir's voice demanded sternly. *"Why reveal that which is already shown? Why proclaim the truth which rises like a mountain in your midst?"*

And then I heard, loud from the high ridgeway, the sharp blast of the carynx; a single long burst, followed by two shorter bursts. The sound rang across the still valley, across the dead lake.

Calbha had returned.

34

Enigma and Paradox

The people rushed to welcome Calbha. Thirst made them fervent, and they acclaimed him with shouts and with singing. But the songs soon trickled away, and the shouting ceased. Calbha had not returned with water—and not so much as a drop remained of the little he had taken with him when he left.

Disappointment was quickly swallowed by dismay when he reported what he had seen:

"Meldron has entered the valley beyond the ridge to the south," he said, climbing down from the saddle. "We counted five thousand on foot, and two thousand on horseback."

"How far away?" It was Llew, pushing through the abruptly silent gathering.

"One day," Calbha replied, "no more."

"Do they know we are here?" asked Cynan, taking his place beside Llew.

"They know. Meldron knows." King Calbha did not blunt his words, and they pierced the hearts of all who heard him. "The enemy is following the trail you made when you returned here from Dun Cruach."

"Bran!" Llew called, summoning the Raven battlechief, who answered from the throng. "We will need watchmen on the ridge."

"It will be done." Bran hastened away at once.

Llew turned to Calbha once more. "Did they see you?"

"It would have made no difference if they had," the king replied. "But no—we waited through the day before crossing the ridge by dark, just to make certain no enemy scouts would see. Still, he needs no scouts. Meldron knows where to find us, I tell you."

"We will hold council at once," Llew said quickly. "Cynan, bring Scatha—"

"I am here, Llew," Scatha called, stepping through the crowd.

"Tegid?"

"I am behind you," I answered.

"Good. Summon Cynfarch," he ordered, "and tell him to join us. We will hold council as soon as Bran returns."

"I will bring Cynfarch," Cynan said, and hurried away.

Goewyn and some of the women approached with jars of water for the riders. "You are weary and tired," Goewyn said, offering Calbha one of the jars. "Drink."

Calbha accepted the jar and raised it to his lips. He glanced around him quickly. "Is there enough for all?" he asked.

"There is enough for you," she said. "You have ridden far on our behalf. For that we are grateful. Drink and be refreshed."

But Calbha refused. "If there is not enough for all, there is not enough for us. We will not drink while others thirst." He returned the jar to her untouched.

Llew raised his voice to the people and bade them return to their rest. As the crowd dispersed, he said to those remaining, "Follow me."

We walked through our shrivelled fields and up the slope to the place where Llew and I had camped when first we had come to Druim Vran. Llew lit a small fire so that we could see one another and we spread oxskins we had brought from camp. Cynan and Cynfarch joined us then, and we settled back to wait for Bran.

Though I could not see their faces, I could feel the fear slithering cold into our midst: intense, desperate, coiling quietly as a snake.

"We began to think you would not return," Cynan said to Calbha.

He spoke just to dispel the mounting apprehension.

"We ranged as far to the north as we could," the king replied, eager to add his voice to Cynan's, "and further than we intended."

"No water?" Cynfarch wondered.

"Water aplenty! We found rivers, streams, pools, springs ... all of them poisoned, all dead." He paused, his voice cracking dry. "There is no good water anywhere. The land is dying."

"It is the same in the south," Llew said.

"Ah," replied Calbha, "I wondered what had induced Cynfarch to join us."

"We outwitted Meldron at Dun Cruach," Cynan said, and related the feat of the fire-shield for Calbha's benefit. "It was glorious."

Cynfarch could not resist adding, "And if you had not squandered your safety for us, Meldron would not now be squatting at your gates. As it is, we have merely exchanged one grave for another."

"Lord Cynfarch," Scatha addressed him firmly, "we are in council here. This is not the place for such talk."

"Is it not?" the king retorted. "If I have misspoken, I am sorry. But if I have spoken truly, mark my words and remember them."

We settled into an uneasy silence, broken only by Bran's arrival. When Bran had seated himself, Llew said, "We will be warned if Meldron seeks an early attack—"

"But he need not attack at all," Cynfarch growled. "We are soon out of water. Thirst will kill us just as surely as Meldron's spears—if more slowly."

"With seven thousand," put in Calbha, "the Great Hound has enough spears to make a swift end."

"Seven thousand..." mused Cynan. "I would know where Meldron is getting water for a host so great."

My mind's eye awakened. I saw before me, not the faces of those gathered at the council ring, but Meldron's vast host streaming into the lowland valley beyond Druim Vran. I saw the slowly advancing line thick-scaled with shields slung on their backs, sinuous and gleaming like a deadly serpent. I saw the sun red in their eyes, the blistering light of day ablaze on shield boss and sword edge. I saw the dust rising in pillar-clouds beneath the hooves of horses and the feet of men.

I saw a pitch sky, black and brooding, smoke-filled where the Great Hound passed; heat lightning shattered the gloom in ragged sheets. I saw the land falling beneath the shadow—a darkness stretching ever nearer the high wall of Druim Vran.

"Well, we cannot sit here and wait for thirst to claim us," said Llew. "We must fight while we still have strength to do so."

"Fight?" Cynfarch scoffed. "He has seven thousand! Even if we survive a battle with a force so powerful, thirst will kill us anyway."

"That is your fear talking, Cynfarch," Bran said coldly. "Llew, tell us what you wish us to do."

It was right that Bran should defer to Llew, and it was nothing new—that was his way. But as he spoke I heard again the voice of Ollathir: *Why reveal that which is already shown?*

Thus the council began. We talked long into the night. Food was brought to us, and we ate. The bread broke hard and dry in our mouths, and stuck in our throats; there was no water to wash it down. The talk grew heated under a baleful moon—voices loud, tempers quick. But I remember nothing of the discussion; I did not taste a morsel of the meal placed before me. For I had glimpsed a sight that removed all else from my mind: the shape of the mountain in our midst.

While the battlechiefs deliberated, images arose in my mind— images of past times when Ollathir was alive, and Meldryn Mawr was king. I saw Meldryn Mawr on his throne in his hall, his countenance brilliant as the torc at his throat...dark eyes searching the crowd before him, confident and wise...his presence glowing bright as the crown on his noble brow...the Great Golden King, Lord and Protector to his people.

And I saw Ollathir, Chief Bard, beside him, splendid in his purple cloak and torc of gold...Champion among Bards, Truth's Warrior, proud and solemn and wise, his strong hands wielding the Penderwydd's rowan staff...in conduct steadfast, upright and unwavering...Lord of the Learned, a trustworthy Servant of

Sovereignty.

I saw fair Prydain as it was before its desolation, a green gem shining beneath radiant skies, and Sycharth rising above the flat land on its proud promontory overlooking grain-laden fields and the ever-changing sea beyond...the strongholds of lords glowing in golden dawn light, and gleaming in the setting sun...high-banked earth and timbered walls...fair woodland, deep forests, rushing streams and stately rivers...Prydain, Most Favored of Realms, the unassailable seat of a most powerful king.

Meldryn Mawr, Great Golden Monarch... Ollathir, Prince of Bards... Prydain, Fastness of Bold Kings...these three together ...together.

Why these three? What was I to glean from this vision?

It would take a keener mind than mine to pierce the mystery to its heart. Meanwhile, our enemies gathered beyond the protecting ridgewall. If the answer was to come, it would have to come soon. Meldron, ever grasping, would not wait to claim his victory.

The war council talked long into the night. But my head was full of the enigma stirring my thoughts like a tempest, and I could no longer sit still. My heart burned within me and I could no longer endure listening to the strident voices. I rose and withdrew from the council ring; my departure went unnoticed.

"Let them talk," I thought. "The enemy gathers round about—I must do something."

But I did not know what to do. So I began walking. I walked, and let my feet take me where they would, tapping with my staff as I went. I skirted the encampment and continued on the path.

As it happened, my tapping disturbed one sleeper, who awoke and joined me on my meandering ramble. Nettles did not speak, but rose and fell into step beside me. Since our flight from Dun Cruach, his presence had become agreeable to me and I welcomed his quiet way. I stopped and turned to him. "Come, we will walk together."

To my surprise he answered, *"Mo bodlon, do."*

His speech improved with each day, as well it might—he worked at it tirelessly. I nodded, and proceeded along the path. The small stranger walked beside me, and we continued in silence for a time.

"Mae trafferthu?" he asked at last.

"Yes," I replied. "There is great trouble."

We walked on, and I found myself beginning to explain to him the mystery that taunted me. I did not know how much he could understand of what I said, nor did I care. It seemed good to me to have someone to talk with, someone who would merely listen.

"When the Wicked One escaped his Underworld prison, where did he fly?" I asked. "When Nudd, Prince of Uffern and Annwn, King of the Coranyid, rode out to despoil this worlds-realm, where did he strike first?"

Nettles, padding softly beside me, made no reply, so I answered my question myself: "He came to Sycharth—the principal stronghold of Prydain's foremost king. That is—"

"Ah," said Nettles, "Prydain!"

I realized once again how quickly his mind worked. Even while I spoke, he was squirrelling the words away. So I spoke aloud my thoughts, slowly, so that he might catch what he could.

"It was Prydain," I said, "that felt the dread Nudd's wrath—but only after the king had been lured away through deception. It was Prydain that the Demon Horde despoiled—but only after its king had been put to flight.

"And I ask you: who did Nudd pursue in his icy hatred? Who endured the cruel blows of Albion's Ancient Enemy?

"I will tell you: Meldryn Mawr. The Sovereign of Eternal Night chose the Great Golden King to face the terrible onslaught of his hatred. It was Meldryn Mawr, Prince of Prydain, Lord of the Llwyddi who endured the Enemy's pitiless attack."

Yes, I thought, Prydain's king endured the onslaught—and more: survived and triumphed.

"But I run ahead of myself," I told Nettles, who walked curious beside me. "Before all that—before Prydain fell, before Meldryn's flight, before Nudd and his vile Coranyid were loosed . . . there was the Cythrawl."

"Cythrawl," Nettles echoed softly. *"Hen Gelyn."*

"Yes," I told him. "The Ancient Enemy. And who was it the Beast of the Pit sought first to destroy? It was Ollathir, Chief Bard of Albion...Ollathir."

"Penderwydd Ollathir," Nettles mused.

"Chief Bard Ollathir, yes—he held the Sovereignty of Prydain! Ollathir alone knew where the Phantarch dwelt!"

Again I was confronted by the three: lord and realm and bard. But there were others—other lords, other realms, other bards—many others. Why these three?

"This is the mystery, my friend," I murmured aloud to Nettles. "Why *these* three?"

I pondered this for a while, and it came to me then that I already knew the answer—the word already spoken: The Song of Albion. So I began to explain to Nettles about the Phantarch, and in explaining to him I began to lay hold of it myself.

"Why these three?" I said. "I will tell you: because these three alone upheld the Song of Albion!"

"Canaid Alba," Nettles said softly.

I halted again. How much did this small stranger understand? How had he come by such knowledge?

"The Song of Albion, yes, that is what the Hosts of Darkness wished to destroy. For so long as it remained, they could not prevail. This is why they ravaged Prydain. This is why they attacked the True King in his kingdom—attacked Sovereignty itself."

"Aird Righ?" Nettles said.

I understood the phrase, but he had got it slightly wrong. "No, not the High King," I told him. "The True King, you see."

"Aird Righ!" he said again, more insistently. And I began to wonder if he knew what he was saying.

"Wait," I said. "Let me think."

Sovereignty...the presence of a True King...who else could uphold the Song but a True King? And might that king also be the High King?

"But how is it possible that Meldryn Mawr could be the High King without knowing it?" I demanded of my diminutive shadow. "It is not possible. No, the thing is impossible!"

Nettles said nothing; I could feel his eyes on me, intense, urgent. What did he know?

"Not the *Aird Righ*," I repeated, and turned. I took two steps and froze. Perhaps it was not Meldryn Mawr who was ignorant of his kingship. Perhaps the only ignorance was mine! Meldryn Mawr and Ollathir might have had good reason to hide it—as they had hidden the Phantarch deep within Findargad's mountain heart to protect the Song.

The realization struck me like the blow of a fist. I swayed on my feet. Nettles reached out to steady me. Blind! I was more than blind, I was ignorant as well—and that was worse.

"Prydain, Meldryn Mawr, Ollathir," I said slowly, so that Nettles could follow, "in these three did the essence of Albion reside."

And now these three strands met in one person: Llew.

I felt my heart quicken like that of a hunter when he has sighted his quarry. "Llew is the center," I said. *"Llew* is the word already spoken. *Llew* is the mountain rising in our midst."

"Llew," Nettles said.

"Yes, my canny friend, it is Llew." I began walking again; Nettles scrambled to keep up with me. "Llew possesses the Penderwydd's awen, because he was with Ollathir when he died, and the Chief Bard breathed the awen into Llew with his dying breath. Llew holds the sovereignty of Meldryn Mawr, because I am now Chief Bard of Albion and I gave the kingship to him. And Llew has penetrated the sacred centers of Prydain: he has traversed Môr Cylch in the Heart of the Heart, and he has twice defended the pillar stone of Prydain on the White Rock—and sained it with his blood!"

My mind sped along this path like a spear flying to its mark. In Llew the three strands came together; Llew, the knot of contention. He was the vessel into which the essence of Albion had been poured.

Ah, but the vessel was damaged, disfigured. He could not exercise the kingship that had been given him. And that was the heart of the enigma:

King and not king, bard and not bard, Llew ruled—yet refused to rule—a tribe which was not a tribe but a gathering of separate clans, forming a realm that was not a realm at all. The paradox was complete. If there was a meaning behind it, that meaning was impenetrable.

Still, thanks to Nettles' innocent mistake, I now held within me a startling new thought: the kingship of Prydain might indeed be the High Kingship of Albion.

Enigma and paradox. What did it mean? I did not know, but I would ponder it continually in the days to come.

I dismissed Nettles then, sending him to his rest so that I might contemplate the revelation I had received. I wandered alone, stalking the glen like a restless beast. My feet struck the path leading to the dead lake. I walked on, reaching the strand, and coming to the water's edge. The stink of the lake repulsed me, but I forced myself to continue along the shore. I had not walked far when I sensed that someone else had come down to the water.

"Who is it? Who is there?"

"Tegid..." replied a voice, and I heard a sob.

"Goewyn?"

I moved towards the sound of her gentle sobbing. Goewyn came into my arms and, face in hands, she put her head against my chest. "Why do you weep? What is wrong?"

"Gwenllian..." she said, her voice muffled and indistinct. I felt her head move away as she lifted her face. "I have seen her, Tegid. I have seen Gwenllian—in a dream," she explained quickly. "She came to me in a dream."

"Ah," I soothed, "I understand."

She pushed herself away from me. "I saw her. She spoke to me. Gwenllian spoke to me."

"What did she tell you?"

Goewyn paused and drew a long, shaky breath. "I do not understand it."

"Tell me."

Slipping her hand under my elbow, Goewyn turned me aside and we began walking along the darkly festering lake. After a while, she said, "I thought to wait until the council concluded...to hear what would be done. But I grew tired. My head felt heavy, and my eyes would not stay open. I thought to rest for only a moment. I fell asleep as soon as I lay down.

"As I slept, I heard a strange sound: like the rustling of birds' wings above my head. The sound woke me...I woke—in my dream I woke. Yet, I knew myself to be asleep, and I knew that I dreamed still."

"I know this kind of dream," I told her. "What did you see?"

"I saw the lake," she answered, her voice growing distant as she entered her dream once more—in memory this time. "I saw the lake as it is—vile and stinking. I saw the waters thickening with the foulness. And I saw someone standing at the edge of the lake...a woman—dressed all in white. As soon as I saw her, I knew that it was Gwenllian. I ran to her. I embraced her, Tegid! She was alive again! I was so happy!"

I did not reply, so she continued.

"Then Gwenllian spoke to me. I heard her voice, and she seemed reconciled—and more than that. She was content. She shone with peace and satisfaction; her face glowed." Goewyn fell silent, awed by the power of the vision.

"She spoke to you. What did she say?"

"She told me to remember the prophecy. She said it was very important. She said that the vision had been truly spoken, and that it would be fulfilled." Goewyn gripped my arm tightly in her excitement. "She said that it is the Day of Strife, but that the Swift Sure Hand was with the *Gwr Gwir.*"

"Are you certain? The *Gwr Gwir,* that is what she said?"

"Yes, but I do not know what it means," she replied. "*Gwir*— truth? Who are the Men of Gwir?"

"I do not know," I said, shaking my head slowly. "Unless the Men of Gwir are any who would oppose Meldron."

The term was part of the prophecy which Gwenllian had given to Llew after the Hero Feat on Ynys Bàinail; he alone had stood against the Cythrawl, and he alone had been given the prophetic word. I had thought about the prophecy many times, searching its phrases in my mind. Llew and I had often argued over its meaning.

"Did she say anything else?"

Goewyn paused, choosing her words carefully. "Yes." Her voice was but a whisper. "She said . . . 'Do not be afraid. There is healing in the water.'"

35

The Gwr Gwir

"Say it again, Goewyn. What did Gwenllian tell you?"

"She put out her hand," Goewyn answered, "and pointed away from me. I looked and saw that she was pointing at the lake. Gwenllian said, 'Do not be afraid. There is healing in the water.' And then..." Goewyn sniffed.

"Yes? And then?"

"I awoke," she replied. "I came here—I ran all the way—" The tears started again. "I came down to the lake...I thought Gwenllian might be here. It seemed so real. I thought she had come back to us...and I would find her here."

"Did she say anything else? Think carefully now. Anything at all?"

Her chin quivering, Goewyn shook her head slowly. "No," she said softly. "There was nothing else. Oh, Tegid...Tegid, I saw her."

I reached out to Goewyn, put my arms around her shoulders and drew her close. We stood for a moment in silence, and then Goewyn straightened and pulled away. She dried her tears and left me to contemplate the meaning of her dream alone.

I did not sleep that night. I walked beside the poisoned lake, the stench strong in my nostrils. My head swarmed with thoughts; my talks with Nettles and Goewyn had left me disturbed and uneasy.

With every step I could feel a dread purpose quickening just beyond the walls of this worlds-realm—inexorable, unyielding. I could sense it, but I could not comprehend it.

Before dawn the warriors assembled. Preparations had continued through the night, and with the coming of daylight they gathered. The carynx called them, and with my inner eye I saw them. Arrayed in battle gear, they stood stout and strong like a forest of tall oaks, waiting to be called forth by the battlechiefs ranged before them.

Scatha, green eyes level, her fair hair gathered and bound beneath her burnished warcap, chose first. Bearing a small round shield on her shoulder and a shirt of leather sewn with overlapping disks of bronze like the scales of a lizard, she raised a white spear with one long, supple arm. She had tied three strips of cloth to the shaft of her spear just below the leaf-shaped blade: two black strips, and one white. These were *meirwon cofeb*—symbols by which to remember her daughters, those for whom she fought this day, and whose deaths and rape she would avenge. Her clear voice called out the names of the warriors who would own the honor of following her in battle.

The Pen-y-Cat, it had been decided, would be the war leader. Supreme in skill, unrivalled in judgment, she was the most formidable of all adversaries, and the most cunning of battlechiefs. Under her training countless warriors had earned their arms, and many had achieved greatness and renown—but none had ever surpassed Scatha. In all, she chose but fifty, and the choice passed on.

Next came Bran Bresal, an oak among oaks, dark hair braided in gleaming plaits, ring of gold glinting on his left arm and torc shining at his throat; he raised his red-painted spear. From out of the massed warriors came the Ravens: Niall, Garanaw, Alun Tringad, Drustwn, and Emyr Lydaw. Like their leader, they wore no cloak, or siarc, or breecs or belt. Like the heroes of song who put off their clothes to fight, the Ravens entered battle naked, their oiled bodies glistening in the sun.

Each man saluted his battlechief as he stepped near—clashing
the haft of his spear against Bran's shield, or slapping the raven
tattoo on his sword arm.

Bran also called others to his flock—warriors he had chosen to
join the Flight of Ravens. When all were assembled the champion
took his place before them, and the choice passed on.

Cynan, blue eyes alight with anticipation, chose next. He stood
with his arm upraised, gripping the hilt of a honed sword in his fist.
His flame-red hair was cut short and greased to his head; his
moustache and beard were brushed full. He called the warriors of his
Galanae warband, and others that he knew. Then he turned to his
father, King Cynfarch, who nodded sagely. Cynan was war leader for
his father, but the king retained the right to approve the choice. This
ritual observed, the choice passed on.

King Calbha, torced and ringed with gold, a massive sword on
his hip, drove the point of his blue-painted spear into the ground, and
gripped the shaft with both hands. In a voice that belled like iron, he
called out the members of his Cruin warband. He summoned them in
ranks of ten, and when he was finished three fifties of men stood
behind him.

Llew, garbed simply in breecs and leather belt, rose from the
rock on which he sat and stood with a sword in his good hand; a
long shield hid his stump from view. He lifted his voice and called
the remaining warriors. Not slow to join him were the men he
summoned; many ran in their eagerness to serve. Each warrior
struck the rim of Llew's shield with his spear shaft as he passed,
and the sound was thunderous. When all had gathered, three
thirties and three stood with him—in honor of the slain bards of
Prydain.

Then Llew raised his sword high, the carynx sounded, and I saw
Rhoedd standing on a rock with the great, curved battlehorn to his
lips. The sound assaulted the air, filling the glen, echoing from the
ridge wall. Rhoedd sounded the horn again, and the Flight of Ravens
moved forward at the run. Scatha and her warband were next, then
Cynan and Calbha, and finally Llew with his triple ranks. Taking up

my staff, I followed the war host and began mounting to the top of Druim Vran.

The people had come to see us away. They stood along the track and hailed us as we passed, banking high the warriors' courage. I saw Goewyn in the forefront, waving a birch branch, and Nettles standing beside her with a holly bough; birch and holly, the twin emblems of strength and valor in the lore of bards.

In the early morning light, I saw the warbands of our tribe fearless and eager to meet the enemy. I saw brave men running to meet death: the Gwr Gwir, hastening to carry the battle to the enemy. I raised my staff as they passed and called upon the Swift Sure Hand to uphold them through the fight; I invoked the Goodly-Wise to guide their steps; I entreated the Gifting Giver to grant them the victory.

We were woefully outnumbered by Meldron's forces. This we knew. But the war leaders had judged the risk carefully: to have any chance at all against such an overwhelming foe, we must act quickly. Our water stores were dwindling rapidly; we could not allow ourselves to be weakened through thirst. To hold any hope of surviving, we must strike now—before Meldron could establish himself in the valley beyond, and while we were still strong enough to lift our swords.

The council had decided to seek out Meldron and attack him. If we succeeded in killing Meldron and his Wolf Pack, it was thought the rest of the war host would likely abandon the fight: chop off the head and the viper dies. We might then send north to a nearby island for water; for we considered that the taint would not yet have reached beyond the shores of Caledon.

The warbands gained the ridgetop and took their positions. By the time I joined them, the host was ranged along the length of Druim Vran—waiting while the war leaders conferred.

We would not attack until Scatha had determined the enemy's strength and disposition; she wanted to see Meldron and learn how he stood before ordering our own ranks. As to that, any weakness in Meldron's position was more than redressed by numbers. The Great Hound's war host spread across the valley on both sides of the river:

thousands ... and thousands more.

"I never imagined ..." Llew shook his head slowly as I took my place beside him. Bran stood at his left hand, gazing down into the valley, eyes hard, his mouth a thin, tight line.

"The Hound of Prydain has succeeded beyond his own inflamed ambitions," I observed. "He has climbed high over the bodies of the murdered and enslaved."

"Then he will fall the further," Bran declared. "I will count it an honor to bring about the ruin he so richly deserves."

We stood on the ridgetop awaiting Scatha's return. Since we could not see Meldron himself, or his Wolf Pack, she and Cynan had gone down for a closer look. When she rejoined us, we would make our final decisions about the ordering of battle.

As it happened, we had long to wait. The sun rose higher, growing hotter as it climbed into a dusty brown sky, and the morning passed. We grew weary of waiting, and the men grew restive—and thirsty. We drank our water ration for the day and watched the fierce sun soar higher. Calbha joined us and we sat together, scanning the valley below. The smoke from their cooking fires spread across the distance, grey-white, billowing like waves.

"They are an ocean," Calbha observed quietly. "And we are but a burn trickling out of the hills."

The sun neared midday before Scatha appeared at last, and with a disturbing report: warriors were still streaming into the valley in great numbers. "But Meldron is not yet with his war host," Scatha told us. "He may be among those even now entering the valley, but we did not see him."

"The war host is not assembled. They are not massing for attack," Cynan added. "They seem to be waiting."

"No doubt they are waiting for Meldron," Llew replied. "If that is the way of it, perhaps we should not wait. Perhaps we should attack."

Cynan looked doubtful, but shrugged. "I would fight the Great Hound rather than his pups, but we cannot sit here any longer. Let us begin."

Llew looked to Scatha. "What say you, Pen-y-Cat?"

She, too, rose. "I do not think we will take them unawares, but they are disorderly and unprepared. Without Meldron they may be more easily daunted. Yes, we will attack."

Bran, Cynan, Calbha added their agreement, and all took their leave, returning to their waiting warbands. "Well," Llew said, drawing his wrist stump through the shield straps, "it has come to this. Will you uphold us in battle?"

"Why do you ask? You know that I will."

"I know." He leaned his sword against his thigh and gripped my arm with his good hand. "Farewell, Tegid."

"May it go well with you, brother," I replied, embracing him tightly.

He turned away then and took his place at the head of his warband. But a moment later, he lifted his sword in a silent signal and the warriors began moving down the ridge to the valley. They soon disappeared among the trees and were lost to my inner sight; I did not see them any more.

I walked along the top of Druim Vran until I found a rock outcrop large enough for me to stand on, and high enough for me to be seen from the valley below. I climbed onto my rock perch and squatted on my haunches until the battle began.

A dull, sullen sun poured white heat into the valley, through which the river oozed like a black, noxious smudge. The river— thick and turgid with its scum of corruption—held my attention for a moment. It formed a natural barrier in the valley; not much of an obstacle, admittedly, but I noticed that the enemy kept well away from its banks. All along its reeking length, the camps on either side gave the river wide respect. No one drank from it, of course, nor did anyone attempt to cross it.

With my quickened inner eye, I scanned the wide valley for sight of bare earth and saw none. The valley swarmed with the horde, and yet warriors streamed through the narrow glen mouth. Was ever such a mighty force seen in Albion?

No; never. I sat upon my rock and gazed at a wonder. Not in the days of Nemed, not even in the days of Nuadha, had such a war host been known. Of horses and men there was no end. The spears of the warriors bristled like an ashwood forest; the glint of their swords in the dire sun flashed with the spiked radiance of the sea, and their shields were more numerous than shells on an endless beach.

Scatha, Wise War Leader, had declined the use of horses—a desperately prudent stroke. Horses would lend us power at the outset, but they would also make it easier for the enemy to identify, surround, and contain us. Our battle plan depended upon penetrating deep into Meldron's forces, finding him and removing him—and that could be accomplished more efficiently by men afoot who, in the chaos of battle, might slip through the ranks unobserved.

I watched the foot of the ridgewall, where the first signs of the attack would come. Scatha had also directed that no carynx should sound the attack. "They will discover our attack soon enough," she said. "But perhaps we can penetrate to the heart of Meldron's host before those across the river even know the battle has begun."

That was our one thin hope: take the center and hold it. This would force the enemy to fight inward upon itself to reach us. We would be surrounded, yes; but there were so many warriors we would be soon surrounded whatever we did. At least, by taking the center, we would create a smaller field of battle, and our own warbands would not be separated.

It was, as I say, a desperate tactic. But, as I looked down upon the masses of warriors encamped below, I understood beyond all doubt the utter hopelessness of our position. We could not expect to overpower Meldron. At best, we could only . . . what? Blunt his attack? Delay his inevitable victory?

Calbha was right, we were but a burn trickling out of the hills. The war host of the Great Hound was as wide and deep as the sea. Once battle commenced, that vast sea would whelm us over and we would vanish without a trace.

Even as this thought took root in my mind, I heard the raw croak of a raven taking flight above the ridge. I turned my sightless eyes towards the sky, and was given the vision of black wings against a filthy yellow sky. I recoiled from the sight and turned away.

Gwenllian's voice came light as a sigh in my ear. The Banfáith had said:

Let the sun be dull as amber, let the moon hide her face: abomination stalks the land. Let the four winds contend with one another in dreadful blast; let the sound be heard among the stars. The Dust of the Ancients will rise on the clouds; the essence of Albion is scattered and torn among contending winds.

Then shall rage the Giant of Wickedness, and terrify all with the keen edge of his sword. His eyes shall flash forth fire; his lips shall drip poison. With his great host he will despoil the island. All who oppose him will be swept away in the flood of wrongdoing that flows from his hand. The Island of the Mighty will become a tomb.

All this by the Brazen Man is come to pass, who likewise mounted on his steed of brass works woe both great and dire. Rise up Men of Gwir! Fill your hands with weapons and oppose the false men in your midst! The sound of the battleclash will be heard among the stars of heaven and the Great Year will proceed to its final consummation.

Yes, it had all come to pass as she had predicted. But the prophecy finished with a riddle:

Hear, O Son of Albion: Blood is born of blood. Flesh is born of flesh. But the spirit is born of Spirit and with Spirit evermore remains. Before Albion is One, the Hero Feat must be performed and Silver Hand must reign.

Silver Hand was the name given to the Champion who would save Albion. It was Llew's name: Llew Llaw Eraint, of whom marvellous things were foretold.

An accusing voice arose within me: *Fool! What have you done?*

I had tried to force the fulfillment of the prophecy by making him king. But I had failed in that. Meldron had shattered any hope that Llew might reign. The Rule of Sovereignty cannot be broken or set aside—not for any reason, not for any man. The Great Hound Meldron had snatched away the kingship when he struck off Llew's hand.

And now, I thought, gazing over the stinking, smoke-filled valley and the enemy spread in deadly array, the Island of the Mighty has become a tomb.

I heard the sound of an approaching footfall soft behind me. Before I could turn, I felt Goewyn's hand on my shoulder. "I mean to stay with you, Tegid," she said, brooking no denial.

"Stay," I said. "We will uphold our brave ones together."

She settled beside me. "I could not wait with the others. I thought perhaps you could use someone to see for you."

We sat together, taking some small comfort in one another's presence as we waited for the battle to begin. And when it did begin, it was as a tiny ripple on the edge of the ocean that was Meldron's host. I saw a swirl like the eddy of a wave in the camp directly below—and even watched it for a time before realizing that it was Scatha's force surging into the foe.

"There!" Goewyn said. "It has begun!"

Calbha's warband entered the fray behind and to the right of Scatha, with Cynan's but a short distance to the left. The three together pushed quickly through the ill-ordered and unwary ranks, striking more deeply and more rapidly than I would have thought possible. The enemy seemed to melt before them, giving ground without a fight.

The Flight of Ravens struck in from the far right, driving towards Scatha. They were a marvel to behold! The speed with which they moved! I could see Bran running headlong into the enemy, scattering whole tribes of warriors before him; Alun Tringad and Garanaw strove to overtake him on either hand, and the rest of the Raven Flight, unhindered by the enemy, scrambled to keep abreast of their leader.

Llew I did not see at first. But Goewyn said, "I see him! To the left, beyond Cynan. There he is!"

With my inward vision I beheld Llew with his warband, flying to meet Scatha. As with the others, the enemy ranks merely opened before them, rolling back upon themselves as the attackers drove bravely in.

I heard a shout from the ridgetop to the left, and turned to see half the population of Dinas Dwr standing on the ridge, and the rest scrambling to find a place to view the battle. Unable to await the outcome, they had all come to witness it.

The shouts soon grew to a chorus of cheers. I doubted whether the warriors could hear the encouragement of their kinsmen, but it poured down upon them in a heartfelt shower of praise. And for a time it seemed as if the impossible had become plain fact: we would, by sheer determination alone, defeat the foe where they stood and drive them from the valley.

A fall of pebbles, clattering among the rocks to my right, gave me to know that Nettles, unobtrusive as ever, had taken his place beside me. Cynfarch, spear in hand, came at his heels, scanning the valley below. If the size of the Great Hound's forces surprised him, he gave no sign. "It has begun well," he observed as he came to stand behind me. "For all their numbers, they are ill-trained and unready."

"Yes, it has begun well," I agreed. I had never seen a war host in such disarray and confusion, and told him so. "Indeed, they do not behave as warriors at all."

So saying, I realized why it was so. These were not warriors. Of course not. How could Meldron field a war host so vast? If I had stopped but a moment to consider the question before, I would have seen the obvious: there were not enough warriors in all of Albion to amass a war host so great. Meldron had swelled his ranks with the helpless he had conquered—farmers and craftsmen, shepherds and untrained youths. He had given them spears and swords but, though they wielded weapons, they were not warriors. That is why, faced with the dreadful desperation of our own warriors, the hapless foemen—ill-matched and unprepared—simply turned and ran, or stood and were cut down.

It was not cause for praise, certainly. But the sight of the enemy fleeing before our rapidly advancing warriors made the people shout and cheer all the same. Glad acclaim rose up from the heights and echoed down the slopes towards the valley in a bright cascade of blessing. With my inner eye, I saw the enemy churning in retreat, ebbing like the failing tide, flowing back and away from the sharp edge of our attack. Farmers and shepherds against skilled warriors! There could be no glory from such a victory. Still, shameful though it was, I dared hope that the bold, decisive assault of our warriors— driving ever deeper, striking into the midst of the invader—would yet turn the battle into a rout.

36

Deadly River

Calbha and Scatha drove deep into the center of the enemy host—alas, their swift advance could not continue. On the near bank of the river the retreat stiffened and abruptly halted. Word of the attack had reached Meldron's mounted warriors who had now had time enough to gather and make the first real attempt at resistance. Still, there were so many frightened people striving to escape that the horsemen could not reach Scatha's warband.

Cynan's force was thwarted by the swiftly thickening press. Escape cut off by their own leaders, the ill-trained enemy turned once more to engage Cynan's withering fury. There were so many bodies pressed tightly together that Cynan could scarcely swing his sword. Bran and the Ravens were likewise obstructed. Though we could not see them clearly, we watched the spear-blade formation thrusting deep into the ranks of the enemy. They still drove towards Scatha, but their progress was slowed to a crawl.

"They mean to fight," Cynfarch observed. "The Dagda have mercy on them."

Llew's warband strove to join Scatha and Calbha in the center. But, as with Bran and Cynan, the arrival of the mounted warriors arrested Llew's progress. Meldron's undisciplined mass formed an unwilling wall; Llew could not advance—there were too many people between him and the center ground where Scatha stood.

But if our own warriors could not further the attack, neither could the enemy retaliate effectively. The battle seemed to have run aground. Like contrary currents in the sea, waves of warriors flowed over and against one another in contending swells—some striving towards the attackers, others struggling away. Our own warbands were islands bounded by these chaotic cross-currents.

The sound of the carynx bellowed from across the valley. Word of the attack had finally reached the enemy war leaders, who now thought to sound the alarm. But they had foolishly established themselves on the far side of the river, and could not now direct their ill-trained warriors, who flailed uselessly.

It did not take Bran Bresal long to resolve his dilemma. Finding it impossible to hack his way through the tangle, he threw his shield before him and simply battered his way forward, overwhelming any who stood in his way. The Ravens followed his lead, and soon they had formed a clear path through the crush of bodies. Over a living road they advanced. I do not believe their feet touched the ground.

"They have done it!" cried Goewyn, as the Flight of Ravens joined Scatha and Calbha in the center of the battleground. "And now Cynan is moving!"

The enemy flowed into the space abandoned by the Ravens. Cynan must have sensed the surge and instinctively moved towards it. What began as a stumbling push ended in a headlong rush: Cynan drove into and through the turmoil like a bull charging a scattering herd; many fell before his blade. The force of their charge carried the warband into the circle cleared by Scatha and the Ravens.

"Now only Llew is left," Goewyn said, clasping my hand as she gazed anxiously into the tumult.

"The horses will cut them off," countered Cynfarch, gesturing with his spear. "Llew cannot move."

Unable to advance on the center, the mounted foemen had turned aside and were forcing their way along the outside towards Llew, effectively blocking his attempt to join the others in the center. Llew's warband would be separated from the main body of warriors and would have to fight on alone—until they could find or force a way past the horsemen.

Though the sun burned hot in the deathly sky, I felt a shadow fall over me. "Now they need horses," Cynfarch muttered. "And chariots. Horses and chariots!"

More enemy horsemen were moving towards Llew's force. Although none had yet joined the fight, I could see that they would, and soon. Goewyn saw it, too. She clutched my arm; her fingernails dug into my skin. I heard a sharp tapping sound and noticed Nettles, a stone gripped tight in his fist, absently pounding his hand against the rock on which he sat, staring wide-eyed at the battle below.

The horsemen drove closer. The others were encircled, and Llew could do nothing to stem the onslaught. It was for me to act. I stood. Taking my staff, I raised it to the fierce and unrelenting sun. As Chief Bard of Albion, I summoned forth the power of the Taran Tafod and loosed it to the aid of our warriors.

I raised my staff and lifted my voice to the heavens, and to the forces beyond. *"Gwrando! Gryd Grymoedd, Gwrando!"* I called, and heard my voice grow loud. *"Gwrando! Nefol Elfenau, Gwrando! Erfyn Fygu Gelyn! Gwthio Gelyn! Gorch Gelyn! Gwasgu Gelyn!"*

The words formed on my tongue and leaped from my lips like flames; I breathed fire. My voice was no longer my own, but the voice of the all-sustaining Word beyond words. I emptied myself of all thought and became a vibrating reed played upon by the willful wind.

"Gryd Elfenau A Nefol Grymoedd! Gwrando! Gorch Gormail Fygu!" I called, hearing only the sound of the Taran Tafod blaring like the carynx. Filling my lungs, I opened my mouth and let the words of the ancient and sacred speech flow from my innermost heart. *"Nefol Elfenau, Gwrando! Erfyn Fygu Gelyn! Gwthio Gelyn! Gorch Gelyn! Gwasgu Gelyn!"*

A fitful breeze stirred; I felt it on my face.

"Gwrando, Gryd Nefol Elfenau! Erfyn Gwrando! Erfyn Nefol!

Gorch Gormail Fygu!" I cried in the voice of the bellowing bull-roarer.
The wind quickened, plucking at my sleeves as I held the staff in stiff
arms over my head. I threw back my head and let the Taran Tafod
thunder forth of its own volition.

And, as if in answer to my cry, I heard the moan of the rising
wind gathering from the four quarters. The dry heat of the day was
quenched as clouds unfurled to obscure the sun. That hot, white sky-
flame grew pale under a pall of smoke and cloud...

...Let the sun be dull as amber...

The wind swirled; howling, it gathered force. A cold blast struck
me full in the face, and another buffeted me from behind, lashing my
back and legs. The people cried out in alarm, and scrambled back
from the cliff edge. Cynfarch hunkered down behind me, and Goewyn
wrapped her arms around my legs—as much to steady me as to
protect herself. Nettles scuttled closer.

*...Let the four winds contend with one another in dreadful
blast...*

The wild winds scoured the empty skypaths and screamed into
the valley, tearing at the rocks and turf, raising pillars of dust,
whirling and heaving it high in darkly billowing streams.

...The Dust of the Ancients will rise on the clouds...

Goewyn clung to my legs, and Cynfarch leaned on his spear shaft
to remain upright. In the valley below, the enemy warriors quailed,
their confusion wonderfully increased. They wailed and shouted in
anguish as the weird gales assailed them.

*...the essence of Albion is scattered and torn among contending
winds...*

Across the poisoned river, the enemy battlehorns blared, their
frightful din all but smothered by the raging squall of the gale. The
sky darkened to false twilight—hard-edged stars burned among the
streaming clouds. Frightened horses screamed and reared, throwing
their riders beneath their hooves. The cries of terrified men mingled
with the shrieks of the dying; the sharp crack of spear on shield
pierced the skyvault. Our brave warriors stood to their work, iron
blades pealing as they struck.

... The sound of the battleclash will be heard among the stars of heaven ...

Darkness passed before my inner eye. Blindness reclaimed me. Amidst the bawl of the tempest I could hear the clash of weapons and the shouts of men rising up from the valley below, but I could no longer see what was taking place on the battleground.

"Goewyn!" I shouted. "Goewyn! Hear me! I cannot see!"

Shifting the staff to my left hand, I reached down for her, took her arm, and she scrambled to her feet. She put her arm around me and together we stood against the gale. Nettles assumed the task of helping steady me; rising to his knees, he snaked an arm around my legs and held on tight.

"My sight is gone," I shouted. "Look for me, Goewyn! Be my eyes!"

"It is terrible, Tegid! There are so many—I cannot see him... Yes! There he is! I see Llew. The warband is with him. The horsemen have reached them, but they are standing their ground. The horses are afraid—they rear and plunge... it is difficult—the riders cannot fight from the saddle. Our warriors strike them at will... the fighting is cruel."

"What of the Ravens?"

"I see the Ravens," she confirmed. "I see Bran. They are pressing forward—they are trying to reach Llew. But there are horsemen before them—and more are coming."

"They are cut off," added Cynfarch. "The Ravens cannot reach Llew."

"And Cynan—what of Cynan? Do you see him?"

"Yes, I see him—" began Goewyn.

"He is at the forefront of his men," Cynfarch put in. "He is fighting. They are all fighting."

"What of the enemy? How do they stand?"

"The enemy has surrounded our war host. Scatha is in the center of the ring. Calbha is to the right of her. Cynan stands to the left. Bran is also on the left," Cynfarch replied, raising his voice to be heard above the gale.

Goewyn added: "Scores, Tegid, hundreds are fleeing—they do not want to fight. But their battlechiefs are making them stand. They jab with their spears, but there is little hurt."

"How many have we lost? How many killed or wounded?"

"I think—" Goewyn began, pausing to assess the numbers, "The enemy has lost many—there are many down. And... oh, but they are all pressing so tightly. I cannot say, Tegid. Some, I think, not many."

My staff had grown heavy; my arm ached from holding it above my head. Tears from the windblast streamed from my dead eyes. I gripped the staff with my benumbed hand, and steadied my trembling arm. Employing the secret tongue of the bards, I called upon the Swift Sure Hand to enfold our warriors and uplift them.

"Dagda Samildanac!" I cried, *"Gwrando, Dagda! Cyfodi Gwr Gwir, Sicur Llaw Samildanac! Cyfodi A Cysgodi, Dagda Sicur Llaw! Gwrando!"*

The wind shrieked down from the ridge. Cold the blast, keen the gale. My limbs trembled with the power surging around me. I heard the searing crack of lightning and the thunder's answering roar. My inward parts quivered; the ground beneath my feet quaked. It was all I could do to stand against the tempest.

"Tegid!" cried Goewyn pressing close. "They are falling back—the enemy is falling back!"

"Tell me, Goewyn!"

"Hwynt ffoi!" shouted Nettles. "They flee!"

"They are all running to the river!" Goewyn confirmed. "They are running away!" The gale tore the words from her lips almost before she could utter them.

I grasped the staff by one end and raised its point to the sky. *"Daillaw! Gwasgu Gelyn! Gorch Yr Gelyn!"*

Again I felt the vibrating pulse in my hands and arms, in my legs and bones and blood. Despite the buffeting winds, I felt the air shudder around me and the heavens convulsed.

The staff in my hand burst into flaming fragments and the hot, dry scent of scorched air filled my lungs as the bull-roar of thunder broke over me. My skullbone throbbed under the blow; my heart stopped beating in my chest. Clear white light burned inside my head.

And it seemed to me that I flew—like an eagle; high, high into the storm-twisted sky, blown by winds. I saw the battleground far below, and the men moving on it. But I did not see them as men: they were waves on a troubled sea, surging and crashing. I saw it all with an eagle's keen eye, and then I fell—steeply plunging, swiftly diving.

Smoke obscured my sight. I fell and fell. And when it seemed that I must strike the ground, the smoke cleared and I saw that I stood in the valley in the midst of battle. All around me streamed fleeing men, eyes wide with terror, stumbling in their haste, trampling their fallen. They fled to the river where, in their desperation to escape, they threw themselves into the vile water.

Heedless, panic-filled, they leaped from the crowded banks into the flowing corruption. The first enemy plunged in to their thighs and staggered forward through the black ooze intent on reaching safety on the other side. But, after floundering a few steps they halted as a new horror overwhelmed them.

Mouths gaping, they turned screaming to their kinsmen in fearful agony. Their cries were appalling. More horrible still was the sight of their shrivelled, suppurating flesh.

For where the noxious water touched the skin it withered, sores appeared and blood gushed forth—blood and yellow pus. Their hands and arms blushed red with sores, and their thighs and legs. The poison splashed into their eyes and onto their necks and chests and faces. The shrill moan of the gale soon mingled with the shrieks of tortured men thrashing in the killing waters.

They staggered and stumbled. Those who fell into the river did not rise again. Yet though their kinsmen rent the air with their hideous cries, more and still more men threw themselves into the deadly flow. They, too, were trapped, mutilated, and killed by the cruel poison. Red blood stained the black water.

Men—screaming, howling in pain like beasts, flesh streaming, lacerated—struggled towards the far bank. There was no turning back: the press of the fleeing throngs behind them drove them on... forced them to their deaths. The black river swelled with floating bodies. None who started reached the far bank alive.

The horror of this strange death alarmed those on the near bank and their panic increased tenfold. Men threw down their weapons and sank to the ground: dead but for the shaking of their limbs. On the far side of the poisoned river, men stood flat-footed on the bank and stared in slack-mouthed wonder at the terrible marvel before them.

I turned from the outrage of this sight and searched for our warriors—for Llew and Bran, Scatha and Cynan. Men surged around me in dizzy, reckless flight. Weapons clattered to the ground. Frenzied with fear, the enemy had turned its back on the battle and now sought only to escape. But of our own warriors I could see nothing.

"Llew!" I cried, staggering forward. I tripped over a body at my feet and fell sprawling upon the ground. Before I could rise, someone seized me...

"Tegid!" I felt hands on me, tugging at me. Goewyn and Nettles held me to the ground as if the wind might take me.

My ears rang with the echo of the thunder as it boomed and rumbled across the valley. I gasped and drew breath. I struggled to my knees. I tried to stand, but my legs would not hold me. Nettles put his arms around my shoulders and supported me.

Goewyn bent near. I felt her hands on my face. She spoke to me, but her voice sounded thin and small. My ears buzzed. I was blind once more.

"My staff... I—where is my staff?" I put out my hands and groped among the rocks around me, striking the ground with numb fingers.

Goewyn seized my hands. "You are hurt, Tegid. Your staff is gone."

"Help me stand."

Goewyn called to Cynfarch, and together the three of them lifted me to my feet. My hands began to ache and then to shake and sting.

"Listen! I hear screams!" Cynfarch said. "At the river! They are driving the enemy into the river!"

"Corruption is claiming her own," I said, and told them what I had seen of those who tried to escape across the deadly river. "But look now and tell me what you see. Quickly!"

"The river is killing them!" Goewyn gasped.

"The wind is gone," Cynfarch said. "The storm is clearing."

"The awen has moved on," I said, more to myself than to the others. Grasping Nettles and Goewyn by the arms, I said, "Come, lead me. Let us go down there. Hurry!"

We began the arduous climb down the ridgewall to the valley below. Cynfarch went before me, and I kept my hand on his shoulder; Goewyn and Nettles walked beside me, supporting me, for my legs were still unsteady. By the time we reached the valley floor, the main force of the enemy had retreated to the banks of the river. Trapped between our warriors and the killing waters, the foemen stood on the water marge in despair of their lives. Many hundreds threw down their weapons in abject surrender. But the genuine warriors among them were making desperate, futile attempts to regroup and renew the battle.

We hastened across the valley floor, stepping over the bodies of the unfortunates who had been killed in the crush of their own numbers. Their twisted limbs jutted up from the ground like broken stalks; many did not even have weapons. Yet they had been made to bear the brunt of the Great Hound's war lust.

We came to the place where Llew had been surrounded in the early part of the battle, and paused to search those lying on the ground. The long dry grass was slick beneath our feet, and the air rank with the sickly-sweet scent of blood. We found Rhoedd, still clutching the carynx in his hand, and others of our own among the dead, and our hearts writhed within us.

"Where is Llew? Do you see him?"

"I think he is among the press at the river," Goewyn answered.

"I see some fighting there."

"Take me there," I said.

We had but stumbled ten paces before Cynfarch halted abruptly. "What is it?" I demanded impatiently. "What do you see?"

Goewyn said, "I see it, too. Dust. Clouds of dust rising across the glen—"

Cynfarch cut her off. "Riders!"

At the same moment I felt the drumming, deep in the earth. "Meldron!"

Defeat

Swift horses racing, Meldron entered the valley to the dull thunder of drumming hooves and the blaring of the battlehorn. My inner vision quickened at the sound and I beheld Meldron advancing across the plain with a warband five hundred strong. He did not lead them, but rode in a chariot surrounded by the elite fifty of his Wolf Pack. Siawn Hy rode beside the Great Hound. The traitor Paladyr was not with them, but I little doubted he was near.

They had come across the hills in order to avoid the river and now came flying over the battle plain, seizing the ground behind us. Even as our war leaders turned to meet the foe, they were ridden down. The enemy was upon us too quickly. There was no time to mount a coherent defence; there was no time to rally, no time to regroup.

All hope was lost before we had even lifted blade against this new threat.

Even so, Bran and Scatha made a fight of it. If they had received the benefit of a warning, who can say what they might have achieved? As it was, Bran succeeded in pulling down three horsemen, and Scatha made short work of four more before they learned to respect her prowess.

But Meldron had no intention of merely overwhelming us and

cutting us down, which he might easily have done. He had something more diverting planned. Instead of committing his warriors to combat, he assembled them in ranks and formed a retaining wall around us. Then he began slowly to press us, step by grudging step, towards the river. Those we had driven to the banks gave way behind until our warriors stood with backs to the killing river and a tight forest of spearblades at their throats.

Bran made a fearless, futile lunge for a warrior who had unwisely edged too close. The man was hauled from his horse and Bran seized the reins and leaped onto the animal's back. For a moment it appeared that he might break through the ranks. The Flight of Ravens made ready to follow him through the gap, but the horse's legs were cut from under it and Bran fell beneath the animal as it thrashed on the ground.

Goewyn, standing beside me, shouted defiantly as they overpowered him and took him prisoner. She might have saved her breath, for we all suffered the same humiliation soon enough. In scalding shame, brave warriors were disarmed: one by one the Ravens were pinned to the ground with spears and stripped of their weapons; their hands were tied behind their backs and they were bound each to the other—Bran, Alun, Garanaw, Niall, Drustwn and Emyr—lashed together, with rope nooses around their necks.

Cynan's warband endured the same treatment. Those who resisted or tried to fight back were beaten until they lost consciousness, or had the tendons in their arms cut so that they could not raise their swords. And when Cynan had been beaten senseless and his weapons confiscated, they turned to Calbha and Scatha's forces.

Only when we were all rendered powerless did Meldron show himself. The Great Hound called out from among his close-crowded Wolf Pack in a bold voice: "Is this the best you could do?" he shouted. "Is this the mighty Llew's invincible war host?"

"Where is Llew?" whispered Goewyn urgently. "I cannot see him."

"Nor can I."

Cynfarch, seething beside me, said, "I think he is there—somewhere in the center. Why does he not resist?"

"I would stand beside Llew," I said, and began forcing my way towards the place Cynfarch had indicated. Goewyn pressed close, gripping my hand in hers. Nettles, trembling slightly, moved silently beside me. An angry cry, and a spearblade sharp in my back, halted us. We could move no nearer.

"Can you see him?" she asked.

"No," I replied.

Meldron, too, wondered where Llew could be found. "Llew!" he roared. "Where are you? Come to me, if you are not afraid. I have come searching for you, Llew. Is this how you receive your king?"

Llew answered from among his men. "I am here, Meldron."

"Come out where I can see you," shouted Meldron. "Foolish to hide from me now, cripple. Must I kill your men one by one to find you?"

I heard warriors cursing as our tight-pressed throng shifted. "No," whispered Nettles, his voice fervent and low. "*Aros ol,* Llew. Stay back."

"Do not do it!" Calbha shouted, and received the butt of a spear in his teeth. He dropped to the ground. His men surged forward and were forced back by a double rank of spearpoints.

"I am here," Llew answered, stepping out from among the captives. "I am not hiding from you, Meldron."

"That is far enough," snarled Meldron from his chariot. "So! Did you think I would not come to smother your small rebellion? Did you think you could elude me forever? I mean to avenge my honor."

"Honor?" inquired Llew coolly. "I wonder you do not choke on the word."

"Bind him!" shouted Meldron, and Llew was taken. With his men around him and his adversary disarmed and bound, Meldron felt safe enough to meet Llew face to face. The Great Hound stepped down from his chariot. I burned with rage to see the scorn on his haughty face and the swagger in his step as he approached. "You will die for that."

Llew offered no reply.

"Nothing to say?" sneered Meldron. I could see his arrogant grin. The Great Hound's vanity had grown great indeed; he would indulge himself to the full. He reached out, stroked Llew's wrist stump, gave it a slap, and laughed. Then, turning this way and that, he shouted, "Where is that blind bard of yours? Where is Tegid hiding? Or perhaps he fears the portion his treachery has earned."

Not slow to reply, I struggled forward and answered in a loud voice, "You speak of nothing but fear and hiding, Meldron. But it is well known that a coward sees cowardice in every man."

Meldron turned towards me. "Ah, Tegid!" He gestured for me to be brought before him, and I was dragged forth. Cynfarch made bold to stop them, and was struck down. "I did not see you—but you do not see me, either." He laughed, and a few of his Wolf Pack laughed with him. "To be both blind and a fool, you must have been born under a double curse."

I waited while they enjoyed their small insult. Then I replied, "It is ever the way of the sick to imagine their disease in others."

By way of answer, Meldron slashed me across the mouth with the back of his hand. "For that you will die last," he grunted, his face close to mine. "After all the others—you die."

It was then that I saw something that made my breath catch in my throat. Bound in gold and hanging from a leather thong around Meldron's neck was a fragment of white stone: a Singing Stone.

My gaze darted quickly to Siawn Hy; he wore one, too! They all did—all of Meldron's chieftains, and the warriors of his Wolf Pack wore amulets containing pieces of stone. Thinking that the Song of Albion would make them invincible, they had made talismans of the Singing Stones and now each man wore one around his neck.

I only had a glimpse, for Meldron turned away, shouting, "Take them to the river!"

My hands were thrust behind me and bound. Strong arms seized me; I was lifted off my feet. Goewyn cried out, and was quickly silenced.

"Meldron!"

It was Siawn Hy. He had been waiting, lurking in the usurper's shadow. Words passed between them that I could not hear. Then Meldron turned, and when he spoke again he said, "I have long desired to see this enchanted city that Llew has built. Is there anything to prevent me, do you think? No? Then I will see it at once."

Then the Great Hound called out to those who had seized us. "Bring them! Bring them all!" he cried. "Follow me!"

We were hauled up the ridge, as the enemy whelmed Druim Vran in their vast number. The feet of the foemen struck the trackways, and our hidden glen was invaded. Our people, standing along the ridgewall wailed to see our defeat. Their outcry struck the ear like the keening of a mother whose child has gone down to death's dark pit. The lament could be heard streaming across the valley and it tore at my heart.

Captives all, we were marched down through the forest to the lake. All our chieftains were bound hand and foot, and we were made to stand on the lakeshore. I wanted to be with Llew, to stand at his side, to face death and die together defying Meldron to his face.

But my hands were tied and I was pressed on every side by enemy warriors. I could not move. Death was close; I could feel the black wings hovering ever nearer with every breath.

Risking all, risking nothing—for I had nothing left—I cried out. "Meldron! Great Hound of Destruction! Scourge and Pestilence of Albion, long may your life endure—so that you may savor the condemnation your acts have earned. Great your guilt, greater still will be your shame. Despoiler! Abomination! Live long, Meldron, revel in the hatred you have rightly won! Delight in the loathing your name inspires! Rejoice in the ruin you have wrought in the land!"

I willed my words to become weapons that would torment him long after my flesh and bones were dust.

"Meldron!" I shouted, "Hear my accusation! King of Hounds, behold your portion!" I extended my bound hands towards the poisoned lake. "Fill your lungs with its stink! The stench is exquisite is it not? Behold the splendor of your reign, Meldron, King of Corruption, Prince of Poison!"

"Silence him!" Meldron shouted angrily, and an instant later a fist smashed into my jaw. A second blow snapped my head back. My mouth filled with blood and I fell to my knees.

When I raised my head once more I saw the foul black water gleaming dully in the white light of the naked sun as it struck the surface of the dead lake. Llew knelt a short distance from me along the shore; he was bound at the wrists, knees, and ankles. Meldron towered over him, gloating with immense satisfaction.

Narrow-eyed, superior, Siawn Hy skulked behind.

I scanned the tight-pressed crowd, and I happened to glimpse Bran and Scatha in the forefront of the prisoners. Calbha stood nearby with his head down; he was bleeding from wounds to his neck and shoulder. All three of them wore nooses around their necks; their hands and feet were bound. I did not see Nettles any more, but Cynfarch stood erect with Goewyn defiant beside him, fire in her eyes. After Llew, they would be next to die.

A boat was drawn up on the shingle nearby. Meldron ordered Llew to be placed in the vessel, and four of his Wolf Pack lifted Llew and roughly handed him into the craft. Then Meldron climbed into the boat with his prisoner and commanded that the boat be pushed away from the shore.

Wicked, and shrewd in his wickedness, I saw then what Meldron intended. My heart heaved within me like a captive beast hurling itself against its cage. I struggled to rise.

"Meldron!" I shouted. Fists struck me down and hard hands held me to the ground with my face a hair's breadth from the noxious water.

The Great Hound meant to murder Llew hideously in view of all his people. He intended that we should see Llew screaming his last breaths as the lethal waters of the poisoned lake pared the skin from his bones. Meldron desired that we should see Llew die in writhing agony, broken and disfigured, his flesh a mass of bloody ulcers.

No doubt this was Siawn Hy's wicked intent—we had been brought to the lake so that we might be tortured and murdered at Dinas Dwr in full sight of all. He wanted there to be no doubt in anyone's mind that Llew was dead and Meldron was king.

"Great Hound!" I shouted. "I defy you! Take me first—kill me!"

Meldron turned his face toward me and laughed in reply, but made no other answer.

I strove to regain my feet. I was cruelly kicked, and the hands that gripped me did not relent. I could but await the inevitable, powerless to prevent it.

Meldron worked the oars and the small boat moved slowly to a place well beyond reach of anyone on shore, yet close enough for all to see and hear what was about to happen. There, with Llew huddled at his feet, he stood and raised his hands in the manner of a generous king bestowing a gift on his people.

The gesture sickened me, for in it I saw the image of his father, Meldryn Mawr, Prydain's Most Noble. I was not the only one to find this mocking mimicry offensive. Bran cried out: "Meldron! I curse you! I, Bran Bresal, curse you to the seventh generation!"

Bran struggled forward to rail at Meldron and received a hail of vicious blows for his effort. The sight of Meldron's scurrilous rabble striking that noble warrior filled me with outrage, and I shouted too, and struggled to rise—until a foot on my neck pressed me to the ground.

The captive warriors cried out against this contemptible handling of their battlechief. They were likewise silenced in a most crude and shameful manner by the Wolf Pack. Meldron's scum even dared attack Scatha, but their repugnant bluster was no match for her daunting dignity. Though they struck her, they could not make her cower before them. Her head remained erect, green eyes blazing with such ferocity that her attackers quickly ceased their assault and Scatha remained aloof from further humiliation.

Cynan I could not see, nor the Raven Flight, so tight-pressed was the crowd of onlookers thronging every side. Still, I little doubted that they, like the rest of us, would follow Llew in turn. I knew that they, like the multitude ranged along the lakeshore, must be watching the appalling event taking place before them.

Meldron, swelling with pride and glowing with self-celebration, stood in the boat with arms upraised. The golden rings on his fingers and arms glistered in the harsh sunlight.

"My people," he called across the dead water. "This day you will witness a triumph. This day you will witness a king placing the whole of Albion under his protection! For even now my last enemy is conquered."

His words were worms in a corpse's mouth.

"You see!" the Great Hound cried. "You have seen how my enemies are destroyed! You have seen how I crush those who think to use treachery against me!"

Meldron seized Llew's arms and hauled him to his feet. Llew was made to stand before him, head forced down in defeat.

"Now you will see how I deal with those who raise war against me!" Meldron shouted, so that all gathered around the lake— warriors and captives alike—could hear. "Now you will see how I claim the vengeance that is mine!"

Llew raised his head, squared his shoulders, and regarded Meldron with unflinching defiance.

Meldron, gripping Llew by the arms, turned him to face the crowd that looked on from the shore. Then, smiling evily, the Great Hound placed his hands on Llew's back and thrust hard. Llew, tightly bound, plunged headlong into the lake.

"No! No!" Cynan shouted. Straining forward, legs and shoulders thrusting, he had somehow gained the water's edge. Now he cried his helpless defiance as his captors hauled him down. "Llew!"

The still air trembled with screams of horror and dismay— piercing sharp, keen as grief. And then the awful silence...

Llew sank instantly. There was no struggle, no thrashing, no tortured death screams such as we had seen and heard at the river. There was only a single splash of black water and then a dread silence as the lethal waters slowly rippled and grew calm once more.

Meldron gazed at the place where Llew fell. He appeared

displeased with the suddenness and serenity of Llew's death. He had hoped to produce a more thrilling spectacle and was disappointed. His lip curled and his countenance darkened with anger as he stared at the lifeless water.

He turned to the throng on the shore. I saw him point as he swung his arm to order Cynan's execution.

But even as he turned, a glimmer from the surface of the poisoned lake caught his eye, arrested him. I saw it too: a faintly shimmering glint, a flash like that of a silver-sided fish darting in a stream. Something moved just below the surface of the tainted lake.

Meldron's arm faltered; his eyes turned again to the place where Llew had disappeared. His expression wavered between frustration and expectation. Perhaps he would have his revenge sweetened by a death-struggle after all?

I thought I saw the glint again, though it might have been the sunlight on a ripple. But Meldron stared. His arm faltered as he beheld a marvel.

Goewyn was first to see it from the shore. Her cry of astonishment sounded like a ringing harpnote across the water. With my inward sight I beheld her—eyes wide in awe, features alight. I turned to look where her gaze rested, and saw a wonder:

A man's hand rising from the water.

Others saw it, too. They cried out with elation and relief. But their jubilation ceased at once. The shouts died in their throats as the onlookers saw that the hand was not flesh: it was cold, shining silver.

38

Silver Hand

A hand of silver, lustrous white and gleaming, rose from the still, black water. Up from the dead lake it ascended and I saw that the hand was attached to a naked arm.

"It is Gofannon!" shouted a man. "It is Llyr!" cried a woman clutching an infant. People gasped in astonishment as a head and shoulders emerged. But it was neither Gofannon nor Llyr; it was Llew's head and shoulders rising from the lake.

His eyes were closed as he surfaced; I thought him dead. Then his eyes flew open: with a sudden inhalation of breath, he shook the putrid water from his face and began swimming.

The crowd recoiled. Their minds filled with the fresh memory of those who had perished in the poisoned river, they expected agony and death. But Llew lived!

Meldron was no less stricken than any other, but he quickly recovered. I heard the metal ring as he drew his sword and I saw the sunlight shiver on its naked blade.

He leaped to the prow of the boat, swinging the sword high. "Die!" he shrieked.

Down he struck. Down he slashed. Both hands on the hilt—his face twisted with hate and rage.

"Llew!" I cried.

Llew turned in the water. Whether warned by my cry, or by a warrior's instinct, he swung to meet the sword stroke falling upon him and raised a hand to fend off Meldron's murderous blow.

Fearfully swift the sword stroke fell. Llew's silver hand flicked up to meet it.

"Look out!" Cynan bellowed from the strand.

That hand...that hand of metal grafted to a stump of flesh...Meldron struck. The silver hand caught the falling blade. The sound pealed like a hammer striking the anvil.

The killing blade shattered; glinting shards spun into the water. The blade broke, and Meldron's arm with it.

The bone snapped with a loud crack, and Meldron looked on in horror as his sword arm buckled and bent between wrist and elbow. His anguished cry sounded sharp surprise in the air as the sword hilt fell from his grasp. But even as he clasped the fractured arm to him, he began to fall.

"Jump!" cried Siawn Hy.

A leap might have saved him, but it was already too late. The boat tipped and, unbalanced by the reckless swordstroke, Meldron pitched into the tainted water. His eyes bulged wide with terror and his mouth gaped in a desperate scream as he toppled from the boat.

He richly deserved his reward, but Meldron's death throes brought no joy to anyone looking on. He flailed wildly as the black ooze sucked him under. As with so many of his hapless men before him, his skin puckered and cracked raw as welts and bloody ulcers formed where the poison touched him, scouring flesh from sinew, and sinew from bone.

He thrashed furiously and screamed in agony, clawing at his own flesh as if to tear it from him. A hideous howl burst from his throat. He writhed and twitched as if spears were piercing him, and his hair fell from his scalp in rotten clumps. Opening wide his mouth, he gasped for breath to utter a last tortured shriek. But the water, the vile corruption, had entered him and he choked on the scream. His head jerked obscenely as death seized and shook him.

Then Meldron slipped beneath the black water. A moment later his corpse bobbed to the surface, floating silent and still, dead eyes staring at an empty sky.

Llew turned towards the shore; he swam a short way, until his feet found a footing beneath him, and then stood. His clothes were gone, and the ropes that bound him with them—the mordant poison had stripped all from him—and now he stood immaculate and unblemished before us. His skin was flawless, clean and whole, his limbs straight and sound. He raised the silver hand and gazed at it in amazement. He stepped forward. Meldron's warriors drew back from his advance. I felt the hands upon my back slacken and relinquish their hold. I scrambled to my feet and ran, stumbling, over the stony shingle. I called to Llew as I ran.

He was yet a small distance from the shore, dripping wet, and still somewhat bewildered by what had happened to him, when he halted. I reached the place opposite him on the strand and shouted again.

"Llew! Come out of the water," I called. Cynan struggled to his feet, shaking his head, staring.

"He is alive!" Goewyn ran to where we stood. She had a knife in her hand and loosed the bindings at my wrists. "Why does he not come out?"

"I cannot say," I answered, my eyes still on Llew, who stood straight and tall, his silver hand upraised.

Cynan thrust out his hands towards Goewyn. With short, sharp cuts she freed him. He spun towards the lake, took two short steps and shouted: "Look! The water!"

My inward sight shifted to where he pointed. I saw Llew standing as before; he had not moved. But flowing in undulating ripples around him, spreading outward in a swiftly widening ring, I saw clean water. Indeed, between the shore and Llew it was already clear, and the ring of pure water was expanding with astonishing speed.

The vile black taint was receding, vanishing, dissolving as encircling bands of clear water swept outward from around Llew, whose presence seemed to flare like a sun blazing in a murky firmament, burning away the fog and cloud-wrack, banishing the blight by the brilliance of its light.

"There is healing in the water," Goewyn whispered, clasping her hands fervently beneath her chin. Tears shone in her eyes.

With her words still hanging in the air, I rushed forward to join Llew.

"Tegid!" Cynan shouted, and lunged to prevent me.

I ran two steps, tripped on a stone and fell sprawling. The lake water splashed over me. My head went under and I felt a burning sensation in my eyes. I came up gasping, dashing water with both hands. Bright light flashed through my fingers; I removed my hands and blinked my eyes.

Everything appeared just as I had seen it before, with my inward eye—but clearer, sharper, keener than before. Inner vision and outward sight had become one: I could see! Dazzling, sparkling, luminous in its clarity, light, brilliant and glorious streamed into my eyes; I closed them and the light was gone. It was true; I was healed!

Cynan dashed into the lake after me. With a wild whoop, he splashed to where Llew stood and wrapped him in a fierce embrace. Goewyn hastened to join them. She kissed Llew happily and clasped him to her.

I rose and ran to Llew and put my hands on him. "You are alive!" I said, touching him. "Meldron is dead and you are alive."

"It is over!" cried Cynan. "Meldron is dead!"

Goewyn kissed him, and Cynan as well. Llew returned their embraces, but as one dazed. He stretched forth his silver hand and held it before us. I took it in my hands. The metal was cold to the touch, polished like a mirror and gleaming bright. The fingers were curved slightly and the palm open in a gesture of offering or supplication.

The smooth silver surface was covered with spirals, whorls, and knotwork—fine lines incised in the metal surface. And upon the palm was the Môr Cylch, the Circle Dance, the maze of life. I blinked my eyes, still unsure of them, and touched a fingertip to the emblem, tracing the superbly wrought pattern of slender swirling lines. The design was exquisitely etched and the lines inlaid with gold. It was a creation of craft and cunning, fabulous in conception, unrivalled in execution—the work of a lord among smiths.

Touching the inscribed maze, I remembered the words of a promise: *I give you the virtue of your song*.

And into my mind came the image of him who had spoken those words: Gofannon, lord of the grove, and Master of the Forge. I had given him a song, for which he had given me a gift in return, my inner sight. Llew had chopped wood for him, but had received no boon from the great lord that night.

"I will give you the virtue of your song," Gofannon had promised, and now he had fulfilled his promise to Llew. For the song I had sung that night was *Bladudd the Blemished Prince*. Oh! What a slow-witted lump I had been! Surely I had sung for the Swift Sure Hand himself.

"Hail, Silver Hand!" I said, touching the back of my hand to my forehead in salutation. "Your servant greets you!"

With a tremendous splash, the people of Dinas Dwr abandoned their fear and surged as one into the lake which was now absolutely pure and clean. They scooped the life-giving water into their hands and poured it down parched throats, drinking their fill. They laved the liquid over their sun-weary heads and were soothed; they washed themselves and were made clean again. Children splashed and frolicked like giddy lambs.

Compelled by thirst and overcome by the sight of so much fresh water, the foemen threw down their weapons and ran to join the glad celebration. Shield and warcap, sword and spear clattered to the stony shingle to be trodden in the rush to the water. The enemy warriors—those who were not warriors at all—could not abandon their weapons fast enough. Freed from Meldron's brutal reign, they knelt in the water and wept with gratitude at their release.

All thought of retribution vanished at their wholehearted thanksgiving; they had been made to suffer the most wicked persecutions; how could we punish them more? They were never our enemies.

Meanwhile, the Ravens and Calbha's warband had captured

Meldron's battlechiefs and the warriors of his Wolf Pack, and assembled them on the strand. Fifty warriors stood grimly awaiting judgment.

Bran raised his spear and called to us. "Llew! Tegid! We need you."

Calbha and Bran stood together, and the warriors ranged behind them on the shingle held the Wolf Pack at spearpoint. We joined them on the strand and, at our approach, Bran and Calbha parted to reveal their prisoner: Siawn Hy. His head was down as if he were contemplating his rope-bound hands.

As we drew near, Siawn raised his head and glared at us from under a baleful brow. A dark bruise swelled on his right temple.

"Fools!" he hissed. "You think you have won this day. Nothing has changed. You have won nothing!"

"Silence!" Bran warned him. "You may not speak so to the king."

"It is over, Simon," Llew said.

At the mention of his former name, Siawn drew breath and spat in Llew's face. Bran's hand, quick as a snake, flicked out and struck Siawn on the mouth. Blood trickled from Siawn's split lip. Bran appeared ready to strike again, but Llew prevented him with a shake of his head.

"It is over," Llew said. "Meldron is dead."

"Kill me too," Siawn muttered sullenly. "I will never submit to you."

"Where is Paladyr?" I asked and received only a sneer of contempt by way of reply.

Calbha raised his sword and pointed at Siawn Hy, and then at the rest of the Wolf Pack. "What is to be done about these?" he asked, his tone cold and pitiless.

"Take them to the storehouses and make them secure," Llew instructed. "We will deal with them later." Alun Tringad and Garanaw took Siawn by the arms and led him away; the rest of the Wolf Pack followed under Calbha's guard.

Drustwn and Niall waded out to where Meldron's corpse floated. They raised the body from the water and rolled it into the boat like a sodden bag of grain. Then, towing the boat, they hauled the body away to be quickly buried and forgotten.

Scatha, watching all this, arms crossed over her breast smiled icily. "I had hoped to see his head on my spear, but this will suffice."

Llew nodded and started after the prisoners. He had not walked ten paces when Cynan snatched up a discarded sword, lofted it, and shouted, "Hail, Silver Hand! Hail!"

Bran leaped forward and retrieved a spear. "Hail, Silver Hand!" he cried, brandishing the spear. And suddenly the whole lake echoed with the sound, as the people of Dinas Dwr and Meldron's former war host ceased their sporting in the water and turned as one to acclaim Llew as he passed. "Silver Hand!" they cheered. "Hail, Silver Hand!"

The cries soared up and up as if to shake the shining sky with their jubilant thunder. And Llew, walking along the shore, stopped, turned to the gathering host, and raised his silver hand high.

We could not celebrate our victory while our dead lay unburied. How could we rejoice with tears in our eyes? How could we feast while the corpses of our kinsmen became food for scavenging birds?

When we had rested, eaten, and drunk our fill of the sweet, plentiful water, we turned once again to the battleground and the reclaiming of our dead—and there were many: almost half of those who had gone down to fight had not returned. Lord Calbha had suffered the greatest loss; the Cruin warband was decimated. The Galanae warriors also paid a fearful price: Cynfarch was shaken to the core. Llew and Scatha had lost fewer than the others, but even one man dead was too many for them and they were greatly distressed. Only the Raven Flight had emerged intact. Fittingly, Bran and the Ravens led the return to the battlefield to begin burying our dead.

Each of our fallen swordbrothers was accorded a hero's burial. As they had died together, we placed them together in one massive grave—shoulder to shoulder, with their spears in their hands and their shields before them. We then covered them with their cloaks and raised the turf house over them.

While this was being done, workmen hauled great slabs of stone from the ridge. When the mound had been raised, we constructed a worthy dolmen to mark the place.

It was late when we finished our task and turned to the enemy warriors. The sun had already set and there were stars shining in the darkening sky. "Let them wait," Cynan suggested. "They were eager enough to gain this ground, let them enjoy the fruits of their labor."

But Llew looked out on the massed corpses of the fallen enemy. "No, Cynan," he said. "It is not right. Most of these were not Meldron's warriors—"

"They fought for him. They died for him. Let him take care of them now," Cynan replied bitterly.

"Brother," Llew soothed, "look around you. Look at them. They were farmers, they were untrained boys, plowmen, woodwrights, and sheep herders. They had no place in this fight. The Great Hound used them cruelly and cast them aside. We have suffered much, but they are no less the victims of his brutality. The least we can do is offer them respect in death."

Cynan grudgingly accepted this. He rubbed his neck as he gazed out across the swiftly darkening plain. His blue eyes glimmered in the fading light. "What do you suggest?"

"Let us bury them as we have buried our own," Llew said.

"That they do not deserve," Cynan said flatly.

"Perhaps not," allowed Llew. "Still, we will do it for them anyway."

"Why?" wondered Cynan.

"Because we are alive and have a choice, and they do not!" Llew replied with passion. "We do it for them, and we do it for ourselves."

Cynan scratched his head. "They will never know the difference."

"But we will," Llew told him.

"It is a good thing," I put in quickly. "But the light is gone, and we are spent. Let us rest now and begin again in the morning."

Llew would not hear it; he shook his head, and I added quickly, "Tomorrow we will erect a dolmen over their grave too. When we see it we will remember what a terrible master fear can be, and how easily it can conquer a soul."

Llew turned to regard the dusky battleground, himself little more than a dark shape against a twilight landscape. "Go then, both of you. Take your ease and sleep. But I will not rest until every trace of Meldron's reign is gone."

He moved off alone. Watching him, Cynan said, "Long he will be without sleep then. There is not a hearth or hill in all Albion that does not bear the taint of Meldron's reign." He turned to me. *"Clanna na cù,* Tegid. Have you ever heard of such a thing?"

"No," I confessed, "I never have. But a new order is beginning. I think we will all learn new ways." I put my hand to Cynan's shoulder. "Order torches to be brought, and food. We will work through the night."

Through the night we labored—and through the long, hot day to follow. The people of Dinas Dwr and their former enemies worked side by side, willingly and ardently. And in the end, two mounds were raised on the plain—one at the foot of Druim Vran where our swordbrothers were buried, and the other beside the river where so many of Meldron's forces fell. It was a noble deed, and the people understood this even if they did not understand Llew's urgency in doing it. He had said he could not rest until it was finished, and I think he spoke from his heart. Indeed, there could be no new beginning until the old had been properly buried.

When the workmen and their teams at last finished putting the capstone on the dolmen, the sun was well down, casting a rich, honeyed light over the turf mound. The shadow of the dolmen stretched long across the green plain. I commanded Gwion to bring my harp and I gathered the host to sing the *Lament for the Brave.*

Long it had been since any among us had heard the spirit-quickening music of the harp and voices lifted in song, and the people wept to hear it—tears of sorrow, yes, but also tears of healing. We sang and the tears flowed from our eyes and from our souls.

When the lament finished, they called for more. I strummed the harp and thought what I might sing, what gift I might give them. It felt good to have a harp nestled against my shoulder once more, and soon my fingers found their way and I began to sing the song that I had been given. I sang and the words kindled the vision once more and it began to live in the world of men.

I sang the steep-sided glen in deep forest, the tall pines straining for the sky ... I sang the antler throne on a grass-covered mound, adorned with an oxhide of snowy white ... I sang the bright-burnished shield with a black raven perched on its rim, wings outspread, filling the glen with its severe song ... I sang the beacon fire burning into the night sky, its signal answered from hilltop to hilltop ... I sang the rider on his horse of pale yellow, galloping out of the grey mist, the horse's hooves striking sparks from the rocks ... I sang the great warband bathing in the mountain lake, and the cold water blushing red from their wounds ... I sang the woman dressed all in white, standing in a green bower with the light of the sun flaring her hair like golden fire ... I sang the cairn, the hero's gravemound ...

While I sang, the setting sun spilled red-gold into the heavens. Clouds stained with rosy fire spread like fingers across the sky. It was the time-between-times, and I stood before a mounded dolmen, a hallowed place; words spoken at such times become sparks to inflame men's hearts. And I knew in my bones that the things of which I sang were yet to come; they would be.

39

Oran Môr

We rested and recovered our strength through the next day. And that day was far spent when Cynfarch and Calbha summoned us to a council. "It is not right that the Great Hound's warband should live to draw breath among us while our swordbrothers lie cold in the ground," Cynfarch said firmly. "Justice must be done."

"He is right," added Calbha. "The sooner we finish this, the better. I say we do it now."

Llew turned to me. "What do you say, Tegid?"

I glanced from one king to the other; they were adamant and would not be appeased until justice had been served. "It is true," I agreed, "the matter must be settled sooner or later. Let it be sooner."

"Very well," said Llew. "We will assemble at the lakeside."

We left the crannog and went to the lakeshore storehouses where the captives had been held under guard since Meldron's defeat. We sat facing the lake on oxhides spread upon the ground; Bran took his place at Llew's right hand, and I sat to his left. Scatha settled beside me, and Cynan, Cynfarch, and Calbha completed our number. Many of Dinas Dwr's inhabitants gathered behind us—among them I noticed the slight figure of Nettles, hovering in the forefront, only just out of sight.

The Ravens brought the prisoners to stand on the shore before us: fifty warriors of the Wolf Pack and Siawn Hy—all that remained of Meldron's warband. Their hands were bound with rope and their feet with chains. Their amulets containing fragments of the Singing Stones had been removed.

Cynfarch was first to speak. Gazing coldly at the prisoners, he said, "Is there anyone to speak for them?" When no one answered, he asked, "Who is leader among you?"

Siawn Hy raised his head. "How dare you pretend to sit in judgment over us. What gives you the right?"

"By the sovereignty of Caledon it is my right," Cynfarch told him. "You and those with you have slaughtered the people and violated the land. You have raped and stolen and destroyed—"

"We followed our king!" Siawn spat. "We served him as your own warriors serve you. Yet you call our loyalty treason, and our fealty an offense against sovereignty."

"You are thieves and murderers!" Cynan shouted. "You have destroyed everything!"

"We have done nothing that you yourselves have not done," Siawn replied. "Who among you has not lifted sword against another? Who among you has not laid hold of a thing that did not belong to you?"

Both Cynfarch and Calbha were suddenly abashed. Siawn smiled with sly satisfaction. "You have done all this and more," he said with slow insinuation, "and you have justified them to yourselves saying, 'We are kings, it is our right.' But when one like Meldron arises, you call him a murderer and thief. Weak men are all alike—they become cowards in the presence of the strong. You are angry and call it righteousness; you are weak and call it virtue. Yet any one of you would have done what Meldron did if you but had the courage. You were content with your small kingdoms, but only because you feared to take more."

"Silence!" Cynfarch roared.

But Siawn Hy only laughed. "You see! It is true. You cry silence because you hear the truth and you cannot abide it. You condemn us for what you lacked: the will and heart to do yourselves what

Meldron did."

Calbha rose to his feet. "Liar!" he raged. "I will not listen to this."

Siawn was not cowed. "How not, Calbha?" he demanded. "Have you forgotten your wars with Meldryn Mawr? Over an insult to hunting dogs as I recall. And you used that as an excuse to seize land in Prydain, did you not?"

Calbha glowered at the smooth-speaking prisoner before him, aghast that Siawn should remember such an old feud and lay it at his feet now. "That was different," the Cruin king muttered.

I well remembered the quarrel Siawn Hy so astutely mentioned. Calbha and Meldryn Mawr had fought a series of battles which had begun over a remark about Meldryn's hounds. The truth of Siawn's assertion could not be denied. With one masterful stroke he had disarmed Calbha.

"Calbha and Meldryn settled their dispute long ago," Cynfarch retorted, coming to the Cruin king's aid. "It is of no concern to us now. It is Meldron who is under judgment."

"And you have settled with Meldron," Siawn replied. "Why do you now judge us for his offenses?"

"He could not have done what he did," Bran said, "if you had not supported him."

"Is it now a crime to support one's king?" demanded Siawn Hy. The Wolf Pack stood easier now, quickly recovering their confidence. "You abandoned your lord, and you think this gives you the right to judge me?"

Bran regarded Siawn as if watching a snake about to strike. "That is not how it was. You twist the truth to fit your lies."

"Do I?" Siawn smirked. "I tell you that if Meldron had won, it would be you standing here answering for your treason. That is the truth. Deny it if you can."

Llew leaned close to me. "You see how he is? He is a master of argument. He will have us surrendering to them, next."

"What would you do?"

He frowned. "This was Cynfarch's idea, not mine," he said. "I suppose we must wait and see what happens." He glanced around quickly, as if searching for someone. "Where is Nettles?"

"He is near. Is it important?"

"Summon him—I think he should be here for this. We might need him."

I rose and went into the crowd behind me. There were now so many more people than when the council had begun that I did not see him at first. But he saw me looking for him, and pushed his way forward quickly. "Llew asked for you," I told him. "He wants you to join us."

He made no reply, but nodded as if he understood; we returned to where Llew sat, and took our places beside him. Calbha was speaking again, so Llew turned to us and said, "Nettles, you are here—good. Listen, there is not much time." He paused. "Do you understand?"

"Yes," replied the small, white-haired man.

"Good. I will try to keep it simple." He indicated the prisoners ranged on the lakeshore before us, their shadows stretching long in the low-riding sun. "They are being judged—you understand?"

"War trial," said Nettles, nodding again. "I understand."

"Good," said Llew, his eyes flicking to me. "Good."

Calbha finished, and Scatha, who had been silent until now, spoke up. "You speak well of loyalty and right," she said. "Yet you attacked Ynys Sci, breaking oaths of fealty that have endured for generations. For this we judge you."

"Ah, yes, Scatha, Supreme War Leader, I bow to you—who taught so many warriors the art of slaughter," Siawn replied, his voice a knife thrust. "So long as your arts were practiced on others, you were content. But as soon as your own realm is invaded, you cry injustice. You taught men to kill, you armed them and sent them out, yet think it an offense when the skills you encouraged are employed. How petty and absurd you are, Pen-y-Cat."

Siawn's ruthless reason mocked them all and his cunning tongue bettered them. Cynfarch and Calbha had not expected this and were unnerved by it. So certain of their course only moments before, they were far from confident now. The council fell to talking among themselves. Llew turned again to Nettles.

"That is Simon," Llew said. "Remember him?"

The small man nodded, watching Siawn narrowly. He said something in his own tongue which Llew answered, and then said to me: "Nettles says that Weston and the others—the Dyn Dythri we sent back—were in communication with Simon. They were trying to reach him. Simon has endangered Albion from the beginning. He achieved his place with Meldron in order to exploit each situation for his own purposes."

"Meldron's place is in Uffern now," I pointed out. "I think it is time Siawn Hy joined his lord."

Siawn, smirking openly now, called out in a loud voice. "You have no right to judge us! Let us go!"

Llew looked to me; I could see him weighing the decision in his mind. "You are the rightful king," I told him, placing my hand over his hand of silver. He glanced down at the silver hand. "Justice is yours to bestow," I said. "Whatever you decide, I will support you."

Siawn Hy challenged the council again and it was Llew who answered him this time. "You have said we have no right to judge you, but you are wrong. There is one blameless who calls you to account."

"Who is this blameless one?" Siawn sneered. "Let him come forward to condemn us if he is here." The Wolf Pack followed Siawn's lead and yapped accordingly, calling for the blameless accuser to show himself, if he existed.

Llew stood. "I am blameless," he said simply. "I have done no wrong, yet I have suffered evil and injustice at your hands. And for this and for every drop of innocent blood that you have shed, I do condemn you."

Siawn's thin smile spread wide across his face in triumph. "Condemn me all you like, friend. You are not a king, therefore you do not possess the right to judge."

"But I am a king," Llew said. "Sovereignty can be granted by the Chief Bard alone. The kingship of Prydain was given to me by Tegid Tathal in the rite of the Tán n'Righ."

Siawn's laugh was loud and harsh. The spite in his voice when he answered was staggering. "You! A king? You are a cripple, my friend! The maimed man cannot be king."

But Llew simply raised his silver hand and flexed the fingers one by one. Everyone—myself included—stared in amazement at this marvel. The hand seemed real!

"As you see, Simon, I am no longer maimed," Llew said. He turned so that all could see, and lifted his voice so that all could hear. "With this hand I take back the kingship that was stolen from me."

"Who owns you king?" retorted Siawn Hy savagely, and I heard desperation creeping into his voice for the first time. "Who follows you?"

"I own him king," said Bran quietly. "I follow and serve him."

"You refused your king, Bran Bresal. You abandoned him when it suited you. Since you claim that right, I say that we should be given the same choice. Let us swear fealty to a new lord."

This caused a discussion in the council. "Perhaps they should be given a choice," said Calbha, a little uncertainly. "But could we trust them?"

"What choice did our dead have?" Llew said. "What choice did those whom they raped and murdered enjoy?" He regarded Siawn and the Wolf Pack with flint-hearted resolve. "Every time they drew sword or lofted spear they had a choice, and each time they chose."

"He is right," said Scatha. "They have chosen many times over whom they would serve."

"I agree," said Cynan. "If you want to give them a choice, let it be this: to die by their own hands, or by ours."

Cynfarch and Calbha agreed. "Then it is settled," Llew said, and turned to the waiting captives. "For your actions in support of Meldron's wrongful reign, I do condemn you. And I demand that the blood debt be paid with blood."

"Llew," said Scatha, "allow me to serve you in this. Any who finds his courage lacking will find mine sufficient to the task."

"So be it," Llew replied.

The prisoners were marched along the lakeside, up across Druim Vran and out to the plain beyond. They were led to the burial mound of their kinsmen and made to stand in ranks before it.

We stood below the mound, the sun setting at our backs. Many of the people had come out to watch the execution, though many more had seen enough of bloodshed and chose to remain at Dinas Dwr. Goewyn and Nettles were among those who accompanied us, however, and stood at the forefront of those looking on as, one after another, the condemned were given the choice: death by their own hand, or by Scatha's.

Thirty men took the sword into their own hands and fell upon it—some with a cry, others silent to the last. The rest refused the sword and faced Scatha's swift blade instead. Not once did she hesitate, nor did her hand tremble. When each man died, the body was hauled up the mound by members of Cynan's warband or Calbha's and there left on the ground around the dolmen for the birds and beasts to devour.

Then, as the sunglow lit the sky in the west, Siawn Hy's turn came to decide.

"Give me the sword," he snarled. "I will do it."

Garanaw and Emyr, who stood either side of the condemned man, looked to Llew for his assent. Llew nodded. Scatha stepped aside as Garanaw pressed the hilt of his sword between Siawn's bound hands, and—

—before Garanaw had even removed his hand, Siawn twisted the blade and swung it sharply down between his legs. The bindings on his feet split and fell away, and Siawn Hy dived forward as Emyr's sword sliced the air above his head. He rolled on the ground and came up running, darting for the river. He shouted something, but I did not catch the words.

Siawn reached the river before any of us could move. Still shouting, he turned to face us—a smile of triumph on his leering face. He raised the sword between his hands in a mocking salute.

Bran's swift spear was already in the air—before anyone realized he had thrown it. The slender missile appeared as a blur in the gathering dusk, a blue-white streak in the fading light. The next we knew, Siawn's sword was spinning to the ground and he was staggering backwards, clutching at his chest where the shaft of Bran's spear suddenly appeared. The impact of Bran's throw carried Siawn Hy to the water marge. One foot in the water, one foot on the riverbank, he screamed again—words I did not understand—and he fell. In the time-between-times he fell.

And as he fell, his body seemed to fade from sight. He struck the water—I saw it! But could I trust my new eyes? For there was no splash...and no corpse to be found when we rushed to the place where he plunged. Siawn Hy had vanished.

"He has gone back," said Llew, gazing at the water. "I always meant to send him home, but I thought he would be alive when he went."

"It was his choice."

"No," Llew said. "It was mine."

Twilight descended over the valley; the first stars had begun to shine and the moon glowed bright just above the horizon. Llew turned to the people of Dinas Dwr, his people, and to the kings and warriors and friends looking on. "Justice has been done," Llew told them. "The blood debt is paid."

"Hail, Llew Silver Hand!" Bran called, lofting his spear. The Flight of Ravens championed the cry, and the people raised the chant. "Silver Hand! Silver Hand! Silver Hand!"

He raised his hand to them; the figured metal shone in the twilight, and I saw in the gleaming silver the radiant glow of kingship glinting bright.

Goewyn appeared, walking along the bank of the river; without a look or word to anyone, she approached Llew. Every eye beheld her slender form clothed in a simple white robe with a mantle of sky blue falling from her shoulders. Moonlight bright in her pale gold hair, she seemed to shine like an earthstar.

She carried a small wooden chest in her hands. The chest was made of oak—inspiration's wood, in bardic lore. Placing the oaken chest at Llew's feet, she straightened, touched the back of her hand to her brow and stepped back. Llew bent down and took up the chest. He opened it, turned the chest, and held it out for all to see. Inside were a number of milk-white stones: the Singing Stones.

Llew withdrew one of the stones and held it before the throng. I saw the silver fingers flex and tighten as he crushed the stone in his metal hand. A sound like chorused thunder broke from the shattered stone—a sound like star-voices clear and clean as gemstones coursing through the endless skypaths—a sound like ten thousand harps united in the heart-piercing music of the Oran Môr, the Great Music—a sound from beyond this worlds-realm, framed by the Swift Sure Hand.

My spirit soared, swift and high; and it seemed that I merged with the matchless sound. I lost all knowledge of myself or where I was; I became one with the melody I felt moving within me. I opened my mouth, yet it was not my voice which struck the twilight air. It was the Song of Albion.

I opened my mouth and the words poured out in a stream of splendid song:

> Glory of sun! Star-blaze in jewelled heavens!
> Light of light, a High and Holy land,
> Shining bright and blessed of the Many-Gifted;
> A gift forever to the Race of Albion!

> Rich with many waters! Blue-welled the deep,
> White-waved the strand, hallowed the firmament,
> Mighty in the power of the One,
> Gentle in the peace of great blessing;
> A wealth of wonders for the Kinsmen of Albion!

> Dazzling the matchless purity of green!
> Fine as the emerald's excellent fire,
> Glowing in deep-clefted glens,
> Gleaming on smooth-tilled fields;
> A Gemstone of great value for the Sons of Albion!

Abounding in white-crowned peaks, vast beyond measure,
the fastness of bold mountains!
Exalted heights—dark-wooded and
Red with running deer—
Proclaim afar the high-vaunted splendor of Albion!

Swift horses in wide meadows! Graceful herds
on the gold-flowered water-meads,
Strong hooves drumming,
a thunder of praise to the Goodly-Wise,
A boon of joy in the heart of Albion!

Golden the grain-hoards of the Great Giver,
Generous the bounty of fair fields:
Redgold of bright apples,
Sweetness of shining honeycomb,
A miracle of plenty for the tribes of Albion!

Silver the net-tribute, teeming the treasure
of happy waters; Dappled brown the hillsides,
Sleek herds serving
the Lord of the Feast;
A marvel of abundance for the tables of Albion!

Wise men, Bards of Truth, boldly declaring from
Hearts aflame with the Living Word;
Keen of knowledge,
Clear of vision,
A glory of verity for the True Men of Albion!

Bright-kindled from heavenly flames, framed
of Love's all-consuming fire,
Ignited of purest passion,
Burning in the Creator King's heart,
A splendor of bliss to illuminate Albion!

Noble lords kneeling in rightwise worship,
Undying vows pledged to everlasting,
Embrace the breast of mercy,
Eternal homage to the Chief of chiefs;
Life beyond death granted the Children of Albion!

Kingship wrought of Infinite Virtue,
Quick-forged by the Swift Sure Hand;
Bold in Righteousness,
Valiant in Justice,
A sword of honor to defend the Clans of Albion!

Formed of the Nine Sacred Elements,
Framed by the Lord of Love and Light;
Grace of Grace, Truth of Truth,
Summoned in the Day of Strife,
An Aird Righ to reign forever in Albion!

I awakened in the dark of night. I was lying on a yellow oxhide in my hut on the crannog, but I do not know how I came to be there. The air was still and calm, the heat of the day lingered even yet. At first I thought it was the echo of the Song that had awakened me. I lay without moving, listening in the darkness. After a time I heard the sound again and felt the faint stirring of a cooling breeze on my face.

I rose then and went out as the thunder echoed across the heavens and the first drops of rain began to fall—fat, round beads of water. And I smelled the fresh scent of cool rain-washed air.

Thunder rumbled again and there came a noise not heard in Albion for far too long: the sound of wind and rain sweeping across the surrounding hills. The storm-music filled the glen and echoed through the forest as the rain swept down from Druim Vran and out across the lake towards Dinas Dwr.

Out from the huts and hall the people came, wakened by the storm. They lifted their eyes to the sky and let the blessed rain splash their upturned faces. Lightning flashed and thunder answered with its booming call, and the rain fell harder. Eager hands cupped water and laved it over dry limbs and heat-wearied heads; men laughed and kissed their wives; children danced barefoot as the water soaked them to the skin.

My inner vision quickened once more to the laughter of rejoicing and relief. With my inward eye, I saw hills greening, streams gushing and rivers flowing again. I saw cattle growing sleek and crops ripening in the fields; apple trees bending under the weight of their fruit, and walnuts, hazelnuts and beechnuts swelling inside their shells. Fish sported in clear lakes, while ducks, geese and swans nested in the shallows. Milk frothed foamy white and mead glowed golden in the bowl; rich brown ale filled the cups, and good dark bread filled the ovens; meat of all kinds—pork, venison, beef, fish, poultry—heaped the platters. All through Albion the hungry ate and were filled; the thirsty drank and were refreshed.

For the long oppression of drought and death was ended. Silver Hand had begun his reign.

BESTSELLING AUTHOR OF
THE PENDRAGON CYCLE

STEPHEN R. LAWHEAD

In a dark and ancient world,
a hero will be born to fulfill
the lost and magnificent promise of . . .

THE DRAGON KING

Book One
IN THE HALL OF THE DRAGON KING
71629-1/ $4.99 US/ $5.99 Can

Book Two
THE WARLORDS OF NIN
71630-5/ $4.99 US/ $5.99 Can

Book Three
THE SWORD AND THE FLAME
71631-3/ $4.99 US/ $5.99 Can

Buy these books at your local bookstore or use this coupon for ordering:
....
Mail to: Avon Books, Dept BP, Box 767, Rte 2, Dresden, TN 38225   C
Please send me the book(s) I have checked above.
❏ My check or money order— no cash or CODs please— for $_____is enclosed
(please add $1.50 to cover postage and handling for each book ordered— Canadian residents
add 7% GST).
❏ Charge my VISA/MC Acct#_____Exp Date_____
Minimum credit card order is two books or $6.00 (please add postage and handling charge of
$1.50 per book — Canadian residents add 7% GST). For faster service, call
1-800-762-0779. Residents of Tennessee, please call 1-800-633-1607. Prices and numbers
are subject to change without notice. Please allow six to eight weeks for delivery.

Name_____
Address_____
City_____State/Zip_____
Telephone No._____   DK 0193